Praise for Autumn Cornwell's
first young adult novel, *Carpe Diem*

"This is self-confessed travel junkie Autumn Cornwell's first novel—and she's hit one out of the park."

—*The Washington Post*

"Suspenseful and wonderfully detailed, the well-crafted story maintains its page-turning pace while adding small doses of cultural insight and humor."

—*School Library Journal, Starred Review*

"Take a traveler as reluctant as Anne Tyler's accidental tourist and add the number of misadventures found in *The Out-of-Towners*, and you have the recipe for Cornwell's hilarious, adventure-packed first novel.... the exotic settings and the wacky predicaments will exercise a strong enough grip to hold readers' imaginations."

—*Publishers Weekly*

"The locale, Vassar's gaffes, and quirky characters—especially Grandma Gerd and Hanks—are what set this book apart."

—*VOYA*

"A witty coming-of-age adventure."

—*Kirkus Reviews*

"…this first novel has its amusements and diversions, including Vassar's share of romance with a self-styled Malaysian cowboy. The best part, however, is the vividly realized setting. Cornwell has obviously been there and done that, and her novel is much the richer—and funnier—for it."

—*Booklist*

Chosen as a fall *IndieBound Pick* (formerly *Book Sense*)

One of *Publishers Weekly's* "Children's Galleys to Grab"

New York Public Library's *Books for the Teen Age*

Nominated for the Missouri's *Truman Readers Award.*

Nominated for the *Rhode Island Teen Book Award.*

Selected as an *International Reading Association (IRA) Notable Book.*

For Shayla~

never
sorry
ever
jolly

Get ready for a
CRAZYTOWN
adventure!,
Cheers!

All he wanted was a date.

never SORRY ever JOLLY

autumn cornwell

FARMHAND INTERNATIONAL, INC

Never Sorry Ever Jolly
First Farmhand International Edition, January 2019

Copyright 2016 by Autumn Cornwell

Library of Congress Control Number: 2017918297
ISBN: 978-1948300-00-1

Cornwell, Autumn.
Never Sorry Ever Jolly / Autumn Cornwell.
Summary: Atheist Collin Uttley joins a church outreach trip to Thailand for the sole reason of scoring a girlfriend.

Published by Farmhand International, Inc
2335 E. Colorado Boulevard 115151
Pasadena, California 91104
www.farmhandinternational.com

Dedicated to Team Cornwell:

Both J.C.s
&
Dexter
&
Clementine

Game on!

A MESSAGE FROM COLLIN UTTLEY

A heads up: I don't exactly come across as a *hero* in this narrative. But the Tacketts told me I should write it up because the "transparency and vulnerability" would be "powerful and freeing."

Riiiiight.

Jack-O said I should share it because it would make people laugh, but he didn't clarify if that meant <u>with</u> me or <u>at</u> me. And the rest of the Team said it would be kind of inspiring—that is, if it didn't freak readers out. (My brothers said it would show you what <u>not</u> to do. Thanks, guys.)

So, here you go. Enjoy the ride—even if you don't believe any of this kind of stuff could actually happen.

I get it.

I was once in your shoes...

ABOUT A YEAR AGO, GIVE OR TAKE

(Names, places, and dates have been changed to protect the innocent, the guilty, and the oblivious. And it's been edited for content so you won't be offended. Much.)

part one

SoCAL

BOLYG

I T ALL STARTED WITH MY FIRST VISIT TO THE
Bread Of Life Church Youth Group, which was not at all
what I expected. I'd barely made it through the front door,
when a dark girl with a lot of natural beauty *and* a lot of metal
(nose stud, brow ring, and grommets in both ears) practically
body slammed me with a hug.

"Hi! Welcome to BOLYG!" She pronounced it *boly-gee*.
"Bread of Life Youth Group. Coffee's over there and worship starts in a few minutes. I'm Ernestine, who are you?
You're new, right? I like—" She stopped abruptly as her eyes
fell to my feet. "What the heck are those?"

The objects in question were the pieces of white fabric
covering the insteps of both shoes.

"Spats. They're *vintage*." I hoped I didn't sound defensive.

Chuckling and shaking her head, she said, "Wow. *Spats.*
Anyway, I like your hair—very Duran Duran." Her own hair
was black and thick with long bangs that almost hid her light
brown eyes.

"Uh, make that rockabilly," I said, lifting up my fedora and
pushing back my own long bangs (that Mom kept nagging me
to cut).

She laughed. "Got it. Well, *Spats*, you better hurry up or you'll miss out on the donut holes. They go fast." Her voice was throaty and she had two dimples that popped in and out. Sure, she was attractive in a "full figured" sort of way, but she didn't have the right style. (And grommets on girls always put me off.)

I wiped her from my mind and moved on.

The hunt continued.

I soon found myself in a huge multipurpose room filled with a hundred singing high school students. Up front, band members in skinny jeans and hoodies led "worship," which I soon learned meant endless praise songs with endless refrains. I made a beeline over to the coffee station where I scored the last remaining donut hole. I chewed slowly, making it last as long as possible, while I tried not to look like I'd never been in a church before.

I scanned the room for potential girlfriend material, which was tough since almost everyone faced the stage.

I finished the donut hole and debated whether or not to sneak out.

I got a cup of coffee instead.

One song ended and before the next one began, I heard—

"Jesus!"

The verbal explosion caused me to jerk my hand, slosh my cup, and send a Niagara of coffee cascading down the front of my vintage button-down shirt and jeans. After swabbing myself with handfuls of napkins, I grimly turned to find out who was responsible for the brown stains that would never fully come out. I couldn't believe a member of the youth group would swear like that—right in front of leaders and all.

It was the girl who welcomed me at the door.

In her torn jeans and 8-eye Doc Martens, she looked like she'd be more at home moshing in a pit than worshipping in a church.

"*Jesus!*" she exclaimed again, waving her hands in the air, eyes closed.

I turned to a lanky guy with an extra large Adam's apple and a skateboard tucked under his arm, who was dumping sugar into his coffee. "Last I checked, she was breaking the... the..." I quickly ran through the Ten Commandments I'd memorized the night before in order to blend in. "...the *sixth* commandment."

He stared at me blankly.

"You know, the commandment that forbids you—I mean, *us*—from taking the name of the Lord our God in vain...? You know, swearing?"

"*Jeeeeeeeeeeeeeesus!*"

"Hear that? I don't get why no one cares about all the cussing going on around here!"

The skater's eyes widened in comprehension as he glanced over at the law-breaker.

"Oh, you mean Ernestine Ketchum. She's cool. That's just how she worships. You know, *charismatic*. Lots of energy. Don't look so freaked, man. She's all right when you get to know her—she's got some great testimonies. You'll get used to her—"

"*Hallelujah!*"

"—eventually," he finished over his shoulder, as he jumped on his skateboard and rolled away across the linoleum.

I almost ditched BOLYG right then and there—the whole experience was way too whacked. However, I needed social interaction. My family had recently moved from Washington State to SoCal (aka Southern California) so my dad could join an environmentally conscious architectural firm, and my mom could research her seventh book on (I'm not making this up) *Mining California's Literary Gold in the Twentieth Century*. The idea was she'd write when she wasn't home-schooling me—and my two younger brothers (wait for it) *Merrick* and *Gareth*. I didn't mind since it gave me even more free time. At twelve and thirteen, my brothers took most of her energy.

Mom had decided to homeschool me years ago after teachers kept saying things like: "Collin read a graphic novel during class again today" and "Collin refused to play Sharks and Minnows with the rest of the students" and "Collin keeps augmenting his school uniform." (Yeah, no one appreciated the fedora or wallet chain.) At school, I was a minnow out of water. But it turned out that the homeschool world was a good fit for me: more freedom, tons of creative outlets, and friends who were interested in the same stuff I was. (Not to mention I could sleep 'til noon.)

Anyway, the move to California didn't impact my education, but it sure killed my social life. So far I'd met zero guys to hang out with and zero girls I'd consider asking out—despite the weekly gatherings with the homeschooling community of Arroyo Seco. Most of the guys were in the geek brotherhood and all the girls were either dating someone else or not my type/style.

Which is why I was still ticked off at my parents for moving during my junior year of high school. Why couldn't they have waited until I went away to college? But luckily, I'd heard through the homeschool grapevine about this "mega youth group," which translated meant "lots of high schoolers in one place, at one time," and more specifically: "lots of high school *girls* in one place, at one time." The group met regularly for beach trips, citywide scavenger hunts, foosball competitions, Japanese *anime* movie marathons, and even all night raves with glow sticks. Plenty of opportunities for male-female interaction. I decided to give it a try.

But there was a slight hitch.

I didn't go to church—didn't even believe God existed. But I was desperate. To be honest, I'd never had a girlfriend before. And I didn't want to start college completely inexperienced, if you know what I mean. Sure, I'd had a lot of girls as friends, gone on a bunch of first dates, but when it came to an "official" *relationship*—no sale. I did come close once with Renata Phrangle—but she dumped me to go to the Homeschool Prom with Sam Whitman instead. (I knew it was because she always hated being two inches taller than me—and he was six feet three. I've personally never had an issue with being shorter than most of the girls I date—but for some reason they sure do.)

So, I ended up sticking it out at BOLYG, despite Ernestine Ketchum's outbursts, and the general awkwardness of being an outsider. I knew it was my best chance of ever getting a *real* local girlfriend organically—without resorting to online dating and social media hookups. (To play it safe, I left the

11

spats at home. Permanently. Some vintage things are old and forgotten for a reason.)

My tenacity finally paid off. It happened about a month after joining the youth group, when I was waiting for yet another bonding activity to start. (I was hoping it wasn't blindfold dodge ball again. The cartilage in my nose hadn't been the same since the last time.) In the large multipurpose room, high schoolers were hanging out, drinking coffee, milling around, and stacking chairs. (Turned out that stacking and unstacking chairs was an activity unto itself.) I was sitting in a corner rereading *The Big Sleep* by Raymond Chandler, hoping some hot Goodreads female would get sucked into thinking I was some sort of mysterious literary stud—when something warm and fuzzy leaped onto my lap and a yellow sheet of paper whizzed dangerously close to my retinas.

"Flounce!"

A black and white spotted dachshund nuzzled my crotch with his wet nose and dropped a saliva-stained paper on my knees.

"Flounce, you were supposed to wait for me!"

And right then, no joke, a golden haired apparition, dressed in a Pepto-Bismol pink vintage dress with a ukulele tucked under her arm—materialized before my eyes.

The sudden close proximity of such a retro prototype catapulted me out of my seat—and my book and Flounce to the floor with a thud and a yip. The yellow flyer wafted onto my brown and tan wingtips—a recent thrift store find.

"Sorry about that. Flounce gets so excited, he just loves helping," said the apparition.

"No problem," I said, bending over and tentatively patting

the top of the dachshund's head. "He's, uh, a… a cute little guy."

In response, she gave me such a huge smile that her emerald eyes almost disappeared. "He's a double dappled dachshund."

I gave Flounce another pat and actually said (which just shows you how hard and fast I was crushing): "Are you double the fun?" In response, he started chewing on my cuff.

"No, Flounce," she said ineffectually.

I gently but firmly pried his tiny incisors off my sleeve and stood up.

She pointed to my striped vest and silver pocket watch. "You do great vintage."

"Likewise," I said, gesturing towards her dress.

"Thanks! I made it myself from a 1954 Butterick pattern."

"Nice." This was too good to be true.

"Well, with the help of my best friend Courtney," she added, "before she moved to Chicago. She had the sewing machine."

"Gotcha," I said in a low tone.

That's right, play it cool.

"Most kids today are so *lame* when it comes to clothes," she said with sudden vehemence. "Totally *boring* and *clichéd.* So, it's awesome to finally meet someone who has some individual *style* for once."

Meet the soul mate you never knew existed.

She laughed at the fixed grin on my face, the grin that was setting my cheekbones on fire. So much for cool. "You're Collin, right? Collin Uttley? From Oregon?"

"Close. Washington. What's your name?"

13

"Shelby Wanderal."

Shelby Wanderal. Whoa. Even her name has style.

"Flounce! Flounce, stop that!" Shelby clunked the ukulele down on a chair, and extricated her canine from my wingtips, where he was methodically consuming my shoelaces.

While she was occupied, I covertly scanned the features of my vintage soul mate: Shelby's teeth were so square and tiny they looked like baby teeth. Her nose was "pug" and her golden blond hair was cut in a short bob. Her pale skin was carpeted in a mass of bronze freckles. But the biggest plus— Shelby was 5'4, the perfect fit for my lean and mean 5'6.

My height has always been my Achilles' heel. A hundred years ago, I'd have been considered average, but nowadays I'm a runt. Which explains the adrenaline rush at finally meeting the mirror image match I'd been searching for my whole life: blond, vintage, and fun-sized.

"Sorry about that," said Shelby, standing up with Flounce now firmly in her grasp. "For some reason he likes chewing on brown things—"

"Do you swing?" It burst out before I could stop it.

Although taken aback, she smiled. "Swing dance? Yeah, I do. How did you know?"

Bullseye!

"Would you... would you wanna go sometime? I heard Brian Setzer and the Stray Cats might be doing a free gig in LA next month. Or... there's this cover band that does a lot of Big Bad Voodoo Daddy..." I trailed off. Why was I so nervous? After all, I'd asked out girls before.

Shelby tilted her head, then said, "Maybe. You know, there's a group of us who swing dance on Thursday nights at

14

Pollards, that restaurant on Olive Avenue. No cover charge, you just have to buy a water or a Coke. Why don't you meet up with us the next time we go?"

Realizing I was staring at her while she waited for my answer, I quickly nodded, "Sure. Yeah, I'd like that. I'd like that *a lot.*"

For some reason, she seemed to be trying not to laugh. "So, anyway, are you applying for the outreach trip?"

"To Mexico?"

"No, not the TJ trip, the one to Thailand to help the orphans in the refugee camps." She picked up the yellow flier that had threatened to slice through my eyeballs minutes earlier and handed it to me. "This tells all about it. The Tacketts asked me to lead worship over there since I've done the last four TJ trips. It'll be my first time in Southeast Asia."

I didn't know anything about the Tacketts other than they were some boring middle-aged couple who volunteered with the youth group. I glanced at the flier and skimmed the first paragraph:

>> BOLYG Summer Outreach Trip to Thailand <<

Trip Description: A five person Team from the youth group will serve the ethnic Katin people group in Thailand during the month of July under the leadership of our own Dr. Peter Tackett (Dentist) and Mrs. Marcy Tackett, R.N. (Registered Nurse), who've served there eight times before. Together they'll create summer camp programs for Katin orphans living in the three refugee camps along

the Thailand-Burma border. The Team will also assist the Tacketts as they provide free dental and medical care to any refugees in need. The Team Members will fundraise before the trip in order to purchase clothes, crafts, food, supplies, and medicine to donate. Only those who turn eighteen by the departure date are eligible to apply...

"If you're interested, you better hurry," Shelby's voice cut in. "The application and references and deposit are due next Sunday."

"That soon?"

"Oh, and the Tacketts do a pretty intense interview. You know, to weed out the kids who just want to score a free vacation, instead of serving the less fortunate—"

"Jeeeeeeeesus!"

I flinched.

"Ernestine's applying," said Shelby gesturing in the direction of the outburst. "We've been on all the TJ trips together."

What?!

I glanced over at Ernestine who was now in a prayer huddle with a bunch of other "exclaimers" of all races and styles: goth, jock, drama club, skater, beard-wearing, and even a lone tech nerd wearing a C++ t-shirt.

However, I refused to let *anything* distract me from accepting this direct invitation from *Shelby Wanderal*. Not the girl with Messianic Tourette's. Not the fact that volunteering in refugee camps was the dead *last* thing I'd ever want to do on my summer vacation. Not the book my neighbor Vassar Spore in Washington wrote about the squat toilets, centipedes, and perpetual sweat in the jungles of Southeast Asia. (You should check it out: *Carpe Diem*.)

I looked Shelby straight in the eye—and was almost blinded by the green that dazzled back at me. "There's *nothing* I'd rather do this summer than serve orphans and refugees in Thailand with *you*—" I broke off, barely restraining myself. "With you *all*. All of you on the Team, I mean. The whole pack of you... *all*."

Once again, she chewed the inside of her cheek as if trying not to laugh. "It would be fun to have you on the Team, Collin."

Flounce yipped in agreement—and then immediately jumped out of her arms and started gnawing on my shoe.

Right then and there, I fell so hard for Shelby Wanderal it felt like someone had thwacked me in the back of the head with a stack of youth group chairs. I immediately began concocting a plan to woo her. Yeah, you heard me, *woo*. I could tell Shelby wasn't like other girls, so I needed to be counter-cultural in my approach. Old fashioned. Gentlemanly. And what better way to woo a prospective girlfriend than on a month-long outreach trip! Talk about a captive audience! I mean, come on! What were the odds of ever meeting a girl again shorter than me—who also *got* me? And who was the epitome of that female vintage style that I found so darn hot? And no wonder I'd never had a girlfriend—I hadn't met her yet!

If all went according to plan, by summer's *end*, my relationship with Shelby Wanderal would have *begun*.

But, first things first: I had to convince the *atheists* at home to let me even apply.

UTTLEY FAMILY TRANSCRIPT

November 3rd

(Transcribed by Gareth Uttley, who happened to be practicing his shorthand at the time.)

Uttley Family Dining Room, 7:30 p.m.:

Mrs. Uttley: *(peers at Collin through bifocals and sloshes glass of wine)* "What??!!"

Mr. Uttley: *(blots red wine on table with yellow Outreach Trip flyer)* "You're telling us that instead of going to the movies on Thursday nights, this whole time you were in fact sneaking off to a—a—" *(coughs spasmodically)* "—youth group!?"

Collin: *(toying with salmon steak)* "Actually, yeah, I—"

Mrs. Uttley: "Why did you feel you had to lie? Have we ever punished you for speaking the truth? Have we? *Have we?!*"

Collin: "Well, no, but I thought that maybe—"

Merrick: *(points at Collin's salmon)* "Gonna finish that?"

(Collin pushes plate towards Merrick.)

Mr. Uttley: *(rubs bald pate)* "Although you know our views on 'religion,' haven't we always given you and your brothers full freedom to explore it openly?"

Collin: "Yes, you have, which is why I—"

Mrs. Uttley: *(shakes her head mournfully)* "Oh, Collin!"

Merrick: *(points at Mr. Uttley's salmon)* "Gonna finish that?"

18

(Approximately fifteen more minutes of similar dialogue, during which Mr. and Mrs. Uttley finish one bottle of wine and uncork a second, and Merrick eats everyone's salmon, then excuses himself from table to work on industrial themed diorama in adjoining room. Finally, at 7:45 p.m., Collin divulges details and logistics of Outreach Trip.)

Silence.

Mrs. Uttley: *(rereads stained yellow flyer and places it on table with a sigh)* "Well, since the Tacketts have made so many trips to the Thai refugee camps, they *presumably* know what they're doing. One would *presume*. But are you certain you want to go through with this, Collin? Are you *certain* certain?"

Collin: *(tilts his head, looks off into distance)* "The plight of the Katin Refugees in Burma has broken my heart—"

Merrick: *(from adjoining room)* "Riiiight!"

Mrs. Uttley: "Tolerance, Merrick! Tolerance!"

(Ten minutes of Collin further waxing poetic on the plight of the aforementioned Katin Refugees.)

Collin: *(concluding)* "—and so, as you can see, I've finally found a cause worth sacrificing for."

(Mr. and Mrs. Uttley exchange looks. Mrs. Uttley takes off her glasses and wipes her eyes.)

Mr. Uttley: *(rubs bald pate)* "We find it odd you want to participate in a *church* outreach trip of all things, but in the end we must both agree (albeit reluctantly) that if you feel so strongly about the cause of social justice among refugee orphans, who are we to stand in your way?"

Mrs. Uttley: *(echoing faintly)* "Yeah, who are we? Who are we other than the parents who birthed you, burped you, reared you, and *will continue to love you no matter what inane pas-*

sions stir you into gallivanting halfway across the globe!?"
(Brief and awkward silence as Mrs. Uttley takes sizeable gulp of wine.)

Collin: "Thanks, guys! Because although I don't *legally* need your consent since I'll be turning eighteen the week of the trip—which, as you know, is the age of majority in California—the Tacketts won't let anyone join the Team whose parents aren't in full support."

Mrs. Uttley: "Well, I wouldn't say it's *full* support…"

Mr. Uttley: *(leans towards Collin)* "Son?"

Collin: "Yeah, Dad?"

Mr. Uttley: "Don't drink the Kool-Aid."

(End of partial transcript. Full transcript available from Gareth Uttley for nominal fee.)

The Imposter in the Fedora
(aka Saint Collin the Soup Ladler)

ONCE I'D FINALLY PERSUADED MY PARENTS to let me apply, the real work lay ahead of me. I'd never put more effort into a project in my life than I did in getting on that Outreach Team to Thailand. I wrote an intentionally bland and believable conversion story ("I asked Jesus into my heart at junior high camp...") so I'd fit in with the rest of the youth group. However, I hit a major roadblock when it came to the three required spiritual references. I had to take a gamble here and hope the Tacketts wouldn't be too nitpicky and require phone conversations, so I just created fake email addresses that would all end up in my own in-box. (Merrick and Gareth came in handy here—they're as left brained as I am right brained.)

I invented a certain "Father O'Malley" with whom I volunteered in the Seattle Soup Kitchen: *"I robustly recommend Collin Uttley as a member of your Outreach Team. I've never seen such compassion for those less fortunate or such an unwavering work ethic in someone this young... Mark my words, future generations will revere him as Saint Collin the Soup Ladler! Ha ha! Although I jest, there is some truth in the statement..."*

Then there was "Hunter Davis," my former youth pastor:

21

"Yes, I'd say Collin would be an asset to your Outreach Team. During summer camp, he singlehandedly saved fifteen kids from hellfire and brimstone through his lanyard ministry alone…"

And finally, good old "Mrs. Elderberry," my next-door neighbor with whom I studied the Bible every day after homeschool: *"That darling Collin Uttley is an utter treasure! When he's not reading the Good Book, he's helping me around the house, taking out the trash, unloading the dishwasher, oiling my walker. Although I'll miss him over the summer, I'll willingly sacrifice him for the good of those poor little orphans!"*

Okay, totally over the top, but this wasn't the time to play it safe.

Then in order to sell myself as a "believer" during the interview, I subjected myself to hours of grueling research. Grueling because since I grew up completely unchurched, I hadn't so much as cracked a Bible in my life. (Mom wouldn't even keep a copy around for literary reasons.) So I read *The Reverend's Good Old Fashioned Bible Basics* and a bunch of church blogs for a general overview, and then skimmed books like *St. John of the Cross* and *Confessions* by St. Augustine for some random historical background. And tortured myself with the you gotta be kidding me bestsellers: *Being a Christian is Just So Darn Fun!* and *What Matters Most to the Born Again Teen?* I figured I didn't need to read the actual Bible, just know enough stuff about it to get by in casual conversation.

I also scribbled down churchy phrases overheard during youth group. ("Just surrender to him…" and "I'm praying for a hedge of protection around you" and "Covered by the blood" and "I want his will not mine" and "Spiritual breakthrough, wooo hooo!")

To really drive it home, I even took an online crash course in Thai and memorized a bunch of conversational ethnic Katin phrases, which I practiced in front of my mirror. (*"Khap Kun Kha! Chai-yoh! Ta blü!"*) Finally, I practiced not cussing—easier said than done. Not that I dropped the f-bomb much normally, but it's strange how when you know you're not supposed to do something, then you *really* want to do it. Around the house, Mom and Dad mainly expressed themselves through the tried and true "Jesus!" and "God!"— and not in the way Ernestine did. (Yes, yes, I get the irony, them being atheists and all.) So I had to wean myself darn quick. But I'm nothing if not a fast learner.

By the end of two weeks, I was ready.

Oh, so ready.

I arrived at Bread of Life Church ten minutes early for my interview, but before I could open the door, a skinny guy in headgear burst through it and slammed right into me, launching a bunch of yellow papers into the air. As he scrambled to pick them up, I expected an apology, but instead he babbled to himself, "Are they crazy? Are they freakin' *crazy?!*"

"What's wrong?" I asked, edging away from him.

His glazed eyes came into focus. "Are you applying for the Outreach Trip?"

"Uh, yeah—"

"Consider yourself forewarned!"

He jumped up, shoved all the yellow pages at me, and stumbled away.

What the heck was that about?

I looked down at the crumpled sheets in my hand.

The headings included *Limited Liability Release Form, Passport and Visa Info, Caregiver Notarized Form,* and…

>> LIST OF VACCINATIONS & MEDICATIONS <<

(NOTE: Consult your doctor about this list—and make sure to get started on the vaccinations at least four to six weeks before we depart. Vaccines need time to kick in and you need to start taking your malaria medication before the trip.)

Here's the list of vaccinations:

1. Measles/mumps/rubella (MMR)
2. Diphtheria/pertussis/tetanus (DPT)
3. Polio virus vaccine
4. Hepatitis A
5. Hepatitis B (Just to be on the safe side!)
6. Japanese encephalitis
7. Rabies (Again, better safe than sorry! There are lots of rabid dogs in Southeast Asia/SEA!)
8. And for malaria, you'll need to take atovaquone-proguanil, doxycycline, or mefloquine (although this one may cause some wacky side effects).

And here's the list of suggested medications:

- Over the counter medication for diarrhea. (Believe me, you'll need it!)
- Medication for pain or fever—like acetaminophen,

aspirin, or ibuprofen
- **Cold & flu & allergy meds**
- **Antacid tablets**
- **Antifungal & antibacterial creams**
- **Insect repellent with DEET**
- **Sunblock (Get the max possible—the sun is brutal in SEA!)**
- **Rehydration packets**
- **As many antibacterial hand wipes and small alcohol-based hand sanitizers you can fit in your backpack! (USE LIBERALLY!)**
- **Moleskin pads for blisters**
- **Eye drops, lip balm, & such for dryness in airplanes**

(NOTE: We'll also have a team first aid kit with the rest of the necessary supplies like Band-Aids.)

"Collin Uttley?" quavered the voice of the elderly church receptionist.

I quickly stuffed the yellow papers into the folder tucked under my arm, refusing to let the medicinal issues of the trip sidetrack me.

I had to focus.

My time had come.

I inhaled.

I exhaled.

Then I removed my fedora, smoothed back my hair, and confidently entered the youth pastor's office, where the

Tacketts were conducting interviews. It was crammed with over-stuffed couches, two worn beanbag chairs, a lone folding chair, tubs full of basketballs and soccer balls, and photos of the youth group taped haphazardly across the oatmeal colored walls.

"*Sabai dii mai?*" I asked boldly, with a sort of half wave, half salute.

The Tacketts both looked up in surprise.

"Nice," said Dr. Tackett with a grin, before replying: "*Chan sabai dii, kop kun maak.*"

I smiled and nodded knowingly—having absolutely no clue what he'd just said.

"Have a seat, Collin," said Mrs. Tackett from the red beanbag chair, gesturing towards the blue one next to her. Dr. Tackett was comfortably sprawled across one of the couches. I perched on the edge of the lone folding chair, ignoring the overstuffed couches and the beanbag chairs that might lull me into relaxing.

Time to be on my A-game.

Dr. Peter Tackett looked more like a weathered surfer than a dentist: tanned with bleached brown hair, a graying goatee, and flip-flops on his feet—despite the cold (for Southern California) winter weather. He was in good shape for his age, despite some thickening around the mid-section. Mrs. Marcy Tackett sat cross-legged on the aforementioned beanbag and was twisting her long blond hair into a bun—which she secured with a Bic pen. Her large protruding eyes, set into an oval face with a high forehead gave her a soulful look. To put it in the Californian terms I was slowly picking up: she appeared less surfer and more granola. And she reeked of patchouli.

The funny thing was that their teeth were so white, so unnaturally neon white, that it was distracting. And didn't seem to fit the rest of their hippie-like personas.

Mrs. Tackett cocked her head to the side and gazed at me with her enormous eyes. Then she gave me a huge gleaming smile (which almost blinded me). "We have to tell you right off that your application blew us away! Blew-us-away!"

"Yeah, you're way more qualified than we are to lead this trip," said Dr. Tackett, with a chuckle that rumbled deep in his chest.

I didn't know how to respond, so I just smiled and twisted my hat.

Darn that Saint Collin the Ladler! I knew I should have toned down those references—

But before I could process further, there came a barrage of questions, which I answered without breaking a sweat—thanks to all those hours of practice in front of the bathroom mirror. They ranged from: "In what ways do you think you can contribute to the Team?" ("First of all, I have a servant's heart...") to: "Are you a vegetarian or vegan or have any food allergies or issues?" ("No way—I'll eat anything that's not moving.") I knew this was a loaded question, since outreach teams had to eat whatever the locals offered them. Then the biggie: "Why do you think you're *called* to go on this trip?" ("Well, I've always been a huge advocate of social justice—especially the cause of refugee children in Third World Countries...")

I could tell they were impressed with my answers—maybe even in awe at how prepared I was.

You got this.

"Okay, a final question for you, Collin," said Dr. Tackett, shifting to a sitting position. "One that isn't on the application."

"Sure thing," I said and leaned back in the chair with cocky nonchalance.

"What's your life verse?"

Doh! "Life verse?"

"Or life *verses*," added Mrs. Tackett. "Some people have more than one—or many throughout their lifetime."

"You mean a verse from the *Bible*?" I stalled, hoping they wouldn't notice the panic rippling across my face.

She nodded slowly and flicked a look at her husband.

What the heck is a life verse???

"Uh, well, that's a tough one… I mean, there are *so* many verses to choose from…" I laughed, shook my head, and gazed off into the distance as if I were visualizing the stacks and stacks of life verses, and the absurdity of selecting just one. "*So* many verses in *so* many books of the, uh, Good Book…"

Think of one, you idiot!

They waited politely for my answer, their brows beginning to furrow.

Come on! You can do this! What was that Psalm about shadows, death, and valleys…? Or that verse you always see on signs with the 3-1-6 on it…???

But, for the first time in my life, my mind was a complete blank. The random bits of trivia my brain generally seems to suck up like a vacuum cleaner didn't materialize this time.

Dr. Tackett coughed gently, as if to prod me into action.

Dang it! Where's that adrenaline surge when I need it most?!

Then suddenly a verse popped into my head. I blurted it out before it could slip away.

"There was no room for them in the inn."

Silence.

"From Luke 2? The story of Jesus' birth?" asked Mrs. Tackett, slightly perplexed.

Sell it, Collin! Sell it NOW!

"Yep. The most life changing *life* verse—ever."

"How so?" asked Dr. Tackett. He seemed genuinely curious.

The question almost derailed me. But I wasn't going down without a fight. "Well, it's a universal symptom. You see, there are times in all our lives when we discover there is, well, *no room in the inn.* That everyone else has a room—our parents have rooms, our siblings have rooms, our friends have rooms, our neighbors have rooms, even the guy at the drive-thru has a room. But *we* don't have a room. We're left out in the cold, all alone. Roomless. Not a room anywhere. A dearth of rooms. So my life verse is a reminder to me to be, you know, grateful for... for... well, my room. *The room GOD gave me.*"

I leaned back in my seat with a fixed smile, and folded my arms with a jaunty confidence I sure didn't feel.

What the heck was that all about??? You just totally tanked it! Talked yourself right off the Team!

But before I could excuse myself and slink out of the room, the Tacketts glanced at each other, and then nodded thoughtfully.

"Interesting analogy, Collin," said Dr. Tackett, scratching his goatee. "Never heard it interpreted in quite that way before…"

I exhaled in relief, but kept my fixed smile in place.

"A couple more things," said Mrs. Tackett. "You don't happen to be needle phobic, do you?"

I hid a smile and shook my head. I knew where this was going.

"Good, because there's a whole boatload of vaccinations you'd have to get," said Dr. Tackett rubbing his arm with a rueful grin. "And some of them hurt like the dickens."

I laughed and waved my hand dismissively. "Oh, pain is my middle name."

A momentary silence, during which I mentally kicked myself.

"Okay…" said Mrs. Tackett. Then she opened a manila folder at her feet and handed me some stapled papers. "You should probably be aware that we have a limit on how many people we can bring with us into the refugee camps. So the Team this year will be a max of five. If you're chosen, you'll have to sign and notarize this before the first Team meeting."

"*Limited Liability Release Form?*" I glanced up inquiringly.

"Basically, you gotta agree that if anything happens to you on this trip, you won't sue our butts off," said Dr. Tackett with a laugh.

"On any outreach trip, there's always a risk of something going wrong," said Mrs. Tackett. Then she added quickly, "But usually very *minor* things."

"Like what?" I asked, more curious than concerned.

"Transportation delays, canceled flights, dysentery, hidden fees, stolen backpacks, the usual stuff that comes with the territory in Third World Countries," said Dr. Tackett. "But nothing really serious. We're just legally required to put it out there."

"Do any of those potential risks concern you, Collin?" asked Mrs. Tackett, blinking sympathetically at me from the beanbag chair, like some big-eyed maternal frog on a lily pad.

I shrugged nonchalantly. "Not really. Should they?" I wanted them to think I was game for anything. By their reactions, I could see I played my cards right. (Now, in retrospect, I really should have paid more attention to those so-called *minor* things…)

Dr. Tackett tossed a stack of yellow handouts onto my lap. "When you get home, look these over, and let us know if you've changed your mind and don't want to be considered for the Team after all."

"And we'll totally understand," said Mrs. Tackett with a sympathetic smile.

"Oh, my mind's made up. I'm in! If anyone was born to go on this trip, it's me! Ever since I popped out of the womb, it's like I've been looking for a way to serve in a refugee camp somewhere, anywhere! Talk about a dream come true!"

Don't do this…

"I mean, I'm in if *you* say I'm in, if you know what I mean. Not trying to be overly confident or anything, but just saying… uh… that I'm really eager… it would be an honor to be considered… Yeah, I'll stop now."

I could see the relief on their faces once I did.

*   *   *   *   *

Did they see through me or not? Did I end up tanking or not? I wondered as I left the youth pastor's office, plopping the fedora back on my head and tucking the folder full of yellow handouts under my arm.

I'd just have to wait and see.

Man, Shelby, after all this, I sure hope you're game.

Excerpts from the Journal of Collin Uttley

(FYI: edited for content)

January 3rd – It's been weeks. I obviously blew it. The Tacketts saw through me. Think I'm an imposter. Or an idiot. Or both.

January 6th – Depressed. Ate four Toblerone bars in one sitting. Why do I care so much? I barely know Shelby.

January 7th – Score! Shelby invited me swing dancing! If I wasn't feeling so edgy about my Outreach Trip status, I'd be doing freakin' BACK FLIPS. LATER: She dances even better than I hoped, and she wore _flats_. When they played Rock This Town by the Stray Cats, we tore it up! And she's up for taking advanced swing lessons together! I think she's diggin' me!

January 10th – I'M IN!!! I'm one of the FIVE! What are the odds??? Makes you almost believe in God. Almost. LATER: Texted Shelby the news. Her reply: "YAY!!!! Was praying you'd make the TEAM!"

YESSS! Shelby + Collin = GAME ON**!!!!**

January 12th - Mom concerned I'll catch dengue fever or malaria or "worse"—what could be worse? Leprosy? She bought me organic bug spray that smells like ammonia. Will inadvertently "forget" to pack.

January 15th - First Outreach Team meeting (of fifteen!). Sat next to Shelby. (Yowl!) Tacketts welcomed us, passed out a bunch more yellow handouts, gave a long backstory of their passion for refugees, and their desire to someday adopt a Katin orphan when all the U.N. red tape gets taken care of. Felt like the odd man out, since the other four teammates are all Born Again Believers and have known each other for years. Luckily, they don't suspect me of ulterior motives and think I'm one of them. (Knock on wood!)

Tacketts suggested we get started on vaccinations and packing list ASAP. You kiddin' me? The trip's six months away, people! Talk about OCD. Shelby is depressed we can't bring all our vintage clothes—not practical in the jungle climate with all the trekking and sweating, so they say. But she'll wear cat-eye sunglasses and retro scarves and I'll wear argyle socks and straw fedora, to keep the vintage vibe flowing...

>> PACKING LIST <<

1. Two pairs of convertible trekking pants
2. Four breathable shirts
3. One pair of trekking shoes
4. One pair of flip-flops
5. Four sets of underwear and socks
6. One sweatshirt
7. One positive attitude! ☺
8. One pair of shorts
9. Sunglasses
10. Earplugs Earplugs Earplugs! (You'll thank us later!)
11. A sense of humor! ☺
12. Small toiletry bag with only *essential* toiletries
13. Portable clothesline
14. Therm-A-Rest mattress
15. Silk sleep sack (no sleeping bag required!)
16. Sun hat
17. Small paperback New Testament
18. Moleskine journal & pens
19. Swim suit (modest)
20. A servant's heart! ☺
21. Rx for contacts or any medication

22. Malaria meds *
23. Paperback book to swap when finished
24. Small digital camera
25. Photos of your family and friends to show refugees
26. Sunscreen and insect repellent (preferably combined)
27. Anti-bacterial hand soap (use liberally!)
28. Travel-size Wet-Naps
29. Travel-size Kleenex packs
30. Pepto Bismal tablets (to take before meals to coat stomach)
31. Travel or pocket size games (like playing cards or Uno)
32. Moleskins for blisters
33. Feminine sundries (sometimes hard to procure...)
34. Granola bars and small packages of trail mix for protein boosts.
35. Waterproof watch (optional, but handy)

* See Vaccination & Medication List for further items to bring.

>> TIPS <<

- Pack in big gallon and quart ziplock bags. This helps keeps things organized AND dry in a moist climate!
- One backpack and one daypack—that's it! And locks for both for when we must leave luggage behind.

- Your backpack shouldn't weigh more than twenty-five pounds if you're average size, thirty-five if you're on the bigger side.

>> LEAVE HOME <<

- Smartphone/Laptop/iPad/Kindle/TV (Think "media fast." And there's little to no phone reception or wifi in the refugee camps anyway.)

- Hairdryer

- Jewelry

- Clothes with political or offensive logos or slogans

- Valuables of any kind

- Self-absorption

Excerpts from the Journal of Collin Uttley

(FYI: edited for content)

January 15th (midnight) – SHOOT! Just read the Expected Behavior Guidelines handout the whole Team must sign before boarding plane to Bangkok... Dr. T said if any Team Member gets caught blatantly (versus accidentally) breaking any of the guidelines, "You'll be shipped back home to California faster than you can say *tom yum soup.*" Refusing to let Guideline #1 bring me down. Will ignore. (Make that: will sign—then ignore.) Will have to be *extra* creative (and cautious) in wooing Shelby. One false step could mean the end of... everything.

EXPECTED BEHAVIOR GUIDELINES
>> BOLYG Thailand Outreach Trip <<
(Handout #14)

I, _____, member of the
Bread of Life Youth Group Outreach Team, promise to refrain
from....

1. *Romantic entanglements.*

2. *Smoking cigarettes, drinking alcohol, or eating any endangered species (even if it's on the menu).*

3. *Any form of disorderly conduct (i.e. using profanity, spitting, making graffiti, brawling).*

4. *Sharing contact information or trip logistics with those "in country" without prior knowledge and consent of the Tacketts.*

5. *Participating in any illegal activities. (Illegal from the U.S. point of view, versus the Thai point of view—important difference!)*

6. *Leaving the group for an extended period of time for any reason, unless authorized by the Tacketts.*

....for the duration of the Outreach Trip to Thailand for my own personal safety and well-being—as well as the safety and well-being of the Team and those we are serving in-country. And I understand and agree that in the unlikely event that *I am* caught intentionally and/or repeatedly breaking any of the above Expected Behavior Guidelines (especially the ones which could endanger the group), I will be sent home on the earliest available flight, and will be held solely responsible for covering any extra charges or expenses related to the change of airplane tickets and additional ancillary transportation. Finally, I understand and agree that the Tacketts reserve full right and authority to decide if and when my deportation is deemed necessary for the safety and well-being of all involved.

Signed:

_____

Dated: _____

Notarized:

_____

Dated: _____

part two

THE MALARIA ZONE

OUTREACH TEAM UPDATE

(Posted from some random internet café in Bangkok on July 3rd because the Tacketts wouldn't let us bring our laptops, tablets, or smartphones, not that we'd have cell service here, but anyway, where was I?)

Sawatdee krup! (Greetings in "Thai"!)
I speak for the entire Outreach Team when I say: your butt goes numb if you don't move for five hours straight. Trust me on this, dudes! (Warning! Don't fall asleep playing old school Pong and Space Invaders in a cramped airline seat. Man, if only they had Xbox—I'm going through withdrawals already.)
Anyway, Jack-O here. We're taking turns posting the lowdown on our trip so far. I think they made me go first because I'm the only one NOT jetlaggin'…
Anyway! Thailand is hot. The curry is hot. The girls are hot. Kidding! (Actually, they are. Steamin' hot. But that's not what we're here for…)
Seriously, folks, the sweat never stops.
Okay, back on track:
After a layover, we landed in Bangkok and spent the night in a business hotel near the airport. We were totally wiped and slept like logs. (We were so dead, it took the Tacketts forever to wake us up!) This morning, we had a team meeting to pray and "debrief," then we taxied into the

city to eat and "acclimate" before we drive to some border town (forget the name) where we'll buy supplies before we officially start outreaching at the biggest refugee camp in all of Southeast Asia, Yai Camp.

Bangkok is pretty much like I imagined it. (Google it and see for yourselves.) Oh, except for way more diesel fumes than the States.

Prayer Request for Ernestine. She hasn't taken a dump yet. (That old travel buddy: constipation. Any tips on getting her regular, send them our way...) The rest of us already have the runs. But the Tacketts say that comes with the territory.

Oh, that's Dr. T yelling for me to get in the van. We're heading to that border town now to buy supplies. Tomorrow: our first of three—count 'em THREE—refugee camps!

Jer gan mai! (See you again later!)
GERONIMO!!!

West Meets East

"**W**HAT ARE YOU WAITING FOR, DUDE?"
"Don't do it, Jack-O!"

"Do it!"

"Yuck! It's totally unsanitary!"

"How do you eat a beetle, anyway? Leg by leg or all at once?" I fanned my dripping face with my fedora.

The Team was clustered around a food stall stacked with baskets of dried bees, ants, lizards, fish, cockroaches, and other "gourmet delights." Shelby Wanderal, Twain Abernathy, Ernestine Ketchum, and I watched beefy line-backer Jack Ogata (Jack-O to his friends) expectantly as he tilted his head and peered through steamed black framed glasses at the four-inch beetle in his meaty hand. Beads of sweat dripped from his spiky tufts of hair onto the insect.

The heat was intense. A maze of ramshackle stalls surrounded us, and a patchwork of blue, red, green, and yellow plastic tarps overhead kept the rain and sun *out*, but kept the humidity trapped *in*. We'd only been inside the local border town market for ten minutes, yet our "moisture wicking" trekking attire was already soaked as if we'd been submerged in one of those carnival dunk tanks.

I was still acclimating—to the climate, to the culture, and

47

to my continual close proximity to Shelby, who, at the moment, was retying a yellow scarf with red cherries over her hair, which was extra curly in all the humidity. And I was also acclimating to my stodgy trekking uniform—going through vintage clothing withdrawals. I sure didn't feel like myself in pants with zip-off legs.

"Sure you want to do this, you big lug?" Ernestine asked Jack-O in her distinctive husky voice. "Remember, the grasshoppers you ate in TJ were way, way smaller…" But despite her "concern," she shoved her digital camera in his face.

"Geronimo!" said Jack-O—and jammed the entire beetle into his mouth.

"Jesus! Have mercy!"

An elderly Thai woman passing by was so startled by the outburst that she almost dropped her basket of guavas.

Twain nodded approvingly as he filmed the action with the Team's official video camera and said in a low, mellow tone: "Nice, dude. Less parts to deal with that way." He sported a crew cut, jungle boots (black leather with olive canvas uppers), mirrored aviator glasses—and towered over the rest of us at the offensive height of six foot five inches.

After a moment of maneuvering the bug around in his mouth with his tongue, Jack-O determinedly began to chew. And chew. And chew.

"Eewwww!"

"What does it taste like?"

"Is it as gross as it looks?"

Jack-O chewed and considered, then said in a guttural voice, "Crunchy, dry. Like chicken wing bones. Or like—ow!" He shifted the contents of his mouth from one side to the other with his tongue, then pulled something out and examined it. "Antennae?"

Shelby's initial awe dissolved into repulsion and she turned to dry heave. After a minute, she stood up and managed a weak smile. "I'm fine, I'm fine. False alarm."

"Good save, Shel. Don't want you upchucking all over the Thai market," Twain said with a mocking grin.

"Vegans are super sensitive," said Ernestine, winking at the rest of us. "That whole *delicate palate* thing—"

"I'm *not* a vegan!" Shelby said defensively. "I just have a trigger gag reflex, that's all."

Jack-O lifted his chin and swallowed the rest. By the look on his face, it must have scraped all the way down. He unscrewed his bottle of water and guzzled the whole thing, sending water cascading down his chin and neck. Then he held his hand out to Twain, "Cough it up, bro."

Twain slapped a twenty on his palm.

"For fifty, I'll eat a lizard or a whole baggie of bees—"

"I'll pass. I only got so much spending money."

"Glad to see you're comfortable with alternative forms of protein, Jack-O," said Dr. Tackett with a chuckle, as he and Mrs. Tackett joined the group, also dressed in trekking attire and also sweating. "But our Thai ministry contact is waiting for us."

"She's down this aisle." Mrs. Tackett gestured for us to follow her, as she fanned her face with a tie-dyed sunhat. Her patchouli smelled extra pungent in the heat and humidity.

It was crazy to think it was barely seven months ago I first met Shelby—and the rest of this oddball Team. After all our meetings, training sessions, and fundraising events, I felt like

I'd known them for years. All of them, that is, except for Twain—he was a tough nut to crack, as my dad would say. Closed off. But Jack-O, on the other hand, was the polar opposite: a goofy, good-natured jock, who always said the first thing that came into his brain. Apparently, he'd applied for the trip because his Japanese American great grandparents had been put in California internment camps during World War II, and he really felt for the refugees.

"What's the grossest thing you've ever eaten, Collin?" asked Ernestine. She fell into step beside me, smoothing back her hair—dyed specially for the trip in bright "fire" streaks of yellow, orange, and red—which contrasted sharply with her bland trekking clothes. She just didn't seem her normal self without a concert t-shirt and thick-soled Docs or worn Chuck Taylors.

"Oh, I don't know…wet bread?"

She laughed and hit me in the arm affectionately. "There's still time."

"Ow! Please refrain from physical contact," I said, leaning away from her and rubbing my arm.

She grinned. "You dork! Why didn't you get your vaccinations in the thigh like the rest of us?"

Despite all her outbursts, Ernestine had begun to grow on me—at least when she wasn't thwacking me in the arm.

She pointed at my trekking shoes. "Aren't you missing something, Spats?"

I winced. "Hey, I told you I tossed the spats. I'm just waiting for you to do the same with your grommets!"

She laughed and fingered the metal in her ear.

We winded our way through the narrow maze of stalls to

the woman who'd be acting as our trip guide, translator, and driver. We heard her before we saw her, the loud and rapid Thai phrases exploding like gunshots in the relatively quiet market.

"Yee sip? Pang mak!"

We turned the corner and there she was.

Jongchit was a high-energy Thai woman with a large moon-like face and hair cut into a pageboy that was mostly shiny black—except for a handful of stray gray hairs that bobbed like antennas when she talked. A pair of glossy red sunglasses shaped like hearts perched on top of her head.

She was surrounded by bags of rice, piles of toothpaste and toothbrushes, bars of soap, cans of bug spray, stacks of folded mosquito netting, and bottles of water.

"Pang mak! Pang mak!"

With a determined smile on her face, Jongchit debated in Thai *(rat-a-tat-tat)* with the stall owner—a matchstick of a man who more than matched her energy. Her voice pierced through the tinny techno music coming from a battered radio in the back of the stall. Finally, she turned to the Tacketts and said in her throaty, animated voice, "He stubborn, very stubborn. Say will give us our price *if* we buy one box more."

"Sounds good. You can never have too much toothpaste," said Dr. Tackett, ready to move on.

Jongchit chuckled. "Aha! Just what he want, the trickster! Tricky, tricky trickster!" She playfully shook her finger at the owner, who gave her a wry grin. "More time. I need more time—more-more-more! Then I wear him down! I wear him down like grains in mortar!" Then she threw back her head and bellowed in delight, launching her sunglasses into the air in a perfect arc, which landed smack on top of an open bag of dried coriander seeds.

I rescued the hearts—shaking off the seeds—and Jongchit replaced them on her head with a hearty, *"Kun sabai dee mai kha!"* Then she grinned at the Outreach Team. We all watched her in awe, not quite knowing what to make of her. She abruptly poked me in the chest.

"How old am I? Guess, boy, guess!"

Ah. That old loaded question that women way past middle age love to ask. I didn't realize it was alive and well in Southeast Asia. The rest of the Team took a collective step back like a receding wave—leaving me the lone shell stranded on the sand.

"Forty?" I asked with a smirk at the others. I knew how to play this game.

She beamed. "Ha ha! You so sweet!" She pinched my cheek.

"Forty-five?"

"More!"

"No way, you can't be fifty?"

"Fifty is a breeze gone by!"

"Fifty-five?"

"So many more summers have passed!"

"Sixty?" I said in a weak tone as if it was unfathomable.

"Do not be startled—I am sixty-five!" she said, pausing for me (and the rest of the Team) to express shock and profuse admiration.

Once she was satisfied with our response, she continued: "But *kha, kha*—I look forty, as you say. Thai weather, it so good-good-good for skin. And the coconut oil." She gently slapped her cheeks. "And my energy, you know I have much-much-much energy! It is from Holy Spirit, he give it to me."

"Okay..." I said, not knowing quite how to respond to this mention of the third member of the so-called Trinity. (A concept I never could wrap my mind around, even after making a bunch of gold foil Russian Trinity Triptych icons in our Art of Religion homeschool class.)

"I am tooooo much! All the time, people say I am too-too much! All the time!"

She threw back her head and chortled with laughter.

The Tacketts had met Jongchit years ago, on one of their many volunteer trips to Thailand. Jongchit was also an R. N. like Mrs. Tackett, and spent a couple decades volunteering in Yai Camp, the largest refugee camp in Southeast Asia. And although the Tacketts had talked about her, nothing had prepared us for meeting her in the flesh.

"Where's Hobab?" asked Dr. Tackett, scanning the market.

"Oh, he outside with the football. Football, football, football! All the time football, the crazy boy!" said Jongchit affectionately. Then, to the rest of the team, "Go, *farang!* Explore market. Eat food. Buy postcard. We have much business here..." Then she returned to haranguing the stall owner.

We looked at the Tacketts for confirmation. Dr. Tackett checked his chunky diving watch and said, "All right, Team, go ahead and explore, but stay inside the market. Meet back here in about *sip haa*—fifteen—minutes."

As the Team headed down the aisle, the radio began to play *Rock This Town* by the Stray Cats. Shelby and I looked at each other and laughed. What were the odds? During the last few months, Shelby and I had bonded over swing dancing, classic movies, and all things vintage. There wasn't a thrift store in LA we hadn't checked out. In fact, we'd spent so much time together I was secretly frustrated that despite my best efforts, we hadn't made it past the friend stage. My parents said I shouldn't be surprised—that the cautious way some Christians dated these days would make Amish courtship look like *Girls Gone Wild.* Not that my parents knew anything more about Christians than what they heard on NPR. And, of course, their dating know-how was next to nil.

Anyway, I really liked Shelby and I could sense she liked me. So either she was playing hard to get—or she was waiting for me to bowl her over with some creative wooing, and if so, *Rock This Town* was the perfect opportunity!

But first—B.O. check. An overpowering plastic scent assailed my nostrils. And although the rest of my body was dripping, my armpits were as dry as chalk. Before the trip, I'd discovered an antiperspirant deodorant called STOP THE STINK LEVEL 10. It was created for Westerners trekking in the tropics.

Confident that I didn't reek, I extended my hand and said, "How 'bout it?"

Shelby stared at me. "What?"

"Let's cut it up!"

"Here? Now?" She glanced around her with a flush of embarrassment.

"What was the point of all those swing lessons if we're not gonna put them to good use?"

"But in the middle of a Thai market?"

"Especially in the middle of a Thai market!"

She relaxed and laughed. "Oh, Collin, you're crazy!"

I whirled Shelby around the dim aisle—narrowly missing an odd stray dog and a near-sighted customer. We rock-stepped and cherry-picked and twirled and dipped until we cascaded with sweat. The stall owners paused to stare at us—some amused and some confused at what exactly these *farangs* (western foreigners) were doing in their market. The Tacketts and Jongchit gave us quick amused glances before returning to business. After dipping Shelby back so far that her curls grazed the ground, she gasped, "No more swinging—I'm sopping!"

"This calls for mango juice!" I fanned my sweating face with my fedora. "I'll be back before you can say lindy hop."

I'M NOT LAZY BUT I'M FUN

A S I MADE MY WAY DOWN ONE OF THE closely packed aisles, my senses were attacked on all sides: the smell of sesame oil bubbling in a wok mingling with the odor of rotting garbage; the sounds of sellers hawking and kids laughing; the vibrant colors of mangos, eggplants, and dried chilies piled high in one stall; and the shiny primary colors of the plastic buckets, dish-tubs, and chairs in the next.

Where were those stalls selling fresh fruit drinks? Was it along this aisle? Or that aisle? Maybe if I took a left here? I tripped over a boy chasing his little sister and ended up toppling into a stack of plastic stools. Then, before I knew what was happening, I was skidding—skidding in *blood!*

I stopped myself just in time before toppling onto a still steaming pig carcass, recently gutted, but I stepped smack right on top of the spleen—which lodged itself under my trekking shoe!

As I crouched down to Wet-Nap the blood that had splattered the bottom of my pants, I noticed Twain walking towards me. I was just about to warn him about the pig blood, when he furtively looked around—oblivious to my presence—then darted out through the plastic tarps into the street. What was he doing? Where was he going? Why leave the group? Why act so mysterious?

I quickly tossed the Wet-Nap into the shallow ditch that served as the market's garbage catch-all and hurried after him. But by the time I peered out through the tarps and scanned the busy street—Twain was gone.

Ten minutes later, I finally tracked down a beverage vendor, bought some Orange Fanta (which was the closest thing to juice I could find), and returned to Shelby, holding the bottle triumphantly as if it were the Holy Grail.

"Here you go."

Although Shelby was in the middle of buying postcards, she paused long enough to drain the contents in one fell swoop. "Collin, you're the best," she said with a gentle burp and handed me back the empty bottle.

"Twain just left the market, which I didn't think we were allowed to do. The *Expected Behavior Guidelines* sounded pretty darn strict," I said. "Do you think he got permission?"

"What? You serious?" Shelby seemed genuinely concerned. "That's weird. I wonder where he went. You don't think he'll get lost or abducted or something?"

I turned to walk away. "Guess I'd better let the Tacketts know—"

"No!" she said with sudden vehemence, reaching out and grabbing my arm. "You can't tell on him until you know what's going on. That's so not *fair*."

Her intense and childish reaction in his defense floored me. But I managed a nonchalant smile and said, "I wasn't going to *tell on him*. Last I checked this wasn't preschool. I was just gonna give the Tacketts a heads up that he might be lost… you know, wandering the streets in a disoriented stupor or something. After all, he went out without a *buddy*. But I won't if you don't think I need to. He's a big boy."

I didn't like the extreme relief that spread across her face.

We returned to the group, where Jongchit had presumably prevailed, for the matchstick man was piling hundreds of boxes of toothpaste in front of his stall. The Tacketts were going over the receipts and filing them in a mini accordion file-folder that Mrs. Tackett kept tucked in her floral hippack.

"Have you seen Twain?" I asked Ernestine, who was holding a pink Hello Kitty t-shirt in one hand and a box of pipe cleaners in the other.

"Hmmm?" She glanced at me briefly, semi-distracted. "He's probably buying souvenirs somewhere."

"Exactly!" said Shelby, giving me an "I told you so" look.

"How many extra pipe cleaners should I get?" Ernestine asked. "I'm not sure we have enough for the lion puppets. I brought extra googly eyes, but not—"

"Are you crazy? We need craft supplies like we need a third leg!" I said with a touch of exasperation.

"You sure?" Ernestine looked doubtful.

I snatched the box of pipe cleaners out of her hand and tossed them back on the table full of random art supplies. "More sure than I've ever been in my entire life." I put my hands on her shoulders and steered her away. "Let me lead you out of temptation…"

Nice one! Way to throw in a biblical reference!

She laughed.

"You may laugh, my friend, but your obsession with crafts borders on addiction." I wasn't entirely joking. The Tacketts had put Ernestine in charge of preparing craft projects for all the orphans and refugee kids. She'd even roped me into a bunch of trips to Michael's and other stores to help her buy mountains of beads, construction paper, glitter, and about a thousand googly eyes.

The other members of the Team had roles to play as well: Shelby was the worship leader, Jack-O was the sports and games organizer, and Twain was our trip documentarian, armed with the church's video camera. And me? I was supposed to be the "Team Rover" and help out as needed. So far, Ernestine and her craft obsession had taken up most of my "roving" time.

"Guys! Guys!" Jack-O ran up.

He was wearing a light blue t-shirt with yellow letters that read: I'M NOT LAZY BUT I'M FUN. "Notice anything different?"

"It makes no sense and the N is blurred," said Ernestine, "so it suits you to a T."

Jack-O turned to me beseechingly. "What do *you* think, bro? Funny, right?"

"Hilarious," came a voice from behind us before I could respond.

Twain. Looking very tall, very nonchalant, and very pleased with himself.

"So there you are!" said Shelby, her face lighting up. "We were getting worried. It was like that time in sixth grade, when the class searched the whole history museum looking for you—"

"And found me climbing on top of a tank in the World War II exhibit," finished Twain with a grin.

Shelby mockingly shook her finger at him. "I should put you in a time out, you naughty boy."

"I'd like to see you try." He tweaked her pug nose and she pushed his hand away, but in the process, dropped her handful of postcards. They simultaneously leaned over to pick them up, knocked heads—then backed away, laughing as if it was the funniest thing ever.

Warning bells rang in my head as I watched this screwball comedy unfold before me. Could Twain actually pose a threat? Although his excessive height of 6'5 was a continual slap in the face, the rest of him was average. *Very* average. Sure, he was muscular and tan, but his gray eyes were too close together under shaggy brows, and he had acne along his jaw line. And it seemed to my discerning eye that his nose was too small for his face. Not to mention he wore braces— and not the "invisible" kind. And probably had to wear *headgear* at night!

I relaxed.

You've got nothing to worry about!

"And check this one out," continued Jack-O, holding up an orange T-shirt with SAME SAME written on the front. He flipped it around to show the back: BUT DIFFERENT. *"Same same, but different!* Get it?" Then he peeled off the blue t-shirt exposing his sweaty torso.

Ernestine turned away as if blinded, "Yikes, Jack-O! Put your clothes back on!"

"Hello! Whatta ya think I'm doing?" he replied in a hurt tone as he tugged on the orange shirt.

I turned to Twain and asked with curiosity, "So… where'd you go?"

The wary look he gave me quickly melted into amusement. "Awww, how sweet. Collin missed me. I was in the *huang nam*—the bathroom. If you can call it that. Subject to interpretation. More like a hole in the ground. The Tacketts were sure right about squat toilets—it does take a while to get your balance right. I mean, come on, how are you supposed to crouch *and* wipe at the same time without tipping over…."

As he babbled on and on about the primitive bathroom conditions, I could tell he was trying to prevent us from asking more questions. There was that mysterious, evasive quality about him again that I couldn't quite put my finger on. Even after months of "team bonding" I didn't feel like I knew the *real* Twain. An invisible wall of emotional protection went up any time things got personal.

I was about to warn Twain about not letting the Tacketts catch him breaking *Expected Behavior Guideline #6*, when I noticed a new duffel bag tucked under his right arm. His right bicep was noticeably bulging under the heft. He paused mid-sentence and shifted it under his left arm when he saw me staring.

"What did you buy?" I asked, more curious than ever.

He blinked at me. Cracked his neck. Then he grinned and said, "This? Oh, just some souvenirs. For my sisters."

"How sweet! Amber and Celia will be so happy. What did you get them?" asked Shelby.

Long pause. "Dolls."

"Really? In traditional Thai gowns? Can I see?" she asked—putting a hand on his arm. (I had to restrain myself from snatching it off.)

Another long pause. "Uh, maybe later, Shel, okay? They're all, you know, wrapped up and stuff."

He no more has dolls under his arm than I have rocks in my head. What was he up to?

THUMP-THUMP!

"**L**OAD 'EM UP, BREAD TEAM!" JONGCHIT called, pulling her red heart sunglasses off her head and securing them on her nose. The Tacketts and the Outreach Team carried the boxes of supplies outside into the street, narrowly dodging beeping *tuk tuks*, the prevalent three-wheeled motorcycle taxis of Thailand. After we loaded up two 4x4 pick-up trucks (one red and one yellow), Jongchit scanned the parking lot, hands on her hips. "Now where is that rascal?"

"Hiya, guys!" called a guy about our age from across the parking lot, where he was playing soccer with some other high schoolers. He ran towards us, laughing and tucking the ball under his arm. He was a couple inches taller than me and lanky, with a mop of shaggy hair, which reminded me of a poster I saw of The Beatles. He wore a shirt with a picture of a soccer player and the name *Ronaldo* stitched across the front.

"Football, always the football," said Jongchit with stern affection.

Jack-O pointed to his shirt and said in a mock scolding tone, "Dude! You should be wearing Pele, not Ronaldo. He's the all time great!"

Hobab laughed and threw the soccer ball into the back of

the truck. His laugh was infectious—half chuckle, half giggle. Without missing a beat, he replied, "Man, you gotta be crazy to think that. Ronaldo is king. Totally king, dude." The fluid English slang coming out of his mouth was a little jarring.

"Pele scored like 1281 goals in 1363 games! He's the top league goal scorer *ever!*" said Jack-O.

Hobab chuckled and swung the bangs out of his eyes. "Goals? Football is more than goals! There's no other player in history with the footwork like Ronaldo's—"

"Enough of the football!" said Jongchit, waving her arms like a referee. "Must meet Bread Team." She tapped his head. "Football for brain."

"I get that a lot, too," Jack-O said to Hobab, nodding sympathetically.

We all introduced ourselves.

Then Jongchit pointed at Hobab. "His Katin dad in Burma. His name Jolly."

"Yeah, he's part of the 12th Brigade," said Hobab. "Fighting the BMJ."

"BMJ?" said Ernestine.

"Burmese Military Junta," Twain said quickly. Then, leaning eagerly towards Jongchit and Hobab, "Is there really a ceasefire right now like they say? Is the BMJ actually playing by the rules this time?"

Hobab and Jongchit exchanged incredulous glances.

"How you know so much about Freedom Fighters, soft American boy?" asked Jongchit, peering at him suspiciously.

"Oh, man! The cause is all I eat, live, and breathe! It's why I'm here," said Twain thumping his chest energetically. "Justice must prevail!"

The impressed look Shelby gave him made me uneasy, so I quickly changed the subject. Turning to Hobab, I asked, "Is 'Hobab' a Thai or Katin name?"

"Do you not know your Bible, Colon Boy?" asked Jongchit. "Hobab is relative of Moses."

"Yeah, *Colon Boy*," said Twain with a laugh, nudging me in the ribs with his elbow.

"Oh, that's right, it slipped my mind," I said, scrambling to cover.

Jongchit turned to Ernestine. "Why you call Ern-es-tine?"

"Uh, well, I was named after my Grandpa Ernesto, who was a pastor in Mexico when—"

"I no like. I call you Mangosteen!"

"Come again?" said Ernestine, totally taken aback.

"Mangosteen. Very delicious fruit. Best fruit in all Southeast Asia. So sweet. Like dessert. Your crazy hairs look like many fruit, dessert of fruit—so very good name for you!" said Jongchit, reaching up to pat Ernestine's red-orange-yellow hair.

"I tell her it looks like one of those Rocket Pop popsicles!" said Jack-O. "Hot and cold at the same time!" He laughed uproariously, pleased with himself, then reached out to touch her fire hair. *"Ssss—hotttt! Red hotttt!!!"*

Ernestine rolled her eyes and said, "Man Child!" just as Jongchit barked, "Time for to vamoose, Bread Team!"

We interpreted that as our cue to climb aboard the vehicles.

"After you, *Mangosteen*," Twain said with a bow to Ernestine.

Just then, Mrs. Tackett's iPhone rang.

The Tacketts were the only ones allowed to bring smartphones, for emergency use only. We were instructed to leave all electronic devices at home, except for digital cameras, because we were supposed to focus on the "here and now" and not be "artificially distracted" by social media, email, YouTube, and iTunes. (Jack-O and Ernestine both went through severe withdrawals within the first 24 hours). The Tacketts had said there was little to no reception in the refugee camps anyway, and in certain areas cell phone use was actually prohibited. They also said it wasn't uncommon for smartphones to be lost, confiscated, or stolen on these types of trips. And there was no way they wanted that kind of responsibility on their hands.

Anyway, it didn't take long for us to realize that something was wrong.

"…are you sure it can't wait?... But don't you think that after the trip would be…" Mrs. Tackett shot a sidelong glance at Shelby. "Well, it's not the best timing… Okay, yes, I understand. I'm so sorry. Hold on." She turned to whisper in Dr. Tackett's ear, and after a moment he gave Shelby a look of grave concern.

Shelby shifted uncomfortably. "What's going on?" she asked in a tense voice. "What's wrong? Something's wrong, I can tell!"

Mrs. Tackett put a tanned arm around Shelby and steered her away from the group. "Your mom needs to tell you something, Shelby," she said in a gentle voice. "Take a deep breath. Another one. Keep breathing, in and out, in and out, that-a-girl…" Then she handed her the phone as they disappeared around the side of Jongchit's truck.

Although we couldn't see them, we could still hear clearly: "Mom?... What is it?" came Shelby's tentative voice.

Suddenly it hit me.

Depending on what this is all about, Shelby might actually be sent home! Too bad there is no God—his involvement could really come in handy right about now.

A few moments later, we heard a piercing wail that made my arm and neck hairs stand to attention.

"Nooooo!"

I instinctively stepped forward, but Dr. Tackett put a re-straining hand on my arm. "Wait."

If it weren't for his iron-like grip, I'd have bolted around the side of the truck. Every garbled syllable and choking sob sent electric jolts of sympathy through my body.

The rest of the Team exchanged concerned glances.

A little distance away, Jongchit and Hobab were in con-versation with a pair of uniformed men, who were gesturing impatiently at the two overloaded trucks.

When the tortuous phone call finally ended, a crumpled Shelby reappeared around the corner of the truck—cheeks wet, eyes pink, chin trembling, and shoulders slumped. The Team immediately engulfed Shelby in a big group hug.

"What is it, Shelby? Come on, tell us already!" said Ernes-tine, her own eyes beginning to water.

"It can't be that bad, Shell-Bell. Can it?" asked Jack-O, wrinkling up his face in concern.

Shelby gazed at us for a moment, and then said with a quaver:

"F-f-flounce!"

It turned out that Shelby's double dappled dachshund had

been run over by a student driver. For some reason, Shelby's family thought she should be notified sooner than later. I could tell the Tacketts completely disagreed. For good reason. What could Shelby possibly do from Southeast Asia? But apparently, her mom thought she'd want some input as to where he should be buried, since they'd gotten a special permit to lay him to rest in their half acre of land.

Poor Shelby.

"Jacked up student drivers!" said Jack-O, shaking his head vehemently. "Those pant-loads should be outlawed!"

After that, the Team took turns praying. (Make that: the rest prayed and I just intoned the occasional, "Yes, Lord." I'd learned that was the key to sounding prayerful, without the need to actually *pray* pray.)

Dr. Tackett was finishing up with, "…and we all know someday Shelby will be reunited with little Flounce—"

"Bread Team go now! Pronto pup!" interrupted Jongchit. "Police give ticket—or we pay bribe. Same same."

"But different!" Jack-O's eyes lit up as he pointed to the back of his new orange shirt.

The Tacketts sat inside the cab of Hobab's truck, with the supplies piled in the truck bed. The rest of the Team squeezed in Jongchit's truck bed, wedged between pieces of luggage. Jongchit revved the engine and headed down the busy street. Shelby hunched in the corner, clutching her ukulele to her chest—small and frail and sad. The Team kept darting helpless looks at her and each other. Although I felt sorry for Shelby, I also knew this was a prime wooing opportunity I couldn't pass up.

I was in the process of scooting over towards her, when Jongchit accelerated onto a highway and our bodies were involuntarily pinned against the sides of the truck bed. Shelby's ukulele case flew out of her arms and slammed against the tailgate! All thoughts of wooing whizzed out of my head as I immediately clutched my fedora to keep it from blowing away.

"This would be so illegal in the U.S.!" yelled Jack-O, his spiky hair now a fright wig in the wind.

"Yikes! Did you see that!? She barely missed that cat!" shouted Ernestine, gripping the side of the truck. Her hair whipped through the air like a red-orange-yellow whirlwind.

"What about those kids?" I croaked, at the sight of the school children walking single file along the edge of the highway. "She almost grazed that girl's arm!"

"Man, it's like that old show... with the racing muscle cars... what's it called? Oh, *The Dukes of Hazard!*" said Twain, as we careened around a corner without slowing down. "No, make that *The Fast and the Furious!*"

During a brief pause while the two trucks stopped at a random traffic light in the middle of the highway, we pried our fingers off the sides of the truck and massaged the blood back into our numb hands.

"This reminds me of that ride at Magic Mountain where you—" But Ernestine never completed her thought, for Jongchit gunned it and once again we were all plastered against the truck-bed walls.

Shelby was mollusked to the side of the truck. Unable to even move her head. Only her wide eyes rolled around freely. I wanted to pat her on the back—but I still gripped my hat with one hand and the side of the truck with the other. Instead, our eyes met in unspoken commiseration.

Those notarized *Limited Liability Release Forms* made absolute sense right about now!

Bam!

"Yip!"

Thump thump!

"What the heck was that???" I asked.

We all swiveled around to see a dog lying on his back, hind legs twitching. But we were going so fast, within seconds it was out of sight.

"Holy Cow!" yelled Jack-O.

"You gotta be kidding me!" exclaimed Ernestine in disbelief.

"Oh, man, this timing sucks," muttered Twain.

The four of us simultaneously glanced over at Shelby, hoping by chance she hadn't noticed.

No such luck.

"Stop! STOP! We've got to *stop!*" Shelby's voice escalated. *"Why isn't Jongchit stopping?!"*

Poor Shelby—as if she hadn't experienced enough dog trauma for one day. I relinquished my grip long enough to give her a quick pat on the arm—then immediately re-gripped the side of the truck. "I'm sure it's already out of its misery and... passed on. Maybe even now it's chasing Flounce across the lawns of heav..." I trailed off at the horrified look on her face.

"At least it won't go to waste," Twain muttered to Jack-O.

"What? What's that?" said Shelby sharply.

"Nothing," said Twain.

"Tell me! What about it not going to waste?" said Shelby. "It'll make me feel a whole lot better if there's a purpose to it all. Tell me!"

Ernestine flashed Twain a "don't you dare!" look and turned to Shelby. "You so don't wanna know—"

"I so wanna know the *truth*," maintained Shelby stubbornly. "Tell me, Twain."

"No, Shel. Forget it," said Twain, avoiding eye contact.

"Tell me!" There was something almost ferocious in Shelby's eyes. "TELL ME NOW!!!"

"You sure you're sure?" He glanced at the occasional small businesses and cafés we were passing. "Okay, look there." Twain pointed to a restaurant. "See that red flag in the window?"

"Yeah? So?"

"It means they… well… they serve K9."

"K9…K9…?" Horror dawned in Shelby's eyes. "You mean *canine*??? They don't really—"

"Sorry, Shel, I told you that you wouldn't want to know," said Twain, shaking his head in remorse.

Shelby turned pale.

"Waste not, want not," said Jack-O with a shrug.

"Shut up!" Ernestine glared at him.

I shot Twain a "now see what you've done" look.

After a couple minutes, Shelby seemed to pull herself together. "No, I'm… I'm sorry for being such a baby. It's just that… that *thump-thump*—" she shuddered, "that *thump-thump* made me think of… think of…"

"Don't go there," said Ernestine, giving her shoulder a quick squeeze.

71

"Thump-thump," murmured Shelby and shuddered again. *"Thump-thump..."*

What should I say or do to comfort Shelby? I'm wasting this prime wooing opportunity!

I scrambled to remember the new "life verse" I'd memorized immediately following that close call with the Tacketts. "Shelby, remember that... that... 'there was no room for them in the—'"

Ooops!

"Uh, I mean, I mean, that when all sorts of bad things go down, in theory, God is actually working for your own good—"

She burst out crying before I could even finish butchering the verse.

"Bad move, bro," said Jack-O in a low tone.

"What? Why? It's *the* go-to verse during tough times—"

"It's *so* not the one to use right now, Collin." Ernestine gave me a pointed look, which I had no clue how to interpret.

But *why* wasn't it the one to use right now?

I was beginning to realize that there were a whole lot of unspoken rules in the church world. So I'd really have to watch my step. Although being discovered as an imposter wasn't on the list of *Expected Behavior Guidelines*, it just might be considered deportation-worthy.

The Wigglewurts

WE LEFT THE HIGHWAY AND BUMPED DOWN a dirt road, dodging potholes and stray dogs—but luckily had no more hits. Jongchit abruptly veered right and we found ourselves surrounded by rice paddies—glimmering squares of water dotted with jade sprouts as far as the eye could see. But before we could fully absorb the view, the truck turned a sharp left, skidded through an open metal gate manned by a sleeping Thai guard, and squealed to a stop.

"Look see! The *Born Free to Live Free AMEN Academy!*" exclaimed Jongchit as she leaped out of the driver's seat.

A stunned silence pervaded the truck bed as the Team realized the insanity had finally ended. Then we stiffly pried our fingers from the metal for the last time and slowly disembarked—stomachs still sloshing.

"Jongchit's gotta have a whole boatload of guardian angels," said Jack-O, smoothing his windblown hair and adjusting his black glasses.

"Make that an entire battalion," said Twain as he grabbed his mysterious duffel and again tucked it under his arm.

I carefully helped Shelby down onto the pavement, where she stood listlessly, sniffing and staring off into space.

Ernestine wobbled over to Jongchit, barely maintaining

her equilibrium, and stammered, "Uh… did you… did you notice back there that you… that you… I mean, did you even *see* that dog? The one you totally plowed over…?"

Jongchit glanced at her in surprise. "Jongchit have super duper twenty-twenty vision. *Di mak!* My eyeball, they miss nothing!"

The words *Born Free to Live Free AMEN Academy!* were painted in bright turquoise on a sign attached to a large, unpainted cement building with shuttered windows and a clay tile roof, surrounded by papaya and banana trees. Piles of building materials were scattered everywhere, and ladders and tools leaned against the unfinished walls.

Jack-O bee-lined towards the trees and plucked a pigmy banana. He peeled it and gulped down the vibrant yellow in two bites. "Heck yeah!" he said with his mouth full. "These make the bananas back home taste like glue!"

Just then, the second truck drove through the gate. Hobab parked slowly and carefully next to Jongchit's truck and the Tacketts got out, smiling and stretching their arms as if they'd just woken up from a long winter's nap. Mrs. Tackett's protruding eyes blinked sleepily as she surveyed our new location.

"So, Team, what do you think of your home away from home?" asked Dr. Tackett in his California drawl—not a bit shaken up or nauseated.

We didn't know what to think.

Next to me, Shelby murmured under her breath, "*Thump-thump.*"

"What's that?" I asked her.

She gave herself a little shake and me a wan smile. "Nothing."

Jongchit was saying: "…twenty-five orphan from Yai Camp arrive next month to *Born Free to Live Free AMEN Academy!* They get education here! Get hope for future here! But need much work. Much-much-much work!"

She led us around the building, sidestepping piles of building materials, including pipes, cinderblocks, and a stack of about twenty empty paint cans—which I bumped into, sending them rolling in all directions over the pavement.

"Strike!" said Twain with a grin, as I scrambled to restack them.

Suddenly, a group of seven Thai ladies—ranging widely in age from thirties to eighties—burst out of the school, talking and laughing. They wore white smocks and plastic shower caps peppered with light blue paint, and carried brushes and rollers, which they deposited next to the empty paint cans.

"*Sawatdee kha!*" They smiled and *waied*—giving us slight bows and pressing their palms together in the traditional Thai greeting.

"Meet the Wigglewurt—my Praying Lady," said Jongchit proudly.

"Wigglewurts," said Hobab, stressing the s.

"That what I say," she scolded, then continued: "They finish prayer meeting now at the school. After some painting. Paint wall *Blue Sky Blue*. Very nice color. But they not good painter—praying slow them down. We all praying together. Every day. For hours and hours."

"Wigglewurts?" I asked.

"You know Smitt Wigglewurt? We name group after him."

Ernestine leaned towards me and whispered, "She means *Smith Wigglesworth*. My Aunt Aurora has all his books. He was this preacher in England around a century ago who healed thousands of people and—"

"What do you guys pray for?" Jack-O asked Jongchit.

"For everything. For our school. For future student. For Thailand. For Burma. For orphan. For refugee. For peace. For—"

"For to get husband!" said a spry eighty-year-old with iron gray hair and prominent teeth.

The Wigglewurts laughed even more uproariously.

"This is Patcharee!" said Jongchit with a chuckle. "She want mate."

"*Kha, kha,* we pray for the impossible," said a tiny middle-aged woman with bright burgundy hair teetering on platform shoes. We later learned her name was Noi—she and Patcharee were Jongchit's closest friends.

"Look at her tooths," said Noi. She extended a tiny finger to Patcharee, who obediently grinned, revealing perfect teeth. "They real!"

"Very nice," I said politely, which detonated a volley of explosions from the Wigglewurts:

"Ha! They not so nice last year!"

"No. Very ugly."

"So so ugly!"

"Black and some missing—very not good. Bad tooths."

"And she have no money to go to doctor. So we pray!"

"Yes, we pray and ask Jesus to make her teeth pretty pretty—"

"So for to get me husband!" laughed Patcharee delightedly.

"And next day, she wake up—and all new tooths!" said Jongchit triumphantly.

"See? Jesus like pretty mouth!" added Noi with a dainty smile.

It took us all a minute to wrap our minds around what they were saying...

"You're telling us that Jesus did your dental work?" asked Jack-O. "That's crazytown!"

Dr. Tackett peered closer to examine Patcharee's teeth and laughed. "Very nice. That'll put me out of business."

"Did that *really* happen?" asked Twain, gazing down at Patcharee skeptically.

"*Kha*, why not?" said Jongchit. "Jesus heal in New Testament—leper, cripple, blind. Even bloody lady not stop bleeding. Why not today? He same yesterday, today—forever!"

Twain shifted his duffel to the other arm. "True... I guess he's still at it..." But he didn't look convinced.

"Sure he is!" said Ernestine. "My Aunt Aurora woke up one morning to find a gold filling in her back left molar as bright and shiny as her wedding ring. Swear to God."

The entire Team swiveled to stare at Ernestine.

"She totally did," she said, frowning defensively. "Don't even look at me like that, all you doubting Thomases."

Twain leaned over and said in a low, mocking tone. "Come on, *Mangosteen*. Did that *really* happen to your aunt? Admit it, you're putting us all on."

Ernestine threw her hands up in exasperation. "Are you serious? You think that's a stretch? Hello! I've seen even crazier stuff than that at my Aunt Aurora's church in downtown L.A.! Once I saw a man's curved spine straighten out right in front of me! And this one old lady had a huge mega tumor on her back—seriously, it was the size of a grapefruit—and it completely disappeared! *Just like that!*" She snapped her fingers.

"But why haven't you told us this before?" asked Shelby, who'd been hovering on the fringes. Her eyes were red and swollen, and she looked slightly hurt. "I mean, we've known you for years."

"Well... I thought it might kinda freak you guys out." Ernestine shifted uncomfortably and fidgeted with the metal grommet in her right ear. "I mean, it's really out there. I barely believe it and I saw it with my own eyes!"

"But our moms are best friends and I've never heard mine talk about it," said Jack-O dubiously.

Ernestine shrugged. "Well, my Aunt Aurora's way more into all the supernatural stuff than my mom."

"Do you think... Do you think..." Shelby paused, then mustered up courage and asked in a rush, "Do you think if my family had prayed for him, Flounce wouldn't have died?"

Talk about gullible sheltered Christians floating around in their big bubbles of denial! Even my future girlfriend!

"Hey, you never know," said Ernestine, her eyes lighting up, "stranger things have happened. One time, my Aunt Aurora's cat got this massive fur ball stuck in his throat..."

I tuned her out as she went on and on about the miracle of the disappearing fur ball. I could *almost* understand the desire to believe in some omnipotent God who supposedly created us on purpose, but this rogue Jesus, who ran around healing willy-nilly? A completely laughable construct, as my mom would say. The last thing we needed was for Shelby to get resurrection ideas about Flounce! No wonder my parents were suspicious of "religion" if this was the sort of whacked stuff that went on. *Don't drink the Kool-Aid* indeed!

As if on cue, Noi laughed and said, "Next we learn to raise dead—"

"Maybe only way we get husband!" croaked Patcharee.

They all laughed heartily.

"Lazarus, come forth—and marry my friend!"

More laughter.

"Anybody need heal?" asked Noi, abruptly glancing at each one of us in turn, hands on her hips.

We looked at Jongchit, who waved her hand impatiently.

"Oh, she want to know if anyone sick. She need practice. So far, we see only one healing. But! We go for more! Volunteer? Or all scaredy cat?"

The Outreach Team shifted uncomfortably.

"Not at this time, but thanks," I said politely.

"Does constipation count?" asked Jack-O.

"Man Child!" said Ernestine, socking him on the bicep.

"Ouch!" he said, rubbing his arm. "What about bruises?"

The ladies laughed good-naturedly, and Jongchit turned to lift a dead duck out of the back of Hobab's truck. (Or a goose. Hard to tell once they've been plucked.) In the momentary silence that followed, we all became aware of a rhythmic sobbing behind us.

Excerpt from Shelby's Journal
July 3rd

Flounce *Flounce* *Flounce* *Flounce* *Flounce*
Flounce *Flounce* *Flounce* *Flounce* *Flounce*
Flounce *Flounce* *Flounce* *Flounce* *Flounce*
Flounce *Flounce* *Flounce* *Flounce* *Flounce*
Flounce *Flounce* *Flounce* *Flounce* *Flounce*
Flounce *Flounce* *Flounce* *Flounce* *Flounce*
Flounce *Flounce* *Flounce* *Flounce* *Flounce*
Flounce *Flounce* *Flounce* *Flounce* *Flounce*
Flounce *Flounce* *Flounce* *Flounce* *Flounce*
Flounce *Flounce* *Flounce* *Flounce* *Flounce*
Flounce *Flounce* *Flounce* *Flounce* *Flounce*
Flounce *Flounce* *Flounce* *Flounce* *Flounce*
Flounce *Flounce* *Flounce* *Flounce* *Flounce*
Flounce *Flounce* *Flounce* *Flounce* *Flounce*
Flounce *Flounce* *Flounce* *Flounce* *Flounce*
Flounce *Flounce* *Flounce* *Flounce* *Flounce*
Flounce *Flounce* *Flounce* *Flounce* *Flounce*
Flounce *Flounce* *Flounce* *Flounce* *Flounce*
Flounce *Flounce* *Flounce* *Fl...*

Uhhh...?!

SHELBY SAT HUNCHED ON THE CEMENT STEPS of the academy entrance, sobbing uncontrollably as she wrote in her journal. Her beige hiking pants were patchy with tears, and her wet curls were plastered to her cheeks. Her hand moved jerkily across the page, which was growing soggy with her tears, row after row—until she finally gave up with a little yowl of grief.

The Wigglewurts exchanged looks, then marched over to her, *en masse*, looking like an army of computer technicians in their white smocks. Jongchit threw the duck on the rope over her shoulder and followed. I hurried after her with the rest of the Team, removing a packet of tissue from my daypack. As the Thai ladies circled Shelby and the rest of the Team stood behind them, I slipped between them and sat down right next to her. In such close proximity, I could smell the Baby Powder Fresh Scent of her deodorant, the slight tang of sweat, and the faintest whiff of jasmine shampoo from our airport hotel.

"Thanks, Collin," she said, taking the Kleenex with a trembling hand, oblivious of the crowd surrounding her. "Sorry I'm being such a baby. After all, it's just a... just a dog."

"Just a dog? *Just a dog?* Your double dappled dachshund? The little fella who loved to chew brown? Stop the crazy talk, Shelby. Flounce was like a little brother to you."

"You're right, he was! *He was!*" And she began sobbing louder than ever into a fresh tissue.

Should I put an arm around her or not? Yes? No?

"Why Chevy cry?" Jongchit asked.

Shelby looked up to see a dozen concerned faces staring down at her and gave a little squeak of shock.

Just put your arm around her! Don't be such a wuss!

"*Shelby's* mourning the loss of Flounce," said Mrs. Tackett. She squeezed through the Wigglewurts, sat down on the other side of Shelby, and quickly put an arm around her.

Blocked!

"Remember the phone call we received?" said Dr. Tackett. "Outside the market?"

"*Kha, kha!* Someone die." Jongchit nodded in remembrance and turned to look at Shelby with growing concern. "Who die, Chevy? Mama? Papa?"

"Her dog—" began Ernestine.

"What? Dog? For dog she cry so big?" Jongchit was first incredulous, then dismissive as she turned away. "I take duck to cook—"

"But he wasn't just a dog," I said hurriedly. "He was like her little brother—"

"Brother? I think you say dog. You confuse Jongchit!"

And before I could clarify, Jongchit handed me the rope that held the dangling duck, and turned to Shelby. She put a hand on each shoulder and peered into her face. "Colon Boy say you lose little brother?"

Shelby jerked her head back, startled at Jongchit's face looming so close to hers. "Uh, well, yeah, Flounce *was* like a little brother—"

"She have big, sad hole in heart," Patcharee declared, thumping her own chest with her hand.

Noi tilted her head and gazed kindly at Shelby. "God, he heal inside body and outside body."

The rest of the Wigglewurts nodded sympathetically.

"Yeah, poor Shel is taking this hard," said Twain, towering over the Wigglewurts.

"*Kha, kha!* We ask Jesus to heal hurt heart." Jongchit barked orders in Thai to the Wigglewurts and they instantly swarmed around Shelby, putting hands on her head and shoulders and back. They began praying rapidly in Thai.

Without turning her head, Shelby rolled her eyes towards me—begging me to rescue her from this awkward situation. But before I could move a muscle—or the duck—Shelby shuddered and slid to the ground, along with her journal—and lay there, *motionless!*

Twain took a step back. "Whoa!"

"What the heck!" Jack-O's eyes looked like they were going to pop out of his head.

"911! Call 911! We need a doctor!" I yelled, jumping up in a panic, the fowl slapping against my legs.

Jongchit laughed throatily as she looked down at Shelby. "You so funny. Jesus the doctor. He working on her now."

I couldn't believe the Tacketts and Ernestine seemed to be taking this all in stride.

"Your turn?" And Jongchit reached towards me.

I leaped back as if burnt. "Uh, no, no. I'm fine. *Fine!*"

She laughed. "You scaredy cat, Colon Boy?"

"The name is *Collin*—"

"That what I say!" And she plucked the rope out of my hand, tossed the duck over her shoulder as if it were a winter scarf.

The Wigglewurts all nodded in satisfaction as they stared at Shelby—who was flat on her back, hands at her sides, still clutching tissues, her short hair a golden halo around her head—and a contented smile across her face.

The Tacketts exchanged knowing looks.

"Was… was that magic?" I asked in a hushed tone.

"Not magic, *miracle*," said Noi with an enigmatic smile.

"God heal tooth, God heal heart!" declared Patcharee, raising her arm into the air triumphantly. Then she and the rest of the Wigglewurts crossed the parking lot, piled into a metallic green mini-van and drove off, tiny Noi at the wheel—barely tall enough to see through the windshield. We could hear a squeal of brakes, then honking, then burning rubber.

Jongchit shook her head solemnly as she gazed after them. "Noi so very bad driver. Her safety take up much, much prayer time."

R. I. P.

WE ALL FOLLOWED JACK-O AND TWAIN AS they carried Shelby through the shiny tiled foyer into a large living room space, where they laid her down on a green leather couch underneath a large black and white framed poster of a soldier in the jungle. The cement was still drying in sections, the walls were half-painted light blue, and there were no doors in the doorjambs.

As we all clustered around Shelby, I took off my hat, ran my hand through my damp hair, and turned to the Tacketts. "Okay, what the heck just happened?"

Mrs. Tackett shrugged her shoulders and laughed weakly, as if she just didn't know where to begin. "God's ways are mysterious, his wonders to perform."

"What?"

Dr. Tackett smiled reassuringly as he slipped off his sandals. "Just God's way of ministering to Shelby right now."

"So it's some kind of supernatural nap?" asked Jack-O, peering down at her through smudged glasses.

"You could call it that. A sort of *power* nap. She's just resting," said Ernestine. I could tell she enjoyed playing the resident expert.

"R.I.P.," said Twain, with a smirk.

Mrs. Tackett lifted Shelby's arm and checked her pulse. "Normal."

"We forgot to warn you that Jongchit's a bit on the... well... *charismatic* side," said Dr. Tackett, rubbing his goatee. "Kinda unpredictable, spiritually speaking. You never know what she'll do—"

"Peter, you're making her sound unbalanced," Mrs. Tackett interrupted. She smiled at us placatingly, her white teeth gleaming. "What he means is that she's a bit of a—"

"Holy Roller?" said Ernestine a touch defensively. "You know, she's not doing anything that's not in the Bible. Remember Paul saying to not get drunk with wine, but *with the Spirit?*"

"*Drunk?!*" I couldn't believe what I was hearing.

"Bring it on!" said Jack-O heartily.

There was an uncomfortable silence.

"Tackett! Please for to come," bellowed Jongchit from somewhere on the second floor.

Hobab bounded down the stairs. "Jongchit wants you to decide on sleeping arrangements."

"We can discuss this more at dinner, Collin," said Dr. Tackett over his shoulder, following Mrs. Tackett up the stairs.

"Can a couple of you guys help me unload the trucks?" asked Hobab.

"Sure thing," said Twain.

Hobab paused to gaze at the poster hanging over the couch and proudly waved a hand. "Meet my dad, General Jolly Mu."

"You serious?!" asked Jack-O.

Jolly was grinning widely, the sunglasses clip on his aviator glasses flipped up revealing deep laugh lines around his eyes. He stood with arms akimbo, a cigarette tucked behind each ear. Although he looked definitely past retirement age, he had the muscular physique of a twenty year old, which was covered with tattoos. I could just make out the ones across his chest:

NEVER SORRY EVER JOLLY

"General of the 12th Brigade of Freedom Fighters for a Free Burma!" said Twain in reverential tones. "Some dad!"

"He looks like one brave warrior," said Ernestine thoughtfully.

"The bravest there is!" said Hobab, his face lighting up. "Once he got shot in the spine and the bullet came out his jaw. A medic stitched him up and he went right back out to the frontline. Man, someday, I'm going over the border and fighting with him, side by side."

"Why not now? The Burma border's only like an hour away," asked Twain, bouncing on the balls of his feet, his eyes shining. "I mean, with the ceasefire it's supposed to be safe, right? What's stopping you?"

"Jongchit doesn't want me to join up." Hobab muttered as he pushed his long bangs out of his eyes. "Says I'm too young—and that I can help my people more with my brain than with my body. It's my fault for getting good grades, I guess."

"Man, that's tough," said Twain.

I shifted impatiently, wishing they'd all just go away already so I could talk to Shelby in private.

"Jongchit must really miss your dad," said Ernestine as she examined the photo.

Hobab gave his half chuckle, half giggle. "Oh, Jongchit's not my *real* mom. She met my family when she volunteered at Yai Camp as an NGO nurse. When I was three, Mom died of pneumonia and Dad was sent back to the frontlines. Jongchit offered to adopt me so I could get a Thai passport and education, and be raised outside of a refugee camp. Dad thought it was the right thing to do for my future." He paused, then added in a solemn tone, "Jongchit may be Thai, but she has a Katin heart—"

"Why you stand around like lazy dog and talk about Jongchit?"

We all jumped as Jongchit came downstairs and strode briskly across the living room into her office. "Time for to unload! Chop chop, *reng reng*, you naughty boy!"

"Aye, aye, sir!" said Hobab good-naturedly and hurried out the front door.

As the rest of the Team followed Hobab outside to the trucks, I dropped to my knees beside the couch and nudged Shelby. "Shelby? Are you all right? Can you hear me?" I nudged harder. "Shelby! Shelby! *Shelby!?!*"

With effort, Shelby rolled her eyes towards me. "Oh... my... gosh..." Her words were slurred.

"What's going on? How are you feeling? What's going on? How are you feeling? What's going—"

I felt a hand on my shoulder—I jumped, not realizing Ernestine hadn't gone outside with the rest.

"Take it easy, Collin. It's all good."

Shelby's tiny smile morphed into a goofy grin. "It feels...

It feels like I'm... I'm... sinking... sinking in Jell-O!"

"Come on," I said, lifting her arm. "Let's sit you up so you can think more clearly—"

She giggled. "No... no... Let me be. I feel all oozy and cozy and... and peaceful..." She closed her eyes.

I stared at her dumbfounded.

Shelby's eyes popped open. "I'm *ooooooozing...*"

I couldn't pry my eyes from Shelby's face. "This is crazytown! It's like she really is drunk."

"Yep. She's slain in the Spirit," explained Ernestine matter-of-factly.

"Slain?!"

"Or *resting* in the Spirit."

"Slain? Resting? In the what?" It was as if she was speaking another language.

She laughed at the expression on my face, then said, "Resting in the Spirit. They used to call it 'Slain in the Spirit,' but it sorta freaked people out. Now they say 'falling out.'"

"Uh, okay. Like that makes more sense. Anyway, what's the point of it all?"

Ernestine tilted her head and toyed with the metal grommet in her ear, considering how to proceed. "Well, the Holy Spirit is sorta comforting and helping her manage her pain. Internally healing her. Basically, it's being baptized in the Spirit. You know, like all the stuff in *Acts*."

I stared at her uncomprehendingly.

"You know, *Acts*? *Acts* in the New Testament?" Then Ernestine said in a flat tone, "Obviously, you haven't read *Acts* and have no idea what I'm talking about. Why am I not surprised."

"Hey! I have too read *Acts!* I just haven't read *all* of Acts," I lied indignantly. "It's so slow going at the beginning..."

"Oh, really? You call the story of Pentecost *slow going?*" Ernestine asked with a peculiar look in her eye.

Uh oh, I'm so in over my head here.

Luckily, I was prevented from having to respond.

"I feel sooooo gooooood!" Shelby's face was flushed and she couldn't stop giggling.

Ernestine laughed and patted her on the head. "You go, girl!"

"What did you mean about drunk?" I whispered to Ernestine once she stood back up.

"Yeah, it's also called 'being drunk in the Spirit,'" said Ernestine.

"Ssssh!" I hissed, but was too late.

"I'm soooooo drunnnnnk!" crooned Shelby, giggling uncontrollably.

"Slain *and* drunk. How sweet. I'm sure this happens all the time in your Aunt Aurora's church," I accused Ernestine.

"Oh, not *all the time.* Just once or twice a month. More during *Pentecost.*"

Was she mocking me? I suddenly noticed her eyes were the exact color of a Toblerone bar—without the almonds or nougat.

"How did your family get into all this craziness anyway?" I asked.

She laughed. "I guess it does seem whacked if you've never seen it before. My dad and Aunt Aurora grew up going to charismatic and Pentecostal churches in the South where this kind of thing was totally normal—it would have been weird if it didn't happen, if you know what I mean. Then Dad moved to Los Angeles for college where he met my mom, who'd experienced revival in my grandpa's church when she was a girl in Mexico. It kinda lit a fire under her butt. She gets intense sometimes—but not as much as my aunt. So a Black Holy Roller Dad and an On Fire Latina Mom created—" she thumbed at her chest—*"moi."*

"The one and only," I said. "Is your dad as into it as your mom and aunt?"

"Sorta. But he's way more low key. He says too much of it wears him out."

Shelby burst into giggles. "I feel soooo *fuzzy!*"

"Ernestine, Collin," called Mrs. Tackett from the second floor landing. "Please help unload the trucks. Then bring your backpacks up here and set up your Therm-A-Rests and mosquito netting."

"Yeah," said Twain, carrying two huge craft duffels into Jongchit's office. "This ain't no Holiday Inn."

"They do have western style showers and toilets, though!" Jack-O wheezed as he carried an enormous cardboard box up the stairs.

"Praise the Lord!" said Ernestine as she headed out to the trucks.

"But what about Shelby?" I called to Mrs. Tackett.

"She'll be fine where she is for now."

"You got that right. Those bunks are back breakin'!" added Jack-O from the top of the stairs. "There's a girls' dorm room and a guys' dorm room, so don't go getting any ideas, Ketchum."

"Shut up, Man Child!" came Ernestine's voice from outside the front screen doors.

So we left Shelby alone to continue resting and (presumably) healing.

The whole weird "slain situation" left me epically confused. Obviously, I didn't buy the whole "Holy Spirit's healing, resting power" explanation. But I couldn't deny I'd witnessed some sort of genuine physical "reaction." There was no way Shelby was faking her symptoms. It would be interesting to know how she felt tomorrow—if any "healing" had actually occurred. After thinking it over, I finally decided there were only three things it could be: autosuggestion, instant hypnosis, or brainwashing.

Oh, man, if my parents ever find out this sort of thing is going on, they'll have me on a plane home faster than I can say "opiate of the people"!

POSTCARD #1

(Photo caption: "Enchanting still life with mangosteens and other happy fruits")

July 3

Hi, Mom & Dad & Aunt Aurora!

Whew! So much to tell you already! I'll just have to wait until I get back—IF I get back. With Jongchit's driving, it'll take a miracle! HA! Keep all those prayers coming for the WHOLE Team. Especially for Collin—I want him to experience the real deal, if you know what I mean. Oh, there's a group of praying ladies here that you'd totally click with, Aunt Aurora! It's like they're the Thai sisters you never knew you had! OH! And Shelby got DRUNK IN THE SPIRIT today! Funniest thing EVER! Pray for SECONDS! ☺

Love you guys! Ernestine (aka Mangosteen)

P.S. Jack-O says to tell his mom "Hi!" since he'll never get around to sending a postcard of his own. MAN CHILD!

Rock Flounce

DINNER WAS SERVED IN A SCREENED-IN porch adjacent to the academy, filled with rows of tables and chairs, which would soon act as the students' dining hall. A primitive kitchen was attached to the back of it, where Yut, an elderly cook with a huge grin and few teeth (calling all Wigglewurts!), prepped and cooked everything from a squatting position. Tonight he'd prepared a feast out of the plucked duck. Unfortunately, we were barely awake enough to fully appreciate the savory meat, rice, noodles, and stir-fry vegetables he laid out for us. That is, except for Jack-O, who'd shoveled down three helpings of everything.

After the meal, Jongchit and Hobab left us alone so the Tacketts could conduct the T.D.T.—Team Debriefing Time. Most of us were too wiped out to "check in," that is, to share how we were doing and make any prayer requests. During dinner, Dr. Tackett had gone on and on about the way the "Holy Spirit ministers to his people today" and how we "needn't fear the unknown." Stuff like that. I confess I zoned out through most of it, I was so beat. Ernestine's explanations made more sense, anyway.

"We'll keep this short and sweet," said Dr. Tackett, with

an empathetic smile as he scratched his goatee. "Since we know the bunks are calling."

"Praise the Lord," murmured Ernestine, more weakly than usual. She was so tired she had to prop her head up with her hand, fire hair trailing in the rice.

"Thank you," said Twain, not bothering to stifle his yawn.

"You mean *khap kun krup!*" said Jack-O cheerfully, then burped loudly. "Ooops! My bad!"

Where the heck did he get all the energy?

A stack of yellow papers made the rounds. The yellow indicated it was one of our official Outreach Trip Handouts.

"So, here's the schedule for our week at refugee camp number one. Marcy and I will be providing dental and medical treatment to the refugees, while you guys play games, sing songs, and do crafts with the orphans. Then at night, we'll meet back together for dinner and worship led by Shelby—"

"It's going to be so much fun!" interrupted Mrs. Tackett, her face lighting up and voice increasing an octave. "I can't wait to introduce you to our friends in Yai Camp. Once you meet them, you'll understand why we just can't stop coming here. They're so precious! Even just one week of encouragement from you will mean the *world* to them! If you only knew how much... how much the children—" She paused abruptly to dig in her pocket for a Kleenex and blow her nose. "If only we could... if only..."

We all lowered our handouts and Ernestine shot me a knowing look. Every time Mrs. Tackett talked about the children or orphans, she broke down. Ernestine's theory was that all these visits just increased her anxiety over wanting to adopt.

Dr. Tackett reached over and gently squeezed her shoulder, his own eyes becoming glassy. "Someday, Marcy, someday…"

"Shelby was supposed to lead us in worship," said Mrs. Tackett in a watery voice, trying to pull herself together. "But tonight you're stuck with me."

She picked up Shelby's ukulele from beside her seat and plunked out a tune.

"I've got a river of life flowing out of me, makes the lame to walk and the blind to see…"

The Team gamely joined in, and I mouthed along. Luckily, it was just one song—her voice was so off-key, I swear I heard a cat yowl outside in protest.

After a momentary reflective silence, Mrs. Tackett set the ukulele down on the table with a clunk and the meeting continued.

"We're getting up extra early tomorrow in order to make good time. Since we're only staying in Yai Camp for a week, leave all unnecessary items here. Questions?" Dr. Tackett paused and scanned our faces.

We stared blankly back at him.

"More than you know," I finally said. "But I'm too jetlagged even to ask them—much less process your answers."

Dr. Tackett laughed. "Why don't you close us in prayer, Collin."

It was a command, not a question.

Unfortunately, I wasn't at the height of my impostor powers at that moment.

"Me? Pray? Uh, okay… Are you guys all ready?" I deliberately folded my hands and closed my eyes. "Yes, Lord—I mean, dear God in heaven, the triune God, three-in-one, majestic Creator—"

"Dude, he already knows who he is," said Jack-O with a chuckle.

"Ha, right, got it," I said, forcing a laugh. Why was this so hard? After all the prayers in youth group and in Team training I'd suffered through, you'd think I'd have remembered *something*. I stumbled along as best I could. "Yeah, so, *Lord*, we'd like to request safety on our trip to Yai Camp—especially for those in the back of Jongchit's truck. *The hedge of protection!*" I said triumphantly. Score! I'd remembered a Christian catch phrase! "That good ol' hedge of protection, yessiree! Anyway, we'd also like to suggest you... um... uh, create abundant opportunities for us to... to be, uh, helpful. In conclusion, we'll do all we can and ask you to do all you can. You know, *quid pro quo*. That is, when you have the time and aren't busy doing more important things like making planets or stopping terrorists. Thank you very much. Oh, and help Shelby not to be too hung over tomorrow."

And then, realizing their eyes were all still closed, I quickly added: "Amen! Amen! All in favor say *aye*."

Jack-O laughed. "Aye, dude!"

Ernestine snorted and shook her head, but it was obvious she was trying to hide a smile.

And Twain muttered, "What the heck was that?" before he was shushed by Mrs. Tackett.

"Uh, thank you, Collin," said Dr. Tackett in a bemused tone.

Gotta bone up on your ad-lib prayer content! The hedge of protection won't bail you out next time. Besides, Ernestine is catching on…

Out of the corner of my eye, I could see her thoughtfully examining me.

"Don't forget to take your malaria pills," said Mrs. Tackett as we pushed back our chairs. "And only use the bottled water." She gestured towards a crate of water bottles on the floor.

As we all stood up and made our way to the door, Jack-O pulled a pack of cards out of his pocket and waved it around. "So, who's up for a little game of Skip-Bo before bed? Anyone? Anyone..? Come on! Mangosteen?"

She laughed. "As if!"

"Are you lacing your water with Red Bull or what?" asked Twain with a yawn as he walked past him.

"Killjoys," muttered Jack-O, shoving the cards back into his pocket.

While everyone else climbed the stairs to the dorm rooms and bathrooms, I walked over to the leather couch and gazed down at my future girlfriend, who still Rested In Peace.

Inspiration hit me—I knew just how to cheer Shelby up!

I slipped outside. It only took a few minutes of searching to locate a small oblong rock. Then I went back inside to rummage through the art supplies left in Jongchit's office. I painted the rock black and white, cut two ears out of black felt and glued them on either side, made a collar from a pipe cleaner, and then added the final touch: two googly eyes.

He lives!

The whole thing took about fifteen minutes.

"Raiding the craft duffel, Colon Boy?" Ernestine popped her head through the office door.

"Uh, well, kinda," I answered, feeling instantly like a four-year-old.

"What's that?" She entered and plucked the rock out of my hand.

"Careful, that part is still wet." Then I added sheepishly, "Rock Flounce. I made it to cheer Shelby up."

She laughed. "Shelby will love it! Googly eyes turn anything into instant cuteness. We gotta do this with the orphans."

I returned to the foyer and carefully placed my creation on Shelby's stomach where she'd see him first thing upon waking. Rock Flounce rode the gentle waves of her breathing, up and down, up and down. I could almost hear a tiny "Yip yip yip!"

Finally, I forced myself to go.

Halfway up the stairs I paused to turn around for one last look—and was just in time to see a large mosquito landing right in the middle of her freckled forehead!

Dengue fever! Malaria! *Or worse!*

I tripped back down the stairs, digging a Kleenex out of my pocket as I went. Standing over Shelby once again, I slowly extended the tissue so I wouldn't scare the mosquito away—always better to kill them, Dr. Tackett had said.

"Hand check!"

My hand jerked in surprise and the mosquito flew off.

"Shoot! Now he's got away," I said, trying to mask my irritation at Jack-O, whose bulk practically filled up the entire front doorway. "I almost had him."

"Cover her with a mosquito net, bro," he said, closing the

door, slipping off his flip-flops, and lumbering across the foyer towards me. "Otherwise your hand's gonna get super tired."

"Where were you?"

He held up a cluster of pigmy bananas.

"But we ate less than an hour ago...?"

"And?" Peeling one of them, he looked down at Shelby. "What's that on her stomach?"

"Oh," I said, sheepishly, "it's, uh, just something to... to cheer her up."

"But what is it? It looks like a turd—"

"It's a Rock Flounce!"

Did I just say that?

Jack-O paused mid-chew, and turned to look at me, his dark eyes at first shocked and then filled with growing realization. "Dude. You know you're not supp—"

"I'm just a concerned friend! That's all! *A very concerned friend.* So don't even go there," I said in a stern tone, crossing my arms as if offended.

After a beat, Jack-O chuckled with his mouth full. "My bad." He leaned closer and said in a low tone, "It's just that I've got a thing for Ernestine, so love is on my mind, know what I mean? It's been going on for years—since our first playdate at the *Fun in the Sun Indoor Playground.* You know, the one on Grove Street? Next to that cupcake shop? Our moms are best friends, so we kinda grew up together. In fact, we—"

"Aren't you guys in bed yet? We have a six a.m. start time, remember." Dr. Tackett's shadow fell across our feet as he walked out of one of the downstairs classrooms he and Mrs. Tackett used as a bedroom.

"Sorry, Dr. T," said Jack-O. He held up his bananas. "Had to grab some potassium."

"As long as it's not another beetle," said Dr. Tackett with a wry smile. "Goodnight, Jack-O, goodnight, Collin."

But I was already halfway up the stairs, taking two steps at a time.

Just What Kind of Sisters Were They!?!

I SAT ON THE EDGE OF MY BUNK IN THE EMPTY guys' dorm room, trying to pull myself together. *Talk about a close call! What if Jack-O had been a little quicker on the uptake? And just how much did Ernestine suspect anyway?* A new thought struck me: what would the Tacketts actually do if they found out that pursuit of Shelby was my only reason for coming on this trip? Even if she hadn't yet reciprocated, would it be considered a rule-breaking "romantic entanglement" that would kick me off the Team and send me home?

But before I could process further, Twain's camouflage duffel caught my eye. After confirming Twain and Jack-O were showering in the guys' bathroom, I pulled it out from under the bunk bed and lifted it up—it had to weigh at least twenty pounds! These were no dolls—unless they were carved out of rocks. I examined the lock. It was sturdy and needed a key; there was no breaking it without a hacksaw. The duffel bag itself was made out of nylon.

I paused to consider my plan of action.

There was only one option.

I grabbed the nail clippers out of my toiletries bag. After

double-checking yet again that the showers were still running, I carefully sliced through the fabric along a seam with the metal file. I'd just have to chance it that Twain wouldn't notice—or assume the seam had burst.

I peeled back the nylon to behold the *very last things* I ever expected to find in an Outreach Team member's luggage—in fact, if *my mom* had popped up like some oversize jack-in-the-box and said, "Aren't you fed up with these crazy Born Agains yet, Collin?!" I couldn't have been more surprised.

Cartons of Marlboro cigarettes!

Bottles of Jack Daniels Black Label whiskey!

Boxes of bullets!!!

Just what kind of sisters were they!?!

I heard one of the showers turn off. Swiftly, I arranged the seams so they didn't look severed, threw the hoodie over the bag, slid it back under the bed, hopped onto my bunk, and tried to act casual.

This is light years away from hand puppets and blindfold dodge ball and praise songs with endless refrains. You've gotta do something—NOW!

The question was: do I confront him? Or go immediately to the Tacketts?

Right then—Twain walked into the room.

He wore a white towel around his waist and metal dog tags hanging from his neck that slapped against his bare chest as he walked. His brown hair dripped and his flip-flops squeaked with every step.

Squeak, squeak, squeak.

"All yours, Uttley," he said, striding past me to his bunk.

Squeak, squeak, squeak.

"Thanks… Abernathy," I said in a constricted voice.

He threw me a look—obviously sensing something.

I opened my mouth to confront him. Then closed it.

"Cat got your tongue?" he asked, with a mocking half-smile.

In response, I laughed way too heartily and said, "Ha! Cat! Good one!" Then I scooped up my towel and toiletries, and casually walked out of the room as he watched me suspiciously.

I paused outside the bathroom where I could hear Jack-O singing his rendition of our earlier praise song: *"I've got a river of pee flowing out of me—"*

Now what???

That's the problem with spying—once you gain information, you're responsible for what you do with it.

Twain's behavior had the potential of endangering our trip—not to mention *himself.* What the heck had he gotten himself into? To be in possession of *one* of those items would be shocking, but comprehendible. But all three? Was he seriously intending to smoke and drink and shoot guns in a refugee camp of all places!? (Not your typical orphan-friendly activities, last I checked.) For a second I thought it was so bizarre that there *had* to be a logical explanation. But just for a second.

I debated confronting Twain then and there. However, at the thought of facing that testosterone-fueled giant solo, sweat instantly secreted from my armpits—despite my STOP THE STINK LEVEL 10. Although I was in good shape myself, I couldn't match his heighth and breadth. If only I'd found the time to master Krav Maga.

104

But whatever Twain is doing, he's obviously gotta be stopped. It's my duty to warn the Tacketts. And hey, all's fair in love and war. It wouldn't hurt to have a reason to squelch any potential crush on Shelby's part. If Twain got sent home, it would sure clear the playing field!

I sped silently downstairs where I could hear the low murmuring voices of the Tacketts, Jongchit, and Hobab coming from Jongchit's office. I shot a quick glance at Shelby's still "resting" figure on the green leather couch, Rock Flounce still surfing her belly. General Jolly Mu grinned down at me from the wall. He seemed to be saying: "I believe you, but don't expect them to."

Everyone glanced up in surprise as I entered the sparsely decorated office, which consisted of a couple long wooden tables, a few chairs, an ancient computer monitor, a metal filing cabinet circa 1950s, and *Blue Sky Blue* streaked walls. Dr. Tackett and Jongchit sat across from each other at one of the tables going through receipts, while Mrs. Tackett and Hobab sat on the floor, dividing the donated clothes and supplies into piles.

"You still awake, Collin?" Hobab tossed the hair out of his eyes as he looked up at me. "Thought you guys were totally wiped."

"You no sleepy?" said Jongchit, looking at me over bifocal reading glasses perched on the end of her nose. "I pray for deep rest—" She half rose from her chair, hand extended.

"Heck, no!" I said, backing away. "I just need to talk to Dr. Tackett about something."

Jongchit chuckled and dropped her hand.

"Sure, Collin, what's up?" said Dr. Tackett absentmindedly, as he wrote the date on a receipt and tucked it into an envelope.

"Well, it's kinda personal... could we talk somewhere in private?"

"Girl problem, right, Colon Boy? Heart hurt for girl?" Jongchit thumped her chest and burst out laughing.

"No way!" It came out a little too quickly. Trying to cover, I added, "I mean, I'm here for the orphans. Full stop."

Hobab grinned and winked at me.

Jongchit laughed again. "Ha ha! Look! Colon Boy face red red red! Girl must be pretty pretty *pretty*!"

The best defense is a quick offence, so I immediately recited, "'*Expected Behavior Guideline Number One*: No romantic entanglements allowed.'"

"*Mai pen rai!*" said Jongchit waving me away.

Mrs. Tackett's soulful eyes rested on me sympathetically for a moment, then she said, "Go on, Peter."

"What? Oh, right, right," said Dr. Tackett, finally sensing the awkwardness of the situation. He pushed aside a stack of receipts and stood up. "Let's use the dining room." I followed him out the door.

Once we reached the exterior dining porch, he held the screen door open for me and flipped on the overhead florescent lights and fans. Night sounds seemed extra pronounced—the rich tones of the chirping cicadas, the deep croak of frogs, the clicking of the geckos running across the ceiling, and the low hum of various insects as they kamakazied towards the window screens in an attempt to reach the light.

We sat down opposite each other at one of the Formica

tables. I plopped my toiletry bag and towel in the center of the table, where a trail of ants carried away bits of rice leftover from dinner. Outside, there was a distant metallic *tink-clunk,* as one of the empty paint cans tipped over and rolled across the driveway.

"Cats," said Dr. Tackett, cocking his head. "Most likely feral. Thailand seems to have a large population of feral—"

"Dr. Tackett, this is *way* more serious than feral cats!" I interrupted, not bothering to disguise my exasperation.

He was momentarily taken aback. Then he smiled at me with that type of condescending kindliness he probably used on all of his root canal patients. "Okay, Collin, what's this all about?"

"It's, well—it's *Twain.*" I took a deep breath and plunged in. "I kind of accidentally discovered some things in his duffel that you and Mrs. Tackett should know about."

"What kind of things?" he asked in an amused tone, obviously humoring me.

"Cigarettes, whiskey, and bullets." My voice couldn't have sounded any more dramatic as the words rang out and then hung motionless in the thick night air.

"Cigarettes, whiskey, and bullets?" Dr. Tackett said blankly. He ran a hand through his sun bleached hair, then repeated incredulously, *"Cigarettes, whiskey, and bullets???"*

I nodded gravely.

He stared at me a moment—then burst out laughing. "For a second there you had me—"

"Follow me," I said grimly, getting up from my chair.

"What? You can't be serious!" He sounded genuinely bewildered.

"I told you it was way more serious than feral cats."

"But… but this makes no sense. I've known Twain and his family for *years*," he said in a dazed tone as he got up and followed me out of the dining area. "His dad and I surf together every Wednesday. It's got to be some sort of misunderstanding…"

I started to feel guilty for doing this when Jack-O might be around to overhear—but then I immediately pushed the feeling aside. The welfare of the entire Outreach Team was at stake! Shelby's potential crush needed to be crushed like a VW Bug at a Monster Truck Rally—and this was turning out to be the perfect vehicle.

Extreme Me

WE PASSED THE GIRLS' DORM ROOM, WHICH was completely silent, and then the bathroom where we could hear Jack-O brushing his teeth. "Don't forget to floss!" Dr. Tackett had the presence of mind to say.

"Yesshure!" said Jack-O, mouth full of toothpaste.

Dr. Tackett followed me into the guys' dorm room, where Twain was now dressed in a t-shirt and shorts, lying on top of his Therm-A-Rest, mosquito netting tucked around him— reading a paperback New Testament.

The hypocrite!

I paused. Now what? Dr. Tackett also seemed unsure how to proceed. But he cleared his throat. "Uh, Twain, would you mind if I took a look in your duffel?"

Twain lowered his New Testament. "Why? What's up, Dr. T?"

"Well, I hear there might be something in there that I should check on... that, uh, doesn't exactly fit the nature of our trip."

"Which breaks *Expected Behavior Guideline Number Two*," I said, wishing Dr. Tackett would be more assertive. *"Refraining from smoking cigarettes, drinking alcohol, or eating any endangered species (even if it's on the menu)."*

Twain sat up and pointed to the backpack next to his bed. "Help yourself."

"No, not your *backpack*," I said. "We want to look in the new *duffel* you bought at the Thai market today."

Twain gave me an inscrutable look.

Since Dr. Tackett still wasn't asserting himself, I took matters into my own hands, strode over to Twain, and dragged the duffel out from under his bunk. "There!"

"You'll need this, Dr. T.," said Twain, then lifted up the mosquito netting and tossed him a key.

I glanced sharply at Twain. What was he up to?

Dr. Tackett sheepishly squatted down in front of the duffel. He was about to insert the key in the lock, when I said: "You don't need that." And I jerked open the bag at the severed seam. A shower of potato chips, packs of Big Red gum, Hershey's chocolate bars, and clothes fell onto the floor. After giving Twain another suspicious glance, I pulled everything out until I could feel the bottom of the bag.

Where were the cigarettes, whiskey, and bullets!?!?

"Sorry if junk food doesn't exactly fit the 'nature of our trip'," said Twain with a smirk. "I had no idea I was violating *Expected Behavior Guideline Number Two*…"

What did he do with it all?

I became a whirling dervish, running around the dorm room, looking in everything and under everything. I wrenched open Twain's backpack and flung his clothes and toiletries across the floor. In my frenzy, I even rummaged through Jack-O's belongings, sending his cluster of pigmy bananas sailing through the air and landing with a plop in the middle of the room.

Where the heck did he stash it all on such short notice?!

"Now, Collin…" began Dr. Tackett.

"Hey, dude, mind putting all that back?" asked Twain with deliberate casualness.

I glared at him. "Where are the *dolls*, then?"

He grinned and shot me a look that said: *Nice try, but I'm way ahead of you.* Then he replied with even more of that deliberate casualness, "Dolls? What dolls?"

"The souvenir dolls you presumably bought for your sisters," I replied through gritted teeth.

"Oh, right. Those dolls."

We stared at each other unblinkingly like two cowboys facing off in the center of town.

"Yeah, *those* dolls."

After a beat, a smirk spread across his face. "Oh, I ended up giving them away to some kids outside the market."

I shook my head in disbelief. "Sure you did—"

"That was decent of you, Twain," said Dr. Tackett as he stood up, completely oblivious. Before I could set him straight, he glanced at me quizzically and asked, "You *do* know what cigarettes, whiskey, and bullets look like?"

"There *were* cigarettes, whiskey, and bullets in there just ten minutes ago!"

"Cigarettes, whiskey, and bullets? Sounds like Collin's got our outreach trip confused with a frat party." Twain's face was so smug I wanted to thwack him one.

"Did someone say frat party?" Jack-O burst into the room wearing a football jersey and shorts, toiletry bag under his arm, and a towel around his neck. He wasn't wearing his glasses, so he peered nearsightedly at us, then tripped.

"Hey! What are *these* doing here?" Jack-O asked indignantly as he scooped up his bananas.

"Sorry about this, Twain," said Dr. Tackett with slight exasperation. Then turning, he put his hands on my shoulders, and gently but firmly steered me towards the door. "Time to go downstairs. I think someone needs to do a little processing—"

"I don't need processing! I need you to believe me!" I tried to wiggle away, but his hands had grips of iron. (Probably from all those extractions.)

"What the heck's going on?" asked Jack-O, peeling a pigmy banana and squinting at Dr. Tackett as he propelled me out of the dorm room. "Is Collin busted?"

"No, he's hallucinating!" Twain laughed—sending malevolent echoes down the stairwell after us.

Once we were downstairs in the foyer, Dr. Tackett released his vice-like grip.

"To be on the safe side, stop taking your malaria pills. Marcy will get you a new prescription in the morning."

"But it's the *truth*, not the mefloquine!"

"Just a second." He entered Jongchit's office and returned immediately with one of the yellow handouts.

"Normally, this sort of thing sets in when you're further along on the trip, but in your case… Well, it's evident you're already experiencing some of the symptoms," said Dr. Tackett, holding out the paper.

After a moment—a *long* moment—I took it.

>> EXTREME YOU! <<
Handout #24

Congratulations! You are now on your way to Southeast Asia. Or perhaps you've just arrived. In any case, NOW is the perfect time to read this—before EXTREME YOU sets in. (Ahem! Resist the temptation to set this aside and pick up the creased PEOPLE magazine in the seat pocket in front of you...)

What is EXTREME YOU? Yes, as a matter of fact, it is the extreme version of *you*. But it's also a side effect of travel along with traveler's tummy, diarrhea, constipation, dehydration, and jetlag. Many times, once the new traveler experiences extreme locales, extreme temps, extreme conditions, and extreme situations for the first time—the EVERYDAY YOU disappears and EXTREME YOU appears.

I'll warn you now—it's shocking to discover that there's another side to YOU. Which you had no idea about and will emerge when you least expect it. Beware: it will be reactionary, extremist, dramatic, angry, overwhelmed, and constantly on the verge of a meltdown.

Say it with me: THIS IS NORMAL.

And again: THIS IS NORMAL.

I stress this because you'll feel guilty about it— thinking perhaps it was a big mistake to go on this trip after all. Your EXTREME YOU will say: You're not cut out for travel or outreach or philanthropy. You'll let everybody down. The refugees and orphans will now be worse off thanks to YOU! You might as well go home right NOW.

You may feel like biting someone.

In this foreign land, you'll be stripped of everything that ever gave you your physical identity. Things like your comforts, habits, home-life, school-life, neighborhoods— even your favorite binge show or fast food won't be available to distract or comfort you. You'll be thrown into situations that you've never been in before—and be expected to go ahead with "business as usual." This will bring that EXTREME YOU right out in all its glory.

And unfortunately, there is no vaccination available for the prevention of EXTREME YOU. But it is treatable— and should be treated quickly so it doesn't spread and contaminate your fellow Team Members. It's highly contagious.

Here are steps you can take to treat it:

1. Pray for strength and calm and peace. (You'll need all the divine help you can get!)

2. Tell someone about it: your Trip Leaders or a Team Member.

3. Journal it. Journaling will help you diffuse the situation and put it in perspective. Help you process what you're experiencing and witnessing. Along with prayer, devotions, and our T.D.T.s (Team Debriefing Times), journaling is crucial for your mental and spiritual well being on this trip.

4. Smile. Pretend you're feeling just fine and dandy. And with the power of suggestion that the mind has— you just might begin to feel that way!

*   *   *   *   *

I remember watching old Alfred Hitchcock movies, where the hero or heroine witnesses a crime and no one believes them—not even their friends or family—because there isn't any tangible evidence. Just their word.

And here I'd always written them off as completely implausible.

I crumpled the yellow *Extreme You* handout into a tight ball and threw it against the wall—where it ricocheted and bounced off my forehead.

I took a cold shower.

I brushed, but refused to floss.

Then I scrutinized myself in the mirror. My pale blue eyes were bloodshot, my blond hair was matted down from my hat, and my facial muscles looked tense. But other than that, the sight of my decent profile and well-defined pecs reassured me that I had nothing to worry about in my continuing pursuit of Shelby.

I was a contender.

I just needed to stop comparing myself to *him*.

I returned to the guys' dorm room and pushed aside the woven blanket hanging in the doorway. The room was in complete darkness except for the glow of a flashlight left on top of my Therm-A-Rest mattress. From the sound of their deep breathing, both Twain and Jack-O were asleep—not that I'd put it past Twain to trick me yet again. But after observing him for a while and confirming he was really sleeping, I snuck over to the contraband duffel, now positioned at the foot of his bunk. Stealthily, I opened it once again at the severed seam and shined the beam of the flashlight on the contents. Potato Chips. Big Red. Hershey's. T-shirts.

Suddenly, I heard a sound that I could have sworn was muffled laughter—but when I flashed my light over at Twain, he was gently snoring, eyes firmly shut. And no headgear in sight.

Just then, I noticed his black Moleskine journal, sitting out in the open, right on top of his backpack. Aha! I snatched it up and eagerly flipped through the pages.

Code.

Every single entry was written in some sort of undecipherable *code.*

Of course they were.

Swearing under my breath, I crept into my sleep sack, pulled down the mosquito netting around me, put in my earplugs, and lay there...

Defeated.

TWAIN'S JOURNAL ENTRY
-DECODED VERSION-

07 03 22 30

COLLIN IS GETTING SUSPICIOUS--BUT THERE'S NOTHING TO WORRY ABOUT--JUST GOT TO MAKE IT TO THE END OF THE TRIP--THEN IT'S GO TIME,

part three

YAI CAMP

It's Renata Phrangle All Over Again!

*T*HUNK!
   Something dropped onto my chest and instantly woke me.

Scrambling to sit up, I tangled in the mosquito netting and banged my head on the wooden slats of the bunk above. Then I muffled an obscenity at the sight of Twain grinning down at me, his braces glinting menacingly in a shaft of light streaming through the window.

"Compliments of the Tacketts."

It was a new bottle of malaria pills.

Our eyes locked in mutual dislike.

Then he laughed and moved towards the door. "Better get a move on if you want any breakfast. We're leaving in thirty minutes."

By the time I'd showered and dressed and headed downstairs with my backpack and mattress roll, breakfast was over and the Team was outside loading up the two trucks with the supplies and donations for Yai Camp. The Southeast Asian humidity was made even more pronounced by the low hanging clouds directly overhead that seemed to trap in the warmth like the tarps in the Thai market. My face immediately began to ooze sweat. As I wiped my forehead, I spotted Shelby leaning against Jongchit's truck, talking to Twain in a low voice while she tied that yellow vintage scarf dotted with cherries around her damp hair. He leaned over her and she looked up at him—*confidingly.*

It couldn't be... Shelby couldn't really be... be *in love* with *Twain Abernathy!?*

Could she???

"Collin?"

Not the dreaded love triangle! It's Renata Phrangle all over again! Will I never get a break? Will the tall guys always rule the dating world? Will I always be such a peon? Such a loser???

"Collin?"

I mentally shook myself.

It's not over until it's over! I'll march right over there and declare what I saw in his duffel! Even if she's the only member of the Team who believes me, it'll be worth it! After all, I'm the one in the power position—

"Hello! Earth to Collin!" Ernestine's annoyed face appeared directly in my line of vision, jolting me out of my reverie. Once again, her beige trekking attire contrasted jarringly with her fire-streaked hair.

"Sorry, Ernestine, did you say something?"

"Only like fifty times." She shook her head in amusement, and raised the eyebrow with the silver ring. "Here." She placed an exceedingly square white toast slathered with marmalade on my left hand, then plopped four prickly red balls into my right hand. I stared at them in distaste. "And you're giving me these because...?"

She laughed at the expression on my face. "They're rambutans. You peel off the skin and eat the white stuff inside."

I examined the spiny fruit doubtfully. "Right..."

"They're legit, you big baby. I've eaten like twelve of them. Sure, they look like hedgehogs, but they taste like grapes."

"Thanks for the toast, but these I return to sender." I tried to hand back the rambutans, but she refused to take them.

"You need more fruit in your diet."

"What? Since when did you turn into my mom?"

"Well, someone's got to look out for you. It's like you live on a whole different planet, orbiting around us, but not quite one of us." She chuckled and licked the marmalade off her thumb. "Yeah, you're one of a kind, Collin Uttley."

"That makes two of us," I retorted—but inside, my mind raced.

What did she mean by that? Had she already discovered the truth? Or was that purely a food pyramid observation on her part? Maybe she's right and I do need to eat more roughage—

"Ernestine, would you grab one of the craft duffels from the office?" called Mrs. Tackett from the trucks. "Just the striped one; the other two are for the next refugee camps."

"Sure thing, Mrs. T!" Ernestine gave me an inscrutable look—then jogged off.

I gazed after her, still confused by the subtext, as I tucked the thorny fruit into the side pocket of my convertible pants to eat later (in theory). Then I turned my attention to the toast and it was gone in four bites. Fortified, I made a beeline over to where Shelby and Twain were still in deep conversation.

"Hey, Shelby. How are you feeling today?" I interrupted, deliberately wedging myself between her and Twain.

"How are *you* feeling today, Collin? Taken your new malaria meds yet?" asked Twain with a sly look as he moved aside.

Ignoring him, I said to Shelby, "You look good, I mean, you know, really *rested.*"

Before she could respond, Twain shoved a pack of Big Red in my face. "Gum, anyone? Contrary to popular opinion, it *doesn't* violate *Expected Behavior Guideline Number Two.*"

"Thanks, Twain," said Shelby, completely oblivious as she helped herself.

He gave me a mocking grin as he popped a piece into his mouth. "Mmm…mmm… gotta love that contraband…"

I picked up the conversation with Shelby right where we left off. "Anyway, I'm glad you're doing so well, because I gotta tell you, that was one crazytown experience."

Her already glowing face lit up even more. She grasped my arm and pulled me towards her. "Oh, Collin, it's a miracle! I'm not at all bummed about Flounce today! I mean, I'm still sad, of course, because I'll always miss the little fella. But I'm not totally depressed and devastated like when I first heard. It's like what those… those *Wigglewurts* were saying. God actually *did* something to my heart. Healed it, I guess. And now I'm so full of *peace* it's like I'm going to explode with happiness!" She threw her arms so wide in exultation that she knocked the fedora right off my head.

I stared at her in disbelief as I stooped to pick it up.

Does she actually believe what she's saying? Talk about orbiting around in your own solar system! Although, I've gotta admit, she sure seems sincere. And at peace.

She leaned forward confidingly. "I was just telling Twain that I sure wouldn't mind being drunk in the Spirit again—"

"More where that come from!" came that familiar voice.

"—but not yet!" said Shelby, backing away from Jongchit as she dumped a cardboard box full of toothbrushes into the back of the truck.

Jongchit nudged Twain with her elbow—narrowly missing his crotch. "You! Come with me! I need big man to carry big box."

"I notice you didn't ask Collin," said Twain for my benefit, as he followed her around the side of the academy.

I glared after his disappearing form. What should my next move be? Twain knew that I *knew* he'd hidden the whiskey and cigarettes and bullets somewhere on this property. However, since the Tacketts didn't believe me, there was only one proactive thing I could do: never let Twain out of my sight when he ventured anywhere alone. Although I wasn't sure that Shelby was interested in Twain in a dating sense—after all, it *could* just be "childhood camaraderie"—I still wanted to prove him unworthy of her love once and for all.

"Collin?" I turned to see Shelby's emeralds in such close proximity that it shook me out of my reverie. "This morning, when I woke up totally happy, for like no reason, it reminded me of that Preston Sturges film we saw. Oh, what was it called…? The one where all those good things start happening out of nowhere?"

"*Christmas in July?*"

"Yeah, that one! That's *exactly* how I feel today."

"Speaking of Christmas, did you happen to notice a little gift when you woke up this morning?"

She looked puzzled. "Gift? What gift?"

"Don't move." Despite the heat, I ran into the academy, raced across the foyer to the green leather couch, and found Rock Flounce wedged in the crease, between the leather and the wood.

I rushed back to the truck, held up the rock, and said in a cartoony voice, "Merry Christmas, Shelby! I'm your very own Rock Flounce—yip yip yip!"

"Oh, Collin!" said Shelby, her eyes lighting up. She snatched it out of my hand and nestled it against her cheek. "I love it! You're so my Santa Claus today!"

I pushed my fedora back on my head, leaned forward, and said in a low tone, "And has little ol' Shelby Wanderal been naughty or nice—"

"Glad to see you got some extra sleep, Collin. That will make a world of difference," came a Californian drawl from behind me.

I leapt back from Shelby as if she was on fire, and landed heavily on Dr. Tackett's toes—vulnerably exposed in his Tevas trekking sandals.

"Ow!"

"Sorry, sorry, Dr. Tackett!"

"Save the swing dancing for the Thai market," said Dr. Tackett, trying to mask his irritation as he rubbed his foot.

"Load 'em up!" yelled Jongchit.

POSTCARD #2

(Photo caption: "Quaint and Charming Thai Market at Sunset Time with Tuk Tuk")

July 4th (Happy Independence Day!)

Dear Mom & Dad & Ava & Kimber & Sausage & Mittens,

I'm doing MUCH better. Still SAD, of course. I can't believe Flounce is really GONE. ☹ (Do Sausage & Mittens notice?) But Collin has been TOTALLY cheering me up! He even made me a ROCK FLOUNCE!!! I never thought I'd find another BFF so soon after Courtney moved away! When I get home, I'll have LOTS to tell you—things that would sound kinda weird if I tried to write them down. Anyway, today we're going to our first refugee camp! SOOO excited!

XOXO Love, Shelby
P.S. This is the market where Jack-O ate a huge black beetle—GAG!

Unfortunate But Necessary

THIS TIME THE ENTIRE OUTREACH TEAM—
Tacketts included—crammed into the back of Jongchit's truck, while all the backpacks, duffels, and supplies were stuffed into her cab and Hobab's cab and truck bed, concealed under blue plastic tarps. I managed to squeeze in next to Shelby, who still clutched her Rock Flounce. Once again, we spent most of our energy trying not to bounce out of the truck as we sped past rice paddy after rice paddy, liquid squares that reflected the cloudy blue sky and palms above.

One hand gripping the side of the truck and the other hand keeping my hat from blowing off, I mentally regrouped after that close call with Dr. Tackett. I sure hoped he hadn't overheard what I'd been saying to Shelby.

I was still berating myself for my stupidity when Shelby held Rock Flounce up to her cheek and mouthed at me, "Yip yip!"

But before I could respond, it *monsooned*. Literally. The sky suddenly parted and dropped a deluge on top of us.

"So this is how Noah felt!" said Jack-O with a gurgle.

Mrs. Tackett smiled as she calmly rung out her ponytail. "Just wait."

Within minutes, the rain stopped as abruptly as it started,

the sun blazed again, and our soaked shirts and pants began to dry. Mrs. Tackett passed around a sunscreen stick, which we rubbed on our noses and cheeks.

After we left the main highway and turned onto an unpaved road, we passed through three Thai Border Patrol checkpoints: barriers made out of wood and barbed wire. Each time, Jongchit unrolled her window and spoke rapidly in Thai, gesturing at the Team. Then she handed the officers cartons of cigarettes, after which they'd wave us through. Marlboros—like the ones in Twain's duffel.

"Is it just me, or does all this security seem overkill?" asked Ernestine, eyes on the guards.

"The Thai Border Patrol doesn't want Katin refugees illegally coming and going," said Twain before the Tacketts could reply. "It's more about them than us."

Dr. Tackett gave Twain an appraising look. "True…"

"What's the deal with the cigarettes?" asked Jack-O, shifting his bulk around in an effort to get comfortable.

"Bribes. Right, Dr. T?" said Twain, nodding knowingly.

"Bribes?!" said Shelby.

"We like to call them *incentives*. It smooths the way," said Dr. Tackett. "Unfortunate, but necessary."

"The Snickers Bars and boxes of Tic Tacs we tried at first just didn't seem to motivate them," said Mrs. Tackett with a laugh.

"We are here *legally*, right?" asked Shelby, looking doubtfully around her.

"Sure. But they could detain us for hours checking our passports and going through all our supplies. This way it's win-win for both of us," said Dr. Tackett, flashing us a reassuring smile. "Believe me, we learned this the hard way."

I pondered this as we drove on. Even though none of us smoked, we were using cigarettes as bribes. Was that ethical? Was the money we raised for the trip being used for this? I scrutinized Twain while he rummaged around in his backpack. He sure knew an awful lot about bribing the border police…

After what seemed like an eternity, but what was in reality about an hour and a half, the two trucks pulled off the road alongside a barbed wire fence with a large metal cattle gate. Bamboo huts with leaf roofs dotted the green jungle and mud hills, even all the way up the sides of mountains. We were surrounded by jutting rock formations, steep cliffs with exposed rock faces, jungle foliage, and a low hanging mist.

"It doesn't really look like a refugee camp, does it?" Shelby whispered in my ear. "More like one of those tropical islands, minus the water. Like—"

"Bali Hai in *South Pacific?*" I knew she was into those cheesy old musicals. One of our few aesthetic differences.

"You so get me, Collin!" She gave me a huge smile—which set my heart thumping like a techno beat.

"Where are the soldiers? Are we going to get to meet some Freedom Fighters?" Twain eagerly asked Hobab, who had pulled up next to us in his truck.

Hobab chuckled as he leaned out the window. "Sure, dude. But most of them are at the HQ with my dad."

Jongchit jumped out of her truck, slamming the door and motioned for us to get out as well.

"Yai Camp!" she said with a wave of her hand. "Time for to unload truck! Pronto pup!"

After unpeeling our wet bodies from each other, and practically tumbling out the tailgate, we lugged our backpacks and supplies from both trucks and made a pile by the metal gate.

"Over fifty thousand refugees live in here," said Mrs. Tackett, pointing to the identical bamboo huts that seemed to multiply like rabbits.

When I'd first heard the words, "refugee camp," I'd envisioned something about the size of a football stadium. But this was like a city!

"Bread Team—passport!"

While we dug into the money belts under our clothing, Jongchit strode over to the bamboo guard shack adjacent to the metal gate. After a few seconds, she pushed her red heart sunglasses off her face, and peered inside.

"Sawatdee kha!"

Two young Thai guards emerged, wearing camouflage and carrying machine guns. One of them yawned as if he'd just woken up. A third guard peered out of the shack window as he took a swig from a glass Coke bottle. All three seemed to recognize Jongchit and the Tacketts.

"Kun sabai dee mai kha!" Jongchit continued, making small talk.

"Sabai dee krap," answered one of the guards.

The Tacketts *waied* politely to the guards and then stepped aside to let Jongchit do her thing. After a cursory glance at our passports, the two guards turned to examine the pile of supplies. Jongchit chatted on and on as they searched. They methodically unzipped and zipped each backpack and duffel.

131

Then with a wink at the Team, Jongchit opened the craft bag and pulled out a lion puppet, put it on her hand, and said, "ROWR!" The officers exchanged startled looks—then chuckled reluctantly, as if to humor her.

A short time after that, they opened the metal gate and waved us through.

Jongchit gave us a big grin. "Okay, Team! Grab supply and follow Jongchit to *Born Free to Live Free AMEN! Orphanage!*"

SEA Urchins

THE EXCITEMENT AT ENTERING OUR FIRST refugee camp instantly evaporated once we learned that the orphanage was located deep in the middle of it—*two* miles away! Which normally wouldn't have been a problem, but we were inching along, each of us carrying a duffel or cardboard box in addition to our backpacks and Therm-A-Rests. With the narrow muddy path, uneven terrain, and intense humidity—it was going to be one grueling slog.

"I wish... I wish we could drive there in the trucks," Ernestine said to Hobab between gasps. She was panting heavily, sweat dripping from her fire hair onto her shirt.

"Don't think Jongchit hasn't tried," replied Hobab, striding along without so much as a drop of moisture on his face.

Luckily, after about ten minutes, a group of Katin refugee men came to our rescue and volunteered to carry the supplies—otherwise we'd never have made it. The Katin people in general had cappuccino colored skin, dark brown hair and eyes—and their average height was slightly under mine. They wore a variety of promo t-shirts obviously donated from Americans (*Diet Mountain Dew, Spiderman, L.A. Dodgers*) and most of them wore colorful *longyis*—a woven unisex skirt popular in the rural areas of many Southeast Asian countries.

Our new friends seemed to find our predicament highly amusing. They chattered and laughed as they effortlessly carried our burdens—*barefoot.*

However, Jack-O refused their help, insisting upon carrying two large duffels in addition to his backpack, daypack, and mattress roll.

"You could strain yourself with all that weight, Jack-O," said Mrs. Tackett, trying to pry the handles of a duffel bag out of his hands.

"No way—these aren't calves, they're cows!" said Jack-O, pointing to his beefy legs. "I was born a pack mule!"

"Well, be careful then," she said, pulling her tie-dyed hat down over her eyes. "This mud is really, *really* slippery."

I sincerely hoped the Tacketts knew where they were going, because Jongchit and Hobab hiked so fast, they were already out of sight! The rest of us trudged past row upon row of huts on stilts, which were jam-packed with families in the top section—and stuffed with dogs, chickens, and the odd pig below. How did they all fit? Squashes, beans, vines, and cucumbers grew in every available space around the huts.

A long line of refugees holding empty containers, waited in line for water. Their faces wore resigned expressions, as if they knew they'd always be waiting in lines for the basics of life and there was nothing they could do about it.

Jack-O paused, his eyes zeroing in on an elderly couple, slightly hunched over, clutching their plastic jugs. "Man, it must have totally sucked for my great grandparents in those internment camps." He took off his glasses and wiped his eyes with the back of his hand.

*   *   *   *   *

We continued on and soon had a cluster of little kids on our tail. They were boisterous and unusually confident for their age, flashing us toothy grins as they gave us pointers in surprisingly good English.

"Watch out—big mud hole!"

"That pig, he bite! Very bad!"

"*Oh… my… gosh!*" panted Shelby, fumbling with her camera. "They're so adorable!"

"I know, right?" said Mrs. Tackett with a huge smile as she glanced around the rowdy pack. "What did I tell you?" I'd never her seen her so animated—it was like she was a completely different person.

"You know what they are?" I asked Shelby. "SEA Urchins! As in Southeast Asia… SEA Urchins? Get it?"

Shelby paid no attention, completely absorbed in snapping photo after photo.

But Mrs. Tackett laughed. "I love it, Collin! SEA Urchins describes them perfectly!"

The SEA Urchins scampered in front of us like mountain goats on the slippery muddy hills. In complete contrast to the Outreach Team, who were awkwardly groping the sides of huts for guidance and taking tentative steps in the slick mud… grabbing any plant, bush, or tree in our path to steady ourselves.

That is, except for Twain, who trekked like a pro, knowing exactly where to place his jungle boot and where to grab hold of the foliage—all the while taking footage with his video camera. And wouldn't you know, while I was watching him, I pratfalled over a rock and slid sideways into a small ditch.

"Nice form, Uttley!" said Twain, catching it all on camera.

"What the heck was that?" asked Ernestine, looking down at me, trying not to laugh. "This isn't *Cirque du Soleil*, you know." She extended her hand.

I waved it away and scrambled to my feet. "Yeah, I'm a little rusty, but I'd like to see you try that move..." I trailed off as I felt liquid ooze down my leg. "You gotta be kidding! I think I'm bleeding!"

But upon further examination, the moisture was coming from the side pocket of my convertible pants. I unzipped it and removed the four squashed prickly rambutans, dripping with juice. "False alarm."

"Oh, Collin! You were supposed to eat them not carry them around in your pocket like some overgrown marsupial," said Ernestine, not bothering to hide her laughter now. "What are we gonna do with you?" She reached out and gave me a head noogie.

Before I could respond, a boy and a girl from our urchin pack popped up on either side of me, each grabbing one of my hands.

"Hello! Hello! We help!" said the girl with an impish smile, showing off a missing front tooth.

"Yes, help!" said the boy with a husky giggle.

They were both barefoot, and wearing such torn and dirty t-shirts that I couldn't even make out what the original graphics were supposed to be.

"Uh, thanks, I mean, *ta blü! Ta blü* very much..." I stammered in an English-Katin hybrid, allowing them to guide me along the path. I didn't want to reject their offer of help—and

I could definitely use some balance. Every time a pothole or ditch loomed ahead, they steered me around or over it, laughing all the while. When I tried to find out their names, they just laughed at my butchered attempts to communicate in Katin.

Their enthusiasm in helping me and their inexplicable happiness despite their poverty really moved me. I couldn't exactly process what I was feeling. But it was intense. Kind of like a dull ache...

As the Outreach Team trudged up the muddy paths through camp in single file, I noticed that Shelby's shoulders had indentations—practically grooves—from the weight of her backpack. The outside pocket bulged, dangerously close to splitting the seams, and the weight seemed to be pulling her backwards—as if one sudden gust of wind could topple her right over.

"Shelby," I whispered, trying not to pant in her ear. "Your pack's way too heavy. Is there anything in there you can get rid of? Like what's that bulging out of—"

"I'm... fine... I'm... fine," she said, panting so hard she could barely speak.

"But, Shelby, your back—"

"My back's *fine*." Her voice had a slight edge.

"Let's take a look," said Dr. Tackett, overhearing us and abruptly stopping to turn around. After removing his hat and wiping his forehead, he reached out a damp hand and lifted Shelby's pack. "Good grief. Collin's right. This pack weighs at least forty pounds! With your frame, you shouldn't carry more than twenty-five max."

"Collin may have a problem with the weight but I don't." Shelby shot me a "now see what you've done" look.

Dr. Tackett responded in his kind but firm professional tone: "You say that but your shoulders and spine say otherwise, my friend. Take it off, Shelby."

Shelby obeyed and Dr. Tackett unzipped the bulging outside pocket. "Well, here's the culprit." He pulled out a large plastic bag and read the label: *"Mauve Mountain Muesli! Ten pounds of organic vegan goodness!* Ten pounds of backbreaking gravel is more like it! Sorry, Shelby, but you're going to have to park this."

"Nooo!" said Shelby in a panicky whisper. "I'll starve!"

I stared at Shelby in surprise. Why this sudden passion for oats?

"You do know they have food at the orphanage…?" said Dr. Tackett, bewildered at her outburst.

"But… but…" she trailed off.

"Calm down, Shelby, we'll let you bring a few ounces to tide you over, if it means that much to you—"

"Let me carry it—*please?* I'm not the one complaining about the weight!" Shelby glared in my direction.

I winced, but held firm. "But Shelby, it's for your own good. Why don't I car—"

"I got it," came a low voice, and before we knew it, Twain had palmed the bag right out of Dr. Tackett's hands like it was a cloud of dandelion fluff and stuffed it into his pack.

"Hey! I was gonna carry that!" I couldn't keep the indignation out of my voice.

"You can have as much muesli as you want, Twain," said Shelby, her voice now as sprightly as her step.

"I'd rather eat asphalt," he replied.

"Move it, Uttley!" came Jack-O's voice behind me.

I dismally slogged after Shelby and Twain, with Jack-O wheezing like a bulldog right behind me.

Real smart, Collin. You just created a scenario that makes Twain a hero!

"Bye, bye, America!" came a childish voice beside me. My two helpers, along with the rest of the urchins, had stopped short at some invisible line of demarcation and would go no further. Parents' orders, maybe? As the cluster waved good-bye, Ernestine hurried over to them, digging into her day-pack.

"Wait! Got something for you..." She pressed a little block of individually wrapped clay into each kid's hand. The high-pitched squeals of excitement as they ripped the plastic off to see what color they got almost burst our eardrums! We could still hear them exclaiming even after we'd hiked out of sight.

"Good... call... Ketchum," said Jack-O, between huffs.

But Ernestine didn't seem to notice—she was too busy looking back over her shoulder and wiping tears off her cheeks.

Hopefully no one noticed the gleam on mine.

A Sticky Situation

T HE TEAM TRUDGED UP A PARTICULARLY steep ravine single-file. I'd almost reached the top, when I noticed something yellow and red in the mud in front of me—Shelby's scarf! I stopped short to pick it up, when—

"Whoaaaaa!" bellowed Jack-O. He cannoned right into me! I grabbed wildly at a nearby shrub just in time to keep from toppling over. But pack mule Jack-O didn't fare so well—all the weight he was carrying plummeted him backwards down the ravine. Shedding luggage along the way, he flipped over a bush, rolled down the incline, and—

CRUNCH!

—smashed headfirst into a jutting rock formation!

Still gripping the branches of the shrub, I stared down at his prone body in shock.

Within seconds, the Team had swiftly gathered around him.

"Oh, my gosh, Jack-O!"

"Jesus!"

"Did you see what just happened!?"

"Are you all right? Is he all right?"

"Can you hear me, Jack-O?"

"He's not moving! He's not breathing—"

"Everyone calm down." Mrs. Tackett's voice of reason cut through the mounting panic.

I slid down the ravine and joined the rest of the Team, who were staring down at his inert form.

Don't let him die! God, if you exist, don't let him die like this! It would be partially my fault! I couldn't live with that—

Right then, Jack-O opened his eyes and gazed up at us blearily.

The Team gave a cheer of relief. My legs crumpled under me and I sat down with a thud.

What a coincidence! Almost like a "god" did hear me and instantly responded.

There was a gash across his forehead and right temple, which bled profusely, and he was covered in mud—but he was *alive*.

"Praise the Lord," murmured Ernestine.

Jack-O looked around. "All I see is blobs…"

"Here are your glasses," said Dr. Tackett, helping him put them on. "Thank God they're polycarbonate."

Our refugee friends retrieved Jack-O's backpack, daypack, Therm-A-Rest, and two duffels and set them in a pile beside him. Then they squatted a short distance away to watch, along with the crowd that was beginning to gather.

Dr. Tackett craned his neck to look up the trail. "Anyone see Jongchit or Hobab?"

There was no sign of them.

"They've probably already reached the orphanage by now," said Mrs. Tackett in a strained voice.

"If only we could get some reception here…" said Dr. Tackett as he checked his cell phone.

Jack-O adjusted his black frames and stared up at us. "Is it half-time?"

We all exchanged concerned glances.

Mrs. Tackett knelt down beside him and pressed a thick wad of Kleenex against his bleeding gash. Dr. Tackett swiftly removed a First Aid kit from his backpack and rummaged through it.

"Jack-O? Jack-O, do you know where you are?" Mrs. Tackett asked in a soothing undertone, her protruding eyes peering unblinkingly into his.

He started to turn his head, then winced. "Ouch. That kills."

"What's your name? How old are you?" asked Dr. Tackett, trying to mask the anxiety spreading across his tanned face.

"I know all that. I know we're on the trip. I just don't remember anything after the airport…. I've had a mild concussion. I've lost my short-term memory. This happened to me three times in football. I'll need a pot and a pail."

"A pot and a pail?" repeated Mrs. Tackett, justifiably confused.

"That's what Coach Linder always gets me. A pot of coffee to keep me awake and a pail for puking. I can't go to sleep for at least twelve hours, you know."

"This has happened to you before?" asked Shelby, her face scrunched in concern.

"I've had a mild concussion. I've lost my short-term memory. This happened to me three times in football. I'll need a pot and a pail."

"Now, Jack-O, you don't really need to be kept awake after a concussion, that theory has been debunked," said Mrs.

Tackett gently and firmly, as if reasoning with a five-year-old. "I've had a mild concussion. I've lost my short-term memory. This happened to me three times in football. I'll need a pot and a pail."

The Team exchanged glances once again as we stood in a semi-circle, chugging water and watching the Tacketts tend to Jack-O. All of us, that is, except Twain, who seemed to be deliberately averting his eyes from the wound, and looking off into the distance. Shelby passed around handfuls of *Mauve Mountain Muesli* to the Outreach Team and our refugee camp cargo carriers—who chewed it thoughtfully, if not enthusiastically.

"Ow—that kills!" said Jack-O as Mrs. Tackett applied disinfectant.

"Good!" said Ernestine spewing flakes of oatmeal into the air. "Maybe it'll teach you not to overload yourself when you're trekking through slippery mud—no matter how macho nacho you think you are."

"Thanks—I guess?" said Jack-O, wiping a stray oat off his cheek. Then to Twain, in a low tone, "Good sign when they're concerned about you, right?"

"Sure." Twain patted him on the back, without looking at him.

"Don't encourage him!" Ernestine whispered to Twain in exasperation. Then to Jack-O, "Of course I'm concerned about you, you big lug! We've been friends forever and I love you—*as a friend.*"

"Man," said Jack-O with a sigh. "She can't even throw me a bone when I've been mortally wounded."

"Take it from me, you're not *mortally* wounded," said Dr.

Tackett dryly as he pulled out a small tube from the first aid kit and handed to Mrs. Tackett

"Isn't that glue?" asked Shelby.

"Are you crazy?" said Jack-O, watching Mrs. Tackett unscrew the cap.

"Yep, Krazy Glue!" said Dr. Tackett, with forced joviality, trying to lighten the mood.

"It's superior to a butterfly Band-Aid, because it seals the cut permanently and allows no germs in," explained Mrs. Tackett as she squeezed a line of glue along the gash, which extended from the side of his right temple around to the middle of his forehead.

"Let's all pray for Jack-O right now," said Ernestine with sudden assertiveness, kneeling so closely beside him that her fire hair hung in his face. "Everybody move in and lay a hand on him."

"Avoid the head," said Mrs. Tackett.

"Avoiding the head is good," said Jack-O, with a slight shudder of his massive shoulders.

We all squatted around Jack-O, putting hands on his shoulders and his back. After the Team prayed for about three minutes—me uttering "Yes, Lord" at intervals—Jack-O's chest started heaving and then he burst out laughing.

"Whoa, man, I'm feeling waaaaay better now. Like I'm...I'm..."

"Sinking in Jell-O?" Shelby asked eagerly.

He shot her a disdainful look. "Jell-O? What are you talkin' about?"

"I thought you might have felt all relaxed and oozy—"

He laughed again. "No way! I feel high! High as a kite,

man! I don't even feel the pain—much."

"Well, that's good… I guess…?" Shelby glanced at the rest of us in confusion.

"Sure, it is!" said Ernestine. "Power prayer affects each of us differently—"

"Skip-Bo!" Jack-O said suddenly. "Dudes! Now's the perfect time for a game of Skip-Bo! Where's my backpack?" As he sat up and looked around—Ernestine screamed and jerked towards him, half-falling into his lap. A clump of the fire hair hanging in his face was now *stuck* to the glue on his wound!

"Ouch! What's going on? It's ruining my high…" whined Jack-O, tentatively touching his forehead.

Ernestine tried to pull the hair off—no sale!

"I'm stuck! I'm seriously stuck here, guys!"

Jack-O laughed. "So you finally admit you're stuck on me, Ketchum!" He put a meaty arm around Ernestine's shoulders, which she promptly pushed off.

Mrs. Tackett tried prying the thick strand out of the line of glue. "Oh, no! She really *is* stuck!"

"What did I tell ya?" said Jack-O with glee, putting his arm around Ernestine's shoulders, which she pushed off yet again.

"Ow!" said Ernestine. "That hurts!" She looked like a marionette puppet, her head strained to the side at an extreme angle.

"I didn't realize it was so fast acting—" began Dr. Tackett.

"Khun kalang tha xari!? What you doing? What going on here!?" came a deep voice in broken English from somewhere behind us.

A Tiny Baby Problem

WITHIN SECONDS WE WERE SURROUNDED BY a group of Thai Border Patrol Officers. The Head Officer was balding and fairly robust for a Thai, dressed in a dark blue uniform with arm patches; the other four officers wore fatigues and camouflage like the border guards at the checkpoints we'd driven through. I tried not to stare at the M-16s in their hands, pointing directly at us. These sure weren't the young kickback guards from the front entrance!

In the blink of an eye, our refugee carrier friends disappeared into the surrounding jungle, leaving the entire Team standing there, frozen in shock.

Ernestine and Jack-O looked particularly ludicrous still glued together, their necks straining, their eyes rolling from side to side, trying to follow what was happening.

"Hiya, folks!" said Jack-O, with a grin. "I'm high as a kite!"

"We're hosed," Twain muttered to me.

Dr. Tackett laughed humorlessly. "Oh, he's just joking, sir. He's had a little head injury."

The Head Officer stared at the spectacle of Jack-O and Ernestine incredulously for a moment, then pulled himself together and asked Jack-O in a gruff voice, "You high? You high on drug?"

Jack-O rubbed his forehead and chuckled. "You called it, dude! I'm high in the Holy Spirit! He's my dealer! Or is *he* himself the drug—"

"Shut up!" Ernestine hissed in his ear.

"Hey!" said Jack-O in an injured tone. "He asked—"

"Let's all calm down," interrupted Dr. Tackett, moving over and putting a hand on Jack-O's shoulder.

"Come on, guys! I'm high!" exclaimed Jack-O, waving his arms in the air and almost smacking Ernestine in the face. "I'm high in the Spirit! Am I right, Shelby? High in the Spirit, drunk in the Spirit—same, same, but different!" He burst out laughing, each shake of his body pulling on Ernestine's stuck hair.

"Ow!" Ernestine jabbed Jack-O with her elbow. "Stop it, you big lug!"

But that just made him laugh even harder.

It was like one of those cringe-worthy scenes in a movie where you want to look away, but you can't.

The Head Officer shifted his gaze from Jack-O to each member of the Team in turn. It was becoming obvious that he had no sense of humor or ability to read nuance—and took everything literally.

Which won't bode well in a sticky situation like this...

The Head Officer turned to Dr. Tackett. "You in charge?"

Dr. Tackett managed to pull himself together and muster up his professional demeanor. "*Sawatdee krup.* Yes, my wife and I are co-leaders of this group of volunteers. Our young teammate here has been injured from a fall and doesn't know what he's saying—"

"Sure, I do!" Jack-O shifted from jolly to belligerent.

"He say he high and drunk," said the Head Officer sternly. "Very forbidden, much much forbidden."

"But he's not high or drunk," said Mrs. Tackett quickly. "He's concussed!" She pointed to his gash.

"And I'm attached!" said Ernestine with some exasperation. "Is anybody gonna do anything about it? Like soon?"

"Scissors?" Dr. Tackett turned to the Head Officer and made a cutting motion with his fingers. "Do you mind if I get some scissors out of my bag…?" He pointed at the first aid kit.

After a moment, the Head Officer nodded and issued a staccato command to his men. In one swift motion, they aimed their guns and rifles at Dr. Tackett's head!

Ernestine jerked her head in shock, which tugged on the thick strand of hair and pulled Jack-O's wound—causing him to yelp in pain.

The rest of us remained frozen.

"What did I tell you?" Twain whispered out of the corner of his mouth. "Hosed."

Although shaken, Dr. Tackett managed to remove a Swiss Army knife and unfold the scissors. With a trembling hand he leaned over and snipped off the very tip of Ernestine's hair—leaving a clump stuck to Jack-O's forehead!

Ernestine gasped.

Jack-O yelped again.

The bright yellow-orange-red fringe sticking out of his head looked so absurd that despite the seriousness of the situation, the entire Team had trouble keeping straight faces.

Only after Dr. Tackett replaced the knife in his backpack did the guards finally lower their weapons.

"Now I'll carry a piece of you wherever I go…" Jack-O whispered to Ernestine.

Mrs. Tackett stuck a large Band-Aid over the gash.

"Hey!" said Jack-O, clapping a hand to his head. "You covered my Ketchum Hair!"

The Head Officer abruptly barked out "Passport!" We all immediately began removing our money belts from underneath our clothes—awkward to do quickly when you're so sweaty your money belt sticks to your skin.

That is, except for Jack-O, who sat cross-legged in the dirt, scratching his head like an oversize kindergartener. "What's up with these dudes? Why are they so cranky?"

Mrs. Tackett shushed him and Dr. Tackett helped him get out his passport.

Two of the border patrol officers gathered up our passports and handed them to the Head Officer, who flipped rapidly through them, glancing at each of us in turn.

Mrs. Tackett clutched her husband's arm and whispered, "Peter! They don't really think we're… we're… ?" She couldn't even finish the thought.

Apprehension crossed Dr. Tackett's face as he removed his hat and wiped his forehead with the back of his hand. "I have no idea, Marcy. All I know is that it's not looking good. And Jongchit couldn't have picked a worse time to go AWOL!"

You know it's not really looking good when your own leaders think it's not looking good. I shot a protective glance over at Shelby, and was relieved to note that she didn't seem scared, only confused. And hot. We were all soaking wet and probably on the verge of heatstroke. Which is why we just stood there, mutely watching the officers search through every backpack, box, and duffel. Once they finished and turned away, Ernestine swiftly darted forward, unzipped the craft duffel, removed something—and stuffed it up her trekking shirt!

One of the border patrol officers glanced over at her suspiciously. She flashed him a huge grin, *waied*, and said, "*Sabaidee mai?*"

After a moment, he looked away.

Now her shirt was bulging. As we watched, she shifted the package up higher and higher, until it rested on her stomach. She looked bloated, like she'd eaten one too many bowls of noodles.

The Team exchanged perplexed looks. What the heck had she hidden?

"Cell phone!" the Head Officer barked at the Tacketts.

The Tacketts exchanged foreboding looks. Then Dr. Tackett cleared his throat and said, "Wait just a minute here, why exactly do you need our—"

"Cell phone!" he repeated. "Cell phone *now!*"

After a slight pause, they slowly removed their cells from their packs.

Prickles ran down my spine and my imagination spun into high gear, when:

"Bread Team! *Reng reng!* Hurry hurry! Snail faster than you…"

Jongchit!

Her bellow had trailed off once she'd absorbed the full implications of the situation. She and Hobab stared down at us from the edge of the ravine. Now here was a bold woman of action! She'd soon clear this all up!

"Border Patrol! *Mai pen rai*," she said in a resigned tone and hurried down the hill, Hobab following behind her. "Cannot Jongchit leave you alone for one tiny minute?"

The Tacketts turned towards her, relief and hope lighting up their faces.

"Jongchit!" croaked Mrs. Tackett.

"Thank God!" exclaimed Dr. Tackett. "There's been some sort of misunderstanding. They think we're high or drunk or—"

"Stop! Don't say a word!" Ernestine abruptly barked at Jack-O, who was opening his mouth to speak. "Not a word! *Zip-your-lip!*"

Eyes wide, Jack-O meekly mimed zipping his lip.

"Here, eat these, dude," said Twain, handing him a large package of trail mix. Then muttering to the rest of us, he added, "That should keep him quiet for awhile."

Jack-O eagerly ripped it open and dug in—and we all breathed sighs of relief.

"*Kha, kha,*" said Jongchit, nodding her head as she assessed the situation. "Jongchit take charge."

She turned to the Head Officer and began explaining voluminously (and rapidly) in Thai. Hobab stood next to her saying nothing, just nodding politely with a fixed smile on his face. Three of the officers stood at attention with rifles across their chest and the fourth kept a casual hand resting on the handgun in his holster. The Head Officer frowned at Jongchit and responded tersely, gesturing every so often at the Tacketts. She seemed to be trying to convince him about something, with little success. At one point, she even pulled out a wad of Thai baht and waved it in front of his face—but he shook his head and refused to take it.

The Team watched in silence—that is, except for Jack-O, who remained oblivious, absorbed in picking out all the M&Ms from the trail mix.

In frustration, Jongchit finally turned away from the Head Officer and huddled with the Tacketts, where they conferred in whispers. After a few minutes, Dr. Tackett turned to the Team, his face tense under his tan. "Keep your backpacks and Therm-A-Rests. They're confiscating the rest for the time being."

"But what's happening?" Twain asked.

"Stubborn," Jongchit shook her head. "He very stubborn man."

Dr. Tackett sighed. "Until this gets cleared up, he thinks Yai Camp would be safer without 'our types' in it."

But before he could explain further, we found ourselves being escorted through camp by the officers. The refugees paused in their activities to watch us pass, but no one said a word nor so much as smiled. No scrappy SEA Urchins shadowed us this time, shouting out phrases in English. No cheerful volunteers offered to carry our backpacks.

"Where are they taking us?" Shelby whispered to no one in particular.

Right then, the sound of children singing in the Katin language filled the air, and the Tacketts paused in front of a large open-air structure made of cinderblocks, topped with a variegated tin roof. With a rueful smile, unable to mask her extreme disappointment, Mrs. Tackett gestured towards the sign above the door: *Born Free to Live Free AMEN Orphanage!*

Jongchit looked back at us and shrugged. *"Mai pen rai."*

The Team exchanged looks. So *that* had been our destination all along!

"Oh, and we were so close!" said Shelby in dismay. She shot an angry look at Jack-O, who was humming tunelessly as he dumped the last of the trail mix into his mouth.

Tears trickled down Mrs. Tackett's cheeks, streaking the chalky white sunscreen and dripping off her chin. She ignored them, staring stoically ahead. A solemn Dr. Tackett put a consoling arm around her shoulders and Ernestine squeezed her arm in solidarity as they continued on.

That strange, indescribable ache in the pit of my stomach returned.

Talk about a bait and switch. More proof that a so-called Divine Creator who cares for orphans and widows does NOT exist...

After eons of slogging, we found ourselves at another entrance, where a couple of Thai camp guards were squatting and smoking. They jumped up at the sight of the Border Patrol Head Officer, dropping their cigarettes and grinding them into the dirt.

Only then did the Head Officer motion to another Border Patrol officer to return our passports. We immediately stuffed them back into our money belts in relief—we all felt vulnerable without I.D. in a sketchy Third World country.

The Head Officer turned and solemnly addressed the Team. His face was stern and his voice was flat and no nonsense. "*First* time in camp. *Last* time in camp. Understand?"

We all nodded rapidly, like a row of bobble head dolls.

The metal cattle gate swung open. The border patrol officers motioned for us to file through, and then the camp guards immediately slammed it shut behind us.

Whew! Safe! We exhaled in relief. That is, until we noticed that...

...the Tacketts were being led in the opposite direction! Towards a large white unmarked van parked on the side of the road! When the Tacketts realized we were being separated, they stopped and turned around to instruct us, but the officers prodded them along.

"They're taking us in for questioning to clear this all up. Wait for us at the academy until we get back," said Mrs. Tackett in a constricted voice, awkwardly craning her neck towards us. Her tie-dyed hat was askew, with damp strands of hair plastered across her forehead—and no gleaming white smile in sight.

"Jongchit, call the American Embassy!" called Dr. Tackett over his shoulder.

"Kha, kha! And lawyer!!*"* said Jongchit grimly, pulling her cell phone with the Hello Kitty cover out of her back pocket—then instantly putting it back at the lack of cell reception.

"Don't worry, Team. It's obviously a big mis—" Dr. Tackett was cut off as he was gently but firmly "guided" into the van. Soon we saw their outlines, barely visible through the tinted windows—still mouthing and gesturing at us.

Jongchit shook her head and said something explosive in Thai—which she didn't bother translating for our edification. Then she whirled around and said something rapidly in Thai (or was it Katin?) to Hobab.

My stomach contorted. If Jongchit wasn't making a joke of the situation, then it must be serious. *Deadly* serious.

"So hosed." Twain removed his olive drab hat and rubbed his damp head and neck.

"Would you stop saying that?" I snapped.

Ernestine seem to be praying under her breath. Her eyes were glued to the van window, where the Tacketts continued to mouth indecipherable instructions at us.

"Where are they taking them?" asked Shelby in a tight voice.

"Hope they're getting food—I'm starved," said Jack-O, waving cheerfully at their dim figures as he crumpled up the empty trail mix wrapper.

Twain shook his head. "Guys, this is really messed up—"

"Baby problem, tiny problem. Tiny baby problem," Jongchit said loudly. "How do you say? Mis-*under*-stand? Yes, misunderstand. You wait, Jongchit take care of everything. I call Hobab when I know more." Then she whispered in Hobab's ear and slipped some Thai *baht* into his hand.

"You've got to do something!" said Shelby with rising panic. "The Tacketts are being arrested! *Arrested!*"

"*Mai pen rai, mai pen rai,*" murmured Jongchit, patting her on the back. "No worry please! God, he very in charge. *Kha,* sometime he seem like one tricky trickster—but he in charge. Return to truck. Back to academy you go—and I must translate." Then she hurried over to the white van—which drove away with a lurch as soon as she climbed in.

Stunned silence.

Then Ernestine lifted up her trekking shirt and a gallon size Ziploc hit the dirt.

"Two thousand googly eyes—and for what?"

Excerpt from Shelby's Journal
July 4th

I just can't sleep after all that's happened. The Extreme You handout said to journal when worried. So I'm hoping this will help me wind down. (And not wake Ernestine up!)

Weirdest day ever! And I thought yesterday was weird! What is going on with the Tacketts???? Have they been arrested or deported or WHAT? No one seems to know! After they were taken away, Hobab asked Twain to drive Jongchit's truck back to the academy. So Ernestine and Collin rode with Hobab, and Jack-O and I rode with Twain. (Which Collin didn't seem to like...) Anyway, Twain drove extra slow and careful—so sweet! But poor Jack-O kept asking where "Coach Linder and the half-time oranges" were.

When we got to the academy, ALL of us (except Twain) wanted to call our parents, but Hobab literally <u>begged</u> us to wait. Said that Jongchit would *clear up this whole misunderstanding with Tacketts by tomorrow, so why worry our families or church for nothing? We had to admit he had a point. Then, at dinner, Ernestine led us in prayer for the Tacketts, but everyone was so tired it barely lasted five minutes. Then when we prayed again for Jack-O's head, he actually did a face-plant in his fried rice and started snoring! Poor guy!*

Twain asked Hobab if he thought we'd be able to go back to Yai Camp or those other two refugee camps we were scheduled to visit. Hobab said, "You kiddin', dude? Not after what went down today." And said we'd probably spend the rest of July painting the academy Blue Sky Blue. Something snapped in Twain after that–like he sorta shut down emotionally. His eyes looked vacant, but you could tell his mind was whirling a million miles an hour. Reminded me of that time in seventh grade when he told me about his parents getting divorced...

Anyway, later on, when I was heading out of the bathroom and into the dorm room for bed, I heard an argument downstairs and looked over the banister. Twain and Collin were standing outside Jongchit's office. Collin was asking who Twain had been talking to on the phone, and Twain said he hadn't been on the phone, and Collin said he totally heard him using the landline, and then Twain said, "You're hearing things, Uttley, just like you've been <u>seeing</u> things." That seemed to really tick Collin off for some reason.

It's just so not like Twain! What is going on around here, anyway???

Why is everything such a MESS!?

Oh, Flounce, FLOUNCE! I soooo miss you!!!

TWAIN'S JOURNAL ENTRY
-DECODED VERSION-

07 04 22. 45

TONIGHT'S THE NIGHT.

Behold, the Feral Cat!

IT WAS ALMOST 1 A.M. WHEN JACK-O FINALLY turned his heft over and the floor shaking snoring ceased. To be honest, my imagination would have kept me up just as long, running worst case scenarios through my brain: *the Tacketts getting deported; the Team getting sent home; Twain stealing Shelby away from me; the Team finding out about me and hating my guts forever; and me getting malaria, dengue fever, leprosy, or worse.* You know, the usual kind of anxiety inducing insomnia.

I couldn't have been asleep for more than ten minutes, when I became aware of the soft, stealthy sound of a zipper being zipped in an attempt to be soundless. As luck would have it, my right earplug had wriggled lose and I heard the "stealth" loud and clear.

Across the room, Twain finished zipping his big backpack closed and hoisted it onto his shoulders. He was fully dressed, jungle boots and all. As I watched, motionless, he attached his daypack to the front straps of his backpack. After a quick look around, he picked up the infamous camouflage duffel bag (which looked strangely deflated), brushed through the woven blankets in the doorway—and was gone!

What the…?!?

Where was Twain going *this* time?

Just one way to find out.

As I scrambled to my feet, I got all tangled up in the mosquito netting and whacked my head on the side of the bunk.

My squawk of pain could have awoken the dead.

But Jack-O slept like a brick.

When I finally freed myself from the diabolical web, I shoved on my trekking shoes, and stuffed a bottle of water and a protein bar in my small daypack. My passport was already on my person, since I never took my money belt off except to shower.

An envelope lay on the wooden slats of Twain's empty bunk—addressed to *The Outreach Team.* I snatched it up and stuffed it into my pocket as I sped downstairs, out the front door—and stopped short. In the light of the almost full moon, I made out the figure of Twain rummaging around in the big pile of empty paint cans next to the stack of 2x4s, from under which he removed:

Cartons of cigarettes, bottles of whiskey, and boxes of bullets!

AHA!

Behold the feral cat!

The "feral cat" that had knocked over the paint can the night I talked with Dr. Tackett.

After stuffing the contraband into the camouflage duffel and hoisting it over his shoulder, Twain strode past the useless "guard," whose thunderous snores rivaled Jack-O's, opened the gate, and headed down the muddy road that ran in front of the academy.

Instead of confronting Twain right then and there, I decided it was time to discover precisely what his secret was. I wished I'd remembered my digital camera. It might have come in handy to document—well, whatever *nefarious* deeds were about to be revealed. As I shadowed Twain from a distance, I briefly wondered if I should have told someone what was going on—in case anything happened.

Too late now.

Twain kept up a steady pace until he reached the main road, which took about twenty minutes. I noticed his left foot had a slight limp. He walked along the main road for another fifteen minutes until the Bus Terminal came into view.

So that's the idea!

Twain entered the station. A few minutes later, he emerged with a ticket in hand and boarded a bus parked out front with its engine running.

Shooooot! Now what?!

There was no way I could ride on the same bus and not be spotted—the only other *farang!*

As I was pondering my next move, a motorcycle taxi drove by.

Bingo!

Normally, I would have taken the time to debate the pros and cons of such a rash action. (A trait I inherit from my parents.) But right then, I didn't give it a second thought—which I now I chalk up to a case of *Extreme You.*

I jogged down the block, staying in the shadows in case Twain happened to look out the window. Down a side street or *soi*, I spotted three *tuk tuks* parked at a taxi stand—and one *mototaxi*, Thailand's motorcycle taxi. The drivers were squatting and smoking and playing some sort of card game. They reluctantly stood up as I approached and greeted me with a lackluster, *"Sawatdee krup."*

I approached a skinny man who was inhaling a cigarette, and sitting on a motorcycle helmet—the perfect cover!

"Mista want *motoesai rap chang?*" he said in a raspy voice, throwing the still smoking butt to the ground.

Using the mini-Thai phrase book I'd shoved into my pocket, I explained that I wanted him to follow the bus.

He spat on the ground as he dug around in his front shirt pocket for another cigarette. "No, no, you not want. Bus slow—so slow. Much fast go round."

"But I don't want to go around—I want to go where it goes."

"*Khrap, khrap.* I take you zoom zoom fast way."

It took a full ten minutes to convince the driver that all I wanted him to do was to inch along behind the bus. He and his friends were incredulous at my desire to "go slow." After pulling out a wad of *baht*, I found myself sitting on the back of the *mototaxi*, wearing the owner's hot pink and black tiger striped helmet with the plastic visor flipped down. There was no way Twain could recognize me if he happened to glance out the window.

The bus pulled out and chugged down the road, and we followed behind. The road grew increasingly windy, with some hairpin curves and sheer drops—I gripped the plastic handle behind the seat and tried not to look down.

When the bus finally stopped at a rest area, I exhaled in relief, ungripped my fingers, then instructed my driver to pull over and wait by the side of the road. Soon Twain disembarked with four fellow passengers, but instead of following them toward the restrooms and food stalls, he put on both packs, picked up his duffel, and headed down the edge of the highway, which was lined with pure jungle. I quickly shoved a wad of *baht* into my driver's hand for the ride (*and* secondhand smoke *and* terror) and ran after Twain as he trudged down the side of the road.

And, what do you know, a half an hour later, Twain was *still* trudging down the side of the road, me skulking about a block behind him. The farther we walked, the more intense my curiosity grew. By that point, I'd have followed him through a leech-infested swamp and over the edge of a cliff to find out what the heck it was all about.

Abruptly, Twain stopped and pulled something out of his cargo pants pocket. After studying it closely, he walked two more yards, paused in front of a pile of discarded rubber tires, and then turned a sharp left deeper into the jungle.

I increased my pace, since I didn't want to lose sight of him with all the thick foliage blocking out the bright moon's glow.

It was a narrow, rocky dirt road—make that *mud* road.

For some reason, I gave zero thought to how I'd ever get back if Twain somehow ditched me. I was probably in survival mode, that ol' *Extreme You*, concerned only with the here and now.

Onward Twain marched, his limp becoming more and more pronounced—apparently, those jungle boots of his just did not fit. Twice he set down the bulging duffel to stretch and switch hands. But he never noticed me shadowing him, thanks to the night sounds of rustling palm leaves, the chirping cicadas, the yips of distant dogs, and snatches of conversation and music drifting out of the rustic bamboo houses lining the road.

Finally, his flashlight beam fell on a weathered silver pick-up truck, where two Thai men sat in the front seat. As soon as they saw Twain limping over—they jumped out.

Enter Needle and Frito

CROUCHING BEHIND THE TRUNK OF A LARGE teak tree, I heard every word.

"*Sawatdee krup,* Mr. Abernath!" said the driver, omitting the "y" at the end of his name. His black spiked hair was bleached blond on the tips, and pitted acne scars covered his cheeks. The other guy was younger, with long black hair in a ponytail and humorless grin. They both wore sleeveless t-shirts and Levi's—and stood a full foot shorter than Twain.

"Needle, right?" Twain asked as he shook hands with the driver.

"*Khrap, khrap.* Needle. Good thing you call. Sooner work better than later." Needle curled his lips back from his teeth in what was presumably a smile. "Him Frito." The other guy nodded, continuing to grin.

Twain stood there uncomfortably for a moment, then shifted his feet, ran his hand through his brown crew cut, and looked around. "Where are the Freedom Fighters?"

"They meet us on other side," said Needle. "Got rest of *baht?*"

"Hold on," said Twain. I could tell he was attempting to maintain some authority in this situation. "Let me get this straight: once I hand over the last five hundred, you're taking me across the river—"

"You bring Johnny Walker and Marlboros and ammo? Show, please."

Annoyed at being interrupted, Twain grudgingly unzipped the duffel and pulled out a carton of cigarettes, a bottle of Jack Daniel's Black Label Whiskey, and a box of bullets.

Needle and Frito exchanged looks.

"You follow directions real good for a *farang*," said Needle in a condescending tone.

"Chai, chai!" said Frito. His voice was higher than expected—almost squeaky.

"Thanks," said Twain impatiently.

"Everything all set. No problem. We do this many, many time before." Needle glanced at a platinum watch on his arm, which was stringy with veins. "But we must hurry. *Baht?"* He held out his hand to Twain, palm up.

Twain placed a white business size envelope on his hand. Needle opened it and rapidly counted the Thai *baht* before slipping it into his pocket. "Good." Then he turned and said something to Frito in Thai, who then hoisted Twain's duffel into the back of the truck.

Needle climbed back into the cab and Twain started to follow him, unfastening his daypack from his backpack.

"Mai, mai—you ride in back." Frito threw him a plastic blue tarp. "Cover up."

Twain started to protest, then Needle said, "Only for first checkpoint. They stop us if see *farang*."

"But I got my hat and sunglasses—"

"Nose," said Frito.

"What?"

"Nothing hide pointy Westerner nose." Frito reached up and touched the tip of Twain's nose and snickered.

Twain was growing more and more disgruntled and barely managed to keep his tone level. "All right."

I watched in disbelief. He wasn't really going with these creeps, was he? As irritating and smug as Twain was, I hated the thought of him in the clutches of Needle and Frito.

Do something! Twain's about to royally jack up his life!

But before I could move a muscle, Frito suddenly jumped in the cab and Needle started the engine. Just as Twain began to climb into the back—VROOOM! Needle stepped on the accelerator and the silver pick-up truck went tearing back down the muddy road the way we'd come. I sunk back into the jungle foliage so the headlights wouldn't illuminate me. As they passed, I heard Frito and Needle laughing uproariously.

Twain fell backwards and hit the dirt, the backpack weighing him down, and his arms and legs flailing. But a second later, he'd mustered up strength, leapt up and run after them.

"Stop! Stop, you…you freakin'… you freakin'…"

Suddenly, the obscenities exploded out of him like water out of a hydrant as he chased them down the road. When he finally realized it was futile, he stopped, dropped to his knees and gave an anguished bellow, like some primeval beast in primordial mud.

It was pathetic. For the first time ever—I pitied Twain Abernathy.

I pushed aside a teak leaf and stepped forward.

"Man, that sucks, Twain—"

Twain screamed and tipped over backwards in the mud,

his limbs flailing like a turtle on its back, unable to turn over.

"What the—*Collin!?!* What the heck are you doing here!?!"

I held out a hand to help him up out of turtle-mode.

"Someone's gotta look out for you."

"Then you saw the whole thing?! How those lowlifes conned me out of a *thousand* bucks?! *A thousand bucks!!!*"

"Well," I said, trying to lighten the mood, "at least the mystery of your sisters' souvenirs has been solved once and for all."

For a full minute he stared at me dully, every last bit of adrenaline and rage draining out of his body. Then he grabbed my hand, and hoisted himself up.

He swore under his breath a dozen more times—all variations on a theme.

The Wannabe Mercenary

AFTER TWAIN HAD FINALLY CALMED DOWN and we were shuffling back down the muddy road, I learned the *full* story of Twain's mysterious behavior. Once he started explaining, it was like the floodgates opened.

"I wanted to go over the border to help the soldiers, to help the FFFFB—Freedom Fighters For a Free Burma, the Feebs—fight the BMJ, you know, like Hobab's dad," he said as stoically as possible, trying to mask his intense emotion. "It wasn't like it was out of selfishness. I'd been planning this since writing a paper on Burma over two years ago in history class. When I found out the Tacketts were heading back to the refugee camps, this time bringing youth group kids, I was totally amped. Here was the good cause worth fighting for— fighting for justice. Like my Great Uncle W.J.—William James—who did three tours of duty in Nam. These are his boots. And my two great grandpas in World War II. I mean, come on! Think about it—less than a couple hundred years ago, we high schoolers would have been soldiers, explorers, or even farmers with our own land. But today? Total waste. All we do is play video games and take standardized tests."

His facial muscles rippled with frustration.

"How did you find out about Needle?" I asked, redirecting him.

"An old school online chat room—can you believe it? Don't get me started on all the forums and websites and social media devoted to Freedom Fighters. There are a lot of wannabe mercenaries out there, looking for a cause worth fighting for." He took a deep breath. "Long story short, looks like I got scammed by Needle. I honestly thought he was legit."

He handed me a manila envelope. "Go ahead. Open it."

I opened it and removed a sheet of paper with a map drawn roughly in pen and a number of sentences in code.

Twain pointed to the map. "Here's where I just met Needle in order to eventually cross the river here. And over there is the Feeb HQ, across The Murk River on the Burma side. My ultimate destination." He jammed the paper back into the envelope, and shoved it into his pants pocket.

"The *Murk* River? I don't think I saw that name in my guidebook—"

"Yeah, because it's a nickname. Some British soldier back during World War II said it looked murky and 'The Murk' sorta stuck."

"Got it," I said.

"All I wanted," he went on in an effort to modulate his tone, "was to make a difference. Not let my life go to waste. To use it or lose it. "

"How much did you give Needle?"

"Over a thousand. More like fifteen hundred when it was all said and done."

"Dollars!?"

He nodded wearily. "Heck, yeah! I worked my butt off at two part-time jobs to save up for this mission. Before we even left the U.S., I Paypaled him five hundred for the soldiers, boat rental, fuel, supplies, and stuff like that. And I had to spend a couple hundred cash that day at the Thai market for cigarettes and whiskey to bribe the check-point guards, and shells for the soldiers."

I shook my head in grudging admiration. "I've got to hand it to you, Twain. There aren't many high schoolers who could have pulled this off."

"Well, I didn't," said Twain grimly.

"True. But you would have if it wasn't for those two—"

"Freakin' scammers!" That set him off on another tirade.

I waited for him to catch his breath. "Okay, I totally get your motivation for setting all this up. It sort of makes sense, now that I've heard it. But your timing sucks. Why try to cross the border *now* of all times? When we don't even know what's happening to the Tacketts!? Or don't you even care?"

"Of course I care! But, come on! What can any of us really do for them? I figure now was as good a time to cross as any, since the trip is off."

We walked on in silence for a minute or two.

"Did you ever think about what would have happened to the Tacketts if you *had* made it across the border as planned? And they had to return to the States without you, and tell your parents that you were never coming back because you were now a *Freedom Fighter?* Did you ever consider how your parents and the church and the rest of the Outreach Team would have felt about you deserting them?"

He shrugged. "I figured they'd be proud of me. At least, once they heard the *whole* story… Besides, I left a letter."

I dug into my pocket. "This one?"

07-04

TO THE OUTREACH TEAM AND JONGCHIT AND HOBAB-

THIS IS A TOUGH LETTER TO WRITE. I MEAN, I WASN'T GONNA CROSS OVER INTO BURMA UN-TIL AFTER THE OUTREACH TRIP WAS FINISHED. BUT SINCE ALL THE CRUD HIT THE FAN, AND EVERYTHING'S ALL MESSED UP, AND YOU'LL PROBABLY BE SENT HOME ANYWAY, WELL, I'M HEADING OUT NOW. YOU GUYS ROCK AND I'LL MISS YOU BIG TIME. (SOME MORE THAN OTH-ERS) . BUT I GOTTA DO WHAT I GOTTA DO AND I THINK THIS IS WHAT I WAS BORN TO DO, IF YOU KNOW WHAT I MEAN. THE KATIN CAUSE HAS BEEN UNDER MY SKIN FOR OVER TWO YEARS. TIME TO DO SOMETHING ABOUT IT, TIME TO FIGHT SIDE BY SIDE WITH THOSE MEN WHO RISK IT ALL EVERY DAY FOR FREEDOM,

ANYWAY, I'M TOTALLY AMPED ABOUT THIS AND WILL TRY TO WRITE OR EMAIL OR CALL AS SOON AS I CAN TO LET YOU KNOW I'M SAFE AND TO EXPLAIN IN MORE DETAIL. (THERE'S A DRAFT EMAIL ON JONGCHIT'S COMPUTER I

WANT YOU TO SEND TO MY PARENTS AND THE
TACKETTS AFTER YOU READ THIS.)
PRAY FOR ME AND THE FREEDOM FIGHTERS|
NEVER SURRENDER|
TWAIN ABERNATHY

It was a deflated Twain who returned with me that night, limping for hours down the dirt roads and grassy embankments along the highway. All the cockiness that gave him his soldierly aura was gone. He seemed oddly humbled and listless and his statuesque frame sagged like a mattress without springs.

He cleared his throat and said awkwardly, "Uh, Collin, I know I don't deserve it after lying to your face, but it would be cool if you, well, you know, if you didn't tell the rest of the Team. At least not until I've figured out the best way to explain it all." He shook his head glumly. "They'll be so ticked off."

I stopped short. Now this was the kind of break I'd been waiting for all along!

He glanced at me with a childlike vulnerability I hadn't seen before. "Well?"

"I won't say anything—on one condition," I said, then paused dramatically.

"Yeah?" asked Twain, warily.

"That we make a deal."

"Yeah?" he repeated, even more warily.

I took a deep breath and said in a rush, before I could change my mind:

"Leave Shelby alone and I won't tell anyone else about your contraband or what happened tonight."

"Leave Shelby alone? What are you talking about? What the heck does Shel have to do with anything?" His wariness dissolved into complete bewilderment.

I sighed. So the big oaf didn't even know she liked him. *The irony.*

"For some reason Shelby seems to be... well, *sorta* infatuated with you." Then I hurriedly added, "But I'm sure it's only temporary."

"You kidding? *Shel?*"

Was it my imagination or was he flattered? Well, as long as it didn't lead to love.

"Unfortunately, yes."

He laughed. "Man, Shel and I go way back. I remember the time in kindergarten when she wet her pants and it got all over the welcome rug—"

"I don't want to hear it," I said quickly.

Twain stared at me incredulously—as if seeing me for the first time. Then he grinned. "Wow. I didn't realize Shel had the *hots* for me—"

"I'm serious, Twain. She can't suspect you care one iota about her. So steer clear." I made my tone as menacing as possible. "You so much as sit next to her, make eye contact longer than five seconds, or speak to her with even the slightest intonation of affection—I spill the beans, right then and there." Now I sounded like a Dashiell Hammett novel.

He shook his head and chuckled. "It's like you're from another planet or something, Uttley. No dude thinks like you do about girls—"

"Well, do you agree or not?" I asked, with a cranky edge to my voice, sick of the whole conversation, sick of people saying I was from another planet, galaxy, solar system.

He paused mid-limp. "Let me get this straight: the only reason you came on this trip was to hang out with *Shelby?* The whole cause of the Katin people and the refugees played *no* part at all?"

After a moment, I nodded. I needed to own this. "Yeah, like you, I had a hidden motive. And I figure, neither of us will look good if the others discover the truth." In my case, the *partial* truth. Hopefully, no one yet suspected I was a total *unbeliever.*

His gray eyes examined my face.

I shifted uncomfortably.

"So that's why you dropped into our youth group out of nowhere—you were trolling for girls?"

What could I say? I shrugged. "All I wanted was a date."

Twain laughed. "What we got here is a stalemate—no, make that a stale*date!*"

"But do we have a deal?" I asked, wanting the whole thing to be over and done with.

He held out a callused hand smeared with mud. "Deal."

We shook on it.

"By the way," I said, pointing to his feet, "you may want to get some new boots. Your Uncle W. J.'s don't fit."

Once we reached the main highway, we managed to flag down a taxi, which dropped us off at the end of the dirt road leading to the academy. Dawn was breaking by the time we shuffled through the gate and once again slipped by the sleeping guard. Within seconds, we'd limped upstairs, and flopped onto our Therm-A-Rests. The entire academy slumbered on—and Jack-O still thundered away.

As I lay there, I couldn't help feeling euphoric. Twain agreeing to have nothing to do with Shelby was the hugest breakthrough I'd had yet. Soon she'd realize that Twain Abernathy had zero interest in her, and the way would be paved for Collin Uttley to take the lead!

The tide was finally turning…

Jump on, Collin, and ride that wave to shore!

That is, I suddenly realized, if we're not all sent packing in the morning…

Mai Pen Rai

M Y HEAD HAD BARELY GRAZED MY THERM-
a-rest, when a booming voice filled my ears.

"*Sawat dii kha!* Rise and shine, Bread Team!"

Although the voice originated from the downstairs foyer, the echoes reverberated all the way up the stairwell and exploded into the guys' dorm room.

Twain and I groggily peeled ourselves off our mattresses, while Jack-O threw back his mosquito netting, bounded out of bed, and yelled, "Jongchit!"

"Downstairs, Bread Team! Pronto pup! *Reng reng!*" came her commanding reply.

Jack-O wore soccer shorts and the light blue I'M NOT LAZY, BUT I'M FUN t-shirt. He had sleep creases on his left cheek, his hair was matted, and his glasses were smudged—but he was alert. He stood in the center of the room, scratching under the Band-Aid on his forehead.

"Are you wondering where Coach Linder is?" I asked tactfully. "Or your halftime soccer oranges?"

"What the heck are you babbling about, Uttley? Is the mefloquine acting up again? I want to know why we're not in Yai Camp?" he asked. "Last I remembered, Mrs. Tackett was attacking me with Krazy Glue."

"The Tacketts got arrested and we got booted out of camp," said Twain with a yawn as he pulled on a T-shirt.

"You're bulldogging me!" said Jack-O in disbelief.

"I wish," said Twain.

"But *why* did they get arrested and us get booted out of camp!?"

Twain and I exchanged looks—and came to an unspoken agreement. It was probably better for him not to know the part he played in their arrest. At least not until he'd fully recovered.

"It's a long story, Jack-O," I said.

"Yeah, dude, why don't we save it for the plane ride home?" said Twain.

"Chop chop! *Reng reng!*" Jongchit's voice was becoming strident.

I stiffly climbed out of bed. Every single muscle ached after trekking through the refugee camp by day and wandering all over the countryside by night. As I stretched my arms and shoulders, I noticed Twain had thick stubble on his cheeks and dark circles under his blood-shot eyes. I'm sure I looked the same.

We glanced at each other in a brief moment of solidarity.

Within minutes, the entire Team—still in sleeping attire—clustered around Jongchit and Hobab in the foyer. Hobab was bouncing a soccer ball from knee to knee. I couldn't stop staring at Ernestine, whose hair was pulled back and encased in what looked like plastic wrap.

And I wasn't the only one.

"What's with the produce bag?" asked Jack-O in bewilderment. "Man, all sorts of stuff's been going on around here that I don't know about."

"I call it my *Dye-Sack*. I invented it myself," said Ernestine. "It moisturizes while I sleep and lengthens the life of the color. These streaks aren't cheap, you know."

"You should patent it," said Twain with a yawn. "Bet there's a huge market for *Dye-Sacks*..."

Despite my sleep deprivation, I couldn't help but notice Shelby's vintage pajamas—a pink ruffled top and with matching ruffled bottoms. I glanced over at Ernestine's shorts and t-shirt, which showed off her fuller... *attributes*. With effort, I brought my attention back to Jongchit.

"Pickle Head better?" she asked, giving Jack-O the once over.

"He seems back to his old self," I said.

"Thank God!" croaked Shelby with as much emotion as she could muster at this early hour.

"Yep! He's totally lucid," said Twain, slapping Jack-O on the back. "He's gonna make it."

"Uh, guys, hello? It's me, Jack-O!" He waved his arms like a referee. "You don't have to talk like I'm not here."

I moved over to Jongchit, Hobab, Shelby, and Ernestine and whispered, "Jack-O doesn't remember anything about yesterday or the part he played in it."

Jongchit folded her arms. "Lucky for him, so big trouble maker."

"God answered our prayers!" Ernestine said, turning to Jack-O. "You're healed!"

Shelby stood on her tiptoes and peeled back Jack-O's Band-Aid to reveal the scar with its yellow-orange-red fringe.

"Ooooh, bummer," she said, shaking her head mournfully. "Not totally healed."

"We pray more," said Jongchit, reaching out towards his forehead.

"Hey, that's my Ketchum Hair. It's not a scar, it's a souvenir!" said Jack-O, clapping his hand over the fringe.

"Oh, brother!" said Ernestine, rolling her eyes.

"So, what's the deal with the Tacketts?" Twain asked Jongchit impatiently.

"Yeah, where are they anyway?" asked Jack-O, peering behind Jongchit as if she'd had them tucked in her back pocket.

Jongchit's laugh rang hollow as she shook her head, the iron gray hairs sticking out of her glossy black hair bobbing like antennae. "*Kha, kha,* the Tacketts. *Mai pen rai.*"

"*Mai pen rai* WHY?" asked Ernestine, not liking where this was heading. "And what does *mai pen rai* even mean, anyway?"

Hobab shrugged. "Depends on the situation. Sometimes it means 'no worries' or 'no problem' or 'don't mention it' or 'it is what it is' or 'never mind.'"

"Well, that helps," said Ernestine sarcastically. "*Not.*"

"Southeast Asia isn't known for being straightforward, you know." He grinned at her.

Jongchit removed her cell from her back pocket. "Dr. Tackett, he leave you memo on my *Hallo* Kitty. They still not get cell phone back. Listen up."

She put it on speaker phone and Dr. Tackett's familiar Southern Californian drawl filled our ears. He sounded tired and resigned:

"Well, Team, it looks like we'll be in Bangkok for at least two more days. The Border Patrol suspected us of being drug traffickers, of all

things, and detained us to 'investigate further.' Obviously, they have no proof. And now it's just lot of legal rigmarole and red tape before they can officially release us. The American Embassy is doing everything possible under the circumstances. They said you can all continue with the outreach trip under Jongchit's supervision until we rejoin you—"

Static, crackle, more static, and then we heard Mrs. Tackett's shrill voice:

"Oh, Team, please don't let our SEA Urchins down! They need some joy in their lives!"

Silence.

We all stared at Jongchit, dumfounded, as she slid the Hello Kitty cell phone back into her pocket

"You telling us the Tacketts got *detention for drug smuggling?*" Jack-O sounded incredulous. "What a pantload! How the heck did that happen?"

"You so don't want to know," muttered Ernestine.

Jongchit exhaled loudly. "Jongchit try everything. Everything! Pray. Bribe. Whine. I whine so good, let me tell you—I wear down officer one by one by one. Except top big shot. He very stubborn. Like donkey."

"There's been a crackdown on *farang*s volunteering in refugee camps," explained Hobab. "Turns out last month there was a drug bust—a group of American ESL teachers smuggling stuff. So they put a new officer in charge of the Border Patrol—the dude you met—"

"Mr. Stupid Big Shot Man!" interrupted Jongchit with distaste.

"—and since this was the Tacketts' eighth trip, and since they kinda look, well, like all the other middle-aged potheads who swarm to Thailand, he assumed the worst."

"Middle-aged potheads...?" repeated Shelby in shock. *"The Tacketts!?!"*

Jack-O cocked his head, considering. "You know, they do kinda look like they're from Portland..."

I had to agree—the Tacketts always did have a sort of hippie vibe about them.

"And you know how strict Thailand is about drug trafficking," added Hobab.

We nodded, remembering how the Tacketts had drilled that into us during training—*"Never agree to take a package from anyone ever!"*

"But why were the Tacketts arrested and we weren't?" asked Ernestine.

Jongchit shrugged impatiently. "You underage."

"But we're eighteen," said Shelby.

"In Thailand, anyone under twenty is minor. Different than U.S.... And you never in Yai Camp before. But Tackett many time. I tell you, it all a big *mis-under-stand.*" Then, grumbling under her breath, "Stupid big shot man..."

"I bet the authorities detained them to save face after not finding any evidence," said Hobab, bouncing the soccer ball. "Their typical MO."

"But why weren't you and Hobab arrested along with the Tacketts?" Shelby asked Jongchit.

"Because we Thai citizen and have special camp pass," said Jongchit. "I volunteer at Yai Camp for many decade."

"Poor Mrs. Tackett in prison!" Shelby shook her head sympathetically.

Jongchit laughed. "Prison? Oh, they not in prison. They stay in nice Bangkok hotel under—how you say? Like house arrest. Order room service. Eat shrimp. Watch cable. They very okay. American Embassy man, he take good care of them."

"Shrimp!" said Jack-O. "Man, I'd kill for some shrimp sautéed in—"

"But what happens now?" interrupted Ernestine.

Jongchit put her hands on her hips and smiled at us encouragingly. "Okay, Bread Team. New plan. Instead of summer program for orphan in refugee camp, you do summer program for orphan in IDP camp. The Tackett, they join us in two day, maybe three, maybe four—"

"IDP?" said Shelby, a touch wearily. "All these acronyms get confusing."

"Internally Displaced People," Twain jumped in, now completely alert and energized as if he'd gotten nine hours of sleep instead of none. "IDP camps are kinda like refugee camps for people in their country of origin."

Hobab gestured towards the cook, who'd just entered the front door carrying plastic bags of groceries and chewing on something that stained his few teeth and mouth pink. "Yut's from an IDP camp."

Realizing we were talking about him, Yut gave us a toothless grin and a thumbs up as he passed by.

"By country of origin," I said, "Are you talking about—"

"Burma!" said Twain, with a huge grin.

"Kha, kha, Burma," said Jongchit, nodding.

I stared at Twain in disbelief at the irony of the situation. Ernestine, Shelby, and Jack-O exchanged startled looks.

"Burma?" said Ernestine in awe. "You serious?"

"Yeah, it's no big deal. You'd finish the outreach trip like the Tacketts planned, only instead of doing it in camps on the Thai side, you'd do it in camps on the Burma side," said Hobab, tossing his bangs out of his eyes with a swift jerk of his head. "Same same but—"

"Different!" boomed Jack-O.

"You got it," said Hobab with a grin. "Man, the IDP kids will so dig it—total once in a lifetime opportunity. And we'll also bring some supplies over for the Freedom Fighters. My dad says they're running low." He paused and then, looking slightly embarrassed, added, "Using your Team's outreach funds, of course. The supplies and cash the Tacketts left behind—for the other two refugee camps that we now can't get into."

"So we'd be crossing the Murk into Burma?" I asked.

"Yep," said Hobab. "We'll be taking boats across and sleeping in tents in the jungle. I'll be straight with you—the accommodations aren't five star."

"No shrimp?" asked Jack-O wistfully.

"Forget the accommodations—what about the legal ramifications?" Ernestine asked. "And the whole safety part?"

Jongchit laughed. "No big deal, Bread Team! Thailand no care if we cross border to Burma during ceasefire since not their country—as long as you carry passport and special border visa I buy for Team. And Burma no care since ceasefire. Burma no care if Westerner bring food and supply to IDP orphan if you stay in IDP camp and village area and not go into jungle."

"I think we can manage that," Twain said cheerfully.

"So, you guys cool to go over border tomorrow to help the IDP orphans and Feebs?" asked Hobab, bouncing his soccer ball off his knee and deftly tucking it under his arm. "If so, we gotta start packing."

"And Jongchit go get Team border visa chop chop!" She turned towards the front door.

"Uh, hold on a minute," I heard my voice say.

Jongchit turned around questioningly. "Problem, Colon Boy?"

Silence. (Or as much silence as there could be in a Southeast Asian country with fans whirling, roosters crowing, and bugs constantly buzzing and flying into things.)

Hobab and Jongchit exchanged looks. Then she shrugged and said, "But if Bread Team want to stay and paint walls *Blue Sky Blue*—*mai pen rai*. No problem."

"What *is* the *problem*, Collin?" asked Twain with a touch of exasperation. "It's not dangerous! It's a ceasefire! Besides, dude, we'd be surrounded by armed Freedom Fighters—a whole lot safer than driving in downtown L.A.!"

Of course, I was all up for going over the border to help the IDP orphans and encourage the Feebs—but my gut told me that if I did, I'd risk losing Shelby for good. Burma was the perfect petri dish to incubate her growing infatuation for the Wannabe Mercenary. I wouldn't stand a chance. Although I wasn't thinking too clearly, I did know one thing: Shelby belonged to *me*. After all, we were the perfect couple—blond, vintage, and fun-sized. She just needed a little more time to come to the same conclusion. So staying put at the academy and painting the walls *Blue Sky Blue* seemed like the best choice all around for our future.

Our future *together.*

"…and also what about Jack-O?" Shelby was saying. "I

mean, we don't want to take any chances—"

"My brain's fine, I'm healed," he said, rubbing his Band-Aid. "I should know, it gets hit all the time. Three times in football, twice in soccer, and once in ping pong."

"Ping pong?" Hobab looked half amused, half confused.

"Those tables are heavier than you think," said Jack-O.

"We get Pickle Head check by doctor today," said Jongchit, poking Jack-O in the side. "Make sure him A-Okay."

"Oh, good!" said Shelby in relief.

"Well?" Twain looked at each of us impatiently. "Are we all in or what?"

Time to stall.

I turned to Jongchit and Hobab. "Can you give us some space to discuss this as a Team?" And then with added emphasis: "To *pray* about it?"

Twain exhaled in frustration. "What? What's there to discuss? What's there to pray?"

But he followed the rest of the Team into Jongchit's office.

Majority Rule

THE BOLYG OUTREACH TEAM SAT MOTION-less around one of the large wooden tables in Jongchit's office. You could practically hear our brains collectively whirling.

"So, who wants to dial and who wants to hang up?" I asked, taking off my fedora and tossing it onto the center of the table. I was impressed I'd remembered that youth group slang, since the last thing the Team needed to find out right now was that I'd been deceiving them.

Ernestine gave me a quizzical look. "I'll open."

"Okay, great, but first, can you take off your, uh, *Dye-Sack*? It's really distracting."

She rolled her eyes at me, but slid off the plastic and set her fire hair free.

"I'll close. Anything to get this over with so we can eat!" said Jack-O.

Then the Team prayed in what I'd learned was called "popcorn style"—short bursts, one after the other, asking "the Holy Spirit for guidance." I even managed to sound authentic for once. To be honest, I was getting anxious about the whole situation, and would have liked to believe that some Big Ol' Daddy Up in the Sky would work everything out.

We opened our eyes to see Twain passing around a stack of yellow papers.

"Not more handouts!" Jack-O groaned.

"Just read it, you'll dig it," said Twain, with a special smile for Shelby. "The Tacketts were gonna have me share this when we were all in the refugee camp. But now's an even better time."

>> THE FEEBS VS. THE BMJ <<
By Twain Abernathy
Handout #28

HERE'S THE DEAL: the Katin Tribes were our allies in World War II while Burma officially sided with the Axis countries. As a result of their war record *and* because they're ethnic minorities *and* because of their religious views, the Burmese Totalitarian Government and Burmese Military Junta (BMJ) got majorly ticked off and began killing them (and other minorities) off through campaigns of "ethnic cleansing."

A ton of Katin people (70,000+) ran for their lives to overcrowded refugee camps in Thailand, like Yai Camp, while tens of thousands remain across the border. Some live in the handful of IDP (Internally Displaced Persons) camps along the Burma/Thai border—but most hide out deep in the jungles of Burma, dodging the BMJ who will shoot them on sight. It's actually the longest civil war in history—over sixty years. The Freedom Fighters For a

**Free Burma (FFFFB or FEEBS)—are some of the rockin'
brave volunteer soldiers who spend their lives defending
the Katin families against the BMJ's attacks.**

**A HEADS UP: This you should know, though. The ma-
jority of Burmese citizens totally oppose the nefarious
BMJ and hope that one day Burma will be FREE from the
evil butt-wipes of the totalitarian military dictatorship.
Oh, and everyone asks why I don't call the country My-
anmar instead of Burma—it's because the military government decided to change the name without consulting
the people. And many political groups and citizens refuse
to call it that because they don't recognize the authority
of the dictatorship to impose that name on them. So
Burma it stays.**

"Man, I dig it, dude!" Jack-O shifted his bulk to give Twain a
high five.

"Great recap, Twain," said Ernestine. "From your Burma
paper, huh? Did you get an A?"

"No, a C, because I forgot to list my sources. And offended my teacher with my 'constant use of profanity.' This is just
part of it—the real thing was sixty pages long... and I got
really worked up towards the end." He grinned. "Let me tell
ya, the last few pages would be rated R."

I had to admit Twain had written a darn moving account. I
felt as impassioned for the Katin cause as the rest of them.
But I didn't like the admiration in Shelby's eyes as she looked
at him, or the tears streaming down her face, dotting the yellow paper clutched in her hand.

"Come on, guys! Isn't this a no-brainer?!" Jack-O burst

out, his chest heaving with emotion. "The kids need us. Man, I don't know about you, but seeing people standing in line for water totally killed me! Water! Water that we get 24/7 and take for granted! What I mean is, I wanna do whatever I can to help people stuck in places like that. Who can't get out. Even if it's just handing out chunks of clay—I'm in!"

Twain slapped Jack-O on the back. "That's what I'm talkin' about!"

"It *is* the whole reason we're here, " said Shelby, her face pink with emotion. "The whole reason we raised all that money, took in all those donations, did all that training, learned all those Katin phrases, and why we're spending all of July here. I'm sorry, but I didn't come all the way to Thailand to paint walls. And we can't let the Tacketts down—we gotta help those *SEA Urchins* in the IDP camp. "

Twain gave her a surprised yet gratified look.

"Preach it, Shell-Bell," said Jack-O, holding out his hand in a high five.

Shelby slapped it a touch sheepishly.

Ernestine slowly nodded in affirmation, as she pulled back her three-toned hair and secured it with a rubber band from around her arm. "I hear ya. There's no way I'm going back to Arroyo Seco without doing some good here first." She wiped her eyes with the back of her hand. "I just can't get those little kids from the refugee camp out of my head…"

Jack-O patted her head. "It's okay, Ketchum Hair."

"Don't call me that…" But Ernestine's voice was more watery than convincing, as she blew her nose.

He kept patting. "It's okay, Mangosteen."

"Okay, guys, we prayed about it and now have a general

consensus." Twain cracked his neck twice rapidly in succession. "Am I right?"

Uncomfortable silence as the rest of the Team darted glances at me.

"Then let's take a vote!" Twain ripped some pages out of his Moleskine journal, tore them in half, passed them out, then grabbed a plastic cup of pens from on top of the metal file cabinet and slammed it down in the middle of the wooden table. "Secret ballot. Two-thirds vote means we go. Anything under that, we stay. Fair enough?"

"Let's do it!" Jack-O snatched a pen and started scribbling on his paper.

Twain leaned back in his chair, ran his hands through his cropped brown hair, and said in a tense voice, "But before we vote, I want to say that this is our one and only chance to level up. To stand out from all the other... other... *dunderheads* our age—"

"*Dunderheads?* Really?" said Ernestine, flashing me an amused look.

"—who do nothing. NOTHING!"

"Here we go again," I muttered under my breath.

"This is our chance to actually *do something* that could make a *huge* difference—not a so-so difference, like recycling bottles or signing some petition outside Trader Joe's. We've got a chance here that no one else in the world has *right here, right now* to physically help victims of oppression. Are we gonna play it safe and paint?" He paused to glare at me, then continued on, his gray eyes blazing. "OR! Since we're all freakin' *eighteen* or older—the age of majority!—and old enough to drive, vote, enter legal contracts, get married, and even fight and *die* for our country without parental consent—will we act like the *adults* we are and step out and risk for the greater good of our fellow humanity? Or are we gonna just be wusses for the rest of our lives, sitting on our butts playing Xbox, waiting for Mommy and Daddy to tell us what to do? Are we—"

"Man, I'd kill for an Xbox right about now!" said Jack-O.

"Okay, okay, Twain! We get it. Let's vote already," said Ernestine, her light brown eyes wide with excitement.

We voted.

Twain snatched up my hat and we all tossed our papers inside.

He quickly counted them and grinned. "Four for going, one for staying. So it looks like over the border we go—"

"Hold on," said Shelby. Her eyes—*luminous* green, green as the rice paddies outside—met mine and held them captive. "Since this is such an important decision, I think it should be unanimous."

Twain gave me a look of his own. I could almost hear the unprintable words he was calling me in his head. He threw my hat back at me just a little too hard.

"Don't you agree, Collin?" Shelby continued. "We should all be unified on this. It's too big a deal." Those eyes were begging me to reconsider.

The four of them watched me, waiting for my reply. Jack-O and Ernestine seemed more curious than concerned. But Twain was visibly tense, clenching and unclenching his jaw— probably worried I'd "mess things up" for him and foil his second and last chance to ever cross the border. And Shelby… it was evident that Twain's cause was starting to bleed into her.

"Collin?" Shelby said again, more gently, those green eyes still captivating, almost hypnotizing mine.

I'm just as on fire about the cause of the Katin people as you are, Shelby! I wanted to say. *In fact, I've built a wall between my heart and those two kids from Yai Camp, otherwise I'd totally lose it. But your love is on the line here—so that's why I can't risk this. Cause or no cause.*

If only I could have downloaded that directly into her brain, so she'd understand where I was coming from!

But in the end, I knew I had no choice.

I had to cross.

You've gotta cross and sacrifice your own happiness for the greater cause. It's what any decent human being would do. And after all, maybe you're overestimating Twain's hold on Shelby…

Just as I opened my mouth to answer in the affirmative, Twain burst out impatiently, "Okay, then! How about this: anybody who doesn't have the *guts* to cross the border can stay and help paint the academy with the Wigglewurts. How's that? And come to think of it, it would be smart to leave an Outreach Team representative here."

So that's how you want to play it…

I'll admit what I did next was stupid and could have sabotaged my whole pursuit of Shelby right then and there. But guys in love do stupid things. And the *Extreme You* thing probably wasn't helping. I stood up, squared my shoulders, and cleared my throat dramatically. "Okay, there's someone here who isn't telling the truth. Someone who's been *deceiving* us, hiding something from the whole Team this whole time.

And this secret needs to be revealed before—"

Twain exhaled impatiently. "What's your deal, Uttley? Why the heck are you bringing all that up now—"

"*You* tell me, Abernathy," I retorted, glaring at him.

He shoved his face into mine. "If anyone here is deceiving the Team it's—"

"All right! All right! You got me!"

To our surprise, *Jack-O* jumped up, toppling his chair!

"Guilty as charged," he said, his meaty hands in surrender position.

Twain and I exchanged bewildered looks.

"What the…?"

Jack-O smiled pathetically as he took off his glasses and cleaned them on his shirt. "Yeah, so my parents made me come on this trip because I was partying too much with the football team."

Dumbfounded silence.

"What? You serious?" said Twain.

"Yeah… it kinda got out of hand." Jack-O yanked down one side of his shorts, revealing a blurry tattoo on the upper right cheek.

"Jack-O!" shrieked Shelby, adverting her eyes.

"Yikes!" Ernestine quickly turned away.

"What the heck is that supposed to be?" asked Twain, trying not to laugh.

I couldn't decipher it either—it looked like a smudged tri-colored blob surrounded by smaller brown blobs.

"It's Elmer Fudd in a hunting cap playing a saxophone with little sausages coming out of it," Jack-O said resignedly as he hiked his shorts back up. "I was drunk at the time—and *not* in the Spirit. That's why the sausages look like turds."

"Oh, man, that bites!" said Twain, chuckling as he picked up Jack-O's chair and gently pushed him back into it.

"So your relatives in those internment camps had nothing to do with this trip?" I asked.

Jack-O shrugged. "Well, kinda yes and kinda no. After my parents found out about my tattoo, they forced me to spend the summer doing something 'charitable.' So I picked this trip because of what my great grandparents went through back in World War 2. Boy, was my mom ticked off when she saw Elmer Fudd! She said she always knew watching all those cartoons would be detrimental to my health."

Ernestine shook her head and said affectionately, "What are we going to do with you, you Man Child—"

"You're not the only one with something to hide, Jack-O," Shelby interrupted, her cheeks pinker than her pajamas.

What?! What was she talking about!? Was she going to admit her *thing* for Twain??? Oh, man, that would not be good. That would be the exact opposite of good.

"That's okay, Shelby," I said, as casually as I could. "Now's not a good time—"

"Actually, Collin, now's the perfect time. You were so right about how important it is for us to be honest with each other. It's time I finally I told the truth about... about..." She paused, her pink cheeks deepening into red.

I ducked my head and shielded my eyes with my hand. I couldn't even look at her.

It's over.

"About... about...being *vegan*."

Vegan!? I breathed a huge sigh of relief as the rest burst out laughing.

Twain laughed. "Tell us something we don't know!"

"How could you think that was a secret?" asked Ernestine. "Shel, your pickiness is *legend* in the youth group."

Shelby looked crestfallen. "That obvious, huh?"

"I'm actually surprised the Tacketts never caught wind of it," said Twain. "But I wasn't gonna tell them. Figured you'd manage all right."

Shelby gave him a grateful smile.

Then he shot me a sly look. "Does *anyone else* have anything they'd like to share?"

Our eyes locked. His piercing gray held mine in a steady, challenging gaze.

"Confession is good for the soul, they say," he said. "You *do* believe in a *soul*, don't you, Collin?"

I froze. Twain was calling my bluff—if I told the Team about his attempt to cross the border, he'd reveal my pursuit of Shelby. And possibly divulge his new suspicions about my so-called "Christian faith." How *dunderheaded* of me not to have foreseen this.

When you fall in love, your brains fall out.

"So?" said Jack-O, looking around. "Who else wants to confess? Ketchum? What's *your* deep, dark secret? Besides your bedtime bread bag?" He waved the plastic *Dye-Sack* at her.

Ernestine tucked a strand of red hair behind her ear and flicked a look at me.

"Hello?" Jack-O demanded. "Deep, dark secret?"

She threw another look at me—and then began to blush just like Shelby!

But before I could compute exactly *why*—

"SOOO? You stay or go?" came a booming voice that made us all jump. Jongchit's moonlike face popped around the corner of the door. "What your answer, Bread Team? If you stay, must order more *Blue Sky Blue*—" Just then, the Wigglewurts pushed their way through the door, tiny Noi and grinning Patcharee leading the way. They wore the white smocks and plastic shower caps completely speckled in blue dots and blobs, and carried paint cans, brushes, and rollers like the first time we'd met them.

"You help Wigglewurts? That very good," said Noi looking up at us with a smile and a tilt of her head.

"*Kha kha!* We old. You young people—very big energy! Paint extra fast! Zoom zoom zoom!" said Patcharee jabbing her paint roller into the air.

Then Noi moved towards Shelby. "How your heart now?"

Shelby smiled shyly. "Good. Really good."

Patcharee laughed and thumped her chest. "What I say? God heal heart! Number one doctor!"

"Stay or go?" persisted Jongchit, completely ignoring their conversation.

There was an awkward silence.

Then Shelby turned to me, her freckled face kind yet questioning. "Collin?"

part four

OVER THE BORDER

A REASSURING EMAIL UPDATE FROM JONGCHIT

(An excerpt, sent July 6th)

Hello, hello! Friend + Family + Bread Church + other Peoples,

Sawatdee kha! My English very so not very good + this computer very old but that A-OK! Kha! Team want Jongchit to update you! The Tackett, they have tiny baby problem. Some mis-under-stand with official men make big headache for them. But good news -- they get much rest in hotel! And much shrimp! But Bread Team, they want help refugee IDP orphan freedom fighter. Halayulah!*>>!! We very glad. They need much, much BIG help + money + help. We very happy they help so yes! Kha, kha! Yes, BABY, sir! Many people HAPPY happy to see them. Pray safe travel over waters + NO runny tummy for Mangosteen + NO more head wound for Pickle Head. Please to tell Bread Church everything A-OK for everybody + NO worry! We have many many gun...

Shoot-Me-Orange

B Y 5 A.M. THE NEXT MORNING, THE OUTREACH
Team was wedged in the back of Hobab's truck, with all
the supplies packed into both cabs, and completely overflow-
ing Jongchit's truck bed. It took over an hour on the windy
smooth roads, another forty-five minutes on muddy bumpy
roads, and then, after parking the trucks, a half hour slog
through the jungle—carrying all six duffels and bags of supplies—to reach the edge of the Murk River that was inacces-
sible by car.

The trip was silent and tense. The Team seemed to be individually mulling over their collective wisdom in making this
decision. And wondering if we still had time to back out.
That is, everyone except Twain. He was, to put it in his terms,
amped—despite having to leave his tight jungle boots behind
and wear trekking shoes like the rest of us. As for me, I'd had
no choice but to go through with it, for although Twain and I
were at a stalemate, he was once again in the power position.

We stood in a row along the edge of the river. Since at that
moment it was overcast and about to sprinkle, the water did
indeed look murky and brown. Palms and lush green foliage
grew along the riverbank, and there wasn't a house to be seen.
Hobab led us over to a pair of wooden longtail boats flanked

by soldiers. They had the same cappuccino skin and dark hair and eyes and slight build of the Katin refugees in Yai Camp—but these guys wore camouflage and had rifles slung over their shoulders. One murmured into what looked like a giant walkie-talkie. The rest nodded at us stoically, but didn't speak.

"Who are those dudes?" whispered Jack-O.

Before Hobab could answer, Twain said with a huge grin, "Freedom Fighters For a Free Burma! Otherwise known as the FFFFB or Feebs!"

"Okay, Bread Team," said Jongchit. "Must put on." She handed out multi-colored plastic ponchos. "Wear hood up and sunglasses on. So Thai Border Patrol not think you *farang*—naughty ESL teacher—come to cause trouble."

"But I thought since we got visas we were crossing legally...?" Shelby said with a puzzled look.

"*Kha,* very legally, *kha,* yes. But Border Patrol make big fuss and slow everything down down down. This Thailand, not U.S., please to remember."

With her red heart sunglasses, pink blouse, and purple flip-flops, Jongchit looked out of place among the soldiers in uniform and the Outreach Team in ponchos.

Twain got an olive green poncho, Jack-O black, Shelby and Ernestine both blue—and I got bright orange.

"Orange doesn't seem a very subtle color," I muttered.

"Shoot-Me-Orange is what I'd call it," said Twain with a grin.

Jongchit chuckled and repeated, "Shoot-Me-Orange! Ha, ha, Mister Twain! He so funny, right, Colon Boy?"

I gave her a wry smile.

The Outreach Team was barely recognizable in ponchos with hoods up and sunglasses on—despite our "pointy western noses."

"Climb in, but take it slow," said Hobab gesturing towards the wooden boat with peeling red paint. "Walk down the center and sit on the sides. No sudden moves or you could capsize us."

While we climbed into the boat as steadily as possible, Hobab helped the soldiers load up the other boats with our supplies and donations. Twain perched on the side, pulled out his video camera, and scanned the alert faces on the boat and the endless jungle on both sides of the river.

"Where are the life jackets?" asked Shelby, looking around her with growing concern. "I don't see any life jackets…"

"Jesus your life jacket," said Jongchit with a chuckle, hands on hips as she watched from the bank.

"What if you don't believe in Jesus?" asked Twain, with a sardonic glance in my direction.

"Ha! Big funny man!" she replied.

I turned away before Twain could see my guilty expression or catch it on film, and noticed Shelby clutching something in her hand—her *Rock Flounce!*

That's gotta be a good sign!

Ernestine flashed me a smile. "Now don't you go capsizing us with your crazy *Cirque* moves…"

"Can't promise anything," I said.

She leaned closer. "You as nervous as I am?"

"Maybe. I'm not sweating bullets yet, but I could be perspiring a bb or two."

As she laughed, I covertly examined her profile. I still

hadn't figured out what had made her act so weird the other day.

Hobab jumped into our boat, pulling his poncho hood over his head, which pushed his shaggy bangs into his eyes. But Jongchit remained on the bank, hands on hips, red hearts on head.

"Aren't you getting in?" Ernestine asked her.

Jongchit grinned. "No sirree, Mangosteen! I cross later with Tackett. And Wiggleswurt. They pray for orphan and soldier. Hobab and Jolly take *jolly* good care of you till Jongchit arrive—"

Just then, an ear-splitting roar, like a lawn mower, filled the air and our boat started vibrating. I looked over—it actually *was* a lawn mower motor!

Jongchit waved energetically from the muddy bank—but we dared not lift a finger as we perched on the narrow sides of the boat, trying not to slip into the churning water! There was a collective hyper awareness of every sound and sensation.

The putt-putt-putt of the motor, the spray of the muddy river, the smell of gasoline—and the realization that the boat was slowly, very slowly, filling up with water.

Slosh, slosh, slosh.

And there was Hobab, calmly bailing with a yellow plastic bowl.

Slosh, slosh, slosh.

Rain peppered our plastic ponchos.

The murky water continued oozing into the bottom of the boat.

As the Team putt-putted further and further away from

the Thai shore, I got hit with a panic attack.

What the heck have I gotten myself into??? After all, once I'm dead, I'm __dead__, and after that comes—__nothingness__. I'm not ready for nothingness yet!!! I want the __somethingness__ to continue!!!

I inhaled and exhaled.

Inhaled and exhaled.

And tried to ignore an increasing sense of foreboding.

Just focus on the water, focus on the water, focus on the water…

"I can swim. Don't know about the rest of you, but I can swim," muttered Jack-O above the motor, more to reassure himself than the rest of us. Every time the wood creaked, his massive frame jerked as if he'd been shot.

Across from him, Twain was grinning to himself, loving every minute of it.

We were about halfway across the Murk, when Ernestine swiped at a mosquito—causing the boat to dip. Shelby, sitting opposite her, quickly overcompensated by leaning back the other way, which temporarily swung her daypack off her back and provided just enough momentum to rip the last seams of the frayed pocket holding her half-eaten jumbo bag of *Mauve Mountain Muesli*—and launched it into the water!

SPLASH!

Shelby grabbed onto Jack-O to prevent herself from following the oats into the deep.

"My muesli!" she shrieked.

Surface bubbles were all that remained of the sinking bag.

A stricken expression covered her face.

No one knew what to say.

I wanted to pat her on the back, but couldn't risk even the smallest movement.

Shelby couldn't pry her eyes from the now distant bubbles.

As I watched her mourn her muesli, a wave of irritation washed over me, along with the hazy sense that Shelby somehow lacked depth. But it disappeared as fast as it came.

Just then, a flag with three large red, white, and blue stripes and sunrays in the upper left corner, appeared against the green of the jungle. *As well as two M-16s pointing directly at us!*

A hand-carved wooden sign read:

Welcome to the Freedom Fighters For a Free Burma 12th Brigade HQ

"The FFFFB!" Twain said, practically vibrating with adrenaline. "Guys, we're in BURMA!"

The rest of us exchanged apprehensive glances.

"I sure hope the ceasefire hasn't ceased," said Jack-O, "otherwise we are *toast!*"

The boats pulled up onto the muddy riverbank, and one by one, we jumped off the end of the boat onto the mud and began a steep climb up a hill, carrying our daypacks and backpacks and as much of the supplies as we could manage. Once we reached the well-worn trail, we proceeded single-file, bookended by the Freedom Fighters who carried most of the medicine, clothes, and supplies—including large tins of pineapple sandwich cookies Jongchit had insisted we bring because they were "Jolly's favorite."

So this was Burma… it looked like a lot like Yai Camp.

Scattered raindrops segued into a torrential downpour.

"The monsoon season," said Hobab, cinching the hood

around his face. "It typically lasts about—*Jack-O, stop!*"

Jack-O froze mid-step. "Dude? What? Gotta take a leak."

Hobab pointed at his feet. "Don't go into the jungle—*ever. Wherever we go from now on, the jungle is off limits.* Everybody stays on the trail." He turned to the rest of us huddling behind him, and repeated emphatically, "*Everybody* stays on the trail. The jungle is off limits at *all* times. Got it, guys?"

We all nodded mutely, wiping the deluge of rain out of our eyes. This was a side of Hobab we hadn't seen before.

What's the big deal about the jungle? Snakes? Leeches? Crazed ESL teachers?

Hobab visibly relaxed and turned back to Jack-O. "There's an outhouse up ahead. Can you hold it?"

"When you put it like that—heck ya!" said Jack-O. "I'll never pee again!"

Just then, a short soldier passed us carrying a large weapon—almost as tall as he was—over his shoulder.

"Oh, my gosh, what was that?" asked Shelby.

"An RPG. Rocket Propelled Grenade," said Twain, trying to hide his boyish enthusiasm. Then, in an undertone to me, "Soon as we hit the HQ, I'm going to join up."

I laughed then realized he was serious. "What? Are you crazy? After all you went through…?"

Twain shrugged. "Why not? I'm here now, aren't I? It would be a waste not to make the effort. And I know *you* won't try to stop me." His expression was one of pure blackmail.

I shot a look at Shelby, who was carefully navigating a puddle, her lips pursed and her pug nose scrunched in concentration. Then I shook my head mutely.

No.

No, I wouldn't.

After five minutes, the torrential downpour abruptly ceased. We tentatively removed the hoods of our ponchos and took a look around—careful to stay on the trail. I tried not to notice that Shelby was deliberately positioning herself next to Twain—who smiled down at her from his excessive height, gently removed a piece of grass from her wet hair, and handed it to her. "Souvenir?"

She giggled uncontrollably as if it was the funniest thing she'd ever heard.

There was that sense of foreboding again...

Never Sorry Ever Jolly

WE FOLLOWED HOBAB DOWN THE MUDDY trail that winded through the Freedom Fighters For a Free Burma (FFFFB) HQ and IDP camp. It began to sprinkle again, so up went our hoods. Several hundred people lived in the rows of bamboo huts on stilts, surrounded by fields of corn, vegetable gardens, and rice paddies. The villagers wore *longyis*—that unisex skirt we'd seen in the refugee camp—and the women's faces glistened with a yellowish gold powder on their noses and cheeks. The soldiers dressed in whatever combination of army fatigues, camouflage, shorts, and t-shirts they could lay their hands on. Most wore flip-flops instead of boots. Some had sparse facial hair, a few wore burgundy berets, and most had amateur tattoos—usually Katin words and sayings and slightly misspelled English phrases like *"Borne Free"* and *"Never Surrendur."*

It stopped raining, so we tugged off our hoods.

"I love how rustic the ink looks," said Ernestine, eyeing a soldier's forearm tattoo of the Katin flag.

"It's made from needles and soot from the fire," said Hobab.

"Don't get any ideas, Jack-O," said Twain with a grin.

212

"Heck no!" replied Jack-O, rubbing his backside. "Elmer hurt bad enough!"

Hobab paused and pointed at a bamboo shed with a roof made of leaves and *W.C.* painted on the door. "There's the water closet, Jack-O."

Jack-O just stared at him.

Hobab laughed. "Outhouse? Bathroom? Toilet? The can?"

Within seconds, Jack-O was hightailing it over to the structure. Soon we heard: *"I've gotta a river of pee flowing out of me..."*

I used the W.C. next—*reluctantly.* Squat toilets were tough enough in the border towns of Thailand, but even trickier in the dim lighting and cramped quarters of a bamboo box in the jungle. I still hadn't mastered the squatting versus sitting technique—always felt I was getting a leg cramp. And the freaky story my neighbor Vassar had told me about getting stuck in a squat toilet on a boat in Cambodia kept popping into my head—which didn't help matters. As much as I hated these SEA bathroom experiences, the Tacketts had warned us not to "hold it in." They'd had one kid on an outreach trip in TJ not poo for a week and suffered major constipation complications. So I forced myself to complete the task, legs shaking and face sweating.

Not a pretty picture.

Once we'd all taken turns in the box of cramp and sweat, we continued on the trail. Soon we had a pack of SEA Urchins tailing us. These weren't as confident as the ones who'd shadowed us in Yai Camp, and carefully kept their distance. They didn't know what to make of us, but they were definitely curious. They couldn't stop staring at us—especially at Ernestine's yellow-orange-red hair.

"They probably think you're from another planet, Ketchum," said Jack-O, tweaking her hair. *"Ssss—hottt! Red hot!!!"*

A couple of little girls ran over to peer closely at Shelby's arm. After a moment, they reached out tentatively to touch it—then abruptly ran away. Shelby shot a bemused glance at Hobab. "What was that about?"

"They don't see many white people on this side of the border, other than the random NGO volunteer," said Hobab. "And you're *white* white—with freckles."

"Maybe they think you're sprinkled with nutmeg, Shel," said Ernestine, laughing.

"What do they think of me?" asked Jack-O, pausing, meaty hands on hips.

Hobab grinned. "Dude, if you weren't so darn big, and were wearing a *longyi*, you could pass for a local."

"Then get me a *longyi*, bro, and I'll blend!"

We passed a group of soldiers in shorts kicking a woven rattan ball over a tattered volleyball net with their bare feet. Despite the intermittent rain and mud, the ball whizzed back and forth across the net with a ferocious intensity.

"Sepak takraw," Hobab explained as we paused to watch. "It's a combo of soccer and volleyball."

"Wow! Their thighs are like granite!" said Shelby in awe.

"Can we play?" Jack-O asked eagerly.

But just then, Hobab abruptly called out, *"Kaw ler ah hgay!"* and beelined towards a cluster of banana trees, where an older soldier squatted.

When the man saw Hobab, a huge grin spread across his

face. He took out his cigarette, shouted something in Katin in a throaty, jovial voice, then stood up and waved us over. As we all clustered around him, taking shelter from the rain under the umbrella-like banana leaves, we recognized him from the wall of Jongchit's office.

"Meet my dad, Jolly—otherwise known as General Mu," said Hobab with glowing pride as Jolly slapped his son on the back and gave him a hug.

"Jolly nice to meet you! Hobab's friends are my friends!" said Jolly in good English—with a surprising British accent.

Jolly looked just like the wall photo—in his sixties, but with the physique of a man half his age. His unbuttoned uniform revealed a six-pack for abs. He had laugh lines that seemed etched into his skin and oversize metal glasses probably made in the 1970s, with a sunglasses clip currently flipped up. And there were the tattoos that we'd noticed in the photo:

On his right arm: *CAREFREE & EASY GOING*

On his left arm: *IN THE HANDS OF GOD*

And across his chest: *NEVER SORRY EVER JOLLY*

Obviously created with soot and needles.

"Jolly Mu." He shook hands with each of us in turn—with a grip of iron.

"Nice to meet you. I'm Collin Utt..." I trailed off at the sight of blood smeared across my hand.

What the heck?

I dug in my pocket for a Kleenex.

"Like your tatts," said Jack-O. "Clear and not smudgy..."

Jolly laughed. "My portable theology." With his finger, he traced the tattoos on his right arm, left arm, and across his chest: "In the Hands of God, I Am Carefree and Easygoing, and no matter what happens—Never Sorry Ever Jolly."

Before anyone could respond, Twain abruptly saluted. "Honor to meet you, sir! You have an amazing track record, sir!" All 6'5 of him was vibrating with the adrenalin of meeting a war hero.

Jolly grinned at him. "At ease, my good chap." Then gesturing with the knife in his hand, he said to the Team, "Make yourselves at home. Pretty dry under here. Be with you in two ticks—finishing this up."

The Outreach Team began saying things like, "Nice to meet you" and "No problem"—until we noticed the blood on the knife. And then we looked down at his left foot. An incision had been made along the length of the big toenail— which was bleeding profusely.

"Fungus. Comes with the territory," said Jolly in response to our stunned looks. "Ceasefire is the best time to take care of it."

We watched in mesmerized horror as Jolly squatted back down and deftly cut into the rest of the flesh, all around the border of the toenail and—

Ripped the toenail right off!

It made a sort of soft tearing, crunching sound that sent chills down my spine and goose bumps across my skin. Reminded me of ripping the shell off a cooked shrimp. Then he added the nail to a growing pile of bloody toenails in front of him… the four other toenails from his left foot!

The Outreach Team took a collective step back.

I couldn't fathom performing this sort of surgery on myself. In fact, it freaked me out when I started losing my baby teeth—instead of wiggling them, I'd just wait for a sticky peanut butter sandwich or a wedge of apple to do the job for me.

I was proud of Shelby. She managed not to heave—she gasped, gulped, and quickly turned away, fanning her face with her hand.

Jolly began cutting into the flesh of the big toe on his right foot.

"*Jesus...*" intoned Ernestine in a weak voice. Fresh beads of sweat appeared across her nose.

"Isn't this overkill? After all, it's only a kind of athlete's foot," said Jack-O. "I get that all the time."

"Yeah, it seems extreme," I said, feeling nauseous myself.

"No monkeying around with fungus in the jungle," said Jolly, as he ripped off the nail. "If you don't remove it all, it spreads. A bad case can put a soldier out of commission for months. Take care of your feet and your feet will take care of you."

Blood pooled in the dirt, mingled with the rainwater, and created burgundy.

"It's not like digging out shrapnel, but that's gotta kill big time, don't you think, Twain?" asked Jack-O. "Twain?"

Something hit my back with such force that I toppled onto Ernestine, who fell against Hobab—who luckily reacted in time to prevent the domino effect.

"Twain!" gasped Shelby.

The mighty Twain Abernathy, the giant with delusions of grandeur, the high schooler who thought he was a Freedom Fighter, the wannabe mercenary—had swooned like a lady in a Victorian stage play!

It took the combined efforts of Jack-O, Hobab, Ernestine, and myself to prevent all 200 pounds of him from hitting the dirt.

"Put his head between his knees!" Shelby barked out.

"He's fainted," I said with satisfaction. "That is, unless he's 'slain in the spirit'…"

Yeah, I was the only one who thought that was funny.

In a minute or two, Twain managed to shuffle over to a wooden bench wrapped around a tree, and put his head between his knees. Of course, I was glad Shelby had witnessed his moment of weakness, but I sure didn't like the concerned expression on her face, or the fact she chose to leave the Team, sit next to him, share her water, and pat him on the back. The blue poncho was way too close to the olive drab.

No wonder in Yai Camp Twain had refused to watch the Tacketts tend to Jack-O's bloody gash—he couldn't handle the sight of blood. Talk about a liability. Some soldier!

Meanwhile, Jolly continued systematically cutting out each remaining toenail.

Ernestine offered him a travel-size bottle of ibuprofen.

He shook his head. "Save it for someone who needs it."

Hobab laughed. "It is no use trying to help my father. He's one of the toughest warriors the Katin have ever produced—been a soldier since he was thirteen. He's spent his whole life protecting his people." He looked at Jolly with pride. "Just like my great grandfather who fought alongside the British in World War II—"

"Which is where I get my jolly good English and my name. Know what Mu means?" asked Jolly, conscious of his captive audience and enjoying every minute of it.

"What?"

"Happy! So that makes me—"

"Jolly Happy!" said Ernestine, Jack-O, and I in unison.

Then I noticed the blue and olive ponchos were still in close proximity to each other. As I "casually" strolled over to check on them, Twain slowly unfolded himself from his hunched position and took the bottle of water Shelby offered.

"How are you feeling now?" Shelby asked in a low, concerned voice, anxiously peering into his face.

"Hosed," he said stiffly, barely moving his lips and refusing to meet her gaze.

"Hosed? Why?" She put a consoling hand on his back. "I think you're being too hard on yourself, Twain. It's no big deal to pass out. Half the high school does every weekend."

He managed a brief smile at her attempt to lighten the mood.

But I wasn't jealous of her attention to him—not even close. The mighty Twain had fallen. His Achilles' heel had been exposed. He was no hero, no Western version of the FFFFB. He was *weak*. If anything, he would inspire pity in Shelby, not awe.

Now let's watch her shallow infatuation shrivel up and blow away!

Neither of them seemed aware of my presence as I hovered nearby.

"Giving blood or seeing blood always kinda messed with my head growing up. But I didn't know I was *this* bad. *This* much of a wuss." He shook his head, as if wanting to rid his mind of the memory. "It's a game changer."

"How do you mean?" asked Shelby, leaning closer.

"Have you ever had to own up to the fact that you weren't who you thought you were? And all the time you'd been on Planet Denial? That you thought you'd, you know, excelled at something, but instead you come to find out you actually suck? It's hard to explain. Forget it." He shook his head dismally. *"Forget it."*

"Twain, give yourself a break! It was shocking. I almost passed out myself watching him pull—" She stopped as Twain abruptly returned his head between his knees.

"Ooops! Sorry, sorry, sorry!"

After a minute, he sat back up and guzzled the water bottle. Then, as he handed it back to her, I could tell from the way he looked at her, the way he said, "Thanks," and the way his eyes met hers—that he was falling.

Hard.

I swore under my breath.

Then over my breath.

But they didn't even notice.

Maybe everything would *not* be all right. Maybe things were *not* coming into the alignment I'd hoped for.

I cleared my throat—neither of them paid any attention. I coughed. No response. I pretended to sneeze. No response. They stared silently into each other's eyes—the tanned manly face inches away from that freckled feminine one. The intensity of their concentration cut me to the quick.

I strode briskly over to them and slapped Twain on the back. "So, Twain, still queasy about those bloody nubs?"

This time, he didn't bother putting his head between his legs, but clapped a hand over his mouth and sped off towards another bamboo outhouse with *W.C.* painted on the door.

The look Shelby threw me actually felt like a wallop.

We stared at each other a moment without speaking. This was a Shelby wholly unfamiliar to me—her face seemed to be set in granite. Immovable, stoic, unfeeling. Like an Easter Island statue. Even her freckles looked angry. Finally, she said in a calm but steely voice, "Don't you and Ernestine have some googly eyes to unpack?"

Without waiting for an answer, she brushed past me towards the outhouse.

Cue panic.

Okay, okay, you gotta just settle down. It's not over yet. This was one minor skirmish in the Battle Over Shelby Wanderal. I mean, come on! How can you expect to compete with weakness? It brings out all the woman's maternal instincts. Maybe next time, YOU'LL be the victim and win her over.

I willed myself to believe this.

Jungle Mess

WHEN I REJOINED THE REST OF THE GROUP, a soldier around our age was bandaging up Jolly's toes while Hobab laughed and chatted with him in Katin. Eventually, Hobab turned to the rest of us, flipped his long bangs out of his eyes, and said, "This is *Saw* Lah Kaw, one of the Feeb backpack medics. *Saw* in Katin means *mister*."

Lah Kaw sported a fauxhawk and a surprisingly square jaw covered with stubble. He wore a sleeveless black t-shirt with VANS across the front and ripped Levi's.

"Call me Lah Kaw," he said in a raspy voice, standing up. He dropped a small pair of scissors and roll of bandages into a woven basket next to him. "American people know about Katin cause?"

Right then, a subdued Twain rejoined the group, with mother hen Shelby hovering beside him. "Heck ya!" he burst out. "There *are* a bunch of us who *do* know and want to support your people *any* way possible and… and…" He trailed off at the sight of Jolly's ten bandaged toes and quickly looked away.

"Cool," said Lah Kaw, mildly amused.

"Lah Kaw's on break from his duties as a backpack medic," said Hobab. He pointed to the basket, which had arm

222

straps attached to it. "He treks through jungles carrying medicine and medical supplies on his back to soldiers and IDPs in all those remote villages."

"Is it dangerous?" said Ernestine. "During the ceasefire, I mean."

"How you say? Tricky, very tricky. Many landmine," said Lah Kaw, lighting a cigarette from a crumpled red and white pack in his Levi's pocket. "Smoke?"

"No, thanks," said Shelby. "We're not allowed to have cigarettes."

"Only use them as bribes," I muttered under my breath.

"Good. They kill you," he said as he inhaled deeply, then coughed. "See?"

Jolly stood up. "Time to eat, don't you think? You all must be spackered."

We followed the compact and muscular Jolly into the large open-air bamboo structure that served as the all-purpose gathering space for the HQ. There were no chairs, just low wooden tables and bamboo matting on the floor.

"Welcome to the jungle mess hall," said Jolly. "Have a seat, chaps."

While he conferred with a small group of soldiers, the rest of us peeled the plastic ponchos off our sweaty cores to let our trekking shirts air dry, and then sat down cross-legged on the bamboo matting around one of the low wooden tables.

As I spread my poncho across the matting, I whispered to Shelby, "Whew! I feel way safer with that shoot-me-orange off my body."

But she didn't laugh or smile or even meet my gaze. She stared straight ahead—her folded arms, pursed lips, scrunched pug nose, and wet curls creating the effect of an indignant kitten that'd just been dunked.

She's still ticked? Just because I mocked the clay feet of her hero?

My stomach sank.

"That is Gimlet." Jolly pointed towards an older soldier sitting against a far wall—a shorter, squatter version of himself, but with iron gray hair instead of black and a grimace instead of a grin. He periodically spat into a battered plastic yellow cup. "Named after grandfather's favorite drink. My second in command—Lieutenant Colonel Mu. An honorable man. Also my brother. But he does not like to talk—he says his English is bad. I tell him, 'My English is *deplorable*, but that does not stop me.'" He laughed heartily. "Do not let my brother's face fool you—he is a clown."

We all turned to observe Gimlet.

He stared back at us, his face expressionless, his eyes blank.

Jolly laughed. "See? Big clown."

Rain pelted the leaves that covered the roof.

"Sounds like it's raining bullet shells," said Twain.

"Been known to happen," said Jolly.

Twain laughed in hearty appreciation.

Gimlet grunted and spat into his cup.

Next to him, another soldier rolled tobacco in a dried banana leaf.

A calendar, a few old black and white photos, and a couple World War II rifles hung on the bamboo walls. A soldier in the corner strummed a twangy western tune on his guitar. Another soldier cleaned his gun. Yet another was painstakingly making something out of pieces of bamboo, wires, light blue polyurethane tubing, and a tin of some sort of dark powder.

"What's he making?" Ernestine asked, after watching him for a couple minutes.

Jolly glanced over. "Landmines."

"You serious?" said Twain with heightened interest and moved over for a closer look.

"But I thought only the BMJ used landmines?" said Jack-O.

"No, we must use them as well," said Jolly. "Part of our defense. We surround the perimeter of our property and headquarters with them in order to be alerted to a surprise attack. The BMJ likes surprise attacks."

"But how do you keep the kids from accidentally stepping on them?" asked Shelby, swapping concerned looks with Ernestine.

"Oh, they all know where the landmines are. We place them many yards away in the thick of the jungle, and also mark them to make them easy to see from our perspective. All the villagers know which places to avoid. Only the enemy, who sneaks in at night, would not see them," said Jolly. "It is one of the Katin villagers' main defenses. See, the BMJ, they use metal landmines that never disintegrate and plant them in fields and inside villages where innocent people can get hurt—a danger for decades to come. Ours are only on the extreme perimeter and disintegrate after a number of months. Let me tell you, the trade off is worth it. Landmines equal extra safety, no landmines equal surprise attack, which means rape, murder, and the burning of the village."

I felt confused and conflicted about landmines *ever* being a solution to *anything*. Being so Western, being such a *farang*, it was difficult to put myself in their shoes—or flip-flops.

"Now do you guys get why I told you to stay out of the jungle?" asked Hobab.

We all shifted and nodded uncomfortably. Except for Jack-O, who said, "Heck ya! I sure learned my lesson: pee within walls."

That broke the tension and everyone laughed.

Twain eagerly leaned towards Jolly. "Hobab said you once got shot in the back and it came out your jaw and after you were all stitched up, you went right back out to fight!"

"This body," said Jolly, pointing to his chest, "is very like that old Timex watch. 'Takes a lickin' but keeps on tickin'.' Now Gimlet here, he was the most injured."

We all turned for a closer look at Gimlet. Since he wore a *longyi*, we could see he had an ancient prosthetic leg stretched out in front of him. Plastic at the knee and ankle area and wood in the space in between.

"He lost that leg during a skirmish in 1998 protecting me from a grenade. Purple heart—that's what he should have. He's a good bloke. No talk, all action."

Gimlet shifted away from us and seemed to be trying to dissolve into the wall—embarrassed at being the center of attention. Just then, to his relief, a couple of the soldiers' wives appeared, wearing t-shirts and *longyis*, and babies on their backs. One held a tray with a large metal thermos, glasses, spoons, and packets of instant coffee, and the other carried a woven basket, plates, a platter of some sort of mixed greens, and large plate of doughy rolls. They smiled at us as they set the trays on the table in front of Jolly, and then disappeared the way they came.

Jolly pulled the top off the basket to reveal rice. "Sticky rice, sautéed vines, and meat rolls. My favorite. Dig in, don't be shy, blokes."

My stomach was growling, so I didn't need to be told twice.

"Smells good!" said Jack-O, helping himself to one of the doughy rolls.

"Meat gives you lots of energy," said Jolly. "Good for soldiers. They need more than rice and vegetables."

"I hear ya," said Jack-O. "Back home, I eat a whole package of bacon and a dozen eggs before every game."

"Wow, this is really good. Reminds me of those barbecued pork buns you get in Chinatown," said Ernestine, chewing a roll with gusto.

Shelby stuck with the rice and greens. But after watching us eat roll after roll, she finally caved and reached for one.

"You could probably use the protein," I said in a hearty voice as if she wasn't ignoring me.

She gave me a relenting smile that buoyed me instantly. "Maybe. I'm feeling kinda iron deficient right now." Then she took a miniscule nibble with her tiny front teeth. After chewing tentatively for a minute or two, she took a bigger bite. "It's better than I thought. I haven't eaten meat in so long it tastes strange. Strange, but good." She took another more substantial bite. Once she finished that roll, she took another, eating so fast her cheeks puffed out like a chipmunk.

Twain and Jack-O ate four rolls each.

"Aw mee wee lee ar?" Lah Kaw asked Hobab and Jolly.

227

"He wants to know if you're finished eating," Hobab said to us. "It's time to pass out supplies to the soldiers."

Shelby scrambled to her feet. "I'd better use the restroom before we go."

"Blaps?" asked Jolly, sympathetically.

"Blaps?" repeated Shelby, mystified.

"Diarrhea."

"Uh, not this time," Shelby said, slightly embarrassed.

"Good one! Blaps! That's better than the runs," said Jack-O, with his mouth full. "I gotta remember that... Blaps...."

"The W.C. is over there to the right," said Jolly, pointing. "Can't miss it."

After grabbing a packet of Kleenex, Shelby hurried out.

Hobab gestured for Lah Kaw to help himself to the last remaining roll.

After taking a bite, Lah Kaw said to the Team, "I very surprise you eat dog. Most Westerner not like taste—"

"Dog?!" said Ernestine, dropping her half-eaten roll into her lap as if it were on fire.

"Dude, you serious?" said Jack-O. He looked conflicted.

Like all of us. Because that dog had tasted darn good.

My belly regions churned.

"You really eat *dog*?" I asked Jolly in a low voice.

Jolly grinned. "Anything that moves, we eat. We can't afford to be finicky. There are only so many pigs and chickens to go around. And we have a lot of soldiers to feed. This dog wasn't a pet, it was a wild dog that bit one of the orphans. Meat rations are low—we finished the monkey last night."

The irony! *The first time in years that poor Shelby relents and eats meat—and it's dog!*

Ernestine, Jack-O, and I exchanged queasy glances. Talk about awkward. We had to be sensitive to the feelings of our hosts, but we also couldn't fight our Western repulsion. That is, except for Twain.

He popped the last bit of roll into his mouth and grinned. "K9. Yum."

"Just wait until the snake bake," said Hobab, grinning back at him, picking his teeth with a toothpick.

We all shuddered.

"You know," Ernestine tactfully, "We're totally fine with rice—"

"Speak for yourself, Ketchum," said Twain with his mouth full of dog.

I glanced over in time to see Shelby emerging from the outhouse. "Not one word to Shelby! Do you hear? *Not! One! Word!* If she ever finds out she ate dog—it would kill her!"

Shelby entered a few moments later, rubbing her hands with sanitizer. After one look at our carefully neutral faces, she asked suspiciously, "What's going on? Why are you guys acting so weird?"

Everyone looked at me.

I cleared my throat and said as casually as possible, "Uh, we were wondering if everything came out all right."

She relaxed and grinned. "No *blaps*, if that's what you mean."

The Outreach Team laughed in unison—way too heartily. But she didn't seem to notice. Poor Shelby! How was she going to survive the rest of the trip?!

Christmas in July

AFTER LUNCH, THE OUTREACH TEAM HEADED back out into the blazing sun to hand out supplies to the entire battalion, who stood in formation in the center of the compound. Jolly asked us to say something encouraging to the soldiers and pray for them while he translated. Talk about a tall order. How the heck do you encourage guys your own age who risk their lives daily to protect their people—while the bravest thing you've ever done is cross a murky river in a Shoot-Me-Orange poncho? Or unknowingly eat dog?

Twain went first. He took off his mirrored aviator glasses and stood at attention in his army fatigues. Even I had to admit that he looked every inch the soldier (despite the trekking shoes) with his action figure build, crew cut, and—of course—immense stature. Deep down, I was impressed with his undying passion for their cause. Not that I'd ever admit it to his face.

His tanned face rippled with emotion. "Man, it's so hard to know what to say to you guys. I mean, in Hollywood, actors play the roles that you live out every day. You're the true heroes in this world. Your sacrifice, your bravery, your faith, your… your… *everything*. Man, I wish I could fight alongside you! It kills me that I can't…" He choked up, but quickly regained his composure and managed to speak about the Freedom Fighters' courage and persistence in the face of intense persecution and opposition, and what an inspiration they were to us all. His last words were: "…and if you see anything wet on my face, it's just sweat."

He stepped back, clenching and unclenching his jaw, and put his sunglasses back on to cover his watering eyes. His dream to fight with the Freedom Fighters For a Free Burma was dead. And although Shelby shot him a sympathetic glance, only I knew the funeral that was taking place internally.

The soldiers stared ahead, expressionless, at attention, and remained this way throughout. So we had no way to gauge their reactions to our speeches.

When Jolly finished translating, it was Jack-O's turn. His speech began, "Man, I can't believe what you Freedom Fighters deal with day in and day out. And so many of you guys are *my age! My age* and you're out there protecting women and children and entire villages! *My age* and you're fighting an enemy who's trying to blow you to smithereens! The only fighting I've ever done is on the football field. It's like we're on the bench, and you're the starting lineup. No, wait, it's more like you're competing in the Super Bowl and we're crashed out on our couch with a bag of Doritos, watching it on TV…"

Jack-O rambled on for about five more minutes, stopping only when he ran out of sports metaphors.

Ernestine followed him, arms raised heavenward, sweat and tears mingling in streams down her face. She took off her hat, shook her red and orange and yellow hair until it stood out like a flame around her head, threw her hands in the air, and proclaimed: *"Jesus! JESUS!* You're totally sacrificing your lives like *he* did! You guys are living sacrifices, that's what you are! You are so inspiring!"* Then she proceeded to sing some old hymn, which ended, *"As he died to make men holy, let us live to make men free!"* Her rich, earthy voice resonated throughout the entire HQ—and made the hairs stand up on my arms and the back of my neck.

But even after that moving tribute, the soldiers continued to stare straight ahead.

Then Shelby stepped tentatively forward, golden and fragile, in contrast to the olive drab and military fatigues in front of her. Her watery green eyes scanned the rows and rows of men. After a protracted silence, she finally said in her silvery voice, "I'm praying right now that God sends hundreds and hundreds of angels to protect you as you protect thousands and thousands of villagers. I pray this ceasefire means the real end of the war. God bless you all." And then she stepped back and dug in her pocket for a tissue while Jolly translated her three sentences.

After waiting to see if Shelby had more to share—she didn't—I reluctantly shuffled forward. I stared into those young, stoic faces, overwhelmed with guilt—Westerner Guilt. First World Guilt. Who was I to give them a pep talk or reassure them that some nonexistent God would protect them? Anything I said would come across inadequate and lame. How could I even begin to relate to them? After all, if I were in their shoes, would *I* risk my life for other human beings? Would *I* intentionally put myself in harm's way? Would *I* die so others could live? Would *I* willingly *cease to exist?*

The very thought of complete and utter annihilation gave me momentary tunnel vision. But at the sight of all those brown eyes waiting unblinkingly for me to speak, I forced myself to man up.

I lifted up my fedora and passed a hand through my dripping hair. "I don't even know where to start. Your bravery and courage speak for themselves. I mean, how you can go forward into battle knowing you could... well, *die*, blows me away. Seriously, you make me feel really, *really* guilty. And maybe that's a good thing. Maybe I need more motivation to literally get out there and help the world. And stop being so darn self absorbed and introspective. After all, since we only have so much time on this earth, we should make it count. So you're like a well-deserved kick in the butt."

Jolly gave me a quizzical look, but presumably translated what I'd said.

And the soldiers remained as immovable and unreadable as ever.

After the speeches, the Bread Team officially presented bags of rice, bottles of fish sauce, tins of oil, water purifiers, soccer balls, volleyballs, and even a new volleyball net to the Freedom Fighters. Oh, and those jumbo tins of pineapple cookies. (Turned out they were a huge favorite not only of Jolly's, but of all the soldiers.) Then we piled our arms high with the personal supplies and walked down the battalion lines passing out mosquito nets, hammocks, ponchos, boots, and cookies to each soldier.

At first, I'd wondered why we needed to hand each item to each soldier individually, instead of just inviting them to help themselves from the boxes and duffels, buffet style. But as I walked down the lines of soldiers, shaking *every single* Freedom Fighter's hand, and presenting *every single* Freedom Fighter with a mosquito net or a pair of boots or even a handful of pineapple cookies, I realized there was a power in *intentionality*. A power that finally melted their reserve—and set them at ease.

Because each soldier gripped my hand, gave me a huge smile filled with thanksgiving and cookie crumbs, and said, *"Ta blü!"*

It was like Christmas in July.

I've Got My Eyes on You

BEFORE WE COULD PROCESS WHAT HAPPENED with the soldiers, Hobab was already leading us down a windy, muddy trail through the huts of the IDP village to deliver an equal amount of supplies to the orphanage school—an open-air structure made of bamboo topped with large teak leaves. The Team was finally getting to do what we'd spent months preparing for—"ministering to the orphans."

Trying not to drop my box of fish sauce bottles, I fell in step with Ernestine, who was lugging the craft duffel. "I had no idea you could sing like that, Grommet Head."

She flashed me an enigmatic smile. "There's a whole *lot* you don't know about me, Spats." Her brown eyes momentarily locked with mine—then she abruptly turned towards Hobab.

But for some reason I couldn't take my eyes off her after that... as she talked animatedly about the orphans with Hobab... as she threw back her head and gave a throaty laugh... as her dimples flashed in and out... as she reached over to give Jack-O a head noogie...

There was definitely something watchable about Ernestine.

As we neared the school, young voices chanting in unison

filled the air. The ABCs? The multiplication tables? The chanting stopped immediately as we entered and deposited our supplies along the back wall. About a hundred elementary age students sat on narrow wooden benches behind narrow wooden tables and gazed at us with eager dark eyes. They wore woven Katin fabric outfits in geometric designs of vibrant red, yellow, and blue.

Shelby grabbed my arm. "Look, Collin! More SEA Urchins!"

"Don't you just want to squeeze those cheeks!" whispered Ernestine as she clutched my other arm.

I shot Twain a triumphant look of "check out the guy with a girl on either arm." But he was busy getting out the video camera.

"Look at their adorable little shirts!" said Shelby, releasing me to grab her camera.

Hobab introduced us to an elderly woman with long silver hair in a bun and a kindly brown face wrinkled like a walnut, Naw Eh Myet, the head teacher, who beamed in delight as she warmly shook our hands. Then, with the help of two other younger teachers, she swiftly lined up the wriggly children into rows, where they immediately burst into a medley of Katin songs, complete with arm gestures.

I had to laugh at one of the tiniest girls, who had prominent beaver teeth, a pigtail on the top of her head, and cheeks like artisan buns. She was so animated that the children around her collectively moved aside to give her more space. She had a bandage made out of a rag wrapped around the index finger of her right hand, but that didn't dampen her enthusiasm.

"What's her name?" I asked Naw Eh Myet.

She laughed affectionately. "Pee Paw."

"What a little cutie pie!" exclaimed Shelby, crouching down to snap a photo.

"What happened to her finger?" I asked.

Naw Eh Myet frowned and shook her head. "Bad, bad dog. Bite children."

Then I'm darn glad he's now in my stomach!

When the songs finally ended and we'd applauded profusely, Hobab turned to Ernestine and asked, "Got anything for the kids now? Like stickers or something?"

"I bet every NGO brings stickers," she said dismissively. "We've got something *way* better. Epic fun is on the way." She hurried over to the craft duffel, and after a few moments of rummaging around, pulled out a large Zip-Lock bag, which she waved in the air enticingly.

"Who wants some… *gooooogly eyes!?*"

Blank stares.

Apparently, epic fun had lost its way…

"Misfire, eh, Ketchum," said Jack-O under his breath, nudging her in the side with his massive elbow.

"Just wait," said Ernestine, not at all fazed by the lack of reception. She turned to Hobab. "Tell the kids to run outside and grab a rock. Any size—small, medium, large, jumbo. And tell them to hurry!"

Hobab rapidly gave the instructions, and within seconds, the kids scrambled to their feet and dashed outside.

The Team set out acrylic paints, paintbrushes, glue, pipe cleaners, stacks of multi-colored felt, and scissors on the wooden table—or at least four of us did, while Mr. Team

237

Documentarian videotaped us in action. Then Ernestine spread out a dozen different sizes of googly eyes, from as tiny as a peppercorn to as large as a golf ball.

"Sustainable crafts," said Ernestine, standing back and surveying the table with satisfaction. "We'll leave all the paints and supplies behind so they can create art long after we're gone."

"I like your M.O.," said Hobab, giving her a thumbs up.

The kids raced back inside, triumphantly holding up their rocks. They squealed when they saw the mother lode of crafts and started to surge towards it—and us!

"Yikes!" said Shelby, backing away from the deluge of bodies.

Hobab and Naw Eh Myet swiftly stepped forward to bar the way, and herded them into little groups. The Team passed out the craft supplies, and the kids immediately set to work. Soon the school floor was covered with rocks painted like monkeys, birds, cats, butterflies—and even cell phones! In one corner, Jack-O showed a group of boys how to paint their round rocks like soccer balls. And in another corner, Shelby watched some older girls methodically transform a dozen rocks into white hens and yellow chicks.

"Aren't they cute?" asked Shelby, looking up at me.

"But not as cute as Rock Flounce?" I asked, half joking, half serious.

She laughed and pulled him out of her pocket. "Who could ever replace Rock Flounce!" She rubbed him on her cheek.

She's flirting with me now! Hope has entered the building!

Something brown and fuzzy rolled across the floor and

bumped into my trekking shoe—and two eyes peered up at me. Pee Paw scampered over and scooped it up and cradled it in her arms, a huge grin on her face. *"Hkaw thà ta͞ ü!"*

Hobab laughed. "She calls it her coconut monkey."

"Hey, Collin, what's that?" Ernestine lunged towards me, dramatically pointing at the ceiling.

I scanned the bamboo poles and leaves arched above my head. "What's what? I don't see anything...?"

"Up there, to the right," she said.

"Are you talking about the gecko? The spider web? The speck of dirt?"

Then I realized she'd moved away.

I shrugged and made a face at Pee Paw. "And I'm the one who supposedly has *Extreme You*..."

Pee Paw giggled and pointed at my feet.

I looked down to see two jumbo-sized googly eyes staring up at me from the tip of my left trekking shoe.

Behind me, there came a chuckle. "I've got my eyes on you, Collin Uttley."

I shook my head and smiled.

That Ernestine.

After they finished, the students carefully lined their colorful creations along the wall of the school to dry. Shelby knelt down to get some close-up shots.

"Some of these kids are crazy talented," she said, pointing at an intricately detailed rooster. "Take that one, for instance—"

But before she could elaborate, Naw Eh Myet shoved the

ukulele case into her arms and commanded, "Team sing now!"

Within minutes, the benches and tables were pushed against the bamboo walls, and Ernestine, Jack-O, Hobab, and I lined up behind Shelby.

Shelby paused, fingers on the strings. "Come on, Twain. We need you."

Right. About as much as a kick in the head.

Twain grinned, flicked a triumphant look at me, and put away the camera.

She strummed and began, *"Father Abraham had many sons, many sons had Father Abraham—"* then broke off as Ernestine moved over to whisper in her ear. Shelby whispered back. The rest of us stood there awkwardly as they carried on an all-whisper conversation for almost five minutes.

Finally, Shelby turned back to the rest of us. "So, Ernestine brings up a good point that 'sons' in this context means *all* children, both sons and daughters. Not exactly politically correct, but since it's an old-fashioned church favorite that's a lot of fun, we'll cut it some slack. Sound good?"

Hobab translated, but the kids just stared at him blankly.

I was right there with them—so many things in the church world made absolutely no sense to me that I'd completely lost count.

"All right, let's try that again," said Shelby flashing them a sunny smile and playing a chord. *"Father Abraham had many sons, many sons had Father Abraham. I am one of them, and so are YOU! So let's all praise the Lord! Right arm!"*

Ernestine, Twain, Jack-O, Hobab, and I waved our right arms in the air in a sort of lumbering chorus line. The kids gamely mirrored us as we continued to sing. Shelby seemed to literally sparkle as she sang and twanged, having as much fun as the kids. (Maybe it was all the sweat?)

"Father Abraham had many sons, many sons had Father Abraham. I am one of them, and so are YOU! So let's all praise the Lord! Right arm! Left arm!"

Now we waved both our right and left arms in the air, sweat streaming down our bodies like lava from a volcano. The interminable song continued in Hokey Pokey fashion (how many sons *did* Abraham have anyway?), adding various body parts at each verse, until finally (to the Team's relief), we reached the grand finale:

"Father Abraham, had many sons, many sons had Father Abraham. I am one of them, and so are YOU! So let's all praise the Lord! Right arm! Left arm! Right leg! Left leg! Nod your head! Turn around! Sit down!"

"Praise the Lord!" Ernestine exclaimed in relief as we all flopped to the ground.

If we'd thought we were sweaty before…

The grinning kids chanted something loudly over and over in Katin.

"Chow time?" panted Jack-O hopefully.

"The orphan, they want *more*," said Naw Eh Myet, her eyes twinkling.

The Team exchanged looks as we wiped our dripping faces on our sopping trekking shirts. *More?*

"You couldn't pay me enough," said Twain, bending over to remove the video camera from the case.

But I knew just what to do.

I sauntered over to Shelby and extended my hand. "They

want more, so let's give them more!"

Shelby backed away, holding the ukulele in front of her face as if to shield herself from the very idea. "Are you kidding? No way!"

"Come on! Let's give these kids the memory of a lifetime. They don't have TV or films or internet—and when's the last time they've ever seen a live floor show?"

The kids started clapping.

"Listen to them! Are you seriously gonna let them down?"

At the sight of the children eagerly clapping, Shelby said in exasperation, "Oh, all right!"

I whisked the ukulele out of her hands and tossed it over to Jack-O—who effortlessly caught it and tucked it under his armpit like a football.

Although her cheeks were bright pink, Shelby stepped forward with her hands extended.

I hummed *Rock This Town* and twirled Shelby across the bamboo flooring. And despite the primitive conditions and our clunky trekking shoes, I gotta say—*we tore it up*. I had way more space than in the Thai market for rock-stepping, swinging, dipping, and flinging Shelby in the air. She kept in rhythm, never missing a beat.

She rocked.

I rocked.

We rocked.

The kids cheered enthusiastically, Shelby gave me a big grin as we whirled around the floor.

"You were right," Shelby panted in my ear. "They love it!"

"Just doing my missionary duty," I replied with a grin.

This is your Victory Dance, Collin! Might as well enjoy it!

"Get ready for that tricky move we practiced," I murmured under my breath. Then I launched Shelby into the air, caught her effortlessly around the waist, tossed her over my back, then slid her between my legs, and popped her back out the other side.

The crowd went wild! The kids cheered, Ernestine shook her head admiringly, Hobab gave me two thumbs up, and Jack-O yelled, "You shred, dude!"

I was a stud.

How could Shelby not feel the chemistry?

How could she not sense we were meant for each other?

That we were *soul mates?*

Then, as I dipped Shelby so far back her curls grazed the bamboo flooring, I threw a look at Twain to see his reaction to such coolness. Everyone else continued to clap and cheer us on—but *he* was videotaping a monkey on a palm tree outside!

I blame *dunderheaded* Twain entirely for what happened next. If he had been paying attention as expected (and if my hands hadn't been so slick with sweat), then I wouldn't have been distracted and stepped on a stray googly eye, skidded backward, fallen on my butt, which launched Shelby over my head, sending her flailing like an airborne kitten across the room where she slammed the bamboo wall!

Some Girl

FLINGING SHELBY INTO THAT BAMBOO WALL (which shook the entire structure) was bad enough, but there was worse to come. She ricocheted off the wall right into *Twain*—who caught her with one arm, while still holding the recording video camera aloft with the other! Even I had to admit that it was an *epic* save. And if the crowd had cheered loudly for me—it was nothing compared to the roof-raising screams of enthusiasm for Twain.

I scrambled to my feet and ran over to her. "Shelby! Are you all right!?! Is anything broken? How do you feel?!?"

Shelby managed a weak smile and then, after catching her breath, rasped, *"Mai pen rai."*

And here I didn't think it was possible for me to be any more in love with her!

Twain laughed and squeezed her. "Atta girl!"

"High five!" said Jack-O.

"She's lucky it wasn't a cement wall," Ernestine said in a low tone.

I shot Ernestine a look, but she'd already turned away.

And then before I knew what was happening, Twain whisked Shelby over to a nearby wooden bench and began massaging her shoulders!

Something jabbed me in the gut.

It was Ernestine's elbow. "Come on, Collin. Time to wrap this puppy up." She conferred with Naw Eh Myet, who hurried away and returned minutes later with an ancient metal thermos in one hand and a battered metal mixing bowl in the other. She set the bowl down on the wooden table in the center of the schoolroom, opened the Thermos, and poured boiling hot water into it.

Ernestine handed me a plastic bag full of multicolored plastic capsules. "Go for it, Collin." She gave me a sympathetic smile, then called to the kids: "Time for Miracle Capsules!"

I was instantly encased in kids—the smaller ones jumping onto the backs of the bigger ones in order to see more clearly. Their dark eyes were shining with excitement and they couldn't stop grinning—especially Pee Paw, who was front and center, her cheeks scrunched up and white teeth protruding like a happy squirrel. (Make that a happy squirrel on a sugar high!) Her coconut monkey now had a string attached to it, which she pulled behind her like a pet.

The collective gusto of the students instantly triggered a sense of fatherly protection for them and the desire to squeeze them all in a massive group hug. I'd do *anything* for these SEA Urchins!

I dramatically counted to three in Katin, holding up my fingers so the children could count along:

"*Ter!*"

"*Kee!*"

"*Ther!*"

On three, I dropped a handful of plastic covered capsules into the boiling water. The kids pressed in closer, holding their collective breaths. A cluster of preschool aged girls glued themselves to my side, the silvery powder on their cheeks rubbing off on my arm.

The kids watched riveted as the plastic outer shell of the capsules dissolved and small sponges slowly emerged and unfolded—then came the eardrum piercing shrieks as I held up one sponge after another.

A red cow!

A green giraffe!

A yellow octopus with tentacles!

The older kids "ooohed" and "aaahed"—as did the villagers and soldiers who were peering through the windows. But the tiniest children stared in silent wonder, as if they couldn't believe their eyes.

Naw Eh Myet shook her head and made clicking noises with her tongue—like this was the most amazing thing she'd ever seen in her entire life. Once I squeezed the water out of the sponges and laid them to dry on the wooden table, eager fingers reached out to touch the exotic shapes.

I glanced over at Shelby, who watched from the wooden bench, flanked by Jack-O and Twain. The affectionate smile she gave me melted my heart like the plastic outer shells of the capsules. (I tried to ignore the fact that Twain was now massaging her lower back...)

Every kid received a sponge animal by the end—even old Naw Eh Myet enthusiastically scored an orange walrus. I spotted Pee Paw standing apart from the group, cradling the yellow foam octopus in her little palm, tenderly stroking the tentacles with her tiny bandaged forefinger. The image seared itself on my mind and heart—and did something indescribable to my insides, like when I encountered those pint-sized helpers at Yai Camp. No wonder the Tacketts found themselves compelled to return year after year after year...

I'd just turned away to furtively blow my nose, when Jack-O jabbed me in the ribs.

"Hey, I caught a couple boys swallowing the extra capsules," he said. "Don't know if that's good for their innards. Should we tell Lah Kaw?"

I laughed. "Oh, they'll come out—*eventually*."

Once Hobab managed to pry us away from the orphans, we walked back to the HQ, debriefing as a Team along the way. Despite being sweaty, tired, hungry—*and* wet, now that rain had begun to fall again—we were exhilarated. Not even the memory of Twain's epic save could dampen my enthusiasm for the kids at that moment. Now I finally understood what a *total high* serving others could give you.

Behind us, a group of older students pretended to swing dance—taking turns twirling each other around and flinging each other through the air. We'd hear the occasional squeal when the less adept ones slammed into a hut or a palm tree.

"Someone's got a little shadow," said Shelby with a wink.

"Shadow?" I turned around to see Pee Paw, dragging her coconut monkey behind her. The yellow octopus now hung on a string around her neck.

She flashed me a big grin. *"Hkaw thà tā ü!"*

"Oh, right, your nice little pet..."

I bent over and gave her monkey a pat—then jumped back, waving my hands in the air as if it had snapped at me.

"Yikes! Back off, you monster!"

That sent her into waves of giggles.

I turned to see Shelby staring at me again with that plastic capsule melting smile.

"Collin, you're the best," she said.

Looks like we're back on track!

"Jesus!" exclaimed Ernestine jubilantly, waving both hands in the air. "Wooo hooo! Praise the Lord, we're *finally* doing what we spent *forever* preparing for!"

"Just wait 'til those kids poop out those sponges!" said Jack-O.

We all laughed.

"We've got to brainstorm our line-up for tomorrow," said Ernestine.

I shook my head. "I don't know how we can ever top to-day—"

"Maybe you can throw someone else against the wall," Twain suggested wryly.

I managed a laugh, but turned to Shelby, who *was* walking a tad more stiffly than usual. "Shelby, I'm so sorry. I can't believe I was such an idiot—"

"Forget it," she interrupted, waving her hand as if brushing away a mosquito. "It was great—until it wasn't. But I'm fine. And it's sweet of you to be concerned. That's what's so great about you, Collin. You're always looking out for me— just like Courtney used to before she moved away. You're such an awesome *friend*."

Was it my imagination or did she stress *friend* a little more than necessary?

"Well, thank—"

She put a hand on my arm, interrupting my response.

"You know what?" she asked, as if the thought had just struck her.

"What?"

"You'd make an awesome *boy*friend..."

What?

"...some girl would be *so* lucky to date you."

WHAT!?!

Blame It on the Betel Nut

*S*OME GIRL? *SOME GIRL!? BY "SOME GIRL" DO you mean YOU, Shelby Wanderal!?! What are you trying to say!?!*

I stopped short—and Jack-O slammed right into me and almost knocked me over. My fedora whizzed through the air and hit the dirt.

"Dude! Can you stop doing that?" he said indignantly as he steadied me.

I automatically retrieved my hat and positioned it at a jaunty angle. Then I grabbed Shelby's arm. The almost slimy layer of perspiration didn't faze me in the least. Nor did her sweat-matted hair or grimy trekking shirt—or tiny smudge of dirt on the very tip of her nose. To me, she was and always would be, my golden girl, my fun-sized *soul mate*.

"Shelby." My voice had a slight quaver, which I hoped she wouldn't notice.

She swiveled away from me and shook my hand off her arm with a laugh. "Don't even think about it! I've had enough swinging for one—"

"It's not that. It's... it's..."

"It's what?"

With as steady a voice as I could muster, I said, "When you—when you said '*some girl*' did you mean *you?* Are you saying you'd—you'd go out with me?"

There! I'd finally asked her what I'd been dying to know for months!

Shelby raised her eyebrows in surprise. "What are you talking about, Collin? We go out all the time."

What the--?! Was she deliberately being obtuse?

She gave me a brisk pat-pat-pat on the back and continued walking.

"Wait!" I quickly caught up with her. "No, what I meant was, would you actually be my girlfr—"

"Hello! Goodbye! We take lady!" Just then, a group of giggling Katin female teachers and students, led by Naw Eh Myet, sideswiped us before I could finish the sentence— finish the *word!* They enthusiastically tugged on Shelby and Ernestine's arms and pulled them towards a nearby hut. Little Pee Paw was particularly giddy, dancing after them, whipping around her coconut monkey and narrowly missing their legs.

"We capture you!" exclaimed one of the younger teachers with glee.

"You gotta be kidding me!" I muttered under my breath.

Was the entire universe conspiring to keep Shelby and me apart?! If so, the planets were working overtime!

"What the heck is going on around here?" asked Jack-O, looking around in bewilderment.

Shelby and Ernestine glanced back at the rest of us in amused surprise, but allowed themselves to be captured. Pee Paw laughed and clung onto Shelby's arm as if to prevent her from escaping.

"Time for to show our tradition!" Naw Eh Myet said to us, her eyes crinkling.

She spoke briefly in Katin to Hobab, who laughed and said, "Looks like it's female bonding time."

"But what are they doing to them?" I asked anxiously as Shelby and Ernestine disappeared into the hut, followed by Naw Eh Myet, who jerked a woven Katin blanket across the doorway.

"Don't worry, they'll be fine," said Twain, videotaping their disappearance.

"How would you know?" I growled at him, still exasperated at the interruption at such a pivotal moment.

"Don't worry, guys," said Hobab with a knowing grin. "You won't be left out of the bonding. Follow me."

I don't know how I managed to keep it together. Not knowing Shelby's precise meaning was *killing* me. It took every ounce of strength I had to keep from racing back to that hut and yanking Shelby out and forcing her to tell me right then and there.

To be honest, I didn't know how much more of this emotional rollercoastering I could take. Did she like me in that way or *not?* I had to know once and for all before I went nuts. Until then, I couldn't focus on anything else, not even the SEA Urchins or the Feebs or the "Cause."

Mom always said I had a one-track mind.

Hobab led us through the HQ, past the lookout shack draped with the vibrant Katin flag, to a bluff overlooking the Murk River. There we found Jolly, Gimlet, Lah Kaw, and a few other soldiers squatting in a semi-circle, chewing on something, and periodically spitting pink streams into the dirt. Behind them, a row of rifles, guns, and RPGs leaned against the wall of the lookout. The men jovially greeted us in Katin as we approached.

"Howdy, chaps!" said Jolly. "Take a pew." He gestured for us to squat next to them.

We squatted. (Not the easiest thing for a Westerner to do for an extended period of time, by the way.)

Twain adverted his eyes from Jolly's blood stained bandages.

"How are your toes?" I asked Jolly.

He shrugged. "It is what it is."

"You should have Jongchit and the Wigglewurts pray for them," said Jack-O.

Jolly laughed. "That I should. Maybe then the nails will grow out in a month instead of a year!"

Gimlet grimaced and spat, revealing red stained teeth. It was the closest thing to a smile he'd ever come.

"Betel nut," said Hobab. He grinned at us and wiggled his eyebrows ludicrously. "Wanna try?"

"You kidding?" said Twain eagerly. "I've always wondered what it tasted like!"

I'd noticed the cook at the Born Free Academy and refugees at Yai Camp chewing on something that stained their mouth and teeth pink, but I just thought it was some sort of natural chewing gum.

"Betel nut?" I asked. "What's that?"

"Dude," said Jack-O, skeptically shaking his head, "been there, done that. All four inches of it, remember?"

"Not b-e-e-t-l-e." Twain laughed. "B-e-t-e-l."

Jolly spat an arc of pink, then said, "It's not actually the betel nut, lads, but the *areca* nut cut into pieces, topped with mineral slaked lime, and then wrapped in green leaves from the betel vine."

"Yeah," said Hobab. "Then you sorta tuck it in the corner of your mouth and chew and suck on it for hours." He pointed to the bulges in the soldiers' cheeks. "Kind of like how cowboys chew cuds of tobacco."

We watched Lah Kaw cut small pieces of the hard nut with a metal cutter, and then rapidly make package after package out of betel leaves, which resembled mini-burritos. He set aside the last one, looked up, and said in his scratchy voice, "Betel nut long, long tradition in Southeast Asia. Four thousand year."

Jolly spat, then smiled at us. "Ready for a sample?"

"You bet! Lay it on me!" said Twain, moving forward and thrusting out his hand.

"You game, dude?" Jack-O peered at me through his smudged glasses. "After all, when in Rome…?"

I shifted uncomfortably. "I don't know if it's such a good idea to put raw green leaves in our mouths. During training the Tacketts warned us about bacteria on uncooked—"

"Chill, Uttley. You don't need to prove your manhood to us." Twain grinned down at me, lifted up my fedora, and patted the top of my head patronizingly. "Feel free to sit—no, *squat*—this one out, little fella."

I pushed his hand away, snatched back my hat, turned to Lah Kaw, and grimly held out my hand.

"There's a good chap," said Jolly with a wink.

Lah Kaw gave us each a little green square package.

Hobab held up his fingers and mimicked me with the orphans: *"Ter! Kee! Ther!"*

On *ther*, we simultaneously shoved the packages into our mouths and started to chew.

I shifted the package to my left cheek and said as clearly as I could with a mouthful of vegetation, "It's like chewing a topiary."

"What's that?" asked Hobab.

"An overly-trimmed shrub."

"More like a salad made out of bark and leaves," said Jack-O, shifting his cud from one cheek to the other. "With dirt for dressing."

"Spicy," said Twain, chewing with concentration.

"I was going to say peppery," I said. "And kinda acrid."

"It's an acquired taste," said Jolly with a pink grin.

"There's definitely something about it," said Twain as he ground the nut pieces in his back teeth. "My tongue is starting to feel numb."

"It has a mildly narcotic effect, about the same amount as a cup of coffee," said Jolly.

Determined not to appear less manly than Twain, I chewed the nuts and leaves with the ferocity of a terrier decimating a doggie treat. Although I was starting to feel nauseated, I forced myself to complete the job.

"Uch, that was brutal," I said, drinking half my bottle of water in one gulp. "No more for me, thanks. One is more than enough."

Hobab and Lah Kaw exchanged confused looks.

"What do you mean?" asked Twain. He peered at me closely. "Collin! Where's your betel nut?"

"In here. Where else?" I slapped my stomach proudly. "Ha! Looks like I beat you, *Twain.*"

"What?!" said Twain and Hobab in perfect unison.

Jolly laughed. "You bloody did what?"

Jack-O glanced back and forth at them in bewilderment. "What's wrong?"

"You weren't supposed to eat it! Just chew on it!" Hobab told me in consternation.

"You know, like a cud of *chewing* tobacco…?" said Twain, jabbing a finger at the wad of betel nut in his cheek.

"What the—?!" My stomach contorted.

Hobab and Lah Kaw spoke rapidly in Katin for a few moments, then Lah Kaw said with gravity, "That very not good for stomach. You must—how do you say?—*get it out.*"

"Get it out…?" I repeated weakly, not liking where this was going.

"He means you gotta throw it up right now!" said Twain with genuine concern—and *his* concern concerned *me!*

I'll skip the gory details of the induced vomiting. It was disgusting and humiliating, and left my throat and mouth raw and inflamed.

It sure took the fun out of bonding.

A little while later, Jack-O, Twain, and I were seated cross-legged on the bamboo matting of the "jungle mess" waiting for dinner. Jack-O was guzzling his fourth bottle of water. He drained it, burped, and then said, "Man, I just can't get that green metallic taste out of my mouth."

"You're telling me," I said in a raspy voice, with an inadvertent shudder.

Twain gave me a friendly slug. "I gotta hand it to you, Uttley. You sure are game."

Ignoring my throbbing shoulder, I glanced at my watch. "I wonder how much longer Shelby—*and* Ernestine—will be?"

"Yeah," said Jack-O, "what weird stuff do you think they're chewing?"

We pondered that silently for a moment.

"I'm starving," said Jack-O, scanning the room for food.

A cockroach ran across the bamboo matting.

"Don't get any ideas," said Twain.

"I'm not that desperate," replied Jack-O, with a grin. "Yet."

Then Twain turned and fixed his gray eyes on mine. Since he rarely made direct eye contact, I found it disconcerting.

"So, Uttley, why do you like Shel so much?"

His question detonated something inside me. After all, I was already feeling raw and surly. I usually keep private thoughts private, but this time, I couldn't stop myself—I burst like a dam that had been building up pressure for years.

Blame it on the betel nut.

"Why? *Why?!* You're asking *why* I like Shelby Wanderal? That's like asking *why* I'd like to win the lottery! Or *why* I like oxygen!"

"Uh, never mind—" Twain began.

"I mean, dude, are you *blind* or what? Does a girl have to be in a centerfold to catch your eye? So someone with vintage style like Shelby wouldn't interest you? Someone who can name every single Preston Sturges movie *and* the year it was made? Someone who sews all her own clothes? Someone who'd rather swing dance than go to the mall? Someone with eyes greener than green and hair golder than gold? Some-one—"

257

I stopped short.

Greener than green and golder than gold? What the heck was that? Shame and confusion instantly filled my headspace. Shame for babbling on and on like a total loser. And confusion because I suddenly realized I'd just recited a bunch of superficial reasons why I liked Shelby, but not one with any real *substance*.

Silence.

Jack-O stared at me with his mouth open so wide, I could see the silver fillings in his back molars. Then he looked over at Twain, who raised his eyebrows and gave a low whistle.

"Dude, you are one whipped puppy," said Jack-O, shaking his head slowly back and forth, turning his blue-black spiked hair into a waving sea anemone. Then realization lit up his face. "So you *did* have a thing for Shelby when you were giving her that turd dog! I was right!"

"Yeah," I said, "Sorry about that."

Jack-O gazed off into space. "And here I always just thought of Shell-Bell as the super nice, curly haired girl in my class who shared her gummies and had an imaginary friend."

"*You* were the one with the imaginary friend," said Twain.

"Oh, yeah," nodded Jack-O. Then after a slight pause, "But the gummies were real, right?"

"So, Uttley, does Shel feel the same about you yet, do you think?" asked Twain in a casual tone, as he closely examined his watchband. "Or does she still happen to still like... that *other* guy?"

My face burned as I clenched my jaw—I didn't trust myself to reply.

"She's no Ernestine Ketchum, but maybe you should ask

her out if you're that into her," said Jack-O. "After the trip, I mean."

"Nothing could stop me," I said, with a challenging glance at Twain.

He laughed. "Nothing?"

I narrowed my eyes. "Nothing."

"You sure about that?"

We glared at each other in standoff style for almost thirty seconds—then simultaneously looked away.

"Let me know if you need any dating tips," said Jack-O, completely oblivious to the undercurrent. "I bet I can remember all of Shelby's favorite foods." He squeezed his eyes shut. "Yep, there she is with her Powderpuff Girls lunch box... now she's opening it and out comes—a baggie of goldfish! A whole-wheat sandwich with avocado and sprouts! Berry flavored Capri-Sun! A baby box of raisins! Some apple slices covered with—"

"Okay, okay, Jack-O, we get the picture," said Twain.

At that moment, Shelby and Ernestine entered the mess hall—and we almost didn't recognize them.

The D Word

S HELBY AND ERNESTINE GLIMMERED WITH
the glistening silvery-beige powder I'd seen on the faces
of the Katin women. It covered not only their faces, but their
necks and arms. They no longer wore their trekking outfits,
but embroidered brightly colored Katin shirts and *longyis*—
which almost matched Ernestine's red-orange-yellow hair.
The males of the Outreach Team stared, mesmerized, at our
female counterparts as they sat down beside us.

"Ta da!" said Shelby, slipping in between me and Twain.
She turned her face this way and that so we could admire the
circles of powder on each cheek and the stripe down the
bridge of her nose. "So, what do you think?"

"Wow!" I blurted out before I could stop myself. The
powder actually did something for Shelby. Made her shimmer
and glisten like *a virtual goddess*. I couldn't pry my eyes off her
face.

"What is that stuff?" asked Jack-O, reaching out a finger.

"Thanaka!" said Ernestine, ducking out of his reach.

"Gesundheit!" said Jack-O.

"Naw Eh Myet showed us how to make the paste out of
the ground-up bark and twigs of the *thanaka*—"

"Gesundheit!" said Jack-O again.

"—tree," finished Ernestine in a slightly irritated tone. "It's only funny the first time, Man Child."

"What's the point of smearing gunk on your face?" Jack-O asked Ernestine. "You look like a clown."

Thanks to her tri-color hair and big dimpled grin, Ernestine *did* resemble a clown more than a goddess.

She stuck her tongue out at Jack-O. "Who asked you, Pickle Head?"

In response, Jack-O peeled off the Band-Aid on his forehead to reveal his bright fire fringe. "Careful, you're talkin' to a piece of *you*, Ketchum!"

Ernestine rolled her eyes. "Oh, brother! Put that back on."

"No way!" said Jack-O, defiantly crossing his arms. "From now on it stays off. I display my Ketchum Hair proudly." He crumpled the Band-Aid into a ball and tossed it at her—right smack in the middle of her fire hair.

I gave Ernestine a sympathetic look, but she shrugged good-naturedly as she fished it out. Then she leaned over to me and whispered, "His juvenile way of showing he likes me. For some reason he thinks we're still in fourth grade."

"Hey!" said Jack-O, pointing at their *longyis*, "when do I get mine?"

"Anyway," said Shelby, trying to bring the topic back around, "we learned that *thanaka* is used for cosmetic reasons, as a sunscreen, and a way to keep the face cool. Like the Southeast Asian version of Cover Girl."

"*Niiiiiice,*" said Twain with a drawl, giving Shelby a drawn out once-over, fully aware how it was affecting me.

It was all I could do not to belt him.

"When are we *ever* gonna eat?" Jack-O shifted his bulk

and scanned the hut desperately to see if food was on its way.

"So, what did you guys do while we girls were getting all beautified?" Shelby asked, looking up at Twain, her curls grazing his shoulder.

"Well," said Twain, "we partook of the ancient tradition of betel nut—"

"Next topic," I interrupted.

"Betel nut?" said Ernestine. "What's that?"

"Skip it. It was messy and gross, so Collin doesn't wanna talk about it," said Jack-O with a conciliatory look in my direction.

"Wait a minute!" Shelby sat up straighter. "Didn't the Tacketts warn us about betel nut? Something about it being addictive and causing a lot of health problems—"

"Well, you don't have to worry about that with us," said Twain. Then he mimicked the Thai Border Guard: "*First* time we try betel nut. *Last* time we try betel nut."

I tried to make eye contact with Shelby in order to gauge her feelings for me—but her eyes were glued to Twain like the fire hair on Jack-O's gash.

Some girl.

"By the way, Shel," said Twain with a sly look in my direction. "Collin has been *very* concerned about you. Thought you'd been abducted or something."

The glare I gave Twain quickly morphed into a smile as Shelby *finally* looked over at me.

"That's because Collin's a *true* gentleman," she said, gazing at me benevolently.

Normally, this would have sent me into instant euphoria. But now…

"You call slamming girls into walls being *gentlemanly*?" said Twain. He stretched his long legs out in front of him and extended his arms high above his head—which pulled up his shirt just enough to reveal his annoyingly ripped abs. Then he bent his legs and rested his flexed arms across his knees. It was completely obvious he was parading his muscles for Shelby's benefit—and it ticked me off.

"Well, he's more of a gentleman than some other self-absorbed baboons around here," said Shelby, looking up at him saucily, her arms folded and her golden head tilted to one side.

"Are you trash-talking me, Shelby Wanderal?" he asked, gazing down at her *thanaka-ed* face with a half-smirk.

"Why, does it hurt your feelings, Twain Abernathy?" she asked, smirking right back at him.

"I'm bawling my eyes out," he said.

"Oh, you poor mama's boy," she said.

His gray eyes locked with her green ones—and their smirks froze.

It was as if time stopped.

I coughed loudly.

They remained transfixed.

Ernestine threw me an incredulous "Are you seeing what I'm seeing?" look.

My stomach hurt worse than when I ate the betel nut.

"Dinner!" I blurted in relief as I saw Hobab enter, followed by a couple soldiers and their wives (faces also covered in *thanaka*), carrying trays heaped with corn on the cob, sticky rice—and strips of meat.

"*Yes!*" said Jack-O, pumping his fist in the air.

But at the sight of more mystery meat, Ernestine and I exchanged wary looks.

Hobab walked over to us and said reassuringly, "Don't worry, guys, this time it's pork, not dog."

"*Dog?!*" Shelby's voice twanged. The word acted like a magnet to instantly draw her attention away from Twain.

The Outreach Team scrambled to cover up Hobab's indiscretion:

"It's just a euphemism for—"

"Just look at that corn!"

"Boy, I'm starved!"

Instead of following their lead, I found myself saying loudly and distinctly: "Yes, *dog*. *Dog* is what you ate for lunch today, Shelby Wanderal. Dog. D-O-G. Dog."

Silence.

I can't justify why I did it. All I know, is that at that moment I wanted to hurt her. Punish her. Make her sorry she ever preferred Twain over me.

Shelby's face crumpled in alarm. Her eyes bulged, her lower lip quivered, her skin turned paler than ever under the *thanaka*, and she actually began to wheeze.

The entire Outreach Team stared at me, flabbergasted.

"Hey, sometimes the truth hurts," I said defiantly.

Shelby fanned her face with her hand. Under the *thanaka*, her normally white freckled cheeks were now almost the same shade of pink as the betel nut spittle. And the look she gave me was exactly the kind that Flounce would have given me if I'd kicked him in his little wiener dog tummy.

She moaned and clamped a hand over her mouth.

Twain stood up and pulled Shelby to her feet as effortlessly as if she were made of styrofoam. "Come on, Shel, let's get you to the W.C." He threw me a piercing glare as they hurried out, Shelby's hand still in clamped position.

As soon as they left, a massive load of guilt dumped on top of me.

I've just wounded Shelby Wanderall! The girl I'm supposed to love! What the heck was I thinking!?! What the heck am I doing!?! I'm screwing everything up! How stupid can you get???

"That was so not cool," Ernestine said slowly, looking at me as if seeing me for the first time and not liking what she saw. No dimples were in evidence now.

I was too gutted to respond, so I just nodded miserably.

"Way harsh, dude," said Jack-O, shaking his head in disbelief.

But although I regretted hurting Shelby, I did *not* regret putting a stop to their inane—make that *dangerous*—banter. After all, I'd been forced into hyper-vigilance mode by Twain's obvious play for her.

The fresh corn on the cob was passed around, still steaming. Ernestine and Jack-O eagerly ripped away the husks to reveal the light yellow kernels.

I passed. How could I eat when Shelby was at that moment heaving out her guts? And probably hated mine?

It had been barely two hours since Shelby had called me "awesome boyfriend material," but I now realized it wasn't for *herself* after all.

Just as I started to get that sinking feeling, something inside me stubbornly refused to admit defeat, refused to concede victory to Twain. As so many war strategists had maintained throughout history: it's not over until it's over.

And right then, I made a conscious decision: I wasn't gonna wallow in my stupidity. I was going to regroup—and *decimate* the competition.

Skip-Bo, Anyone?

AFTER DINNER, GAMING COMMENCED IN THE jungle mess hall. Jolly asked some soldiers to rig a generator for an overhead electric light so the Outreach Team could play chess, backgammon, dominos, and the other games we'd brought for the soldiers. Once night fell, the sounds of rustling palm leaves and clicking geckos magnified, and the pungent smells of jasmine and smoke from a multitude of cigarettes intensified. The air was still heavy with humidity and our skin continued to ooze sweat.

The Team was exhausted. We'd been up since five a.m. and had been going full throttle all day in the depleting Southeast Asian climate. But we plastered smiles across our faces and prepared for battle.

After all, it was what we'd come for.

"Anybody up for some Skip-Bo?" asked Jack-O in a lackluster tone, holding the card game in the air.

To his amazement, Lah Kaw and a large group of soldiers instantly surrounded him.

"You kiddin'?" he said incredulously, scanning the crowd. "I've finally found my peeps!"

In no time, a rowdy game ensued, with shouts of "Skip-Bo!" in broken English peppering the night air.

"Wanna play chess?" Ernestine smiled down at me, where I sat banished in a corner, all my passion drained out of me. The *thanaka* on her face had smeared and had frosted parts of her hair—giving her the look of a mischievous clown child caught in the kitchen playing with a bowl full of raw cookie dough ingredients.

I glanced dully over at Shelby who was absentmindedly strumming her ukulele as she watched Twain play chess with Jolly. The tune was *Rock This Town*.

Ouch.

"Sorry, Ernestine," I said loudly. "Being shunned just doesn't put me in the mood for games." But Shelby didn't seem to hear—nor care. She hadn't so much as made eye contact with me since her return from the W.C. Talk about taciturn. Actually, taciturn didn't even begin to cover it— icicles weren't this frigid.

So much for decimating the competition.

"Suit yourself," said Ernestine, shrugging. "But moping won't help anything."

"I'm *not* moping," I said indignantly. "I'm... I'm *meditating*."

She gave me a look that indicated she definitely didn't buy *that*.

Hobab invited her to play Scrabble with him and a couple soldiers.

"It's supposed to improve their English," he said. "But beware, they use proper nouns."

"Like Pele?" asked Ernestine with a grin.

"No, like *Ronaldo*," he said, grinning back.

"Pele all the way, dude!" said Jack-O, without even looking up from his cards.

Ernestine joined the Scrabble game, but once again, I passed.

"Don't just sit there, Collin—get playing something!" said Jack-O, shuffling cards. "Jump in here if you want."

"You mean… *if you dare*," said Lah Kaw in his slow and deliberate English, running his hand through his fauxhawk.

"*Mop-ing…*" murmured Ernestine in a sing-song voice.

To keep her quiet, I stood up and reluctantly joined the rousing game of Skip-Bo.

"Stalemate? You gotta be kidding!" Twain said to Jolly, gazing down at the chessboard in disbelief. "That's never happened to me before!" Then with a pointed look in my direction, he added, "At least not in *chess*."

"We Katin have decades of experience…" said Jolly, lighting up a cigarette.

I don't know exactly when I first noticed that the ukulele had stopped twanging—and that Shelby and Twain were missing. But since I was actually winning at Skip-Bo—decimating the competition to be exact—I couldn't just stop the game and search then and there. However, in between turns, I scanned the jungle mess to see if I could spot the duo tucked away in some dim corner. Jolly was now playing chess with Gimlet, who streamed betel nut into his battered plastic yellow cup between moves.

"Skip-Bo!"

"Your turn, dude!" said Jack-O loudly in my ear, causing me to jump and scatter my cards. "Hey! Party foul!"

I scrambled to pick up the cards.

"Look alive, *Colon Boy!*" Hobab called over from the Scrabble game.

"Do you know where Shelby and Twain went?" I asked Jack-O as I scanned the cards in my hand, looking for one to discard.

"I don't know, the W.C.? Your turn, bro! You're holding up the show."

Where the heck were they???

Somehow, I managed to play the rest of the game. But I was so distracted, I ended up losing to Lah Kaw, who cackled in triumph.

"Victory! But I give rematch—if you dare!" he said with a grin, shuffling the cards under my nose.

"Rain check—I gotta go!" I said, under the pretense of needing to use the facilities. I grabbed the flashlight out of my daypack, and then slipped out of the bamboo hut and into the night.

"Don't forget Kleenex!" Ernestine called after me. Then to her fellow Scrabble players: "Wait a second! Kleenex! I can play that!"

Going. Going. GONE.

LET ME MAKE THIS CLEAR: I WASN'T *SPYING*, I was *chaperoning*. After all, Shelby was a vulnerable girl in the barbaric jungles of a war-torn nation in the clutches of a wannabe soldier who'd stop at nothing to achieve his desires—

Okay, okay.

I was jealous.

Pure and simple.

And, once again, it's not over until it's over.

I couldn't stand the not-knowing-for-sure-if-they-were-a-thing-or-not. After all, just because Shelby was temporarily *ticked* at me didn't mean she didn't *like* me. Then again, it didn't mean she *did* like me.

The not knowing was killing me.

I'd never be able to concentrate on anything else until I knew for sure, *without a shadow of a shadow of a shadow* of a doubt.

After using the squat toilet in the steamy outhouse—which was like going to the bathroom in a crockpot—I silently circled the compound, shining my flashlight into every dark nook and cranny. Other than the occasional cluster of sol-

271

diers smoking or lone villager strolling home, there was no one else to be seen. No one else, that is, named Shelby and Twain.

I was on the verge of heading back to the jungle mess to see if they'd returned during my absence, when I heard:

"Oh, Twain!" followed by distinctive laughter.

My ears pricked up like a pointer's. I rushed towards the source of those musical notes, down the dirt path to a clearing near the cluster of banana trees under which we'd met Jolly tearing out his toenails. I crept closer and closer under the cover of various trees and bushes until—

There they were.

Twain and Shelby sat side by side yet again on the wooden bench that wrapped around the trunk of a large palm tree, positioned against the very edge of the HQ property—their backs to the jungle, their faces to destiny. It was the very same bench where Shelby had comforted Twain after passing out— only this time Twain didn't have his head between his knees.

If only.

I thrust the obstructing palm leaves out of my face, but they ricocheted right back, one leaf lightly slicing the skin of my left cheekbone. I barely noticed.

The two of them nestled on the bench, Shelby perfectly fitting into Twain's side like a puzzle piece, the dark green jungle behind them providing sharp contrast with their pale forms. The moon was bright, so the shadows of the banana leaves were crisp against their faces. I figured if I could somehow sneak through the foliage directly *behind* them, I could observe them much more closely without being seen— and actually hear what the heck they were saying. So I crept stealthily—those now familiar sounds of the tropics (rustling bamboo, chirping cicadas, buzzing insects) more than masking any movements I made.

I plowed into the thick jungle, making a wide arc in order to eventually end up directly behind them. Carefully pushing aside the leaves and branches, my trekking shoes soundless on the dense floor of moss and ferns, I kept going until their silhouettes were semi-visible smack dab in front of me. Now I was in the right position—but unfortunately, about thirty feet away, unable to hear a single syllable.

So I inched forward as quietly as possible until I could just barely make out what they were saying.

"...no, don't rub it off," Twain was saying in a low voice.

Shelby continued wiping the *thanaka* off her face with a Kleenex. He grabbed her hand. "Leave it."

"Really?"

"Yeah, it does something for you." His voice, moving from low to downright husky, trailed off as he gently touched the tip of her nose. "Makes your eyes greener than green, your hair golder than gold..."

Plagiarist!

"What?" she said, transfixed.

He laughed. "Never mind."

"You mean *mai pen rai?*" She cocked her head and gave him an impish grin.

He laughed again and moved closer—if that were even possible. "What I'm really trying to say is that I've always, you know, liked you. But I didn't get *how much* until *now*. Seriously, since that day you peed your pants all over the welcome rug in kindergarten, and I gave you my blue sweatshirt to wear

273

around your waist until you got home, well, I've kinda had a thing for you, Shel—"

"Oh, Twain!"

His silhouette merged with hers.

My worst nightmare.

Unfolding in real time.

And I'm front and center.

After a muffled giggle, they finally broke apart. A shaft of moonlight highlighted their faces. There were now smudges of *thanaka* on Twain's nose and chin and forehead. Shelby seemed dazed as she touched her lips with her fingers.

I pressed closer, stepping over a clump of dead leaves, barely restraining myself from yelling something along the old school lines of, "Unhand her, you cur!" or even the more direct, Jack-O inspired, "Hand check!"

I could see Twain's arm muscles pressing against Shelby's woven fabric top, pulling her tighter and tighter against his chest… his long tanned fingers fondling those sacred golden curls…

My heart began to beat so rapidly and loudly that blood pounded in my ears.

Speak up! Step in! Do something!

But I was frozen.

And besides, what was I supposed to *do?* After all, he was doing exactly what I'd be doing in his place!

"Tut tut, Twain Abernathy!" said Shelby in a sing-song voice. "You're breaking *Expected Behavior Guideline Number One! No romantic entangle—*"

"Oh, I'll *entangle* you, Shelby Wanderal!"

I can't even begin to describe what this did to my insides.

A weed whacker would have done less damage.

When they finally broke apart:

"Uh, you know what?" Twain's throaty voice sounded slightly apologetic. "For the longest time, I thought you had a thing for Collin."

"*Collin?*" Shelby laughed.

For the second time that day, I felt walloped by Shelby. The incredulity and genuine amusement in her voice caused me more pain than anything in my life up to that point— including my combination nasal septum operation and tonsillectomy in seventh grade.

"Come on, don't act so surprised. Back home, you guys were always hanging out, swing dancing, watching old movies, stuff like that. And he's always talking about you and doing sappy things for you—like making that rock dog. Seriously, he's crushed so hard for you, Shel, it's dead obvious to everyone but you."

"Oh no, it's not what you think. I mean, we're best friends. Like how Courtney and I were before she moved. Actually, he's more like a—"

"Brother?"

"Totally! Like a brother."

"You mean a *little* brother." Twain made a gesture with his hand to indicate *short*. Then he started singing a children's song about some height challenged man that they both seemed to know. "*Zacchaeus was a wee little man, a wee little man was he…*"

They laughed.

I instinctively jerked backwards as if someone had stabbed me through in the heart.

Because someone did.

LOSER.

For now… *now* I knew *definitively* without a doubt that there was *no* hope.

NO HOPE.

No hope of dating Shelby. No hope of marrying Shelby. No hope of future little blond Shelbys drinking juice boxes and falling off play-structures. No hope of spending my last days with Shelby in Leisure World Retirement Community swing dancing in our orthopedic shoes.

NO HOPE.

My dream died.

I could see it wilting, crumbling into pieces, and scattering into the wind.

Going.

Going.

GONE.

For even if Twain wasn't in the picture, Shelby would *never* consider me dating material. *Never* see me as more than a best friend. Apparently, she *did* consider me awesome boyfriend material—for some *other* "some girl." But not for her. The mantel of truth dropped upon me as heavily as a death shroud.

"Sorry to break it to you, Shelby Wanderal," said Twain, in a voice now so low it was practically a rumble, "but I have more than a *brotherly* affection for you…"

Shelby giggled and Twain's arm wrapped more tightly around her waist. Her rapturous face tilted up once again towards his intense one. Suddenly, it was as if his frame swallowed hers up—he completely engulfed her!

Where are his hands?! WHERE ARE HIS HANDS!!!???

Twain said in his throatiest tone yet, "Oh, *Shel…* "

His lips covered hers once more.

My body lunged forward through the thick foliage. It didn't matter if *she* didn't want *me*—I didn't want *him* to have *her!*

As I surged, I yelled the first thing that came into my head. *"SKIP-BOOOOOOOOOO!!!!"*

Their stunned faces turned towards me, then—

BOOOOOM!

part five

THE GAP

??????

PAIN.

Fragments. Bits. Pieces. Various shapes and colors and hallucinations.

PAIN.

Distorted faces looming in at me.

PAIN, PAIN, and more PAIN.

BLOOD, BLOOD, and more BLOOD.

Lah Kaw the Backpack Medic bandaging up something on my body somewhere. The blurred faces of Shelby and Ernestine merging into one, streaked with *thanaka*, peering down at me. Wailing. Crying. Shouts. A sense of urgency.

A phrase echoed over and over in my ear: *"I told them to stay on the trail! I told them to stay on the trail! I told them to stay on the trail!"*

Numb. Physically and emotionally.

Later, I found myself lying on a mat in a dimly lit hut, staring straight up at a bamboo and leaf ceiling. Although my body was inert, my senses were alert:

A mosquito tiptoeing across my cheek…

People breathing nervously…

Someone's nostril hair whistling…

Pain pulsating through every tissue and nerve...

And a throbbing pain so intense in my left foot that I threw up—then passed out.

R.I.P.
(Rest in Pieces)

*J*OLLYJOLLYJOLLYJOLLYJOLLY

I blinked rapidly.

SORRYNEVERJOLLYEVER

The dark blue letters floated in front of my eyes, rippling in and out of focus.

JOLLYSORRYNEVEREVER

Then, finally, the letters settled down and became:

NEVER SORRY EVER JOLLY

After a few minutes, I realized the letters were tattooed on a brown muscular chest—and looked up into the hazy face of Jolly Mu.

"What hap…" I began, but trailed off. My dry, cracked lips stung.

"You had a little misfortune, my lad," said Jolly gravely, his dark eyes meeting mine. His kindly weathered face was strangely comforting.

I tried to sit up—and then gasped at the pain shooting through my left leg.

"Easy does it." Jolly gently pushed me back down on the damp mattress, which I realized was my own Therm-A-Rest and silk sleep sack. He handed me a water bottle with the lid already off.

With a shaky hand, I gripped the bottle and gulped down the contents, water streaming over my chin, down my neck, and soaking my already wet t-shirt.

I lay back. My eyes shifted towards my bandaged left foot, where most of the pain was localized. Then they shifted back towards Jolly's eyes behind his metal framed glasses. I stared at him mutely, willing him to answer the unasked.

"It was a landmine. You stepped on a landmine," said Jolly slowly, making sure I was tracking. "You're lucky to be alive, my lad."

"Land…mine…?" I racked my brain to recollect how on earth I'd been anywhere near a *landmine*. The last thing I remembered was playing Skip-Bo.

"You seemed to have lost your way back from the W.C.," said Jolly. "We found you beyond the HQ boundary line, in the no-go zone. You had us worried there for a minute—we thought you were a casualty of a BMJ surprise attack. Fortunately, it was a half-disintegrated landmine, otherwise you wouldn't be lying here talking to us now."

All at once it came flooding back: tracking down Shelby and Twain in the moonlight; hiding out in the dark foliage behind them; witnessing that kiss; and the most humiliating of all, *"Zacchaeus was a wee little man, a wee little man was he…"*

I winced—and not from physical pain.

Jolly smiled sympathetically. "It hurts like the dickens, doesn't it? We're working on getting you something stronger."

"But how… bad… is it?"

Part of me didn't want to know, but the other part

couldn't stand the suspense. What was the extent of the damage???

"So sorry, but you lose… you lose…" came Lah Kaw's disembodied raspy voice, somewhere behind me in the hut.

"Lose what? Lose *what!?*" I croaked, as panic welled up inside me. I tried to rise up from my mattress again, but the pain was too intense. My entire body felt pulverized. I felt frozen, then on fire, by turns. I tried to sense what I'd lost— but with everything throbbing and pulsating, it was impossible.

"Easy, easy now," said Jolly, putting a hand on my shoulder to gently yet firmly lay me back down.

I slowly craned my neck towards Jolly, and managed to blurt out: "What… did… I… *lose???*"

There was a brief silence.

I braced myself.

Jolly seemed about to speak, when:

"We very sorry, but your *kàw mu*, it is gone," said Lah Kaw, now materializing in front of me, carrying a tin tray covered with white gauze and tubes and ointments and syringes.

I stared at him uncomprehendingly. "My *what* is gone?"

Jolly shook his head sadly, "Bloody sight worse than fungus."

Alarm bells went off in my brain.

"You mean…?"

"Yes, your toe, it is gone."

"My toe," I said numbly.

"Yes, your *kàw mu*," said Lah Kaw. Although he said it sympathetically, he was all business as he pulled on latex gloves and began to gently unwrap the bandage on my left

285

foot—the foot that looked like a mummy.

"My toe? My *toe* is gone?" I fought the urge to laugh.

Jolly and Lah Kaw both nodded solemnly.

The whole thing seemed so completely nonsensical.

My *toe* was gone?

Any minute now, I'll wake up, I told myself.

Wake up, Collin, wake yourself up!

I closed my eyes. Then opened them. Nothing changed. Lah Kaw continued to remove the bandages on my foot, and Jolly continued to watch me expectantly.

"Which… which toe?" I asked as calmly as I could.

Lah Kaw paused the unwrapping, and looked at me. "The large one, he is not here."

"My *big toe!?*" I said, all calm evaporating. "You're talking about my *big toe!?*"

"Yes," said Lah Kaw, shaking his head sadly. "All gone. So gone."

"It blew to bits, don't you know," Jolly added helpfully.

It blew to bits.

My toe blew to bits.

"What else is gone? What about… my nose? *My nose!?*" I lifted shaking hands towards my face.

"No, no, your nose, he not gone. He still there. He fine. The small toe, they cut and hurt and burn, but still all there," said Lah Kaw. "And you have many bruise and—how do you say? *Lac-er-ate* from plastic and bamboo shard. Your leg have many, many red scar…"

My big toe exploding, fragments of skin and tissue and bone whizzing through the air, pelting the hut roofs like rain.

The imagery passed through my mind over and over again, as if on a continuous film loop.

"Want to see now?" asked Lah Kaw, removing the last of the bloody white cotton and gauze. "Or later?"

Dread washed over me.

My breath came in shallow rasps.

A hand squeezed my shoulder. "No harm in waiting, my lad."

A wave of relief rinsed the dread away.

I leaned back and closed my eyes.

Then my eyes flicked open of their own accord, and zeroed in on my left foot.

A bloody, scabby mess—with a GAP where my big toe had been.

Everything went black.

Excerpt from Shelby's Journal
July 9th

OH. MY. GOSH. OHMYGOSH OMYGOSH OMYGOSH. I still don't understand what just happened!!! We are all SO FREAKED OUT!!!! I don't blame Twain for passing out again—I mean, the BLOOD splattered all over us. I probably would have fainted, too, but I was too busy throwing up.

I can't help feeling that this was ALL MY FAULT. Ernestine said Collin has been IN LOVE with me since day one. DAY ONE! It ~~blew me away~~—I mean, really shocked me. Sure, I knew he liked me a lot as a friend, but he never seemed to take anything seriously, so I thought everything he said was sort of a JOKE. Like in those screwball comedies we both love.

Twain says I was BLIND. Even Jack-O says it was a 'no-brainer.' And if he says it, then I must have been completely OBLIVIOUS of the obvious!

But the three of them say I CAN'T BLAME MY-SELF. It was a TOTAL accident. (Easy to SAY–much harder to FEEL.)

* * *

Just came back from dinner. (Noodles–whew!)

NOW THAT I THINK ABOUT IT, deep, deep, deep down, in the deepest part of me, where I don't like to look, I kinda think I subconsciously knew Collin liked–loved–me. (!!!!!!) But that I didn't set him straight on my feelings, because finally here was a guy paying attention to me after ALL those years of Twain NOT. And Collin was SO MUCH fun to be around and we had so much in common–he was like my new best friend! Maybe deep down, I wondered that if I told him that he couldn't be my boyfriend, he wouldn't want to hang out anymore...? No more movie nights, swing dancing, or thrift store outings?

But maybe if I'd told Collin the truth, he'd still have his big toe.

Will he EVER forgive me?

A Casualty of Love

I'M NOT SURE EXACTLY WHAT KIND OF PAIN medication they administered, but it didn't work. The pain was so excruciating that I briefly lapsed into shock, letting things be done to me like an inert tilapia on a fishmonger's slab. My entire body throbbed and stung from the cuts, bruises, burns, and lacerations the landmine had inflicted—not just my left foot.

Apparently, I was "lucky" that Lah Kaw was stationed at the HQ that week. No one else had such extensive medical experience of treating injuries in primitive and hostile conditions. Although he looked like he should be fronting a rock band or racing a BMX in some extreme sport contest, he was super competent. He changed my bandages and oversaw my medical care, while Hobab and various soldiers took turns feeding me, giving me medicine, and helping me go to the bathroom in a series of buckets and plastic bowls. The pain was so intense I didn't mind the awkwardness.

I hadn't seen the Outreach Team since *it* happened. But I was fine with that. I couldn't handle their pity just yet.

Most of my thoughts were incoherent.

I felt shattered.

Raw.

Peeled like an apple.

Internally blown to bits.

I was incapable of processing anything. So it just hardened into an immovable lump inside me that grew and grew.

I did not feel like myself. Collin Uttley no longer existed. Someone new and lacking a big toe had taken his place. Someone with a GAP.

Now all I could think over and over again was *no toe... no toe... no toe...*

My moods were erratic.

One minute I'd be full of gray-black gloom.

Minutes later—dazed.

Then numb.

Then I'd bawl like a baby.

The next minute I'd laugh hysterically for no reason—freaking everybody out.

I was told I was "lucky" I hadn't lost my foot or leg or *life*. But it was impossible to shift my focus from what I *lacked* to what I *had*. Being *grateful* to be alive and mostly intact after a major trauma just wasn't doable.

At least not for me.

Never Sorry Ever Jolly? Riiiight...

It took a long time for the shock to completely wear off. The whirlwinds of injustice, pain, betrayal, anger, and horror blew unceasingly through my brain like a desert windstorm, and so overwhelmed me that I could barely form a coherent thought.

And any possibility of belief in a so-called Divine Being disappeared completely. After all, any God who would allow something like this to happen would have to be untrustworthy. Apathetic. Cruel.

Why do bad things happen to good people? I thought of Jolly. Never Sorry Ever Jolly. Despite all that happened to him and his people, he seemed to think his "God" was good and would ultimately work everything out for good.

I'm a good person and now I got no toe.

Does not compute.

Also, I had a reoccurring dream of me standing on one side of a huge ravine with a figure standing on the other side. I couldn't make out who it was. The gap prevented any access between us, because there was no bridge. In fact, as I stood there, the gap grew wider and wider and wider, until they disappeared from sight.

Did I think about Shelby Wanderal? *NO.* I blockaded her and Twain from my mind with a wall of mental bricks.

Did I think about my family and their future reactions? *NO.* I couldn't risk going down that path—I'd never find my way back.

To be honest, I blocked everything and everyone from penetrating my heart. I refused to relive the trauma. I was too injured and vulnerable to sustain even one more wound. I didn't have the mental bandwidth to process even one more feeling or experience.

My emotional capacity was zilch.

Actually, it was Gimlet who provided the most comfort. He would come and sit next to me in the hut, lean against the wall with that prosaic prosthesis of his stretched out in front of him, and do nothing but chew and spit betel nut. Did nothing. Said nothing. Just sat and chewed and spat pink streams into that battered plastic yellow cup. But for some reason, it consoled me.

My sense of time was out of whack, but it must have been around three days later, when Hobab was patiently feeding me spoonfuls of (what I hoped was chicken) broth, when the thought struck me.

"Do my parents know about...?" I gestured feebly towards my left foot.

Hobab refilled the spoon. "Dad got a call through to Jongchit right after it happened, so she called the Tacketts and had them call your parents to give them the lowdown. But you'll probably have to wait to talk to them yourself until you get back to the Thai side—the reception sucks over here. It's been scrambled since... since..." He trailed off uncomfortably, fighting back tears. A moment later, in a half angry, half grieving tone, he blurted out: "Why didn't you listen when I told everybody to stay out of the jungle?! What the heck were you doing? 'Guys, stay on the trail,' I said. 'Guys, don't go into the jungle—'"

"It's not your fault," I interrupted, waving my hand weakly. "I was like a kid running into traffic. Wasn't thinking."

Hobab looked stricken, then mortified at what he'd just said. "Sorry! Sorry! Man, I'm so sorry! I didn't mean—"

"No, seriously. I'm the dunderhead here." No one else needed to suffer for my idiotic error of judgment. Enough harm had been done.

He wiped his eyes and managed a smile.

At least one of us felt better.

After swallowing more broth, I asked, "So when can I return to Thailand?"

"You gotta wait until you're stable enough to cross the Murk. Don't worry, dude. Lah Kaw is doing all he can for your foot until we can get you back. You're *lucky* he's here."

That word again.

"But where are the Tacketts and Jongchit? Shouldn't they be here by now?"

He didn't respond.

"Hobab?"

He seemed reluctant to answer me. "Uh, well, dude, turns out that your landmine kinda created some... *confusion*. The Thai Border Control heard it and thought the war was on again and clamped down on any border crossings for awhile."

"Is that the *real* reason I can't go back?" I tried not to panic.

"Chill, man." Hobab gave me a reassuring smile. "It's gonna be okay. Dad's trying to work something out with the Border Control so Jongchit and Wigglewurts can cross over here to—"

"But what about the Tacketts?"

He shrugged. "They're still in Bangkok ordering room service."

"What? You're kidding!"

"Nope. The red tape takes forever in Thailand." Hobab set down the empty bowl and handed me a pigmy banana. "You ready for visitors yet? The Team's totally dying to see you, man. How about after your nap?"

My stomach sank.

I wanted to refuse, but knew I couldn't put it off forever.

So Jacked Up!

FOUR PAIRS OF EYES STARED AT ME—EMERALD, dark brown, gray, and Toblerone.

"He's awake!"

"Sssshhh! You don't want to freak him out."

Silence.

Staring.

A nervous cough.

Then the gentle voice of Shelby: "Collin? Collin, can you hear me?"

The Outreach Team was clustered around my Therm-A-Rest, looking down at me, their faces anxious and sympathetic.

I gazed up at them mutely.

My body felt like it had been jammed through a paper shredder then ineptly taped back together by a five-year-old. Every expanse of skin, every tissue, every sinew, every tendon, every muscle throbbed with pain—even more than the last time I was conscious, if that were even possible. After a couple of moments, I rolled my eyes to catch a glimpse of my left foot—I was in too much pain to risk even moving my head. To my extreme relief, it was fully bandaged. Another view of The Gap would have sent me over the edge.

Shelby, Twain, Ernestine, and Jack-O stared at me awkwardly in the silent semi-circle I'd been dreading all along, not knowing what to say or where to look. Hobab remained in the background, leaning against the hut wall, tossing one of those woven rattan balls from hand to hand. A *longyi* covered me from the waist down. The Team darted covert looks at my bandaged left foot protruding out from under it—that is, except for Twain, who stared straight ahead as if he had blinders on.

I tensed for the landslide of emotions that seeing Shelby again would trigger. But, strangely, as I gazed into her glistening green eyes—I felt nothing. Absolutely nothing.

I was numb.

I zeroed in on Jack-O's light blue t-shirt.

I'M NOT LAZY BUT I'M FUN

Those yellow letters made about as much sense as my life did right then.

I'M NOT LAZY BUT I'M FUN

I squinted my eyes and watched the letters blur together… Wasn't it a decade ago he bought that shirt at the Thai market?

"Jesus!" exclaimed Ernestine in a higher octave than normal. She dug a Kleenex out of her pocket and blew her nose so violently her silver rings clinked together.

Shelby's face was taut and pale, and she nervously twisted something in her hands. After a couple moments, I realized it was my 1950s Knox straw fedora. When she saw I'd noticed it, she handed it to me. Sweat stained, misshapen, tattered around the edges, more beige than white, and emitting a strangely musty odor—yet mine just the same.

She managed a trembling smile and said with forced enthusiasm, "I thought you'd feel more like your old *vintage* self with it..." Then she trailed off as I slowly lifted the hat and placed it on top of my head. At the sight, she abruptly burst into tears. "I'm sorry, Collin! I promised myself I wasn't going to cry..." She turned away.

In response, I slowly leaned over and removed something from the backpack next to my mattress. After a moment, I handed it to Shelby, my eyes averted. "Here."

"My scarf?" Shelby said in surprise as she looked down at the cherry sprigged yellow fabric in her hand.

"You dropped it."

"When?"

"Oh, a while ago now..."

After a moment's hesitation, Twain awkwardly reached out and gripped my shoulder. Although it killed, I forced myself not to flinch. His gray eyes met mine. They were humble and sympathetic—and moist. "Man, Collin, this is so—"

"TOTALLY JACKED UP!" bellowed Jack-O indignantly. "IT'S FREAKIN' NUTS!"

"Sssshhhh!" said Shelby and Ernestine together, nudging him with their elbows.

"Sorry, dude," said Jack-O in a quieter tone, running his hand through his blue-black spikes. "It's just so... so... so... *lame*. Sorry! I mean, it totally sucks."

But for some reason, Twain's and Jack-O's responses did something to me. It felt cathartic to have others upset on my behalf.

"Can we pray for you?" whispered Ernestine in an almost

inaudible tone, as if speaking any louder would somehow damage me further.

"Later?" If they tried anything like that right now, I'd start bawling like a baby. And besides, what was the point?

Ernestine retracted her hand.

I knew then that I'd have to be strong enough for all of us. They needed me to "be okay," so they could feel less guilty for being the survivors. Survivor guilt. I had to play the role that so many injured and dying had played before.

I managed another half smile, and said thickly, "If you think this is gonna stop me swinging, you got another thing comin'." As cheesy as it sounded, they all visibly relaxed.

"We're here for you, bro!" said Jack-O impulsively. "You name it, we'll do it!"

"How does your foot, you know, *feel?*" asked Twain, leaning forward with curiosity.

Shelby and Ernestine gave him reproachful looks.

"Sorry, you don't have to answer that," he added quickly.

I shifted, sending streaks of pain throughout my body. "Well, I can still feel *it.* My... my toe. I know that sounds weird, but Jolly said it was normal. He called it the... the Phantom Limb Syndrome." It wasn't my voice, it was someone else's—flat and distant. The only way to speak about my toe, was to divorce myself from emotion.

The Great Divide.

"You mean the Phantom *Toe* Syndrome?" said Jack-O with a chuckle. "Sounds like an old *Scooby Doo* episode." Then he said abruptly, "Sorry, man. Didn't mean to joke about it."

I managed a weak smile.

"But at least it's just your big toe," he continued, "and

you're not missing a couple limbs or totally dead—"

"Jack-O!" Ernestine and Shelby exclaimed in horrified unison.

"Sorry, dude, sorry! I keep sticking my foot in it—" He stopped. "There, see? Did it again!"

I gestured limply with a finger as if to say, "It's all right." Then I said, "You guys were right when you thought I acted like I was from a different planet. I'm not one of you. I only came on this trip to, well… I mean, I'm not even a… I don't even believe in…"

They smiled and nodded at me sympathetically, probably feeling it was healthy for me to express my feelings.

I took a deep breath. "I… don't… believe… in… God."

They continued to smile and nod sympathetically.

"Did you hear what I said? *GOD. DOES. NOT. EXIST.*" Then, when they still didn't seem to be catching on—I lost it and let loose with a geyser of profanity that rivaled Twain's after his run-in with Needle and Frito.

When I'd finally finished spewing, I noticed they were still smiling and nodding sympathetically—but now kindly patting me on the back and shoulders.

"Get some rest, dude," said Jack-O, ruffling my hair.

"Yeah, you'll feel way better in the morning," said Ernestine in an artificially bright voice.

"You're just not yourself, Collin," added Shelby.

Of Course I'm Not Myself! I wanted to shout. *I'm Collin With A BLOODY GAP!* But by then, I was too tired to speak any longer—much less argue. I was already drained from their visit. So I closed my eyes and pretended to sleep. My sole survival tactic.

Silence.

A sniffle.

An uncomfortable cough.

Another sniffle.

The sound of someone passing gas.

"Jack-O!"

"Hey, it wasn't me!" Jack-O sounded indignant. "Ewww! It reeks!"

"Sorry," said Ernestine sheepishly. "The roughage here just doesn't agree with me…"

After a few more whispers and sniffles, the Outreach Team moved towards the door of the hut. Despite their low tones, I could still hear them clearly.

"He seems so… so *dismal*," whispered Ernestine.

"Do you think he's really lost his faith because of this?" asked Shelby, trying to keep the tremor out of her voice.

"Man, talk about *Extreme You*," said Jack-O.

"Don't worry, guys, he's so messed up he just can't think straight right now," said Twain.

"Yeah, Lah Kaw thinks it's ASR," said Hobab.

"What's that?" asked Ernestine.

"Acute Stress Reaction," said Twain in a low tone.

"Or it could be PTSD—Posttraumatic Stress Disorder," whispered Hobab. "There's this dude in one of the border clinics, who's an expert on amputations and landmine trauma. He'll know how to treat Collin."

And on that note, the Outreach Team silently filed out.

I started to open my eyes, but quickly shut them when I heard someone reenter the hut.

They walked over to me and paused.

After a moment, I felt something gently placed on my stomach.

Then the footsteps shuffled out.

Alone at last.

I opened my eyes to behold... Rock Flounce.

I cried like a baby.

Excerpts from the Journal of Collin Uttley
(FYI: edited for content)

July 12th – They told me journaling would help me process, come to terms with what happened, and heal. ALL LIES. I've never felt more ticked off in my life. And writing about it just fuels the flame. Accentuates the random-ness and purposeless of life. (And death.) I'm ticked off at losing my toe. I'm ticked off at God for not existing. I'm ticked off at Shelby for choosing Twain. I'm ticked off at Twain for choosing Shelby.

Everything seems flat and meaningless and gray.

All I want to do is sleep.

July 13th – Lah Kaw wants me to get up and move around a bit, to get used to how to navigate and bal-ance without a big toe. He made crutches out of bam-boo and duct tape. Awkward and painful and embarrass-ing. If I thought I was ticked off before...

It's insane just how much you need a big toe for balance. That whole youth group analogy about how every single part of the human/church body is important, and if you're missing a pinky or an ear, you'll really notice the difference—well, now it makes *much* more sense.

Does this mean I'm going to be getting a FAKE TOE!?!

Dreading the day when I'll have to face my parents, my brothers—the world. Being an object of pity for the rest of my life.

July 14th - The Team continues to feel guilty they weren't injured and keep trying to cheer me up.
Shelby: "I can't wait to cut the rug with you when you're better."
Me: "I'll never dance again."
Shelby: "But you said your injury wouldn't stop you from swinging...?"
Me: "Don't believe anything I say."
Ernestine: "You will so dance again, you big Eeyore!"
Me: "Excuse me, but I think I'll go nap."

July 15th - I'm DONE. Decided it's time to tell the Team the *whole* truth and nothing but. After all, what the heck do I have left to lose?

Confession Is Good for the Soul (If You Have One)

I DECIDED TO CONFESS AFTER WE'D WASHED but before we went to bed. That is, after the rest of the Team had separated into guys and girls, tied on *longyis*, and took turns dousing themselves with water scooped from a square, cement reservoir. I'd opted out. That kind of movement was still way too painful and required at least two others to assist me. So "washing" for me meant swabbing myself with a bunch of Wet-Naps.

The Team now sat on a raised sleeping platform next to the row of individual nylon pup tents that Jongchit had sent with us, thinking it would be much more convenient than mosquito netting. The Team agreed with the convenience of the tents, but said they were like marinating in your own sweat—said I was "lucky" I still slept in the hut. (If I heard that word just one more time...) From the platform, we could view the rapid brown currents of the Murk and the smudge of green on the opposite bank. In the far distance, I could just barely make out a long-tailed boat full of mollusk-hatted locals cruising up the river. But dusk was falling and soon we wouldn't be able to see a foot in front of our faces.

The tangy smell of sunscreen and bug spray mingled with the pungent smoke from a village fire where someone was roasting more mystery meat. At the opposite end of the platform, two soldiers swung in hammocks with M-16s resting across their chests, chatting in low tones, and smoking endless Marlboros. I leaned against a wooden pillar, bamboo crutches beside me and left leg stretched out in front of me, my foot still encased in the mummy-like bandage.

Ernestine had called the T.D.T.—Team Debriefing Time—so they could pray for my toe. However, little did they know I had a completely different agenda. I glanced around the circle at each familiar face. Despite their recent wash, they made a motley group. Their shirts and pants were dingy, stained with sweat and dirt. Shelby and Ernestine had stopped applying makeup days ago, and their faces wore a perpetual sheen. A piece of Katin fabric made into a scarf now covered Shelby's matted curls, and Ernestine's hair was less "fire" and more "pilot light." Twain's stubble had sprung into a full-fledged beard, and even Jack-O's chin and jaws were lightly peppered with black hairs. Both Shelby and Twain had red sunburn and peeling noses. And Jack-O had finally scored a *longyi*, which did make him pass for a local— make that a local with access to a whole lot more food than the rest.

The Team's combined body odor created a musky scent that was overpowering—even when seated upwind.

"All right, guys," said Ernestine, "time to lay hands on Collin." She smiled at me, flashing her dimples. "We're not taking 'no' for an answer this time—"

"I don't need you to pray. I need you to listen," I said in a flat tone. I rubbed my jaw—which was also becoming increasingly furry.

Pre-explosion, they probably would have protested, but post-explosion they just (yep) smiled encouragingly and waited. They'd been treating me as if I was Baccarat crystal for days—and I was sick of it.

A gecko rapidly climbed up the pillar, making clicking noises as he went. The Team members watched him disappear from sight, then shifted their mildly curious gazes to me. Although I was about to expose myself, I felt absolutely nothing. Once again, I was divorced from my emotions, as if everything was happening to another Collin Uttley up on stage and I watched from the audience.

All eyes were on me.

Now's the moment you've all been waiting for...

"I'm not one of you. I'm a piece of—I'm an imposter. I lied on my application, I lied to the Tacketts, and I've been lying to all of you this whole time. I came on this trip for one reason and one reason only..." I nodded curtly toward Shelby. "And by now, you all know why."

Shelby shifted uncomfortably. "It's okay, Collin, you don't have to say any—"

"There's more." I glanced at Twain, who seemed to sense where I was going with this. "You've probably guessed already, but I was dead serious when I said I didn't believe in God. That wasn't just the pain or the meds talking. I'm really not one of you. I'm *not* a believer. Never was. I was raised an atheist. God the Father, God the Son, and God the Holy Spirit were just the fictional subjects of Renaissance paintings and Russian triptychs in my extra credit homeschool art class.

I mean, sure, it's conceivable that a man existed named Jesus who had a thing for carving end-tables, but not that he was 'divine.' He's just a swear word—one I've been trying not to say this whole time."

They stared at me mutely.

I quickly added, "I *wish* I could believe, but my mind just won't let me. Sorry."

Silence.

Then Twain nodded. "I figured."

"Same here," said Ernestine with a shrug and a sympathetic smile. "After a while it was pretty obvious."

But Shelby and Jack-O stared at me with slightly hurt, shocked expressions.

"You mean you never asked Jesus into your heart at junior high camp?" asked Jack-O peering incredulously at me through his smudged lenses.

"Pure fabrication," I replied dully. "One of many."

"Oh, wow," murmured Shelby. Her eyes fell from my face to her lap.

I don't know what I expected after dropping my truth bombshell, but all I felt now was anticlimax and a skid mark of sadness.

They all just sat there, not quite meeting my eye.

Somewhere in the night a stray dog yipped.

"Dinner?" quipped Twain, trying to break the tension. Then, with a quick glance at Shelby, he added: "Kidding, kidding."

"Well," I said, gasping as I painfully pulled myself up with the aid of the bamboo crutches, "I'd better get back to my hut. Don't want to further taint you with my pagan presence."

"Dude! You mean you planned *all this*, went through *all this*—just for *Shelby???*" Jack-O burst out. "*Shelby?!* Shell-Bell with the Powderpuff Girls lunchbox and gummies???"

"Hey, man, that's harsh," said Twain, shifting uncomfortably.

Jack-O turned to Shelby. "No offense, but no girl is worth that!"

After a momentary flicker of hurt, Shelby nodded. "Yeah, you're right. I was so not worth it."

I gave her a half smile. "Now ya tell me…"

"Oh, Collin!" said Shelby, her freckled face crumpling.

And before I knew what was happening, the Team surrounded me and encased me in a group hug—a big sweaty, smelly group hug.

"We love you, man!" Jack-O bellowed in my ear.

Someone gave me a head noogie.

And someone had extra-pungent B.O. that would have made my eyes water—if I wasn't crying already.

As the Team helped me off the platform so I could return to my hut, Ernestine gave me a squeeze and whispered, "You'll always be one of us."

Excerpts from the Journal of Collin Uttley

(FYI: edited for content)

July 15th – (LATER) I confessed, so why do I still feel like a total pantload? (As Jack-O would say.) I'll never forgive myself for lying to a group of people who—it turns out—really <u>do</u> care about me. And then there's the whole toe thing. If God exists (which obviously he doesn't) then this is his stern rebuke. His biblical way of teaching me a lesson. Which I'm sure I completely deserve, but it sucks all the same.

God is *not* love.

God is LOATHE.

He loathes me.

I loathe myself.

Why didn't he just blow me up while he was at it?

part six

CRAZYTOWN

Guess Who?!

I JOURNALED IN MY HUT UNTIL I FELT TIRED—
make that *depressed*—enough to sleep. I eased myself down
on my Therm-A-Rest and tried to remember the last time I
took my pain meds. The next thing I knew, I was jolted out
of a deep sleep by boisterous laughter and babbling voices.

"*Sawatdee kha!*"

"We have arrive!"

"*Sabaidee mai?*"

Before I could figure out what time it was or even *where* I
was, a cluster of village women wearing *longyis* and woven
bamboo mollusk hats, swarmed around me! They peered
down at me and examined my left foot.

"Who…? Wha…?"

"Prayer time, Colon Boy!" one of the village woman an-
nounced as she whisked off her conical hat to reveal she was
the one and only Jongchit!

The rest of the "village women" removed their hats to reveal the Wigglewurts in all their glory! There was old
Patcharee grinning at me, her gray hair flattened into a helmet
by the bamboo hat, and pint-size Noi teetering on her stiletto
heels!

"Surprise!" shouted the Wigglewurts.

313

Then they dug around in their backpacks, and within seconds, the air was fluttering with multi-colored silk flags! They danced and waved them around me with robust enthusiasm! Some twirled one flag and others, like Noi, twirled two. I spotted Ernestine Ketchum in rumpled shorts and her pink Hello Kitty t-shirt hovering in the doorway, and desperately motioned her over.

"What's… what's going on…?" I could barely get the words out, my throat was so dry. "How did they even get here?"

"Colon Boy not come to Jongchit, so Jongchit come to Colon Boy!" exclaimed Jongchit before Ernestine could answer. Her face hovered over mine like a pale dirigible. She seemed to be trembling with anticipation or excitement. I couldn't tell which—after all, I wasn't even sure that this wasn't all just a dream.

"*Kha, kha!*" The ladies all eagerly bobbed their heads and whirled the silk flags in the air.

"We dress like local and putt-putt-putt right past check point! Thai Border Patrol think we farm lady!" Jongchit chortled with glee.

"*Kha, kha!* Work in rice paddy!" added Patcharee.

The Wigglewurts seemed to think that was especially hilarious. They laughed and fluttered.

I stared at them. Were they the "locals" I'd seen in that long-tail boat on the Murk River?

"But why are you *here*? And why aren't I *there*?" I didn't mean to be a jerk about it, but I was exhausted—and in pain.

"How your foot today, Colon Boy?" said Jongchit.

In response, I gave a startled wheeze—for she was gently

and slowly removing the bandages that covered The Gap, my non-toe.

This is an ambush! An invasion of my physical and personal space, and I'm not going to just lie here and be prayed for by a group of crazies with fabric swatches!

I clenched my jaw and hissed through gritted teeth, "Lah Kaw said I was supposed to wait for the border clinic doctor—"

"We your doctor now!" Patcharee chortled, clapping her hands in glee.

"Hal-le-lu-jah! Hal-le-lu-jah! Hallelujah! Hallelujah! Hal-le-lu-jah!"

One of the Wigglewurts strummed Shelby's ukulele and another shook a tambourine with more zest than skill, as they warbled the *Hallelujah Chorus* from *Handel's Messiah.*

A scarlet silk flag tickled my cheek.

The tambourine rattled in my ear.

My stomach began to sink.

How much more humiliation will I have to take!? Isn't losing my future girlfriend AND my big toe enough for one week?!? And now I have to lose my self respect as well!?!

The other Wigglewurts surrounded me, a giggle here and a flutter there, as I laid on my Therm-A-Rest, staring up at them in disbelief. Patcharee was particularly enthusiastic with her orange flag, whipping it around my face with gusto—so much so, she almost sliced my cornea. It reminded me of my meeting with Shelby and Flounce and the Outreach Trip flyer—how long ago that seemed! (And how *sane* compared to this!)

"For the Lord! God! Om! Nip! Po! Tent! Reign! Eth!" they gamely warbled on.

"The time has come, Colon Boy!" said Jongchit hovering over me. "God say last night we must come here today and pray for you ASAP like Smitt Wigglewurt! For God want to heal your toe *now!*"

Right.

Some big and distant Being cares enough about __me__ to send a bunch of whacked, healing-obsessed women into the danger zone specifically to pray for my __toe__.

"But I don't believe. I don't believe *at all*. You're wasting your time," I said thickly, hoping they'd cut it short and leave.

Jongchit chuckled. "No worry. We believe for you."

I gestured towards the flags and ukulele. "What's… what's all this for?"

Jongchit smiled. "We praise God for what he do before he do it."

"That called faith," said Noi primly.

I deliberately switched topics. "But where's Hobab? Lah Kaw? Jolly? The rest of the Team?"

"Team sleep like baby-baby," said Patcharee with a chuckle and a swish of her orange flag.

"Especially Pickle Head," said Jongchit with a laugh.

"He rumble like monster truck!" said Noi primly as she rocked on her heels and expertly twirled her two purple flags.

"And scare bird away!" laughed Patcharee.

"But we have Mangosteen! She good girl. She ask to pray with Wigglewurt," said Jongchit, jabbing a startled Ernestine with her elbow. "She have much, much faith."

"Faith for what?" I asked suspiciously.

"Mai pen rai," said Jongchit, with a sly smile.

"Kha, kha! Mangosteen have faith for whole army!" chortled Patcharee.

"Maybe... maybe you wish it was Shelby here with you," said Ernestine in a subdued voice, fiddling with the grommet in her ear.

"No!" It burst out before I could stop it.

Ernestine looked pleased.

"Why don't you start with one of the Feebs?" I asked Jongchit in desperation. "Shouldn't soldiers have first priority? Like Jolly! Hello! He's got fungus!"

Jongchit just chuckled, shaking her head in amusement. "One at a time, Colon Boy. One at a time. We get to soldier and orphan next. But for some reason, God say to start with *you.*"

"We no argue with God!" said Patcharee as she thrust the orange flag at Ernestine, then pulled out a large brown glass bottle from her backpack and handed it to Jongchit.

"What's that?" I edged away, my suspicions multiplying.

Ernestine sensed my rising panic and laid her hand on my shoulder. "It's totally gonna be okay, Collin. Trust me on this one." She smiled, flashing those deep dimples, and gave me a wink as she waved Patcharee's orange flag over me. "Besides, what's the worst that could happen?"

I managed a rasping laugh. "Don't get me started—"

"Oil," interrupted Jongchit, holding the bottle high. "For we anoint you, Colon Boy, and pray for healing! *Kha, kha!"* She put a restraining hand on my other shoulder as if to prevent me from sprinting for the door.

"We go for healing for you!" said Patcharee with glee,

snatching her flag back from Ernestine. "You no need flag. Use that." She pointed at Ernestine's red-orange-yellow hair.

"But—but the bleeding has already stopped! And it's all cauterized and Lah Kaw said it was healing fine and that once the swelling went down…" I trailed off at the disconcerting gleam in her eye.

"Wigglewurt!" Jongchit turned and addressed the ladies in rapid-fire Thai. In an instant, they surrounded me. I felt hands everywhere—on my head, neck, shoulders, arms, right leg, and even—ever-so-gently—on my left foot.

Jongchit grasped my chin and looked deep into my eyes. She spoke slowly and carefully, over-enunciating each word. *"Co-lon, Co-lon, list-en to me now.* Listen up! *Listen, listen, listen!* In book of James, it say if people sick, put oil on them, pray, and they be heal. Understand?"

"James 5:14," murmured Ernestine in my ear.

I nodded mutely—as best as I could with Jongchit's hand still firmly grasping my chin, pushing my cheeks together and lips out like a puffer fish.

"Now time for to anoint you…" Jongchit prayed rapidly in Thai as she smeared oil on my forehead and, once again, ever-so-gently on my left foot.

What was that smell? It reminded me of the market stalls…

"Sesame?" Ernestine sniffed my forehead. "Sesame oil?" She turned to Jongchit in confusion. "Aren't you supposed to use anointing oil—"

"Same same. All oil work same," said Jongchit briskly. Then she placed one hand on my head and one hand on my left foot—and began praying so intensely it sounded like groaning. The rest of the Wigglewurts did the same. Some began to sob and wail. Ernestine's hand was still on my shoulder—but gripping it more tightly. I could feel her silver rings digging into my shoulder, and hear her praying softly under her breath.

Jongchit shifted in and out of English, Thai, Katin, and some other language that I couldn't identify.

I wanted to laugh at the absurdity of it all, but suddenly I felt lightheaded and woozy. Like after swallowing the betel nut. I started to experience tunnel vision.

"*For! The! Lord! God! Om! Nip! Po! Tent! Reign! Eth!*" warbled the ladies.

Swish, swish! Went the flags.

"Grow! Grow! GROW!!!" thundered Jongchit.

And the ladies prayed and sang and sobbed on... and on... and on... *and on! Why wasn't anyone rescuing me from this insanity???*

The ruckus must be waking the entire HQ!

This is totally ridiculous and humiliating! I'm not standing for any more of this!

Right as I opened my mouth to yell "Stop!"—unexpected warmth began oozing across my body. Warmth that blazed into intense heat on my left foot. Then my entire body began to tremble—face, shoulders, arms, fingers, and remaining toes began vibrating. Slowly at first, then faster and faster. I couldn't stop them from moving! No matter how hard I tried to control myself, I couldn't. In fact, the more I attempted to stiffen my limbs, the more dramatically I shook!

What the heck is going on?!?!? Why am I shaking!?!?

Jongchit broke off mid-prayer and boomed at me: "Relax!

Relax! Must relax and let Holy Spirit do his work!"

"Hal-le-lu-jah! Hal-le-lu-jah! Hallelujah! Hallelujah! Hal-le-lu-jah!"

One of the flag waving ladies danced over to me, whirled her flag over me, then burst out with, *"Jesus God kha kha!"* so vehemently that I was sprayed with spittle.

"Amen! Mister Jesus! Mister Jesus, we love you!" croaked Patcharee.

"Kha, kha! Peuang di!" said Noi. "So good friend to us, Jesus!"

"We want your miracle, Mister Jesus! Like blind man, leper man, dead girl!" yelled Jongchit.

Whip-whip-whip! Swish-swish-swish! Swathes of silk fabric grazed my head and billowed above me in a rainbow of pink, purple, blue, red, orange, yellow, and green.

I'm hallucinating! It's the pain meds and malaria pills and ARS and PTSD __and__ betel nut all rolled into one! EXTREME YOU!!! That's what it is!!! Why didn't the yellow handout cover insane international women who think they're Smith Wigglesworth!?!

Abruptly, all the Wigglewurts clustered around my left foot. Every single hand was now on my left foot and leg, which was shaking so hard I thought it would haul off and smack one of them in the face.

Jongchit turned to Ernestine. "Mangosteen! Hand on wound, hand on wound!"

"Me?" Ernestine's mouth dropped open. Her hand had remained on my shoulder the entire time, gripping it so firmly in solidarity that her rings indented my skin.

Jongchit nodded her head ferociously. *"Kha, kha,* YOU, Mangosteen! God say Mangosteen lay hand on foot!"

"*Kha, kha,* YOU!" echoed Noi and Patcharee and the other ladies in unison, with definitive slashes of their silk flags.

After prolonged prodding from the Wigglewurts, Ernestine removed her shaking hand from my shoulder and placed it tentatively on the very end of my foot—on The Gap.

That instant, an electric shock pulsated through my entire body! Before I had time to react, there was another jolt! And another! And another! One right after another—currents of electricity racing through my veins! ZAP! ZAP! ZAP! It was as if I'd grabbed a live electric wire!

"I'm hurting him!" said Ernestine in a panic, and began to remove her hand.

"No! Stay, Mangosteen, stay!" said Jongchit with glee, clamping her hand over Ernestine's. "God send healing fire! Fire from Heaven!"

Ernestine watched me tentatively as the electricity continued to zap and jolt my entire body. My eyes and cheeks and mouth involuntarily contorted in pain and shock with each onslaught of power.

I was on the verge of passing out, when for the first time in my life I felt an urgency to pray—*pray* pray, not fake pray. My teeth were reverberating so violently, I couldn't speak audibly—but I could still cry out mentally: *God, IF you actually exist, what the heck is going on!?! Why am I being electrocuted??? This is way out of control! I am out of control! I can't stop shaking! Is this really you, God? Or is this some sort of dream? Or nightmare? Or are Jongchit and her friends completely bonkers? Or wait—am I the one who's bonkers???*

An especially powerful electric jolt ripped through my body, causing me to burst out: "MY GOD!"

Suddenly, there was an explosion of light and I was somewhere else.

I was not in the hut.

I was not on my Therm-A-Rest.

I was standing—STANDING! I was standing on BOTH feet! I looked down and, yes! There was my old friend, Mr. Big Toe, back in place on my left foot!

Then I looked up—where the heck was I?

In a bright hallway with terra cotta tile and white stucco walls, apparently. Through a recessed window in the wall, I could see blobs of green and an expanse of blue outside. Nature?

Well, wherever I was, it sure was no dream.

Just then, I heard swift footsteps coming up behind me. Before I could turn around—

"Ooof!" I was tackled to the floor!

My assailant jumped up, laughing. "Collin! You made it!"

I scrambled to my feet. A man stood there, grinning down at me, panting slightly. It was a happy face with a beard and laugh lines crinkling around his eyes and—was that a dimple? Or just a shadow? After a moment, he reached out and slapped me lightly on the arm.

"Tag! You're it!"

Then he whirled around—and raced down the hallway!

I stared after him, stupefied.

That can't be… that can't actually be…

"Slowpoke!"

Suddenly, I knew.

I didn't have to be told.

I just *knew* it was *him*. The certainty instantly downloaded into my brain. That guy running away from me was *Jesus!* The Carver of End-Tables! He was REAL! And he'd tagged me! He'd actually *tagged* me!

"You remember how to do it, right? Put one foot in front of the other...?"

And now he was mocking me! With a (wait for it) *twinkle* in his eye!

This was Jesus?

I'd never pictured Jesus as a prankster who would tackle you, but more as a solemn "about to be crucified" pale Jesus, with dark circles under his eyes and a golden halo over his head.

Right then, something unfamiliar and euphoric bubbled up inside of me, and that old Christmas carol, *Joy to the World, the Lord is Come* started ringing in my ears.

Running down the hallway ahead of me was *Lord Joy himself*—apparently in the middle of recess.

"Wait up!" I yelled and sprinted after him.

He paused to turn and grin at me. "Don't worry, Collin. It'll come out all right."

Then he was gone.

The bright hallway was gone.

And I was back in the hut.

Shrimp Stir Fry

THE FIRST THING I SAW WAS *TWAIN* KNEELING at the end of my Therm-A-Rest, videotaping my foot—and he wasn't passing out! Before I could fully process this, I noticed Shelby next to me, crying so hard she was laughing, shakily snapping photos with her digital camera.

"*Oh, my gosh-oh, my gosh-oh, my gosh!*" she gasped.

"GOD, YOU ROCK! YOU ARE SO FREAKIN' AWE-SOME!!!" boomed Jack-O's voice in my ear. I turned to see him bouncing up and down on the balls of his feet, waving four silk flags furiously above my head, two in each hand, like some sort of oversize drum majorette! "GOD, YOU BRING IT, MAN! YOU SO BRING IT!"

Slish! Slash! Slish! Slash!

Every Wigglewurt—and *every flag*—was still present and accounted for.

What was going on in here??? How long had I been out, anyway???

I wanted to share what I'd just experienced, but the pain in my left foot and leg was excruciating. *Worse* than before—if that was even possible!

Jongchit's gleaming face abruptly appeared, inches away from mine. Sweat from her forehead mingled with tears on her cheeks.

"Colon, look! LOOOOOOK!!!"

She abruptly pushed aside Shelby and a couple Wigglewurts to give me a perfect view. The perfect view of…

…my big toe.

My big toe growing out.

I repeat: MY BIG TOE GROWING OUT.

MY BIG TOE GROWING OUT!!!!!!!!

For once Ernestine was not exclaiming—she was staring dumbfounded at my toe, her hand still on my foot. Surrounding her, the Wigglewurts rejoiced at the top of their lungs, Patcharee boisterously banged the tambourine against the hut wall, and Noi furiously strummed Shelby's ukulele with her tiny fingers, continuing to lead them in Handel's *Messiah*.

"*Hal-le-lu-jah! Hal-le-lu-jah! Hallelujah! Hallelujah! Hal-le-lu-jah!*"

"*Oh, my gosh! Ohmygosh! Ohmygosh!*" Shelby intoned breathlessly in my ear.

The toe—if you could call the white mass a toe—was extending just fast enough to be perceptible to the human eye. The new skin was very white and smooth. You could see the blue veins faintly underneath.

A shard of toenail glimmered.

I couldn't believe it. How could I?

This had to be a dream—maybe I'd gone from one dream to another dream within a dream.

But—the pain was so intense that I almost passed out. And the shocks and zaps continued to come in waves.

"Jesus! Jesus! Jesus!"

"Praise the Lord!"

"Jesus, He is so good!"

325

"*Oh, my gosh! Ohmygosh! Ohmygosh!*"

"COME ON, GOD! KEEP IT GOING! YOU'RE SOOO ROCKING IT, DUDE!"

Since the hut was so jam-packed with people, it was getting extra humid.

"This is *crazytown!*" Twain intoned, eyes still glued to the video cam.

He took the words right out of my mouth.

I was sopping wet.

Shelby's exhilarated face was cascading with sweat and her golden head was dripping wet, as she continued to snap photo after photo.

"*Oh, Collin! Oh, my gosh, Collin!!*"

When had the Team arrived? How *long* had this been going on???

"*Hal-le-lu-jah! Hal-le-lu-jah! Hallelujah! Hallelujah! Hal-le-lu-jah!*"

If it wasn't for the pain, I'd swear I was hallucinating. I had absolutely no grid for what was happening—then it hit me!

St. Augustine! In my research before my Team interview, I'd learned he'd healed an amputee! He'd prayed for an official in the city of Carthage… doctors had removed part of his leg due to gangrene, but when St. Augustine prayed, it grew back! On the spot! Of course, at the time I'd just read it as a piece of fiction—now I realized it had to be *true!*

There *was* precedence!

Obviously, Collin! After all, even you *have read the part in the Bible that says that Jesus healed lepers! And leprosy causes noses, ears, fingers, and toes to all fall off. So presumably, they all grew back…?*

I peered down at my left big toe: it looked like an elongated larva emerging from a cocoon.

"Hal-le-lu-jah! Hal-le-lu-jah! Hallelujah! Hallelujah! Hal-le-lu-jah!"

"Oh, my gosh! Ohmygosh! Ohmygosh! Oh, my goooooooooosh!"

"MORE, LORD! MORE TOE FOR COLLIN! GO, TOE, GO! GROW, TOE, GROW!!!" roared Jack-O like a crazed Dr. Seuss. He jumped up and down in rhythm to the words, shaking the bamboo flooring, and endangering everyone's eyeballs with his wild flagging.

Jongchit whisked the ukulele out of Noi's hands and shoved it unceremoniously into Shelby's arms. "Play baby guitar!"

"What? Me? Now?" In her shock, Shelby fumbled the ukulele and almost dropped it.

"Kha, kha, Chevy play!"

"But what song?"

"Any song! Go, go! *Klay klay klay!"*

After a moment's hesitation, Shelby strummed the ukulele and sang in a wavering voice, *"Father Abraham had many sons, many sons had Father Abraham! I am one of them and so are you! So let's all praise the Lord! Right arm! Father Abraham had many sons, many sons..."*

Why did she pick that, of all things? Well, at least it's not the offensive "wee little man" song.

The growth was excruciating! I'd never felt so much pressure, tearing, stretching, bursting! It hurt *way* more than the actual landmine explosion itself!

A shrieking noise like the whistle of a steam locomotive filled the hut—on and on and on and on and on. It almost distracted me from the pain—almost but not quite. Especially when I realized the shrieking noise was coming from *me!*

I couldn't stop myself—my mouth was wide open, emitting the loudest unmanly squeals I've ever heard before or since.

I looked over to see Twain's reaction. But I couldn't see his face—it was glued to the video camera the entire time.

"...right arm, left arm, right leg! Father Abraham had many sons, many sons had..."

"JESUS!" exclaimed Ernestine, waving one hand in the air, while the other one continued to clutch my foot.

"YEAH, JESUS!" shouted Jack-O, bouncing in rhythm to his words. "YOU ARE A ROCK STAR!!!"

I felt so completely out of control that I even—I'm embarrassed to admit—peed a little. Not that anyone noticed, since I was drenched with sweat.

"...right leg, left leg, right toe, left toe! Father Abraham had many sons, many sons had Father Abraham..."

The hot flashes became more and more intense—my entire body began to reverberate so intensely, I found myself literally bouncing on the Therm-A-Rest mattress! The heat and bouncing and smell of the sesame oil combined to create the effect of a shrimp being stir-fried!

Ernestine continued to clutch my foot and wave one hand in the air. Jack-O bounded up next to her, flagging with intensity and yelling, "GO, TOE! GROW, TOE!" Her waving hand accidently grazed his head, and upon contact, he shimmied as if electrocuted—then immediately thudded to the ground, sending the four flags whizzing across the hut, almost impaling two different Wigglewurts, and toppling Shelby on his way down!

"GOD!!!" howled Jack-O. "YOU SLAY MEEEEEEE!"

Then he passed out, spread eagle on the floor of the hut, a smile of bliss on his lips.

"*Oh, my gosh! Ohmygosh! Ohmygosh!*" babbled broken record Shelby in a daze, sprawled on the floor, one leg under Jack-O's back, and one hand clutching the ukulele.

Twain's only reaction to the drama was to silently shift the camera to record Jack-O for a moment, then immediately return to my toe.

"*Pa tu! Pa tu!*"

Just when it couldn't get any more surreal, the hut door burst open and Jolly, Gimlet, Lah Kaw, and a bunch of Freedom Fighters burst in, guns aimed, shouting commands in Katin and English.

"*Pa tu! Pa tu!* Stop! Stop!"

A frazzled and almost crying Hobab followed behind them.

The Wigglewurts' flags froze mid-whirl. There was a *tinkle-crash* as the tambourine hit the floor. Twain lowered the video camera in stunned amazement. Shelby sat motionless, her hand still holding the ukulele up in the air. Ernestine was so shocked she squeezed my foot—and I let out a bark of pain.

Only Jongchit seemed unfazed.

"Ut ut ut! Even Mister Big Shot General Mu must wait his turn for healing!" she said with mocking sternness, shaking a finger at his bandaged toes.

Jolly lowered his gun and grinned at the rest of us. "My apologies, folks. You'd think I could bloody well tell the difference between a BMJ surprise attack and a Jongchit revival meeting..."

Hobab looked genuinely upset. "Sorry, guys, but it sounded like Collin was being tortured in here!"

In a matter of speaking, I was and still am.

Twain motioned with his free hand. "Jolly, Hobab, get a load of this!"

They stepped over "slain" Jack-O, and made their way through the frozen Wigglewurts over to me.

Jolly bent over to examine my foot, then suddenly staggered backwards. "Holy smokes!"

"Holy *Spirit,*" said Jongchit reprovingly.

Hobab frantically gestured towards Lah Kaw and the rest of the soldiers and shouted, *"Heh la ēē! Gwa la ēē!"* Which sent them scrambling over to my side.

After that, I don't remember what anybody said or did.

The throbbing escalated. My pain threshold had been far exceeded minutes before—and my head felt like it was about to implode.

At that moment, I (thankfully) passed out.

I'm not sure how long I was unconscious. This time there were no visions of heaven or games of tag with Jesus. When I awoke, my new toe still throbbed, but with far less intensity—and I was no longer slipping and sliding on my Therm-A-Rest like a seal on a rock. I lay like a motionless sea cucumber in a tide pool, drenched in salt water.

It took a good minute before I remembered where I was and what was going on.

When I was finally able to bring the blurs into focus, the

first image I saw was of Ernestine—staring in dumbstruck awe at her hands.

Then Jongchit's moonlike face loomed into my line of vision, so closely I could feel her breath on my face.

"Colon? Colon Boy! You back with us now? You awake?" she asked with the most gigantic grin imaginable practically splitting her face in two. I blinked twice. She seemed to take this as an affirmation, and continued in jubilant tones, pointing at my left foot. "Look see! LOOK SEE!"

I looked and saw.

There it was! A brand new toe! Complete with a brand new toenail!

NO MORE GAP!

"See? See miracle?" asked Jongchit. "See crazy surprise gift from God?"

In my wildest imagination, I had never, ever EVER conceived of a NEW BIG TOE GROWING OUT OF MY BODY!

My whole paradigm of—of *EVERYTHING!*—exploded!

If God could do this, well, then, it followed that he was darn well capable of doing ANYTHING! AT ANYTIME! IN ANY PLACE! WITH ANYONE!!!

Jesus was one wild and crazy guy!

My inner being exploded with JOY!

I would never be the same again.

"JESUS!" I heard someone exclaim.

And that someone was me.

Aftermath

THE OUTREACH TEAM, THE WIGGLEWURTS, and the Freedom Fighters surrounded me, sweating and staring down at my miracle. (That is, except for Jack-O, whose arms and legs were still stretched out across the floor as if he was making a snow angel.) The adrenaline and euphoria were wearing off, and it seemed like everyone was now experiencing a surreal mix of catharsis, anticlimax, and delayed shock. I could manage nothing more than lying flat on my back on the Therm-A-Rest—and breathing. And even that hurt!

Earlier, a kind soldier had shoved one of those pineapple cookies into my hand… but I'd been too weak to lift it up to my mouth. The cookie had since disintegrated in my sweaty palm, the crumbs sticking to my fingers.

No one spoke.

Just stared.

And dripped.

Dripped droplets of sweat down on me, as I gazed up at them.

My new metatarsal had skin so white that it was practically transparent and looked years younger than my right one. It literally seemed to glow with the intensity of a firefly in the dim hut. The effect was as if someone had sculpted a foot out of tan clay, then added a big toe in neon white. (Why had God bothered to grow out my toe in such a dramatic way— but not blend it with the rest of my foot? Not that I was complaining!)

I don't think if I'd died and rose from the dead that it would have been such a spectacle. After all, when you hear about those kinds of enormous miracles, you always wonder whether they'd been "really dead" in the first place. But a blown-up toe is a blown-up toe. A missing toe is a missing toe. A gap is a gap. No getting around the evidence of negative space. There *was* a toe, there *wasn't* a toe, there *was* a toe.

It had definitely *not* sunk in yet. If I thought I was in shock before, it was nothing like the shock I was experiencing *now*.

Hobab, Jolly, Gimlet, Lah Kaw, and the other Freedom Fighters shifted towards Twain, to watch the footage on the video camera monitor. Their expressions ranged from disbelief to disgust to incredulity to amazement—that is, except for Gimlet, who remained stoic to the last, still spitting pink into that plastic yellow cup.

After the last frame of miracle and mayhem had been viewed, Jolly gripped my shoulder with fingers of iron. I yelped. "Well, my lad, this what I call true R & R—Rest & Regrowth!"

Lah Kaw dramatically clutched his head, ruffling his fauxhawk, and said in a wild tone for someone usually so low key, stumbling along in broken English, "My mind hurt! I do not un-der-stand what happen to *kàw mu!* Con-fuse! Very con-fuse!"

"Yeah, what does this all mean?" Twain asked Jongchit.

"Does Collin's toe set a precedence? Or is it just a one-time regeneration?"

She shrugged. "Jongchit not God. Only God know."

"But should we expect more miracles like this?" pressed Shelby.

Jongchit shrugged again. "Only God know. But! We pray for healing first and last and alway. God work through us for healing on earth!"

Jolly turned to Gimlet. "If God heal toe, why not leg?"

Before he could respond, Jongchit gave Gimlet a hearty slap on the back. Her face was gleaming with sweat and joy. *"Kha! Kha!* That what I say!"

Gimlet stared stoically ahead.

"Wigglewurt!" commanded Jongchit.

The Wigglewurts, though weary from the recent Healing Party, rallied, and began to surround Gimlet. Patcharee even mustered up her orange flag, which she began to wave in businesslike fashion over Gimlet's head. Noi picked up Shelby's ukulele and began to strum.

Gimlet didn't move a muscle.

Then Jolly spoke to Gimlet rapidly in Katin.

To our surprise Gimlet replied in a clipped tone.

Jolly laughed.

"What did he say?" asked Ernestine.

"He said he never gets fungus on these toes," said Jolly, pointing to Gimlet's wooden foot.

Jongchit chuckled and nudged Gimlet with her elbow. "You stubborn old goat! But you not too stubborn for God! He like old goat!"

"First, fake leg off," said Patcharee, extending a wizened hand towards his prosthesis.

But before she could touch it, Gimlet leapt back, dropping his cup, splattering betel nut spit everywhere—then bolted for the door! There was a collective gasp of surprise as he sped across the compound and into the night.

A moment of stunned silence.

"Dang! He's sure fast with that fake leg," said Twain, laughing as he wiped betel nut spit off the camera lens.

"But even more fast with new leg," said Jongchit briskly. "Come, Wigglewurt! Healing Fire Power, Round Two!" She jabbed the air in a one-two punch.

"But you'd think he'd *want* healing," said Shelby in confusion, peering out the door.

"You'd be surprised how many people resist it," said Ernestine, shaking her head sadly. "It's like the unknown scares them more than the chance of wholeness. As my Aunt Aurora always says—"

"Mangosteen? You come?" Jongchit interrupted. "Lay fire hand on stump?"

Ernestine managed a weak smile, then replied, "You know, I'm beat. I'll have to sit this one out."

Jongchit tut-tutted, but smiled and said: *"Kha, kha!* Miracle take much, much energy! Me sixty-five—sixty-five! And in here—" She jabbed a thumb at her chest. "—more energy than whole Bread Team!"

"I'll go!" said Hobab, swinging his bangs out of his eyes, an impish look on his face. "I'll support you, *Mom!*"

Jongchit gave him a wide grin. *"Dee mak!* Very good, *Son!*"

Then she barked out orders in Thai, and the Wigglewurts

snatched up their backpacks, flags, and jumbo bottle of sesame oil—and marched out. Tiny Noi teetered after them on her high heels, plinking and plunking Shelby's ukulele, and warbling:

"Fa-ther Ab-ra-ham! He have many son…"

The Human Starfish

ONE BY ONE, JOLLY, LAH KAW, AND THE OTHER Freedom Fighters pried themselves away from my toe, picked up their guns and departed—automatically stepping over Jack-O, who continued to lay blissfully comatose in the middle of the hut. Soon only the Outreach Team was left.

Ernestine passed out bottles of water, pigmy bananas, guavas, and packets of cashew nuts from a plastic bag that had somehow materialized in the hut. For a few minutes, they drank and ate in silence. My water, pigmy banana, guava, and packet of cashews sat untouched on my lap—I was too weak even to pick them up.

Jack-O grunted and shifted, but his eyes remained closed.

Twain carefully put the video camera into a black leather case.

"How come... how come you didn't pass out while filming that whole time?" I asked weakly. The last of my energy was ebbing away. My eyes involuntarily shut. With effort, I forced them open again.

"Yeah, Twain!" said Shelby, her mouth full of cashews. "I was wondering that, too. I mean, this was *way* grosser to watch than Jolly's toenails."

"Miracles are messy," said Ernestine with a knowing nod.

Twain gave us a half smile. "Don't know. Maybe the camera acted like a kind of buffer. Made it seem surreal somehow, like I was just watching a mov—"

"KETCHUM HAIR!!!" Jack-O sat up and slapped a meaty hand to his forehead.

Ernestine choked on a cashew, Shelby sloshed her water, and Twain almost dropped the camera—but I simply blinked. By that point, *nothing* could have startled me.

"Whew! Still there!" said Jack-O, as he felt the yellow-orange-red fringe. He struggled to sit up. "Holy Cow! What a trip! What a ride! What a nap!" His face was gleaming and his normally tufted hair was plastered flat. His shirt was stuck to his beefy chest.

"Welcome back, dude," said Twain, slapping him five.

"What'd I miss?" asked Jack-O. His eyes fell on the bag of provisions, and for a few minutes, all that was heard were the sounds of gulping and chewing and burping. These were so rhythmic and soothing that they put me right to sleep.

Sometime later, I heard my name. I was too exhausted to open my eyes, so I just lay there, half-listening, half-dozing, to Ernestine's low, urgent voice.

"…can you even begin to comprehend what this means for Collin? Just wait until the Tacketts, our parents, and BOLYG all hear about this!"

"Everyone's gonna freak out!" Shelby sounded dangerously close to freaking out herself.

"I don't know about you guys," said Jack-O, "but this has totally changed the whole New Testament for me. I mean, all that healing-miracle-power stuff is really *real* real! Who knew? Seriously, guys, *who knew!?*"

"Uh, anyone who bothered to read Acts," said Ernestine dryly.

Twain laughed. "I'm uploading the footage on YouTube. I bet it goes viral in minutes—"

"What? Shouldn't you ask Collin's permission first?" asked Shelby.

"What's the diff?" countered Jack-O. "Wouldn't he want all the world to see his freakin' awesome miracle?"

"Well, it's *his* big toe, *his* life," Ernestine replied tartly.

"Man, oh, man, oh man, oh man!" said Jack-O. "Collin will be famous—he'll probably meet the Mayor! The President! The Queen! What if they make Collin an ambassador? Then he could go all around the world showing people his big toe. Wearing a giant toe costume—"

"What are you babbling about, Jack-O?" said Ernestine.

Before he could answer, Shelby burst out: "It's still so unbelievable! I keep thinking this is a dream."

"Yeah," said Jack-O, "and we'll all wake up separately and find out we were all just in the exact same dream—"

"Isn't there a movie about that?" asked Twain.

"But do you guys know what this *means*? What this *really* means? That God grew out a toe?" Ernestine's voice escalated.

There was a momentary silence.

Then came Twain's sardonic voice, "That regeneration isn't just for starfish anymore?"

"Yeah!" exclaimed Jack-O. "That's what Collin is—a human starfish!"

"Seriously, guys," Ernestine continued, "have you really thought about it? If God actually does something like *this*, then what *else* is he up to? What if these type of healings are about to happen all across Burma? Across Southeast Asia? Across the *world!?*"

Silence.

"Healing people one by one like Collin? Or like—*shazam!* In some sort of instant healing wave *tsunami?*" asked Jack-O, genuinely interested.

"Who knows?" said Ernestine. "Remember how Jesus said we'll all do greater things than he did? If that's really true, then—"

"I… I saw…" My throat was so dry I could barely speak.

All four of them whirled around to face me.

"Dude! We thought you were sleeping!" said Jack-O.

"How are you feeling, Collin?" asked Ernestine, getting up. "Do you need something?"

"Jesus… Jesus…" I rasped.

They all leaned forward expectantly.

I took a deep breath and stuttered: *"Je-sus…t-tag-ged… me…"*

They gazed at me uncomprehendingly, then exchanged concerned glances.

Jack-O looked me over, then laughed. "There's no spray paint on you, bro—"

"Ssssh!" Shelby nudged him.

Twain said to the others in an undertone, "I'm sure this is a normal side effect of—"

"Guys! Guys! You gotta check this out!"

Hobab burst through the door, laughing so hard he could hardly speak. Outside, we could hear boisterous female voices shouting in both Thai and Katin.

"What's going on?" asked Shelby.

"Oh, man!" said Hobab breathlessly. "That Jongchit! She and the Wigglewurts have been hunting down Gimlet this whole time. They finally ambushed him coming out of the W.C., where he was hiding out. Right now, they're praying for his leg, but he's trying to escape! Patcharee's got an iron grip on his good leg and Jongchit's holding down one arm." He popped his head around the corner of the door—then burst out laughing again. "Now he's swinging his fake leg at them like a machete!"

"No way!" said Jack-O, moving towards the door. "This I gotta see!"

"Bring the video camera!" Hobab called to Twain over his shoulder.

"Wait for me!" said Shelby, scrambling to her feet.

Ernestine smiled down at me and gave me a head noogie. "Get some rest, Miracle Boy. We'll talk about Jesus *tagging you* later." And she followed them out.

The hut was empty.

Did she believe me?

I don't know how long I'd been sleeping when I woke up to see Ernestine sitting cross-legged next to my Therm-A-Rest.

"Did… did Gimlet's leg…?"

She grinned and shook her head. "He escaped again. For some reason he's having none of it. You should have seen his face when Noi poured that sesame oil over his head and it ran into his eyes…"

Her detailed description of the messy prayer session almost lulled me back to sleep. That is, until I heard:

"So… what's all this about Jesus tagging you?"

The words hung in the air. How surreal and immature they sounded spoken out loud. For a brief second, I doubted it had happened. But then I remembered those crinkly laugh lines around his eyes…

"Come on, Collin, spill! I'm dying to know what happened!" She leaned forward expectantly.

"Um… well… okay… you asked for it." After I slowly and haltingly described my experience, she sat there silently staring at the floor, tugging on her grommet, and periodically nodding her head.

I shifted uncomfortably. Did she believe me? Or had I overshared?

Finally, she looked up and said matter-of-factly, "Colossal. Totally *colossal.*"

I felt a wave of relief. "So you don't think I'm crazy?"

"You kidding? I can't tell you how many encounters like this I've heard about. I just want it to happen to *me*, already!" She leaned over and gave me a swift hug, which was awkward and sweaty. "Thank you for sharing, Collin."

As her light brown eyes stared intently into mine, my eyelids became increasingly heavy… I blinked slowly… Then blinked again… And again…

Revelation

"**C**OCK-A-DOODLE-DOO!"

The piercing sound penetrated my brain and jolted me awake. For a second, I thought a rooster was stuck to my head, its beak in my ear, and talons digging into my scalp.

With effort, I pried my gummy eyes open. Daylight permeated the slats in the bamboo walls and shafts of light crisscrossed my body, each one filled with motes. The hut was hot and muggy and still.

"Cock-a-doodle-doo!"

The rooster thankfully crowed on the other side of the thin wall—and what I thought were talons digging into my scalp, turned out to be a raging headache. My stomach growled and rumbled like a caged tiger trying to break free.

The first thing I did was reassure myself that my new big toe was still there.

A tiny face grinned at me from the end of the bed.

"Aaahh!" I yelled, scrambling backwards.

The tiny face followed—leering at me.

I heard a familiar chuckle beside me.

"Sorry, couldn't help it," came Ernestine's husky voice.

Peering closer at the face, I realized it was my miracle toe, in all its Day-Glo Glory, sporting a Sharpie grin across the nail—and a tiny googly eye on either side.

I laughed—which immediately morphed into a moan as pain ripped through my body.

"We named him Bob." Ernestine's fire hair was pulled off her shoulders into a high ponytail and she wore the same grimy pink Hello Kitty t-shirt, shorts, and flip-flops I'd seen her in last. She sat cross-legged next to me, with three water bottles, mango slices, hardboiled eggs, and basket of sticky rice piled on her lap.

"What… what time is it?" I rasped. My mouth was so dry it felt like a paper bag.

"You mean, what *day* is it. You slept like thirty hours straight! They sent me in here to wake you up and make you eat something."

"Thirty hours?" I struggled to sit up. But my silk sleep sack was so soaked with sweat and my entire body was so stiff and achy, that I slid all over my Therm-A-Rest until Ernestine efficiently propped me into a sitting position.

I gulped down an entire bottle of water and then polished off a second one.

"Here, you'd better have some food." Ernestine held out the basket of sticky rice and I barely restrained myself from snatching it out of her hand.

I wolfed down the rice, mangos, and eggs in minutes.

"Whoa! Pace yourself or it'll be coming right back up!"

I leaned back and belched.

"You've got some mango juice…" She leaned forward and wiped the juice off my chin with her silver-ringed fingers.

"Thanks," I said, blotting my chin with my silk sleep sack. Then I paused, shocked at the length of my stubble—I was heading into full-on beard territory!

Ernestine grinned, releasing those dimples of hers. "Wish you had a mirror?"

"I bet I look like a lumber jack!"

She tilted her head and pursed her lips as she gave my appearance a once over. "You know, I gotta admit, it kinda does something for you."

"Seriously? You're not just saying that?"

"You boys are so darn vain! Yes, *seriously*. It gives you a manly vibe, more rough and tumble."

I rubbed my beard, and chose to take it as a compliment.

"Anyway, word's gotten around the HQ and the village. Your big toe is big news. Everyone wants to take a look at *Bob*."

"Speaking of everyone—where's the rest of our Team?"

"Playing soccer with the soldiers. Then we're doing crafts with the IDP kids—making *papier-mâché* bobble heads with these." She held up the Zip-Loc bag of googly eyes. "Luckily, we have just enough to go around. It's our last chance to hang out with the orphans, since we're crossing back tomorrow."

"Tomorrow? That soon?"

"Yeah, Jolly managed to convince the Thai Border Patrol that the landmine explosion was an accident—thanks to Twain's toe footage."

"Really? It helped?"

"Once they saw it was just some crazy *farang* causing a ruckus and not the BMJ, they opened the border again. The only thing is…" she trailed off.

"The only thing is what?"

"Well, we're still waiting for the Thai Border Patrol to return the videotape. Twain's getting kinda edgy." At the concern on my face she quickly added, "Not that it's a big deal. Jolly will take care of it."

Hearing that the evidence was out of our hands made *me* edgy! How could I expect anyone to believe my crazytown miracle without proof? I sure hoped Shelby's photos turned out...

"Oh, and the Tacketts finally got released from their hotel house arrest," Ernestine continued. "Jongchit said they'd each gained ten pounds from sitting around eating *pad thai* and watching game shows all day. They're waiting for you at the *Born Free Academy*."

"I wonder what they'll think about it all... And what everyone else will think of my miracle. Like my parents. Merrick and Gareth. My extended family. The other homeschoolers. Those church people—"

"Brace yourself, Miracle Boy," she interrupted, holding up a hand as if to stop that thought in its tracks. "You'll be surprised who believes you and who doesn't—even with the evidence staring them right in the face. When my Aunt Aurora got that gold filling, her best friend didn't believe her at all and still hasn't talked to her to this day."

"That's harsh." I shifted my legs and groaned as pain ricocheted through my body. "Eowww! Why didn't Jesus heal *all* my wounds and pain while he was at it? Why was the healing so localized? And why does God choose to heal one person and not another? It seems so arbitrary—not that I'm complaining."

"Yeah. That's one of the biggies. No one can really answer it."

"Not even Aunt Aurora?"

She chuckled. "Not even Aunt Aurora."

"I know I'm new to the whole God thing, but I just don't get why he does what he does. It makes no sense."

"That's because it's a mystery. *He's* a mystery. Think about it: if our finite human minds could understand and explain every single thing about our infinite God—then would he really be God?"

She had a point.

"But why did I get healed, but a war hero like Gimlet *didn't?*"

"*Only God know,*" she mimicked Jongchit. "In his case, he was literally trying to *escape* from healing prayer, so that always changes things up. Actually, Jongchit thinks some sort of healing did happen *internally* during Gimlet's prayer time, because this morning at breakfast we actually caught him *smiling.* Smiling! *Gimlet!* Can you believe it? Jolly said that was a miracle in and of itself. So, basically, everyone's healing's gonna look different."

"But still—"

"God shows us love specifically *and* individually," she went on, "like how Jesus usually healed one by one, seeing each person as someone to be loved, not just a box to be checked off of his Social Activist To Do List or something." She pretended to hold a clipboard and pen. "Healed a leper— check! Opened blind eyes—check! Grew out or reattached (same same) severed ear—check!"

I laughed.

"Anyway, he's all about *relationship*. Does this make any sense? Or does it all sound like yammering?" She opened and closed her hand as if it were talking. "Like '*wah-wah-wah-wah*'?"

Ernestine is so darn cool. And she knows so much. You can ask her anything. You can tell her anything. Nothing fazes her.

After a minute or so, I realized she was staring at me. "Sorry, did you say something?"

"I said that whether people get healed right away or not, we're still suppose to risk praying for healing *every* single time," she said with a smile, twisting the grommet in her ear for the umpteenth time. "And leave the results—or lack of results—to him."

"Sounds good," I said, still only half listening. I found myself taking in her high cheekbones and thick eyelashes. Of course, I'd always noticed her dimples and those Toblerone eyes—but why hadn't I ever appreciated the rest of her charms before? Like her clavicle? That was some clavicle!

Jack-O sure had.

"What did I just say?" Ernestine demanded.

"Uh…" Shoot! What *did* she just say? Oh, right! "Something about whether healing happens immediately or not, you've still got to, you know, risk it… risk praying for them…"

I knew something was up when I found myself staring at the hut wall through the grommet hole in her ear—and it didn't creep me out. All her metal was actually starting to grow on me.

With effort, I pried my eyes away from her.

There was a moment of silence, while we both watched yet another gecko crawl across the bamboo-slatted wall. Then I turned to her and blurted out:

"You never told the Team your secret."

Where did that come from?

"My what?" She seemed genuinely confused.

Awkward. I nervously cleared my throat. "Uh, during 'true confessions' after Shelby admitted being a vegan and Jack-O flashed his smudgy tattoo, you kinda seemed like you were about to say something. You know, right before Jongchit interrupted…?"

Her eyes shifted from the gecko to me.

After a moment, I tried to pry my eyes away, but those mesmerizing Toblerones refused to release their hold.

"Let me tell you," she said, putting her hands up in a surrender pose, "I didn't think I'd *ever* fall for a guy who actually wears *spats,* of all things. *Spats!*" She let out a deep belly laugh.

I pretended to be offended. "Hey, I don't '*wear* spats', I *wore* spats once—*once!* Don't get me started on your *grommets!*"

She shot me a startled look, then giggled. "Grommets and spats! *Grommets* and *spats!*" Then she burst out laughing again.

I stared at her, mesmerized, watching her dimples flash in and out, in and out, in and out…

All this time, I'd been *overlooking* her. *Looking over* her *at* someone else.

So I sat there, *looking straight at* her for the first time ever, my eyes clear enough for the first time ever, to see…

…into the very core of the real Ernestine: the creative Ernestine, the spiritual powerhouse Ernestine, the goofy Ernestine, the adventurous Ernestine, the miraculous Ernestine, the generous Ernestine, the *hot ("Ssss-hot! Red hot!")* Ernestine—who, I suddenly realized, was *exactly* my height!

I once was blind, but now I see!

She was now laughing so hard that her whole body shook, and tears zigzagged across her face. And every time she tried to stop, one look at my expression would set her off again.

I continued to watch those dimples of hers flash in and out, in and out…

After a few minutes, when she finally seemed to be segueing into mild chuckles, I ran my hand through my damp hair, nervously cleared my throat and said, "You know, Ernestine, all this time I never noticed… I mean, never realized that… that you… that you…um… that I…" I trailed off, then burst out: "But, come on! What do you see—"

This was embarrassing.

"Yeah?" she prompted.

"What the heck do you see in *me*? I mean, come on, I was chasing Shelby the whole time."

There was a long pause.

We stared at each other.

Finally, Ernestine smiled and shrugged. "You got me. There's just something about you… It's like my Aunt Aurora always says, 'Sometimes you just see the gold in folks that other people don't.' And you have a heck of a lot of gold underneath all your scruffy stubble and…"

Here she made air quotes.

"… *'vintage style.'* It's like you're not afraid to be *you*. No matter what other people say. Also, you have a lot of tenacity and creativity—and you totally make me laugh. That's a huge plus."

Before I could respond, she added, "If only you weren't so darn white-bread! *Spats!*"

We were soon laughing so hard that our guttural sounds

ricocheted off the walls of the hut. I had no idea why we thought this was so funny, but we did. Some things are just inexplicable. Period.

Like this *thing* between Ernestine and me.

I paused mid-chuckle to spit out: "Grommets and—"

"*Spats!*" Ernestine's laughter had actually escalated into a squeal, when—

"What the heck's going on here?"

SAME SAME BUT DIFFERENT

JACK-O BARGED INTO THE HUT, WEARING HIS orange SAME SAME BUT DIFFERENT t-shirt and carrying a soccer ball under his arm.

Startled at the interruption, Ernestine snorted and stopped mid-guffaw, and my own laughter morphed into choking fit.

"You all right, dude?" he asked, giving me a once over. "It's like you're having a conniption or something."

"I-I-I'm fine…" I managed to stammer, and then grabbed the third bottle of water. Jack-O took off his Aussie hat to fan his dripping face—and there, across his forehead, he'd written *KETCHUM HAIR!* in Sharpie, with an arrow pointing to the fire fringe. "Get the lead out, Ketchum! Bobble head time. The troops are getting restless."

Ernestine wiped her eyes with her t-shirt, then stood up, staggering slightly. She glanced over at me.

"Spats!"

"Grommets!"

Which set us laughing once again.

Jack-O glanced back and forth at the two of us in exasperation. "Holy Cow!"

"Holy *Spirit!*" we said in unison, then doubled over in laughter once again.

"You gotta be kiddin' me," muttered Jack-O, shaking his head as he watched us.

Once we finally stopped laughing, I indicated the soccer ball and tried to steady my voice enough to ask, "So... who won?"

He stared at me through his smudged glasses with growing realization. Mixed emotions played across his face, before his eyes narrowed and he said, "*You* did. Who can compete with a miracle?"

"What?" But I knew full well what he meant.

Ernestine also pretended to be oblivious as she blotted her face again with her shirt.

Jack-O shifted his bulk to face Ernestine and jabbed a thumb at his *KETCHUM HAIR!* "So this counts for nothing, huh?"

"What are you babbling about?" she asked, still wiping her face.

"I get it—it's because I only got *half* healed. Because I didn't get blown up and grown out. Or is it because I'm a jock? No, I know—it's because I'm yellow, right? Or is it because you're brown? Wait—it's because of this orange t-shirt, huh? You always hated this—"

"You big lug!" she said in affectionate exasperation. "It's because you're a twelve-year old boy trapped in a line backer's body! You need to grow up before you can date anyone. Or at least get the heck out of adolescence..."

He stared at her glumly, his mouth drooping and his chunky black glasses sliding to the end of his nose.

"I mean, come on, Jack-O," she said more gently, "your idea of a date is TPing houses and egging cars."

"So?"

"See what I mean?" Ernestine said to me.

"Actually, Jack-O," I said, full of genuine sympathy, "I'm sure there's *some* girl out there who'd consider TPing houses and egging cars the highlight of her week."

Ernestine looked at me in surprise. "You're totally right! Who am I to judge?" Turning back to Jack-O, she said, "I'm the loser here because I can't appreciate you. Face it, Jack-O, you're a total catch. I mean, you're a lot of fun and you've got more muscles in your right arm than Collin has in his whole body."

I threw Ernestine a pained look.

"True," said Jack-O, looking me over appraisingly.

"And you've got cool hair, insane amounts of energy, a heart of gold—"

"I'm sure he gets the point," I interrupted.

"Keep it coming," said Jack-O, waving a hand.

"But best of all, you're a *great* friend, a *loyal* friend," she said. "And I hope you'll always be *my* friend."

A second later, they were hugging.

"Change your mind and you could still get some of this," he replied with a grin, jabbing a thumb at his fringe.

"Man Child," she said, socking him on the arm.

He sighed heavily and bounced the soccer ball. "Our moms are gonna be so bummed. They always wanted us to get together… after all those years of VBS, Awana, and Veggie Tales. I mean, every time I hear that song about tomatoes and potatoes it's gonna slay me."

Ernestine laughed. "Oh, you'll get over it."

I had no idea what they were talking about. All I knew was

that my bladder was about to explode. Those three bottles of water had already made their way through my system.

I scanned the hut desperately for the bucket I'd been using as my own personal toilet, but for some reason, it had disappeared. I'd have to use the W.C.—which was probably preferable, since I had enough pee to fill a pool.

I rose unsteadily to my feet. The abrupt movement made me dizzy, and I began to sway. Odd sensations quivered through my foot as I put weight on my new toe for the first time.

"Whoa, there!" said Jack-O. He immediately dropped the soccer ball and put a massive arm around my shoulders.

"Careful—you haven't tried Bob out yet," said Ernestine, as she also wrapped an arm tightly around me.

"W.C.!" I said abruptly in a tight voice, as the urge to urinate intensified. "A.S.A.P.!"

"Lean on us," said Ernestine, suddenly all business, gluing herself to my side. "Are you in pain? How do you feel right now?"

I gave her a half grin through gritted teeth. *"Never sorry, ever jolly."*

She smiled in approval. "Atta boy."

I slowly and carefully slipped on my flip-flops, every move sending fresh twinges through my body. Then, bookended by Ernestine and Jack-O, I painfully limped over to the flimsy bamboo door.

Reaching Out

A S WE SHUFFLED THROUGH THE DOORWAY, I almost keeled over in surprise. Hundreds of squatting Freedom Fighters and IDP villagers surrounded the hut! And what looked like a battalion of BMJ soldiers squatted behind them! As soon as they spotted me, the crowd stood up in waves, like a field of undulating wheat. No one said a word.

Stood side-by-side.

At ease.

Watching *me*.

"Sorry, dude—should have warned you," Jack-O murmured.

Hundreds of pairs of eyes bored into me. I opened my mouth to speak, then snapped it shut.

What did it all mean?

However, at that point, I wasn't remotely capable of navigating all the surprise, apprehension, and confusion somersaulting through my head. I stared blankly at the crowd before me. Then I slowly began to pick out familiar faces here and there: a grinning Jolly giving me a salute; Hobab and Lah Kaw kicking a soccer ball back and forth; Twain and Shelby helping Naw Eh Myet pass out craft supplies to the group of orphans; and Jongchit and the Wigglewurts flanking Gimlet, who spit into his yellow cup—which now had two googly eyes stuck on it! *And* he actually *grinned* when he saw me!

Then my eyes fell on Pee Paw—the little girl with the big buckteeth, pigtail sprouting on top of her head, and artisan bun cheeks—marching towards me, a solemnly determined expression on her round face. She wore the same colorful woven outfit as before, and the yellow foam octopus still hung around her neck—although by now it was on the grimy side. And she still dragged that coconut monkey behind her.

The crowd watched in absolute silence, as the tiny figure doggedly advanced, the coconut pet bouncing over the dirt and rocks.

Within moments, Pee Paw stood splay-legged in front of me, hands on hips.

We stared at each other for a moment.

Then Pee Paw looked down at my new big toe—and giggled at the googly eyes.

"*Saw* Bob," I said with a smile as I wiggled it.

"*Saw* Bob," she repeated and giggled again. Then she abruptly extended her right hand. With intense concentration, she slowly unwound the dirty rag from the forefinger. *The top digit was missing—from the tip to the first knuckle.*

So that dog had actually bitten off part of her finger!

My stomach contorted—and this time not from hunger.

The urge to urinate evaporated.

There was a collective murmuring as the crowd leaned forward in anticipation, like a wind had sent a ripple through the field of wheat.

"Oh, man!" whispered Jack-O. He and Ernestine exchanged glances.

I looked down at my new big toe, then back into Pee Paw's dark eyes. They were expectant. *Hopefully* expectant.

She scrunched up her cheeks in a big smile, revealing those prominent beaver teeth—and extended her finger.

"*Bah ywā.*"

I didn't know what she said, but I knew what she meant: *I want what happened to your toe to happen to my finger.*

I looked over at Ernestine. She smiled and gave me a slight nod. She didn't say anything, but I knew what *she* meant: *GO FOR IT.*

I looked down at my new toe.

I looked at Pee Paw's finger.

At my toe.

At her finger.

Toe.

Finger.

Toe.

Finger.

Then I extended my hand towards hers.

My hand was shaking.

Pee Paw was grinning.

I paused, my hand frozen mid-air.

"This is freakin' killin' me!" Jack-O moaned.

Is this even legit? I mean, I'm no Jongchit or Wigglewurt. Will God heal her like he did me? If so, will it be physical or emotional healing? And will it be instant or eventual? Or is all this just a NO GO?

Only one way to find out.

I took a deep breath, and reached out—

A MESSAGE FROM COLLIN UTTLEY

Use this space to write down exactly what you're feeling right this second—your first impressions. Your second impressions. Third. Seriously, go ahead, grab a pen and write on this page. (That is, if you own the book, otherwise you should probably write on something else.) Put down what you think happens next, and what you wish would happen next...

_____

_____

_____

_____

_____

_____

_____

_____

_____

_____

_____

_____

_____

part seven

STATESIDE

THAI SMILE FUN
(one year later)

"WHO WANTS MORE RICE?"

"Pass it over here, dude."

"I'll take seconds of *tom kha kai.*"

"Hey, bro! You're hogging the noodles!"

"Shouldn't we wait for the Tacketts?"

"They said they'd be late, remember?"

"Are they bringing *her* with them?"

"That was the plan."

Scraping plates and thunking bowls were heard as the Bread Team dug into their lunch. I leaned back in my chair and scanned the familiar faces. I couldn't believe it was already the one-year anniversary of our outreach trip—and of my crazytown miracle.

Ernestine sat next to me eating *pad thai.* Her hair was now what she called Easter Egg: pink, yellow, and light blue. Other than that, she looked the same. And (cue drum roll) we'd officially started dating a month after returning from SEA.

I, Collin Uttley, had finally scored a girlfriend.

As if reading my mind, Ernestine turned and flashed me a grin, and then said under her breath: *"Spats!"*

"Grommets!"

"You guys never let up, do you?" Next to her, Jack-O shoveled one stick of *satay* after the other into his mouth. He wore the ol' I'M NOT LAZY BUT I'M FUN t-shirt, which was practically see-through after multiple washings. He'd finally forgiven me for stealing his girl, but it obviously still stung. He paused in his meat consumption to gave me a good-natured sock in the arm. "You don't need to rub it in, dude…"

"Speaking of romantic entanglements, have you two set a date yet?" Ernestine asked Shelby and Twain, who sat across from us. The couple hadn't changed much in the last year—Shelby still wore vintage and Twain still looked like a Wanna-be Mercenary. The only difference was Shelby's new annoying habit of twisting her engagement ring around and around and *around* her finger.

"Stop asking that," said Shelby, setting her Thai iced tea down with a bang. "You know we promised our parents we'd wait until we graduated from college."

Ernestine, Jack-O, and I exchanged knowing looks.

"Riiiight," said Jack-O. He dug around in his pocket, pulled out a crumpled $20, and slapped it on the table. "This twenty says you guys don't make it the full four years."

"Hey now—" Twain began.

"Forty bucks says you'll only last a year," I interrupted, tossing my wallet on the table and looking Shelby straight in the eye.

After a beat, she sheepishly looked away.

Ernestine grinned mischievously and threw a Target gift card on the pile. "I bet you the sixty dollars and fifty-two cents left on there that Shelby caves in less than six months and you move into married student housing by January."

Twain laughed and put his arm around Shelby. "Preach!"

"You guys are throwing your money away!" Shelby said with mild exasperation, pushing the stash back across the table at us. But I could tell she was secretly pleased.

Twain's gray eyes zeroed in on me. "So, what about *you*, Uttley? When are *you* gonna cough up the cash to buy *your* girl a ring?"

Ernestine and I both shifted awkwardly, then began babbling at the same time:

"We don't want to rush things—"

"What's the hurry—"

Twain laughed. "Take it easy. I'm just messin' with you." Then abruptly changing the subject, he added, "Nice to finally see your face, dude. You were turning Moses there for a while."

"Don't you mean Father Abraham?" Ernestine joked, flicking a finger at my smooth jaw. Last week I'd finally shaved the thick beard I'd started growing in SEA—so with "short back and sides" and long bangs (hanging in my eyes), I looked exactly the same as when we all first met—down to a new fedora. (That old one was toast.) Even my miracle toe practically blended with the rest of my foot—although, there was something about it that looked different, even if you couldn't put your finger on it.

Suddenly, a series of loud pops exploded outside the window. We all froze, then burst into laughter. For we weren't in a ceasefire on the Thai-Burma border—we were in the THAI SMILE FUN café about a block from the Bread of Life

Church in Arroyo Seco, California. And tomorrow was the Fourth of July.

"Dude! The last time we heard an explosion, someone lost a toe!" said Jack-O with his mouth full.

"No joke!" said Twain, fingering the dog tags around his neck. "Wonder how Jolly and the Feebs are doing?"

Shelby shuddered. "I still get nightmares sometimes."

I laughed. "How come you do, but I don't?"

"Survivor guilt, maybe?" offered Ernestine as she passed me the rice.

"Speak for yourself, *Mangosteen*," said Shelby with a smile.

"No one else will ever understand what we all went through," said Twain.

"Never," I said with feeling. And the rest all nodded solemnly.

The truth was that our return to the States hadn't gone as planned. We'd expected everyone to freak out about my toe, but instead the focus seemed to be more along the lines of:

"What the heck were you guys doing over the border in BURMA, of all places?!?"

"Landmine!?!? Why on earth were you anywhere near a LANDMINE!?!"

"Who authorized this trip?"

"What do you mean the Tacketts weren't with you?!?!"

"House arrest? Why weren't we told about that!?!"

Etc... etc...

Ernestine had been right: about half the people we told about my toe growing out believed it, but the other half thought we'd all experienced a mass hallucination or were making it up or that my toe hadn't been completely blown off in the first place.

Since Twain's footage hadn't been returned yet—apparently Jolly was *still* working on getting it back from the Thai Border Patrol—the only evidence we'd had was Shelby's digital photos. Which unfortunately, as it turned out, were totally blurry because of moisture on the lens in that steamy hut.

So that meant people pretty much had to take my crazytown story on *faith*...

Which brings me to the reactions of my parents and brothers. To my surprise, Merrick and Gareth had listened open-mouthed to my entire story and believed every single thing I told them. I kept catching them staring at my toe when they thought I wasn't looking.

"I wanna go on an outreach trip!"

"Can we join the youth group, too?"

But Mom and Dad were less enthusiastic.

I'll hand it to them—at least they didn't sue the church. It was a close one, because Dad consulted his attorney and the law firm thought they had an open and shut case of negligence.

I tried to convince my parents that despite all the crazytown insanity, the trip had been life-changing in a good way. This is what went down...

UTTLEY FAMILY TRANSCRIPT

July 28th

(Transcribed by Gareth Uttley, who just so happened to be practicing his shorthand *yet again*.)

Uttley Family Dining Room, 7:30 p.m.:

Mrs. Uttley: *(shakes head mournfully while dishing out penne pasta)* "I'm sorry, Collin, but your father and I are more convinced than ever that the Bread of Life Church is a cult. You haven't been the same since the trip."

Mr. Uttley: *(spears pasta with his fork)* "She's right, son. There's something totally different about you—"

Merrick: *(interrupts, with mouth full)* "But we think it's a *good* difference!"

Gareth: *(pauses while transcribing)* "Yeah. He's not such a jerk."

Mr. Uttley: *(smiles patiently and rubs bald pate)* "Collin, we're concerned about that group of young people you spend so much time with. Are you sure they're a *good* influence?"

(Collin laughs.)

Mrs. Uttley: *(polishes bifocals on shirt)* "Like that girl you've been seeing so much of..."

Collin: "Ernestine?"

Mrs. Uttley: *(puts on glasses and peers at Collin)* "I just don't know if she's the right fit for you. She seems a bit... *extreme.*"

Collin: "Extreme because she believes in miracles or extreme because she has rainbow hair and grommets in her ears?"

Mrs. Uttley: *(after a slight pause)* "Well, both..."

Collin: *(smiles)* "Come on. You can't blame my friends for *my* behavior. You gotta admit that having a toe blown off and then grown out will have a major impact on someone."

Merrick: "Mind-blowing!" *(makes the sound of an explosion, despite having full mouth of pasta)*

Mrs. Uttley: *(wipes face and then hands Merrick a napkin)* "Wipe up those pasta bits!"

Mr. Uttley: *(furrows brow)* "Your mother and I believe random freaks of nature *can* occur now and again in the evolutionary process. So while we don't consider what happened to you *'a miracle from God,'* we do understand how unsettling it must be emotionally and physically."

Collin: "But you know I believe in God now, right?"

(Silence.)

Mrs. Uttley: "Who wants seconds?"

(After their sons consume seconds and thirds, and then leave the table, Mr. and Mrs. Uttley scoot their chairs closer together. The transcriber admits to eavesdropping at this point.)

Mrs. Uttley: *(low tones)* "But aren't you concerned?"

Mr. Uttley: *(whispering)* "Brainwashed. Just give him time..."

Mrs. Uttley: *(mostly inaudible)* "...psychologist?"

Mr. Uttley: "Oh, he'll get over it. *Eventually.*"

(End of partial transcript. Full transcript available from Gareth Uttley for nominal fee.)

A Same Same But Different Kind of Miracle

I DIDN'T EVEN BOTHER TRYING TO TELL MY parents about Jesus tagging me. What was the point? Apparently the rest of the Bread Team had difficult conversations after returning to the States as well. Because while most of their family and friends believed in the *idea* of the miracle of the toe, without any proof they didn't see it as the life-changing experience we all did. (Other than Ernestine's Aunt Aurora, that is. She couldn't get enough of our stories about the Wigglewurts.) Some of our fellow youth groupers called us *extreme* (that word again) for wanting to pray for healing and miracles, and you know, go for the "greater things."

But how could anyone expect us to live life *as usual* after what we went through?

Impossible.

I felt a nudge in the ribs.

"Collin? Wake up, bro!" Jack-O's voice boomed in my ear.

Twain leaned across the table, waving a hand in front of my face. "Hey, man! Did you hear what Jack-O just said?"

I turned to Jack-O. "What's up?"

Pushing his black framed glasses up on his nose, he leaned forward. "Two words, dude: *team tattoos*. You in?"

Everyone laughed.

"I told him it makes total sense," said Twain. "After all we've been through together, we're bonded for life—like soldiers packed in a foxhole."

"It would be fun to have permanent matching souvenirs." Ernestine grinned as she toyed with the grommet in her left ear. "I've always wanted ink."

"As long as Jack-O doesn't design it," I said. "We don't want matching turds."

More laughter.

"*Touché!*" said Jack-O, giving me a head noogie.

"Don't you mean *tush?*" said Ernestine with a smirk.

"What about NEVER SORRY EVER JOLLY?" said Twain. "Now that would be cool."

"It's cool, but it's also long—I don't want to be a walking billboard," said Shelby, reaching up to give Twain a head noogie.

"Yeah, we only got so much skin," I said.

"What does *Mallory* think about you getting another tattoo, Jack-O?" When he didn't answer, Ernestine gave him a head noogie. (I never did get the whole head noogie thing.)

He actually blushed.

"Jack-O and Mallory sitting in a tree, K-I-S-S-I-N-G," teased Shelby and Ernestine in sing-song voices.

Once Jack-O had realized Ernestine would always be a best friend but never a girlfriend, he was finally able to check out the other girls at BOLYG. And he soon connected with a game-for-anything girl named Mallory, who pranked him during youth group by stealing his Bible and underlining all the juicy bits in the book of *Song of Solomon* with a neon pink highlighter. (Apparently, it's quite the love poem. I haven't made it there in my reading of the Old Testament... *yet.*)

In return, Jack-O TPed her house. Then she retaliated by covering his entire car with tortillas and whipped cream.

It was a match made in heaven.

"Mallory's chill," Jack-O managed to finally get out as he self-consciously ran a hand through his hair.

To think that in the span of a year and a half, the Bread Team had morphed from total strangers into my closest friends. Even Twain and Shelby, who at one point had *macheted* my heart.

Now that we'd graduated from high school, the next year was going to be one of epic changes all around. Shelby had enrolled at the Fashion Institute of Los Angeles, Twain had joined the ROTC, and both Jack-O and Ernestine had been accepted at the same Christian liberal arts college in Orange County—Jack-O on a football scholarship, no less.

And me?

Well, I was taking what the Brits and Europeans called a Gap Year. Spending an entire year traveling and figuring out what to do for the rest of my life. And exactly what part Ernestine would play in it... My first stop? Volunteering for a month at the *Born Free to Live Free AMEN Academy*.

"*Sawat dii kha!*"

Speaking of Southeast Asian friends...

The Bread Team swiveled around to see Dr. Tackett and Mrs. Tackett making their way toward us through the maze of tables in the THAI SMILE FUN café. The couple still had the same California beach style vibe—except for a few more wrinkles on their face and gray in their hair.

"Tacketts in da houz!" bellowed Jack-O, jumping up and almost toppling his chair.

We stood up to welcome them, and gestured to the three empty seats...

For they were not alone.

There, walking between them, as self-composed as if she was still in her orphanage on the Burma side, was *Pee Paw*. She had the same artisan bun cheeks, buckteeth, and pigtail on the top of her head. But now she was wearing a neon pink summer dress and white leather sandals, and carried a little flowered purse.

"Bro hug!" said Jack-O, and the Bread Team surged forward to engulf the tiny girl in one massive group hug.

She laughed delightedly and gave each of us a high-five in turn.

"Five!"

"Five!"

"Five!"

"Five!"

When she got to me, she paused and looked down at my left foot. She pointed and said, "*Saw* Bob!"

Then she held up her finger... the same finger I'd prayed for a year ago.

It looked exactly the same.

"Five!" She gently slapped my hand.

For although the miracle of a finger growing out hadn't happened, the *miracle of adoption* had. Pee Paw had been highlighted by our Team and, as a result, Jongchit helped the Tacketts spend the entire last year navigating the endless amounts of red tape in order to adopt her. And this monumental event opened the door for other refugee kids and orphans to be adopted by American, Australian, and European families.

The Tacketts' dream had *finally* come true. And their dream had enabled others to dream.

"I'm glad you started without us," said Mrs. Tackett, gently helping Pee Paw take her seat. She was so full of love for her new daughter that she couldn't pry those bulging eyes off her.

"When do you leave for Thailand?" asked Dr. Tackett, easing himself down into the chair next to me. His goatee was now totally gray and he'd definitely gained a few pounds.

"Beginning of September."

"When the rest of us have to be in *school*," said Jack-O with a fake whine.

Dr. Tackett winked at Ernestine and gestured towards me. "You gonna miss this guy?"

Ernestine laughed, slightly embarrassed, and tucked a pink strand of Easter Egg behind her ear. "Sure, but next time I'm coming with—"

"We're *all* going next time!" interrupted Jack-O.

"Jongchit mentioned you guys wanted to return next summer," said Mrs. Tackett, heaping rice onto Pee Paw's plate.

"Yep," said Twain, leaning forward eagerly. "Bread Team Part Deux. Hobab emailed last month and said Jolly wants to take us deeper into the interior to bless some remote village that never gets visitors."

"And Jongchit wants us to help the underground church in some *undisclosed location*," said Ernestine in a mysterious tone.

"Well, that gives them a year to fight it out," I said.

"And gives us enough time to earn money for our tickets and expenses," said Shelby.

"And for our team tat—" began Jack-O, before he was jabbed in the side by Twain, who gave him a *"Shut up!"* look.

"*And* for our parents to get used to the idea," added Ernestine hurriedly.

"From the sound of it, Jongchit and the Wigglewurts already have your entire itinerary planned out," said Dr. Tackett with a chuckle. "I don't know if Jolly will have much say."

"Man, I believe it!" said Jack-O. "Those were some bossy ladies!"

Dr. Tackett turned to me. "So, Collin, have you finished writing up the story of last summer?"

I gulped down the last of my Thai iced tea. "Almost."

He smiled. "Good. What happened to you deserves to be told."

"What's it been like delving into the past?" asked Mrs. Tackett, finally prying her eyes off Pee Paw and shifting her unblinking gaze to me.

"I don't know," I said. "Therapeutic, maybe—"

"Happy toe!" said Pee Paw abruptly, grinning up at me, her mouth full of rice.

"Happy toe?" I repeated. Why did that simple phrase make me want to bawl like a newborn? I smiled down at her. "Exactly. Happy toe. I couldn't have put it better myself."

And if there was a gleam on my cheek, it was just sweat.

A MESSAGE FROM COLLIN UTTLEY

Well, there you have it. All I wanted was a date—but I got so much more. Thanks for reading my crazytown story. If you liked it—great! If you didn't, then blame the Tacketts. It was their idea, remember? Now get out there and give some of those "greater things" a try!

AUTHOR'S NOTE

The backdrop of this story was *very* loosely based on outreach trips my husband and I led to Southeast Asia over the years, specifically the times we spent in Thailand and Burma/Myanmar beginning in 2004. The various groups depicted here are fictionalized versions of real life counterparts, including the Katin, who were inspired by the *Karen* people group (I actually borrowed their language for the novel) and other ethnic religious minority groups living in Burma and Thailand.

The Karen National Liberation Army (KNLA), the Free Burma Rangers, and various other brave souls we encountered provided ample material for the fictional Freedom Fighters For a Free Burma (FFFFB/Feebs). And the nefarious Burmese Military Junta (BMJ) was based on the Burmese (oh, so *ironically* named) State Peace and Development Council (SPDC). Some location names and places were changed as well—for example, the Moei River along the border of Thailand and Burma became the *Murk*, and Mae La Refugee Camp and other smaller camps combined to become *Yai Camp*.

The courage, faith, and joy of our Karen friends in the face of ongoing persecution *blew me away*. It was an absolute honor to sit cross-legged on bamboo matting, listening to their stories and sharing their rice. Sadly, the civil war between the Burmese military and the ethnic and religious minorities like the Karen continues to this day, despite repeated attempts at "ceasefires." Although there have been many positive breakthroughs in recent years, there's still much more to be done to bring political, personal, and religious freedom to Burma and other parts of Southeast Asia. It'll take a miracle. (But I happen to believe in miracles—do you?)

For more information on the various experiences, locations, and people who inspired this novel, visit my website:

www.autumncornwell.com

DEDICATION

This book is dedicated to Team Cornwell. For both J.C.s in my life: one died that I might live and the other almost killed himself helping me bring this book to life! (My husband is a virtual saint dropped from heaven, I tell ya!) *Never Sorry Ever Jolly* would not exist without either of them. And to my two adventurous, creative, and game-for-anything kids, Dexter and Clementine, whose whacky and unpredictable childhood is a result of their mom's unorthodox calling. I can't wait to see what "greater things" Team Cornwell steps out in faith to attempt—even when it looks downright crazytown! *Game on!*

ACKNOWLEDGMENTS

Khap kun kha! Ta blü! **Hearty thanks to all my *jolly good* family and friends who've rooted me on over the oh-so-many years it took to write this book. (Especially those who believe all the stuff in it *could* actually happen.) A special shout-out goes to:**

My parents, William & Patricia, for providing me with a childhood full of faith that moves mountains, unconditional love, generous support, freedom to risk—and a likeminded sister, to risk with. It all started with you!

My sister and best friend, Danica (who read multiple drafts, listened to my *endless* brainstorming, and generally encouraged me nonstop for *years*), my bro-in-law Steve, and nieces Thorne and Pippa. Fellow adventurers—physically, creatively, *and* spiritually! (C + C FUN FACTORY!)

My in-laws, Patiane & Geno, who've so enthusiastically and so generously supported my writing and ministry—and even babysat Dexter, so his crazytown parents could cross the Burma border! And Stan & Abbey, those prayer warriors who kept us surrounded with a "hedge of protection" (ha!) while in SEA, and continue to encourage me as a hybrid wife-mother-author.

My literary friends, specifically Ruth ("Auntie Ruth!"), for her abundant generosity, encouragement, and camaraderie through the years, as well as her thoughtful insights on the work in progress. And Catherine, for her Spirit-filled wise counsel when I needed it most and helpful feedback on the manuscript. As well as my highly valued Beta Reader friends: Linda, for her meticulous attention to detail, and Minji, who gave me such a great last minute plot suggestion!

Those chums who add such joy to the ongoing journey of life: Sophia, for our inspiring adventures in travel, ministry, and *boba;* and Amy, whose friendship has provided me with laughs, spiritual kinship, and aesthetic surprises.

The many churches, organizations, NGOs, and compassionate individuals who made our trips into Burma and other parts of Southeast Asia possible—especially the indomitable Mimi and her family, who led us all over SEA. And of course, our intrepid outreach team members: Audra, Clement, Jenny, Mike, Kahle, and Mick. (Although our trips were a *wee* bit different than BOLYG's, eh?) Thanks for the inspiration!

Those at home and abroad (and even in these acknowledgments!) who provided extra flavor for a few of my completely fictional characters. (You know who you are. ☺) Also, my dad and Uncle Jim, who risked their lives for their country—and inspired Twain's Uncle W.J.

Finally, all the *real* Jollys and Jongchits I met throughout Southeast Asia—who I'm unable to name for their own safety—who risk their lives daily, so others can live, worship, and laugh freely.

ABOUT AUTUMN CORNWELL

Sooo, I know you're just dying to know my *life verse*. Okay, okay, it's Nehemiah 8:10, said in a jovial, booming tone—*"For the JOY of the Lord is your strength!"* (Wait, or is it actually: *"I awoke and looked around. My sleep had been pleasant to me"* from Jeremiah 31:26?) Close one. Anyway, when I'm not adventuring internationally, I can be found adventuring physically, spiritually, *and* creatively in Pasadena, California with my saint of a husband, J.C., and two angelic (most of the time) children, Dexter and Clementine. (*Gooo, Team Cornwell!*) My first young adult novel, *Carpe Diem*, was published in the U.S., Germany, Netherlands, and China. To connect with me, or to find out what *crazytown* things I've been up to these days, head over to www.autumncornwell.com. (Where I promise not to pester you about your life verse. That is, unless you'd like to share.☺)

BOOK CLUB
DISCUSSION QUESTIONS

Since *Never Sorry Ever Jolly* can be read either as a work of complete fiction or as a novel filled with experiences and miracles that could *actually* happen, it seems the perfect book for some rousing discussions!

1. What was your immediate reaction to *Never Sorry Ever Jolly*? How would you describe the story to a friend? Did the events seem believable to you? Or completely fictional, as in they could *never* happen in "real" life?

2. How did you feel about Collin as the protagonist? Did his first person narrative draw you in? Why or why not? What was your favorite chapter or scene? Least favorite?

3. Which character(s) resonated with you the most? The least? Who would you have liked to spend more time with? Who bugged the heck out of you?

4. Would you want to travel through Thailand and Burma with this particular youth group? Why or why not?

5. Which characters seemed to change and transform the most in the story? Did your opinion of them change or stay the same?

6. What's the strangest (or grossest) food you've ever eaten? Would you eat dog or beetle? Are you vegan, vegetarian, lactose intolerant, gluten free, or (fill in the blank)? How do you handle that when you travel?

7. What kind of traveler are you? The kind who's over-prepared? Or do you fly by the seat of your pants? Are you more introverted or extraverted with fellow travelers and locals?

8. What's your spiritual background? Do you believe in God? If so, what did you think of the depictions of Jesus and the Holy Spirit? If *not*, did this novel change or challenge or even confirm your beliefs in any way?

9. What's your opinion of miracles and healing today? If you attend a church, what's their theology about it? Does it mirror your own?

10. Have you ever felt completely shattered like Collin? Or full of grief like Shelby? Whom did you turn to? Compare and contrast Shelby's loss with Collin's loss. Do you think Shelby overreacted? Why or why not? What kind of loss have you experienced?

11. Jolly called his tattoos his "portable theology." What phrase, picture, or verse would encapsulate your perspective on life?

12. Do you keep a journal? If so, do you use it more to document your life, process your feelings, or keep track of creative ideas?

13. What did you think of the ending? What do you think happens next? What would you *like* to happen next?

14. If you had the chance to take an outreach trip like the one in the novel, would you jump at the chance, or stagger back in horror?

15. How did you feel about the Freedom Fighters and their ongoing battle to protect their people from extermination? Is war ever justified? What did you think about the Tacketts bribing the Border Patrol on an outreach trip?

16. Did you empathize with Twain and his passion for the Katin people group? Would you have voted with the majority of the team to go over the border?

17. What social justice cause especially moves you today? Are you doing anything about it?

18. In the chapter entitled *Christmas in July*, Collin ponders whether or not he would ever sacrifice his life so others could live. Would you?

19. What do you think the Bread Team tattoos should be?

20. What's your stance on googly eyes? ☺

ADDITIONAL QUESTIONS FOR JESUS FOLLOWERS, YOUTH GROUPS, OR CHURCHES

1. Sooo, did you happen to "ask Jesus into your heart at junior high camp"...? ☺ If not, what was your "born again" experience?

2. What word would most describe your Christian life in this season? (Comfortable? Adventurous? Boring? Confusing? Fun? Experimental? Traditional? Messy? Or...?)

3. When's the last time you've stepped out and risked for your faith? Was it a physical, emotional, spiritual, or creative risk?

4. While all healing is miraculous in some capacity, Collin's physical healing would be classified as a "creative miracle," because something came out of nothing. Have you experienced a creative miracle? Do you believe they are possible?

5. While grieving, Shelby received emotional healing in a totally unorthodox way. What are your thoughts on the various ways the Holy Spirit heals our hearts and minds?

6. Have you read any books about Smith Wigglesworth or others like him? What Christian biographies and autobiographies have inspired you?

7. How did you feel about Ernestine and the Wigglewurts and their charismatic behavior and theology? Did you identify with them? Or did you find their actions uncomfortable or offensive or intriguing or...?

8. What does it *look* like or *feel* like to put God in a box? (Safe? Predictable? Stifling? Cozy? Or...?) And how does it look or feel when He's *not* in a box? (Scary? Exciting? Uncertain? Creative? Reckless? Or...?)

9. Have you ever felt abandoned by God? How did you respond at the time?

10. In light of all the challenges in the world today, how would you personally apply Colossians 1:27 ("Christ in you, the hope of glory.") and 1 John 4:4 ("He who is in you is greater than he who is in the world.")?

11. How do you feel about Collin's spiritual journey from unbeliever to believer? Does it ring true? Why or why not?

12. What do you *really* think about Jesus? How would you describe your relationship with Him? What's He *like?* Does He resemble the Jesus Collin encountered in any way?

13. What are your thoughts on the Holy Spirit? How would you describe the Holy Spirit's ongoing work in your life?

14. And what are your feelings about God the Father, the Creator? Do you feel like a child of God? Why or why not? In what ways do you create like your Creator Father?

15. What do you think Jesus meant by "greater things" in John 14:12? How would you apply it personally? What greater things have you attempted? Partnering with God, what greater things do you *want* to attempt?

16. Also, what were the things that Ernestine and others did that were "small" and yet also "great"? Those *small great things*? (For example, those things we do every single day that may take extra effort on our part—like saying hi to a stranger, offering to help out when it's totally inconvenient, taking the time to craft an encouraging text or email, sharing half of your burrito with the friend who forgot her lunch *again*, etc.) What small great things have you done lately? What small great thing do you feel the Holy Spirit nudging you to do this week?

17. Have you ever had a *crazytown* experience? (i.e. being slain in the spirit, getting miraculously healed, experiencing visions or visitations, etc.) What do you think the purpose of such experiences are? Did your experience draw you closer to Jesus? Why or why not?

18. Sooo, what's your—yep, I'm going there—"life verse"?

FEEDBACK & SHARING

Ta blü! Khap kun kha! Thanks for reading *Never Sorry Ever Jolly!* If you've experienced any *crazytowns*, have feedback or comments, or are willing to share what you wrote at the end of this book, then head on over to www.autumncornwell.com and join the *Jolly Good* Community. We'd love to hear from you!

48316239R00240

Made in the USA
Columbia, SC
07 January 2019